Give or Take

Patricia Duffy

To Ralph, who taught me about chocolate éclairs.

Contents

Chapter 1

Overheard in the girls' bathroom –
Burt's Bees
No, Carmex
Burt's Bees
I'm so addicted to lip gloss.

Mizbie cycled in high gear, her scarf flying. Maneuvering her bike down the sun-parched slope and into the circle drive of St. Bartholomew's, she spotted Seth with his violin case.

"You're here early, Seth." She forgot how late she was and broke into a smile. "Are you helping Mr. Barton with the orchestra fundraiser?"

"Hi, Miz B." He smiled back, a sophomore on a mission. "I'm collecting bake sale money, then we have to reset chairs and stands after jazz band messed 'em up."

She stepped to the side and looked around him. "Something's different about you," she said, looking at his goofy smile and sun streaked hair. "It must be all that cross country practice." This was going to be a better year for Seth. She could feel it.

Seth stood there; his cheeks and ears grew red. Mizbie could see he had something to say, so she waited. "I gotta go. See ya second hour," he said.

෴

Wearing a dress that swayed at her knees, Renee walked into the office. Turning her back to Krahler, she looked over her shoulder and asked,

"What do you think? Does this dress make my arse look fat?" Facing him again after showing off the offending arse, she continued to joke with him even though he was no longer a fellow teacher she had once chided, but the new principal.

Krahler widened his eyes with the befuddlement of a married man with kids and a job that put him under the community's microscope. "I . . . it's . . ." but having been asked this question by his wife, especially since the birth of their third child, he said, "You know, there are women who work out at the gym every day and would be happy to have their arse look like that."

Renee, true to her Irish South Boston roots, winked and laughed, leaving the school office fishbowl. She passed the two secretaries, who remained cheerful despite barrages of morning students lined up to retrieve forgotten locker combinations and lost backpacks.

"Hey, not so fast with that cash box, buddy." Krahler tried to stop Seth as he exited the walk-in safe in St. Bartholomew's main office.

"I need the box for the bake sale. Mr. Barton sent me up for it."

"Wait just a minute. Tell me your name and let's see what's in here." Krahler's loud voice made Seth back up and sit on a stool reserved for students waiting to be suspended.

"Really, mister, I'm late. I gotta go," Seth said.

Mizbie stepped beside him. "It's okay, Seth," she said. Seth gave her a grateful look. He took the box and dashed away.

"What are you doing here?" Mizbie turned, her nose nearly touching Krahler's.

"Look, it seems there's a misunderstanding." His voice was loud and Mizbie could smell coffee on his breath.

"Where's Smithfield? And what do you mean bullying a student like Seth? You don't know what he's been through and here you are treating him like a thief or a truant. He is neither. You need to find out about things first before you go jumping to conclusions, *buddy*!"

Mizbie glared at him and turned on her heel into the teacher's workroom. What was going on?

Renee was there pulling mail from her box. "Remember Krahler? Smithfield left for the Middle East yesterday on another National Guard deployment, so they brought Krahler up from his post at Newberry Elementary. He taught math here a few years ago."

"It's so sudden." Mizbie was stunned. "I'm going to miss Smithfield."

"Me too. You sure made an impression with Krahler," Renee said.

"That blathering blowhard. He was scaring Seth." Mizbie had spouted off again, but she had to defend the boy. Now Krahler would be watching, waiting for opportunities to lambaste her for embarrassing him in front of students and the office staff on his first day at the high school.

"Just remember," Renee whispered and pointed her thumb at the principal's office next door, "who's listening."

"How's it goin' with your four classes of freshmen?" Renee said louder than she needed to. She stopped pulling papers from her stuffed mailbox and looked at her friend.

"What's so bad about it?" Mizbie looked at her. "I've got some sophomores too."

Mark spoke up from the corner of the room, looking over his glasses. "What did you do, Mizbie, scratch the IT scheduler's new VW? I get one class now and then, maybe two, but I'd collapse teaching more than 100 freshmen a day."

"Let's see who you have," Renee grabbed Mizbie's papers from her backpack. "Look who's taking freshman English for the second time!" She pointed to three names. "That's what you get for having last year's stellar test scores. Our class scheduler from IT had instructions to put every do-over he could think of in your classes. You're screwed, I tell ya." She grabbed the rest of her own papers and headed to her classroom, heels clicking away. She looked back at Mizbie and laughed, an eerie tremolo that echoed down the hall.

Mizbie shrugged. Renee had no more bite than her tiny Yorkie lap dog. "See if I make you any more chocolate ganache brownies," Mizbie called after her. No matter. Even if her kids were handpicked to win "Most Irritating" student awards, the challenge would be worth it. Already this term she felt the satisfaction when lightbulbs turned on, not to mention the look she imagined on Renee's face as she ate her words. Mizbie walked toward the classroom fixing her scarf, an African batik that Renee and her husband brought back for her. It felt good, that electric Monday pulse, even though it was tempered with her sleepless Sunday night.

Since the school open house last week, she'd been curious about the direction her students would take this year. Parents trooped through with children reluctant to give up their summer tans. Parents and students looked her over, decided if her age was worthy of respect and asked how much homework she gave. A Brooks Brothers dad stood with his carbon copy, button down son next to a Howard Stern dad with a curly mane of hair, earring, open shirt revealing a silver chain, and a daughter in a black leather bustier with black mascara ringing her ready-aim-fire eyes.

Education professors tell future teachers what to expect when they walk into a room full of students. Books have been written about setting the tone, not accepting less than their best, or instilling motivation in the individual student. Nothing could have prepared Mizbie for this homeroom class that she would scoot up the ladder to the next grade, rather than the treadmill of summer school. Mizbie didn't feel competitive, but when she walked in the room feeling the Monday them-versus-me vibe, she knew she would win. They would not wear her down.

"Tell me what you know about what it means to infer?" She paused. No one answered.

"Let me tell you a story of something that happened to me –"

"Yeah, right, whitey," came a voice from the back.

Mizbie's ears and eyes landed on the speaker at the opposite end of the room.

"So what happened to you, Miz B. righty white? Desmin smiled.

Tension spread across the class and Mizbie sensed a moment, exhilarated by her claimed progeny. They were all hers, every one of them, these charges, who thrived on distraction and sound networking, all hers for an hour each day.

"Excuse me?" Mizbie said, louder than necessary. She directed a high beam stare into his eyes and her expression became serious. "Let's think about this, Desmin."

Her story on inference would have to wait. Here was a window for another kind of teaching. She walked back to stand beside him, but directed her words to the class. "Let's think about what we say and what it means about what we really want. We have our own microcosm right here with our homeroom class."

"What those words you use?" said a girl with almond eyes and straight, black hair down her back.

"I'll write them on the board, and you can look them up for tomorrow," Mizbie said. "Now," she turned back to the class, "Turn to the person next to you and look into each other's eyes. What do you see?

Students turned. Some leaned in; others backed off.

"Black eyes."

"Brown eyes."

"Washed-out blue eyes," said Robin, covering his own.

"Hey, they're gray."

"Keep looking. Look more closely," Mizbie said. Tension eased to curiosity. The room became stuffy, so she opened some windows.

"I see myself. I see a reflection," said Rashmi, her long, black braid nearly reaching the floor. She smiled at Mizbie and both knew they had an ally.

"Tell us where you come from, Rashmi."

Rashmi had a faraway look as she spoke of home. "I come from Jaipur. It is the capital of Rajasthan, known for its great history and natural beauty. It is called the Pink City."

"Yeah, India with all the slums," a boy with a shaved head said.

She turned to him, lifting her chin. "We have no slums in Jaipur," she continued in an assertive voice. "Many people in Jaipur are vegetarian. We do not want animals killed for food."

"Thanks, Rashmi. Maybe you could bring in pictures of Jaipur some time." Mizbie walked by and smelled the unmistakable scent of curry. "So what you see is a reflection of yourself or another you." She spoke louder to the class. "Let's think of each person in our homeroom as part of our school family where we not only respect one another, but treat others with caring." She stepped back to Desmin.

"Indian, huh. You get two Indians together and you know what you get? A political party! Get it? They can't agree on anything." He laughed at Rashmi.

She glared at him and turned to the front of the room.

"Desmin," Mizbie paused. His right arm and the side of his face were covered in disfiguring scars, some lighter and others darker than the rest of his coffee-colored skin. He had to make sure his words shocked before his face did. "You are my other me." She looked into his eyes. "I will treat you with respect and care."

"You gotta be shittin' me, man," Desmin shifted in his seat. His hands pushed on the top of his desk.

"Desmin, *respect and care*." Mizbie stared into his eyes. "Everyone turn to the person beside you. Look into their eyes again and tell them. Say, 'You are my other me. I will treat you with respect and care.'"

"This is just weird," Shannon mumbled.

"That's what my brother said last year. She made him read a book, so my mom stuck me in her class, too. She does weird stuff every day," said Nathan.

"Did I hear someone whine? Whining has no credibility. We don't drone, mutter, grouse, jabber, yap, fuss, or babble because we are the class with cred. Say that to the person next to you. Look them in the eye when you say it."

"We are the class with cred," they grinned and repeated.

"Mizbie," Mr. Krahler stood at the door. "A word –"

She stalked to the hallway. Didn't he know not to interrupt a class? Should she show him how to send an email or leave a note in her box?

Krahler chirped and flapped about some at-risk student named Edward, released from the juvenile facility, a boy who had been tossed from school to school and how this was his last chance if she could get him to pass by the end of the year. Mizbie nodded to speed up the story and get him to leave, agreeing to meet the boy later.

"By the way, you have a student trying to crawl out the window," he pointed.

Mizbie turned to check, and when she looked back, Krahler was gone. She raced to the window and grabbed the shirt of the girl at the window, trying to remember her name. She chided herself for taking so long to learn students' names. How difficult would it be this year to get 90 percent of her students to pass the state test? Test scores swung wildly from one year to the next for every instructor. It was partly perseverance, partly dumb luck of the class list, partly finding friends she could sound off to (who would still speak to her the next day), and partly knowing her students needs better than they knew themselves.

∾

St. Bartholomew's, the only high school in the town of Astor, used to be a religious school until the 1950s when it lost funding due to an indiscretion and was sold to the town fathers for a small sum, with the stipulation that they keep the name. That was fine with the community. St. Bartholomew's had a solid reputation with new families coming to town after World War II, and the name gave the newcomers comfort and confidence that morals and values would be a step up from a school named Central or West. Besides, the name on the sign in the front and all the school stationary were already printed.

In 1951 when the town council looked into the history of the name, they found Bartholomew to mean plowman or farmer in ancient Aramaic. They liked the connection, because most students came from farm families. By unanimous vote, they decided to hold a Bartholomew Fair with contests for the best pie and an area for carnival rides. The date was the weekend after September 11th, the day Bartholomew's martyrdom was commemorated in the Coptic calendar.

A community near London, had such a fair since the Middle Ages, giving the whole idea a sense of history. Because one of the miracles surrounding Bartholomew's sainthood involved a group of children lifting his heavy body, which had been washed ashore, the council decided to have one of the activities be a tug of war over a mud bog. The tradition continued for decades until the date of September 11th took on a new meaning in 2001.

The Bartholomew Fair then morphed into August with the Bartholomew Back-to-School Bash and 5-K Run. Booths from local insurance companies gave away free grippers for opening jars. Those who didn't run could get a free blood pressure check from the drugstore booth. Proceeds from the run were donated to the Astor Child Advocacy Group.

∾

Mizbie hauled the girl back to the window. She let go of the shirt and stood face to face with her. "What's that all about?"

"I just felt the need to escape for some fresh air." She blinked and checked her shoes.

The class snickered.

Without turning away, Mizbie's hand shot out toward the class like a traffic cop. "Yes, your name, Mara Jade," she remembered the name. "Is that from *Star Wars*?"

The class listened.

"Yeah, from a *Star Wars* character. That's right." Mara Jade grew thoughtful and sat down.

For once Mizbie was glad that her boyfriend, Carl, was a *Star Wars* geek, otherwise she wouldn't have made the connection. She walked through the rows, and reminded a few students to put away cell phones. In front were the Indian students whose parents came to work for PharmaTek. The boys in madras shirts had their hair cut short. Rashmi sat with them.

By the window two boys with sandy tousled hair, Nathan and Gilbert, sat next to each other. Both wore black T-shirts and tapped their fingertips on the desktops. "You guys look like twins today," she stopped in front of them.

"Heck no. We're just friends. He lives down the street," the one on the left said.

"We have three classes together, besides band," the other said.

"Drummers, right?" Mizbie said.

"I am. He plays trumpet." Gilbert spoke for both of them.

"You're not even cousins?"

"He doesn't look like me. Look, we have different eyes."

It was true. The eyes on the left were a darker shade of blue.

In the middle of the room sat the farm kids, no strangers to hard work. Mizbie could smell the fresh air on them. She continued her walk through the back left corner where the tallest guys sat. They smelled strongly of girls' favorite body spray, and they sat like coiled steel, ready to spring to action. Their attention focused on a quartet of girls in front of them. The girls, drowsy looking, glanced back through mascaraed lashes, their pouty lips turning to smiles. Tight colorful T-shirts matched their nail colors and occasional stripes were sprayed into their hair.

"Jenna . . . it's good to see you," Mizbie said. Jenna had just been added to her class.

"Hi, Miz B. Just want you to know, I'm not anything like my sister was," she said.

"What your sister do?" Desmin asked.

Mizbie coughed. "Okay, my little seedlings." She changed the subject. "Light that match; find that energy; access that control center. Let's open the books."

The lesson had veered off course a bit, but Mizbie was not unhappy with the result. When the bell rang, Mara Jade headed toward the window, but Mizbie's stare changed her direction toward the door. They couldn't wait to escape.

❧

After dinner, Mizbie walked through the park behind her apartment to the pond, an area the pharmaceutical company had refurbished in exchange for 100 acres of wetlands. PharmaTek filled in the wetlands and built its huge research facility, creating jobs that transformed the small former agrarian village. A few blocks from Main Street, the old oaks and maples in the park surrounded the new pond and created a calming, albeit commercially landscaped, respite. With issues jockeying for position in her brain, Mizbie walked to the top of the recycled plastic oriental bridge that was supposed to last forever.

She peered into the water, cleared her thoughts, and put space between the old drama and the new. Staring at her own reflection, far enough away to replace street noise with nature sounds, she thought about this spot a few generations from now, when no one would know any of the people of Astor had even existed. What would all of this matter? Cares and concerns of descendants of these people would crowd out memories of their ancestors who would become a mere wonder of another time, much like the memories of her parents clouded and hazed with each coming year. A spotted carp swished its tail and disappeared under the bridge.

Mizbie had Jenna's sister, Loni, last year. Today in class Jenna hadn't wanted to mention her sister. No wonder. Loni had rarely asked a question, but assignments were carefully carried out in tense handwriting. Guys in the seats around her stared at the glow of her long, brown hair. One day last spring, Loni waited for the other students to leave. Loni's brown eyes were rimmed in red. She kept looking toward the door to make sure no one else heard.

It was a tragedy, everyone said. At the house after the funeral, Jenna found Mizbie and began to talk. "My sister said she could talk to you," Jenna said. "I want to tell you what happened."

The family had thought she was out with her boyfriend that night. But when Jenna walked to the back shed with the compost from the evening meal, she looked up to see her sister, still and tall. The moonlight cast a bluish tone to her skin and clothes. There was a slight breeze, and as she tossed the compost into the bin, she saw her sister's body swing slightly, her hair covering her face, which it never did. Her feet were off the ground, her face expressionless. Jenna touched the clothes and drew back her hand. Loni didn't respond. The rope around her neck was one she recognized from a game of tug-of-war with their cousins the week before. It was long, and she had looped it around one of the boards that supported the shed roof.

Jenna's first thoughts were about how she would be the only one left to do dishes and fold clothes from the dryer. She would have to read *It's Raining Meatballs* 1,000 times to their little sister –, *her* little sister –, instead of just 100 times. Loni was just mean to do this. Her sister's face was so calm. Jenna wanted to feel that calm instead of the feeling she couldn't name, the many feelings crowding in on one another. Too many feelings.

Jenna ran back to the house and upstairs to her room. On her bed was a note that said, *Good-bye.* That's all. "She told me why the night before, but I'm not telling, not even Mom and Dad. I won't tell anyone ever because she asked me not to. It's all I can do for her now –, keep her secret."

Mizbie imagined Jenna living with the vision of her sister and her secret burden. So much potential was lost, a life cut short so young.

Jesspin9
to MBax20
12:22 p.m.
September 6

Hey Miz,

I got the message from the Herrod House's publishing division and it wasn't what I'd hoped for. Funds aren't available "at this time." They might send me in the fall or not at all. I'm my uncle's only niece, so I thought he could do more for me. I feel like a kid on Christmas morning, who woke up to see the tree and gifts taken away. Or it's like a dream deferred. My dream isn't entirely deferred, but it has some serious sag. I'm wallowing in my disappointment,

Jess

Chapter 2

Heard outside honors English class--

--He's like my music Sherpa, man. He has all these songs nobody's ever heard of. I'm just following the path.

Haven't you heard anything? He ranted about my paper like a soul-sucking Dementor. That was an A paper.

Lynn sat across from Mizbie in the workroom wearing her short skirt, and tall boots. All the windows were open on the unseasonably warm day, because the school office was the only air-conditioned room. Both of them were trying to ignore the after-school staff meeting as long as possible. Lynn, who had one freshman English class, was civil but cool, probably because of the dustup they had last year. She flipped over a paper she had been correcting. "Look at number eight. The question was 'How did the character Louise really die?' Her answer was 'It was karma.' Can you believe it? She said karma!"

Mizbie excused herself and, without another option, headed toward the library for the dreaded staff meeting. Here was another friend she would stay in touch with only in a Christmas-card way, another friendship strained by her feisty temper.

The staff meeting had begun five minutes before she sneaked in.

"Our mission statement is not just a collection of words; it's something we feel in our guts, a direction we have taken, a commitment we've made . . ." Principal Krahler continued.

Mizbie sat down, trying to melt into the group. "This is Krahler warfare," Ryder whispered to her. "Another stillborn mission statement killed by the systemic disease of bureaucracy." Mizbie watched Ryder stretch out his long cowboy legs, the alligator boots extending under the library table.

Principal Krahler considered himself a Renaissance man, a reformer. He approached being principal as if it was his calling, a vocation. He had made some big changes since he became principal of St. Bartholomew's these past weeks, sweeping a pathway of resistance as if he was destined to do it with his dour countenance alone. Principal Krahler attended Calvin College, named for the religious reformer of more than five centuries ago, but Krahler relished the reformer role, like Calvin.

There were those who felt he was depraved last year at Newberry Elementary when he proposed his "Run-It-Up-the-Flag Wednesday," where all students were strongly encouraged to gather voluntarily fifteen minutes early each Wednesday morning to plan their goals for the week and tell it to the flagpole in front of the school. Krahler wore his National Guard Reserve hat to these gatherings. Although he never served in a war, he was a fervent military supporter.

The student group grew smaller as the year pressed on, but Krahler persevered with his flagpole goal setters even as mornings grew colder, his rugged individuals predestined for great things, the talk of goals by the voluntary few.

Mizbie's mind wandered as the cramped library grew warmer with the 80 tired staff members waiting and listening. The books on the shelves were mostly old and outdated, but there were two rows of computers from a federal grant a few years ago. Her eyes followed the black cords and cables up near the tall ceiling where Pewabic tiles were inlaid in the wall around the perimeter. The muted colors depicted gods, goddesses, and heroes of Greek myth. Why had the monks chosen these embellishments instead of mosaics of saints?

There was Demeter with her quiver of arrows and Poseidon presiding over his sea of blue tile. Of course, some of the tiles had fallen, and being too expensive to replace, revealed occasional squares of naked gray cement. She imagined the Franciscan monks of St. Bartholomew's so long ago, who had built the school and supported themselves by teaching and selling their wine. The order had dwindled, so the town inherited the high school and the graveyard, final home to the many monks who dedicated their lives to teach here.

The old building was expensive to keep up and was always in need of repair. State funds gave them a well-equipped computer lab here on the second floor, but the computers made the room swelter with a tropical humid heat in fall and spring. Wires and extension cords snaked around the floor, and students walked over duct tape to their seats. The roof was perennially patched, and it wasn't unusual for custodians on the roof to create a vibration that loosened the plaster on the ceiling so it would hail down on some unsuspecting student.

". . . and remember our homecoming game against Mayville next Friday. We'll need some volunteers to take tickets starting after the parade at 6:00 . . ."

Astor's covenant was the bonding spirit of football. The sport didn't need to be carved on a stone tablet, for citizens to feel the promise in their hearts at the end of every summer when adults hung out at the pre-season practice sessions watching players run drills and play scrimmages, making bets on who would be the season's star. In a town deeply ingrained in football, Mizbie knew all too well the little wiggle room left for other obsessions. The Hornet team had become an unfailing belief, a uniting force, and a sign of obdurate strength.

Football games in Astor could draw 2,000 fans, even more for the homecoming games, such as this one against their rival, Mayville. An anonymous benefactor provided a nearly two-million-dollar indoor practice field and weight room. The first half hour of practice was spent on homework with tutors, so players would be eligible for the college scholarships offered by this same benefactor. People who grew up here, grew up with football as the most important event of fall. Winter was cross training, spring was spring training, and summer was getting fired up for the next fall season. Area towns celebrated cherry festivals or blueberry parades. Astor pride sparkled in its annual Kickoff Parade each homecoming, with punt-and-pass contests, bands, floats, and players waving from the back of Chevy Silverados.

Football boosters had pumped it up this year, because Coach Maxfield hinted that he might be thinking about retirement. After 30 years, he was ready to spend frostier fall days teaching his grandchildren the game. With a 25 – 5, season-win record, the Hornet Boosters weren't looking forward to the prospect of losing him. Even though they knew he had at least another whole season to go, hometown fans were already lamenting the loss, mourning before he even left. Their hope was in the Nameless Benefactor who might pay for a new coach with money the school system didn't have.

Not only did the Hornet Parent Boosters voice their concerns, but also the Stingers Alumni Club. Even the Fifty Yardliners, a tailgating group that kept stats on players from at least 20 years back, grumbled about the loss over coffee at the Bean and Leaf shop in town. The mysterious Yellow Hornet, an unnamed student in an eight-foot fuzzy hornet suit, buzzed around on the sidelines at every game, posing for an occasional picture with fans. His stinger served as a portable seat when he plopped down on the sidelines during a play, so fans could see through his antennae. Every three years, a secret ceremony bestowed the costume on a deserving sophomore. Many vied for the honor, granted by the departing senior, another oath of anonymity sworn, continuing the tradition.

After 25 state championships, 5 against Mayville, the 100-piece marching band, also winners of state championships but with threadbare uniforms and no booster group, continued to fire up the crowd in rousing fashion. A quiet minority of citizens wrote editorials and initiated petitions to divert a tiny fraction of the bountiful profit in football game ticket sales to the Hornet band, Quiz Bowl competition bus fare, or science fair programs. Eventually the football euphoria won out over any alternative. Money from Stinger hats and hoodies made possible state-of-the-art weight-lifting equipment or new press box sound systems. Extra funds in Stinger accounts needed only an alumni whim to be spent.

With an unemployment rate above the national average, the team was a point of pride and diversion for the entire community, more than a high percentage of college graduates could ever be. In all its fun and all its seriousness, to understand the people of Astor, one had to appreciate its total devotion to football.

∾

Friday night in her apartment, Mizbie wasn't in the mood for a pub crawl. Carl was out of town on business and Renee was having her ego massaged and fed at the Larkspur Spa and Dude Ranch. When Mizbie opened the mail, there was the ancho pepper pork rub she'd ordered. How could there be a better way to spend a Friday night? Fingers flying across her laptop, she clicked enter and waited for a pulled pork recipe to appear. She looked around at her living room, free of knickknacks and dust catchers. Possessions weren't something she longed for. Her parents had kept a sparse home, and as far as she was concerned, it meant less to dust and clean, less to worry about, and less to take care of. Her closet had never been crowded with clothes.

The only exception to her sparse lifestyle was the kitchen drawers. Mizbie loved to cook and eat. Her kitchen drawers were filled with various spatulas both firm and flippy, knives of several lengths and weights, and spoons from demitasse tasters to squat rice spoons and hefty ladles. She had a tiny whisk small enough for one egg, and one big enough to stir spaghetti sauce. Wooden skewers waited for soaking in cinnamon water for her grilled shish kafta. Micro planers of three sizes grated everything from lemon zest to a dusting of Parmesan Reggiano. She loved the feel of her wooden spoons and chose particular ones depending on the task –, a long-handled one for her barbecue sauce, a bigger bowled one for her rum custard zabaglione.

At any given time, Mizbie might be out of milk or eggs, but she was rarely without a good supply of cooking chocolate. Her favorite chocolate recipe was a simple dark chocolate ganache, which she drizzled over cakes and pastries. Friends at school would request it, if they were making a special dessert. She occasionally made caramel of three flavors (Chambord, espresso, or hazelnut), and gave most of it away. When she

16

asked students about their passions as a writing topic, she confessed to them her passion for cooking.

After massaging the pork rub into the meat, she prepared the simple dinner and retired to the couch, tucking her legs under her. A cup of hot oolong tea made lazy steam curls beside her.

She glanced at a 1966 paperback copy of Kurt Vonnegut's *God Bless You, Mr. Rosewater* that she'd picked up at Inkslinger's New and Used Books. It had a coffee stain on the back cover and the inside smelled like musty wood and incense. Maybe the original owner had just returned from a protest of the Vietnam War or was smushed in the back of a van and reading on the way to Woodstock in 1969, getting high off the smoke. Used books spoke to her, their imagined histories sprouting what-ifs in her mind.

Her eyes scanned several partly read books camped out on the floor like tents, their spines up. She passed over *One Hundred Years of Solitude, Lolita,* and *The Unbearable Lightness of Being,* and chose *A Moveable Feast.* After a sip of tea, she read a few pages before her mind wandered to the Horace quote about power, "Force without wisdom falls of its own weight." There was the idea of "eternal return" of events, fortuitous coincidence, and the heavy burden of eyes that wouldn't stay open, succumbing to sleep.

∾

Mizbie called on Brandon, whose animation could not be contained. "Ya know they're doing research for earthquakes like the San Francisco one we read about in Jack London's story. They're studying those things, like those dishes." Brandon's turn for current events made him seem more like Dorothy's straw man than the testosterone-fueled spark plug he usually appeared to be.

"Tectonic plates?" Mizbie asked. She clamped her mouth tight and struggled to look serious.

"Yeah . . . those plates. When plants in the ocean die, they turn into carbon after a long time and they're kinda recycled into the earth."

Brandon bounced in his seat. "Carbon is pulled out of the atmosphere so we don't get so much of the greenhouse effect. We'd overheat the planet without tectonic plates."

The reason Brandon was falling apart, sat next to him. Tessa was oblivious. "I'm afraid of clowns," she blurted, as if this had anything to do with what they were talking about. "Clowns and Thai food and Kurt Cobain."

Brandon looked at her as if she had just promised him the moon; Dante longed for his Beatrice. "Their shifts bring nutrients and water to Earth that exists on no other planet we know of."

His earnest voice reminded Mizbie of the Ukrainian student, Brandon's Beatrice from last week. Oola tried so hard to cover her Ukrainian accent, longing to sound American. In her home country's tradition, she brought a small pumpkin to school and presented it to Brandon, who kept stopping by her locker, asking her out. "This means no, I won't go out with you," she said, as she pushed the pumpkin into his chest and walked away. He looked stunned, standing there staring at the pumpkin.

"Brandon, you are on this! Maybe you could turn tectonic plates into an article for the school paper!"

Genevieve and Haley had dressed in matching yellow hoodies with the Hornets logo on the back. Their school spirit extended to their alternate colors of nail polish: yellow and blue. "Miz B, our moms won their Roller Derby meet last night. That's news, isn't it?" Genevieve said.

"They sound brave," Mizbie said.

"Both our moms skate for the Fat Tracks team. Mine's been skating for about seven years and she's broken a bone almost every year she's skated." Haley pointed to her elbow, her tibia and her femur to show the bones. "She calls herself Burning Woman,"

"That's scary," Tessa said.

"My mom's a hairdresser by day, and then she turns into Sonic Mom. She's only been skating for a few years, but she's broken her wrist and sprained her elbow," Genevieve said.

"And they still want to do it?" Mizbie asked. "They think it's worth the broken bones?"

"It puts her in a good mood when she gets home," Haley said.

Desmin walked in with a late pass. He wore a bright yellow shirt, unlike his usual choice of sportswear. The shirt was inside out. When everyone looked, he said to the class, "Krahler say somethin' 'bout my shirt inciting unrest and like that." He stood in front of the Indian students. "I say I have freedom of expression, to express myself, ya know what I mean?" He jutted out his chin. Rashmi looked at Desmin with curiosity. "He say my freedom ends when I step on somebody's toes. That man's toes mighty big –"

"Desmin, what was on your shirt?" Mizbie asked.

"The shirt say, 'Gun Rights – Shoot Immigrants.' Got it from my dad."

Mizbie was sorry she asked. "Desmin – have a seat. We'll talk later."

Instead, he turned toward her, and she looked up at him, standing so close she could smell Mountain Dew on his breath. At least it was just Mountain Dew. She returned to her desk and gathered the papers, put them in a desk drawer, and slammed it shut.

"If you think 'bout callin' him, get out you head," Desmin said, clenching his fists. "He don't stay in the same place two nights in a row, 'cause he think the govment's after him. He don't trust no one." He took a buzzing cell phone from his pocket and checked it. "He don't trust no cell phone."

"Somebody's probably after all of us," Mizbie said. "We'll just deal with it. But in class you have to give up this technological teat," She took the phone from his hand.

"Get out my mouth. You said teat," he said. "Whoa, looka you stylin' Jessica," he said. Did I see you at a cage fight in Detroit last summer?" He sank into his seat. "My aunt, if she see you right now, she say you look casket sharp. Yeah."

This is the underbelly of the freshman class. But they're my underbelly. "Okay, get your writer's notebooks out for a journal write. Let's gather some ideas first. Tell me what your neighborhood is like."

"It's always raining and dark," said Tessa.

"Mine's not really a neighborhood, just a dirt road. I walk down the road alone like an elephant," said Gilbert.

"I remember a police car coming to my brother's apartment, taking him to jail," said Rip.

"Just cows to be milked, chickens to be fed, and rows of greenhouses, no neighbors," said Seth.

"I think of summer block parties. Everybody comes out and barbecues in their yards. They close off the street and we play soccer," said Rico.

"My neighbor has a pool and we all go there to swim," said Noel.

"I hear the neighbor lady rabidly shrieking at me for yelling at her dog to get out of my yard," said Nick.

"Rabid lady," Brandon said.

"Don't yell at my dowg," Robin sang *dowg* like a lonesome coyote.

Mizbie's traffic cop hand shot out at them. "Genevieve?" she said.

"My uncle was in jail too, but he's back now," Genevieve's ran her hand through her hair with colors beyond naming, complex shades with iridescence, such as bubinga, purpleheart, and wenge woods, deeper and shinier than any parquet floor. Mizbie saw the boys around her watch as she flipped it back. "He has a license to pick up roadkill?"

Genevieve said it as if it was a question. Mizbie gave Robin a look for making dead dog faces and motioned for Genevieve to speed up her story.

"So he collects these dead deer and raccoons and muskrats along the side of the road, takes them to his shed out back, boils and scrapes the bones, then grinds them up like fee - fi - fo - fum! He is kind of a giant guy too." She opened her hands wide. "But really, he's an artist. He had a show in Grand Rapids last month. He makes these molds of claws, fills them with the bones and resin and sells them. He says the claws symbolize the way people claw out natural areas and steal them from the wild animals that should be able to live there, but end up as road-kill instead."

"Does he work around here?" Mizbie asked.

"Yeah, he's in the apartments by the park."

That was Mizbie's apartment complex. She imagined a neighbor boiling bones on his stove and shuddered.

Robin continued his comedic commentary in the back of the room. As Mizbie approached him, he tried to defend himself. "I'm working on my opening monologue for when I'm the first Asian ever on late night TV." He pushed his chair against the back of the wall, balancing on two chair legs.

"Robin, Robin, get all your legs on the floor. If I didn't have to teach you, you'd be hilarious. But the problem is, I have to teach you! What students wouldn't rather listen to your jokes than take part in class?"

"Okay," Robin appeared broken, like a piddling puppy.

Chastising Robin was like trying to stop Tahquamenon Falls. Robin breathed comedy. Inhale breath, exhale a joke.

"So let's pick up on our discussion of satire from yesterday. Remember satire makes fun of an issue to bring attention to it or to improve a condition. Like Jonathan Swift's *A Modest Proposal*. What do you know about the essay?"

"Isn't that the one where a guy wants poor people to sell their babies so they have enough money to eat? Then the rich people buy them to boil and bake them?" Edward said.

Mizbie was surprised to hear Edward speak up, but this was the kind of writing subject he would read on his own.

"Eeww, gross!" Genevieve said.

"That's from the Irish potato famine, isn't it?" Shannon sat up from her slump. Her concrete expression broke. "My great great, and a bunch more greats, Irish grandmother took her six kids for a walk. Her husband killed himself. She had to get the kids out of the house, right? The potatoes were like, bad. She walked 50 miles from Killarney to Cork. They were starving. They tried to find stuff left in the fields. Two of the kids died and that's when she started to hear the voices." Shannon's eyes glazed.

"What happened, Shannon?"

"That was in the 1700s. Now my mom hears the voices," Shannon's voice wavered. "Says it's our Irish grandmother. It's scary when my mom hears voices. I hope I don't ever hear them." Shannon folded her arms tight around her.

"It's the voices! I have to do what they say," Justin's hands flailed around him.

"Stop! It's not funny." Rashmi looked worried.

"Okay, Shannon's concerned about her mom. Let's talk about satire later. Justin, see me after class."

"What'd I do?"

"Just back up a minute and think, Justin."

"Shannon's always saying weird stuff. You can't believe her. I'm –"

A desk clattered. Mizbie turned. The window was open. Mara Jade was gone. "Mara Jade, get back inside the room. Now."

"I was hot." Mara Jade sighed heavily and climbed back in the window.

"So you opened the window and climbed out onto the sidewalk? What were you thinking? Don't answer that."

"Ms Baxter. A word." Mr. Krahler's voice.

Mizbie turned to see Krahler at the door with Nick's mom, Mrs. Huntsman. "I was just coming in when I saw a student climbing out of your window, Ms Baxter," Mrs. Huntsman said.

"I don't like having to explain to the school board president why a student would be climbing out of a window. Do you have an explanation?" asked Mr. Krahler.

"Tessa was telling us about her fear of clowns." Mizbie motioned to Tessa. She nodded. "She was agitated at the thought of being trapped in the room with clowns and what would happen if there was a ... fire. So Mara Jade was demonstrating how easy it was to escape to safety."

"I'm sure these demonstrations won't happen again, am I right?"

"Not unless we're overrun by a bevy of clowns," Mizbie said. *Note to self: requisition screens on windows.*

∞

On her way to lunch, Mizbie saw Heuster chase Desmin out of the locker room door. The gym teacher's whistle bounced on his shirt. "D-man, your pants are sagging below the equator. In L A, they'd fine you a hundred bucks plus community service. Pull 'em up!"

Desmin didn't turn around but gave the back of his jeans a tug.

She noticed that Heuster moved fast for a big man.

"Hi, Mizbie. You have Desmin, don't you?" Heuster slowed to walk with her.

"He's one of mine, yes. How's he doing for you?" Mizbie couldn't really concentrate on Heuster's answer. She thought about a July night when she and Carl had "taken a break" and she braved Tikki Cove Speed Date night. For $10, Sylvia, the owner, gave everyone two beers, pizza, and an hour of speed dating. Mizbie was more of a wine lover, but she felt the beer would put her in the mood, so she took a drink from the first beer and spilled half of it down the front of her blouse.

After a visit to the restroom, she noticed the timers were already set. She sat in her previous seat and there across from her sat Heuster. He knew she was seeing someone, and he looked surprised to see her there. She was puzzled by his nervousness, because he always seemed so full of himself. Mizbie waited an eternity for the timer to ring. The next man was at least 60, nearly twice her age, dressed in a polyester jacket and a fish tie. Sweating profusely, he spoke little about himself but described himself as a naturalist. Trying to put him at ease, she made conversation about a National Geographic special she had seen and suggested he might enjoy it.

"Is it violent?" his eyebrows shot up. "I've seen enough violence in my life. I can't see any more violence."

The next man was even older. Mizbie looked over her shoulder trying to see where men her age were. This man had two offending hairs plastered over the top of his shiny pate. She smelled mothballs. *How do I get out of this?* The timer mercifully buzzed. She saw Heuster sneak away to the main room where a band played, so she joined him. Over beer, they recounted their speed-dating skirmishes.

◉

"Desmin's got a poker chip on his shoulder," Mizbie finally answered, "But I don't think we have anything to worry about with him."

"He's having a tough time in gym. He's not real coordinated, and when Brandon had a few words with him –, you have Brandon too, right?"

Mizbie nodded.

"He said he'd been expelled in Detroit for hitting a kid over the head with a lead pipe and putting him in the hospital. It scared the hell out of Brandon."

"That's just talk," Mizbie said. "Desmin told Rashmi to quit looking at him funny or the same thing that happened to a guy in Detroit, would happen to her. They never saw that kid again. I couldn't believe he'd say that to gentle Rashmi."

Mizbie had called Desmin's aunt that afternoon. She'd said, "Des' from Detroit, you know. My little bro is his dad and he couldn't handle Des'. Des' got in with the wrong crowd after his ma took off, so I said I'd take him. Des and me, we gonna get along just fine. I'm a prison guard with the Department of Corrections. I'm Army Reserve too. I'll whip him into shape, honey. Tough love, you know? With the accent on tough. I'll whip him upside the head I hear talk of him bad mouthing that girl again. Already got him doing 50 pushups with me every day. He scared, that's all, this a new place, the way he look and everything. He make up stories to cover up he's afraid. He find his way. He smart, you see. I make sure he catch up."

"Fifty pushups a day? That can't hurt." Heuster smiled.

"His aunt, Ms Gray, isn't giving up on him yet."

Although Mizbie had seen Heuster in the copy room, she rarely had a real conversation with him. Her first impression was not all that great. It was on a professional development day when there were no students, so he'd come to school in a shirt that barely covered his chest but show-cased his body builder physique, every pec and bicep. Squaring off by the mailboxes, a chemistry teacher turned and locked eyes with him. "Hey, Heuster," he sniffed, "keep it in the locker room, will ya?"

"You sayin' I stink? Huh? Smell this!" He raised his sculpted arm and stood face to face with his accuser to reveal a clean-shaven under-arm. His voice commanded, "Go ahead. Smell my armpit!"

"Whew . . . smells like 'roid rage to me." The chemistry teacher backed off.

Mizbie saw amusement in Heuster's eyes, but the confrontation made her grab her copies and leave.

Heuster toured in bodybuilding events on weekends – probably with the help of some body-building enhancements. He told the guys in gym class and the wrestling team that it was clean living and eating right. In the teachers' workroom, he gave renditions of protein shakes, chest shavings, Vaseline shining, bench press prowess, and the bicep size that inched out other body builders more experienced than his 27 years. But now she found him easier to talk to than the fatherly speed daters, and he seemed an agreeable listener; she liked that.

∾

"The next newspaper deadline is in six days and we don't have a lead story. What have you got?" Mizbie and her school newspaper reporters brainstormed between bites of their lunches.

"I say we interview Singer," Mara Jade looked at him. "You did a cross-country motorcycle trip last summer."

Singer nearly knocked his Coke on the floor. "This trip . . . a couple guys read *On the Road* and it just sounded like a good idea." He looked doubtful. "It's nothing to write about really."

"Was it a feeling of wanting to escape from Astor?" Mizbie asked.

Singer replied, "We didn't do it 'cause anybody dared us to or anything. We didn't do it to tell everybody we did it. We didn't do it to look like we were living the life. We did it – we were just a bunch of guys pushing out, just because we wanted to."

"C'mon, Singer," Mara Jade balled up her kale chips bag. She sat on her knees and leaned in his face. "Give me something I can use."

"I don't know . . . we just started talking about it so much, we felt like we had to. It was something we had to do or we'd be worse than dog crap for wanting to do it so bad and then not doing it. I felt like if we didn't do this, it would torture me the rest of my life. Like the guy who dies at the end of a movie, not to do this thing would always be my big regret. And now that we've done it . . . not that it was SO GREAT or anything –, but it makes me wonder if each thing I choose to do makes me different."

"Singer, your decision carried so much power." Mizbie grew animated. "Had you ever made a decision like this yourself?"

"Decisions about what direction to take, experiences I'll have or won't have. Before I was like a pool ball and my life was the table. I was shot from bumper to bumper and for a change this was a shot I got to call. Like that."

"Singer, you've got to save these thoughts." Mizbie picked up a marker and began writing on the white board. "You've got to write it down and maybe put it in a song for your band. Everyone, think about the meaning out of what Singer said. We'll get a good lead article out of this. Headlines, anyone? Something about seeing your life differently?"

"Aw, geez, writing it down would completely mess it up." Singer winced, but his hand over his mouth hid a grin.

"Writing it down preserves the ideas, Singer, it doesn't spoil them. When you're 35 and have eight daughters, you'll want them to read this," Mizbie said.

"I can't write anything about the trip."

"Look, you have to give us something," Mara Jade rifled through her backpack for a pen.

"Write it like you said it. The same way. Don't even think about how it sounds."

"But once it's written, it doesn't change. If I write down what we did, it stays that way forever. I don't want that. This way it changes every time I tell it, then what I tell becomes the truth. Not that this is a lie, I really did it, but when I talk about it, I think of new stuff that it means to me, like thinking out loud. There isn't such a thing as a lie, only different versions of the truth; that's what my dad says."

"Be Walt Whitman, Singer," Mizbie said. Singer had told her that each time he sang songs with his band, the songs changed a little. "You know how many revisions Whitman made in *Leaves of Grass*?" As she spoke to Singer, other students began paragraphs of the article, piecing it together. Singer's page was still blank.

Jesspin9
to Mbax20
9:00 p.m.
September 20

Hey Miz,

They made the offer, and I've decided to go. My uncle's publishing house in Chicago will give me a stipend, and I think it'll be enough for about four months if I'm frugal, and you know how I can stretch a dollar, or in this case a Euro. I've spent too many years wishing for a chance. Now it's my turn. The plane leaves JFK on Tuesday, and I'll be on it. I'll buy a ten-speed in Amsterdam after I arrive. Everything I need will be in my backpack.

Basically, they hired me to hang out. I'll hang out in hostels, pubs, beaches, anywhere with a good bike trail and decent street food. I hope to make it down through France, maybe follow the Loire for some good local cheese and wine, western Spain or wherever they have tapas, although I'd like to make it to Madrid and up to the beaches at San Sebastian and the other Basque areas. Then on to northern Italy, maybe Fiorenza. Maybe I'll catch up with my brother and his family in Belgium. What will my big banker brother think of his little sis now?

I'll email a draft chapter back to them once a week and maybe drum up interest ahead of publication with my blog. Here in Chicago I met a couple from Amsterdam, and they gave me the location of a good falafel-and-crepe vendor in Amsterdam. I'll think of you back here teaching school while I'm away. The thought of this adventure is terrifying and compelling. Wish me luck.

Jess

Mizbie sighed and replied to the message, trying to keep the envy out of her words. She offered to watch Daphne the cat while Jess was away.

Turning to the window sill she looked at the lucky bamboo plant that had flourished when Carl had given it to her two years ago. Now it had lost leaves and those that remained had yellowed. The twisty stalk was still green, so Mizbie couldn't allow herself to throw out a plant that had the possibility of a comeback. She soaked the pebbles surrounding the stalks.

A snappy knock on the door. *Carl.*

Mizbie raced to the bathroom mirror. A blue streak crossed her cheek. "You ink-stained wretch," she said to the mirror, rubbing out the mark. She had just finished the 12th melancholy paper on Blake's "Tyger Tyger, Burning Bright." She grumbled and ran a brush through a wave of her hair. "You look like you've dredged up a reliquary of dead thoughts!" A lick of lip gloss later, she made it back to her door with a few long steps. He had come probably right from the airport. Even though he'd had a five-hour flight from Italy, business class, his suit looked Armani fresh in contrast to her monochrome army green T-shirt and jeans. She stood face to face with him, tense and expectant.

"That suit looks hot. Take it off," Mizbie said.

Carl removed his suit jacket and tossed it on a chair. "Milan was . . . productive." He looked like he was going to say more, but just looked at her. "I brought you something," He showed her a shiny, dark box. They sat down and Carl's arm wrapped around her.

"Oh, Carl," she said. Her fingers loosened the silver ribbon and broke the tape on the azure paper. The satin-lined box of the same color opened to reveal an orb.

His head touched hers. "It's Murano art glass."

"Oh, it's . . . resplendent," Mizbie said, puzzled and pleased. He knew she didn't like to dust, but clearly he had put some thought into the gift. "I've never seen anything like it." She turned the glass sculpture around in her hand. Light from the window played through two birds with feathers, or perhaps two fish with scales. The figures faced each other to form an abstract heart shape in brilliant blues and iridescent hues.

"So what do you want here? We're starting from scratch. Let's create something new." He leaned closer.

He's undergone a reptilian shed. He thinks he can reinvent himself in some new persona of altruism?

Mizbie smelled the cologne he had worn when they first met. The memory made her legs give an involuntary quiver.

"How about some wine?" She jumped up. "I have a new Italian table wine. We'll celebrate your homecoming and my three-day weekend."

"I had something else in mind," Carl leaned back and straightened the creases in his pants. "But wine is good."

What did the gift mean and why did she pull away? It bothered her that Carl knew more people, was more disciplined, more widely traveled and far less impressed with Mizbie's life than she was with his. She brought two glasses nearly full of red wine back to the living room, and handed one to Carl. He accepted his glass and examined the jewel tone. In a sonorous Italian accent he said, "Look . . . flushed ripe and round with beautiful legs . . . in army green jeans." He took a sip. "Ahh . . ."

Mizbie laughed. He set both their glasses down and took her hand, wrapping himself in her arms. He moved them both to a dancing rhythm of his own music. With a smile, he whispered in her ear. *"Bellisima! Andiamo!"*

He had me at flushed and ripe. Her trust radar, usually right out in front like cats' whiskers, took a long lean stretch and purred.

Mizbie put on the sound track to *Il Postino* and, with Carl's help, cooked and served dinner. The aroma of homemade lobster ravioli won out over the balsamic in the Caprese salad with its Leelanau cheese instead of traditional buffalo mozzarella. Carl said he was starving and asked for just another little piece of ravioli. The bubbly Prosecco she served carried over to the dessert, a cocoa-sprinkled tiramisu from her favorite *Cook's Illustrated* recipe, which she had made the night before. Carl rounded off the edges of the remaining tiramisu, insisting each bite was his last.

Leaving the dishes on the table, Carl took her hand and led her to the living room. He found a song for a slow dance. Mizbie lit a candle on the table. They danced until the music stopped and eventually found their way to the bedroom, where they fell into bed. Carl pulled her T-shirt over her head. He whispered in Italian and kissed her deeply. His love-making reminded Mizbie of sailing lessons in the little Lightning boats on a brisk day on Lake Huron. When she recognized the right breeze coming up, she would grip the tiller and angle the boat to catch the breeze just right, and just before the sail caught full of wind, there was a tiny tremble in the tiller. She loved the tremble, the anticipation.

Carl was high-maintenance, craving attention, but he understood her, and sometimes recognized what she wanted before she knew it herself. He put into words on a Friday night, what she wouldn't have realized until Monday morning. In Mizbie's mind, the words *Carl* and *mate* often came together like a game of ball magnets swinging apart, and then resting together.

"Acch . . . I'm a friggin' salmon swimming upstream trying to spawn," Carl's mood changed as he tried various positions with his full stomach.

Unlike most men Mizbie had dated, just when she thought she knew Carl, his prickly temperament resisted her efforts to figure him out. She asked him if it was time to go home, but sensed his reluctance to leave. She wanted to be with him and needed to get away from him too. She needed closeness, freedom, dialogue, and quiet. Having one made her long for the other. She didn't decide to fall in love, like she had decided to make the lobster ravioli for dinner. There was not thought or decision involved any more than the jazzed feeling from impulsively eating one chocolate kiss, then wanting the rest of the bag.

"Descend, Mr. Salmon," Mizbie arched her back and Carl dove.

The next morning was Saturday, and they lay nestled between pillows – the pure luxury of sleeping in. Lying there with Carl, wanting to suspend the moment, she said, "You know me, Carl. And here you are anyway."

Carl grunted contentedly. "Imagine us fossilized like two hermit crabs together forever." Mizbie nearly said it was that their bristly temperaments sometimes stung them both, but thought better of it.

Carl listened to the neighbors arguing in the hallway, unable to distinguish words but able to hear the impatience of a child and a consoling parent. His mind wandered, longing to find the magic of getting women to do what he wanted them to do without feeling cocooned by them. He thought of the trophy wives he'd seen on the arms of men at business functions, listening to the husbands boast about these women who apparently turned into tigers afterward in the bedroom.

In the meantime, Mizbie showered and sang to an old Phil Collins song. "Jimmy Mack, Jimmy Mack . . ." Her hair dryer stopped. Mizbie's father had taught her well, so rather than call on Carl, who couldn't hammer a nail straight, install a computer printer, or bring back to life any household appliance, she performed these duties for both of them. *Carl had other strengths,* and the hair dryer hummed in minutes.

Carl pictured her singing into her hairbrush microphone, her shoulder-length, wet hair swinging while she swooped and hopped to the beat, naked before the bathroom mirror. Married men seemed, for the most part, content. *They knew this magic.* Carl wanted that contentment and satisfaction. Like Ayn Rand's Atlas, he relished holding up his black-and-white world himself, even as it became more difficult, the power and wealth that his business generated was becoming more important than how he got it. Feeling the power made him desire more. *How much was enough?* So far, he hadn't discovered the magic that others seemed to have to make it happen, that feeling of having enough, being content.

Chapter 3

Writing on the Nick Huntsman's T-shirt –

Pro life! Support the death penalty!

Astor was a town that could've had a motto along with the Elks, Optimists, and Moose emblems welcoming newcomers along M-58. The motto would read, "Astor: True to Our Beliefs." True, the *Astor Index* had conducted an informal survey in which 71 percent of the population believed team loyalty defined Astor. With few exceptions, Astorians built up personal narratives to support their belief systems, ignoring pesky facts. A giant human skeleton found in the Arabian Desert? Of course. Moon landing? A Hollywood hoax. The Earth was flat in Astor. Astorians who couldn't trust the government, but could trust their little pebble in the big pond, hid behind their bunkers of constructed beliefs. Some truth was too painful. Townspeople didn't ask questions, if answers would put voice to the great distance among its citizens. But there were exceptions.

The Astor *Index*, that liberal bastion, had an editor with a nettlesome way of dredging up uncomfortable facts to counteract local rumors. But Astor preferred to believe the rumors anyway, refuting them even more so after facts were published, including town councilman Eli Smith, whose judicious use of tax money included a convention in Las Vegas where he lost $26,520 at the blackjack tables. Local merchants preferred to remember it was Smith who brought federal funds to build a $1.5-million model-railroad history museum that brought dozens of hobbyists to Astor each year for its annual model train convention.

Actually, it was Smith's father, Earl, who owned the local hobby shop that sold model cars and trains. Earl wrote the letters and became a fly in the ear of Congresswoman Williams who got the bill passed while glad-handing Eli. Beyond councilman, Eli's career life was questionable since being thrown out of his dad's business at age 19, yet he took all the credit for the little museum.

The word at the Bean and Leaf coffee shop was that Mayor Stevens's popularity had plummeted, all because of a bucket of beige paint. It seems no one knew or cared much about the combination mayoral and school board presidential election last year. It didn't come close to the excitement of the previous three mayoral elections among stray cats and dogs. Because Astor was the county home for the Humane Society, Astorians decided to bestow the mayoral honors one year on a cat named Cat, and the following two election years on the same dog, appropriately named Dog.

The mayor-president was brought on a leash to every city-council/ school-board meeting and the council found it a pleasant experience to reach consensus on nearly every vote that way. Dog sat at the feet of council-board members with the countenance of a bloodhound, appearing to listen to the discussions of street name changes or snow plow consolidations with all due gravity. Unfortunately, now that PharmaTek had brought so many jobs to Astor, council-board members, including Carl, felt a shift in local politics. The new PharmaTek board members suggested that a human mayor might up the town's respectability and stature.

Barb Stevens had no previous political experience beyond her membership in the town council-board. She did have some popular ideas about educating local students and saving money. "We want dedicated teachers, not those hot shots who are just in it for the money," she said. The council-board members weren't fond of opinionated women, but they liked the way she talked. "PharmaTek wants to build a new biotech facility. That means more jobs. They need us to give them a tax break of 6 percent. If we lower teacher salaries by 6 percent that should take care of it."

Carl reminded the members that they had just lowered teachers' salaries 4 percent last year and offered a compromise of 5 percent, figuring the remainder could be made up by taxes from new employees of PharmaTek. They agreed that a 5 percent salary reduction was clearly a generous offer.

"You know, Mayville is really saving some bucks next year. They'll be Mayville Charter Academy." Barb Stevens looked around. No one had heard this bit of news.

"How does that work?" Carl tapped notes on his notepad.

"Miller-Smith is taking them over. They'll let all of the teachers go and hire cheaper ones fresh out of college. All services are outsourced, so they're cheaper too. None of that art or music stuff anymore. Kids can't make a living learning art or music."

"So what's their track record?" Carl was looking up Miller-Smith, a Fortune 500 conglomerate.

"Their track record? They've got a great business model. That's what we need, to run schools like a business with the students as a product. It's golden."

"It looks like they've opened a dozen schools in a three-state area in the last year. But the COO gets a half mil a year for each school. How's that cheaper?" Carl was still searching for an education model on the company website.

"Look, you've got to pay for good leadership, Carl. With all the cuts to teachers, it's still cheaper. Miller-Smith's even got this deal where each school advertises and attracts all the community kids in the fall so they have a big enrollment. As soon as the Fourth Friday Count is over, they get rid of any kid who needs special ed services. Special ed teachers are too expensive, so they don't hire them. They send those kids back to public school. For discipline problems, they kick the bad actors out too." She pointed her pencil at him for emphasis. "The school gets all the Fourth Friday Count state money from the special ed kids and troublemakers, but they get rid of the kids. It's a win-win."

Carl reminded himself not to tell this to Mizbie. She waited outside the door, ready to present a request for funds for St. Bartholomew's. If she heard half of this talk about Miller-Smith, she'd be a raging conflagration all weekend. "Doesn't that put a burden on the public schools that are left?" Carl found a website comparing salaries of principals. They could hire five of them for the price of Miller-Smith's COO.

"That's the thing. The troublemakers and special ed kids don't score well on standardized tests, so it makes the charters look great next to the public schools. And there's not so much dang accountability or oversight for charters, so they can get away with creative accounting and reporting, ya know what I mean?" Barb smiled and raised her eyebrow. "They spend millions on advertising. Just think, St. Bartholomew's Charter Academy. Of course, we'll still support the football team; that's a given."

"I don't know, Barb. What about the students?" Carl was looking at websites of the Miller-Smith's charters and couldn't find much beyond mission statements about a new path to value. "The company's only been in education for a year. Don't you think it's too soon to tell how it's working out?"

"That's the best part, Carl. We'll spend less per student than we do now. Less per teacher too. Students are such a drain on taxpayer money. Miller-Smith will run it like a business and we'll be able to lower taxes."

Carl opened the door for Mizbie to join them, but Barb was still talking. "If teachers were doing their jobs, kids wouldn't spend their summers playing video games and eating junk food." Barb leaned in to make her point. "They'd have a work ethic." She looked at Mizbie. "Why should we pay higher wages to teachers when our trash haulers really do more to keep Astor a good place to live?"

Mizbie used every ounce of jaw-clenching, fist-tightening, self-control and faced Barb with a smile. Mizbie spoke of summer math and reading programs staffed by volunteer teachers. She assured Barb that none of the programs included video games or eating junk food. Her voice grew louder and she explained the PowerPoint slides she brought. Robotics students were working under a ceiling of falling plaster. In another slide, science students watched their teacher, her work friend, Mark, conduct one experiment when they should have had supplies to conduct their own experiments. Council-board members barely looked at the screen. Mizbie picked up the textbook Mark had given her for the meeting.

"See this 10-year-old science book?" She slammed the tattered book on the meeting table and gained their attention. "According to this, Pluto is still a planet." Her English texts were even older. She saw Barb look at everyone around the table. No one but Carl would argue with Barb.

"And remember the band uniforms," Mizbie fought to keep the edge out of her voice. "They were promised two years ago, but the order was never completed. Uniforms are 12 years old and falling apart."

"Music again," Barb pointed her pencil at Mizbie. "We don't have money to spend on the band. Music does nothing but cost money."

Mizbie braced herself. "Take a look at what *Science Daily* has to say about music. And PBS, and the *New York Times*." She walked around the table and gave each board member stapled sheets of printed graphs from studies she'd prepared. "When children learn an instrument, the brain power also transfers to other subjects, especially science. Music learning stays with students for life. St. Bartholomew's student deserve better."

"Hah," Barb pushed the papers away without looking at them. "*Science Daily*, PBS, just a bunch of shrinks. And the *New York Times*? Left-wing nuts, all of them. You wouldn't hear Fox News saying such nonsense."

The PharmaTek public relations representative rented a bus and took the city council-school board to Grand Rapids for a pricey dinner. Despite the council's lack of enthusiasm toward the additional cost of paying a mayor, after a few drinks and prime rib, the council began to see the wisdom of PharmaTek's idea. Shortly after, Steven's name appeared in a blitz on local TV4 and billboard ads. On voting day, the ballot read

Dog

Barb Stevens

Anthony Vizente

Voters picked the most familiar name, the one that looked most mainstream. Who had time to think about issues and wonder whether

Barb Stevens promoted hauling Canadian toxic trash into nearby land-fills or not?

The first executive decision made by Mayor Stevens after her land-slide election victory, was to remove the Native American mural that had graced the central wall since the city hall was built. The hall had celebrated its sesquicentennial the year before, and in celebration, the aging mural had a thorough cleaning from a company that special-ized in such work, coming all the way from New York. During the cel-ebration, half the town walked in, curious to gawk at the rehabilitated mural, the first image that greeted citizens when they walked in the door. Too Spirit, a homeschooled, native Ojibwa student, gave a speech in her native dress. Someday she would lead her tribe. Mayor Steven's decision to remove the mural came, she said to the city council, in a dream. Dressed in her customary red blazer, she straightened her lapel with the diamond columbine pin, a gift from PharmaTek the day before she declared her candidacy for mayor of Astor.

She certainly didn't mean to insult the ancestors of the displaced Native Americans whose land the Astorians relieved them of nearly two centuries ago. The town's founding fathers had named half the new roads, made from Ojibwa trails, with native names as a tribute to them. The Ojibwas were use to it, having previously been relieved of their land near Chillicothe, Ohio, before settling in Astor. But now the chronically civic-minded town council thought it would be a tonic in these economically difficult times to rename Anougons Street, named for the Ojibwa warrior Little Star, to Maxfield Drive, homage to the retiring football coach. Despite an opportunity to obliterate five min-utes of spare time at the end of their meeting to scuttle out early and possibly preserve the memory of Anougons, the council didn't hesitate or table the vote to encourage further thought, but voted on the street name while the thought was fresh. It unanimously passed.

The street name change was just one of the kindnesses Mayor Stevens saw as respect to the new eastern Indians who were becoming a larger percentage of the conservative voting population, thanks to the growing pharmaceutical plant. Seeing the mural would be just too con-fusing for them, too off-putting. Now instead of a 20-foot work of art with lush green Michigan flora and fauna, Native Americans building hogans and planting crops, and an orange sun lowering over a sparkling Lake Ojibwa, citizens were greeted with an expanse of calming beige paint, an update she called it. The tax assessor's door in the middle was kept with its original oak wood trim.

～

Genevieve walked in the classroom, looking like they'd make an exception and drop the velvet rope just for her. Her chichi oversized bag swung off her shoulder and landed with a thunk on the desk. From it she pulled a comb, bent it, and tested its tensile strength. Slipping into her seat, Genevieve played with the hair of the girl in front of her. Today it was tiny braids. Last hour it was Robin's hair she gathered in tiny clips all over the back of his head until he pulled them out and scowled at her with a firm, NO! Students sitting in front of Genevieve understood this was something she was born to do. She had a passion for hair. Often before class started, they just let her do it, enjoying the tug and smoothing brush of her hands against their heads and hair, a personal pleasure in a public place.

Her jeans, tight as guitar strings, drew the guys' attention and her gaze held them like catnip. Behind the gaze that appeared as if she was mind crunchingly bored, or was less capable of thought than a dust bunny, she watched through her invisible mirror. Her mirror allowed her to see and understand her friends, their wants and their differences. But left her feeling as if no one would ever understand her or even bother to try. How different she felt. It wasn't that she wanted to be more conventional, but just understood. If someone would only try to take a step through the mirror.

Papers rustled. Poems were pulled from notebooks. "Okay, we're listening for voice and style, whether you use broad beautiful phrases or simple compact prose. The writer, E. L. Doctorow, once wrote that the ideas in poems come out of their emotions, and the emotions are carried on images. He also said words have music in them, and thinking the word, you can hear its sound. Remember the images in "The Highwayman" poem? They were musical and rhythmic, carried on emotion. You're not lemmings ready to jump off a cliff after one another. You think for yourselves."

"This better help my grade. I gave up four hours of work at the batting cages last night to work on this sh . . . thing,"

"Ah, Desmin . . . 'Oft in jest have I heard truth!' That's Chaucer. But you don't have to give up work to write. Work is the material of writing. Stolen moments make writing."

"Yeah, but you get paid to say that. I lose pay to write this sh . . . thing."

Mizbie took in a breath but didn't say what she was thinking. "Amanda, could we hear yours first?"

Amanda was reluctant to do anything that brought attention to her. Her voice was tentative. "It's called 'Hidden Papers.'"

I've been looking for the divorce papers since
We moved here from Ohio,
And I found them last month tucked away
In a sewing machine cabinet where Mom
Didn't think my brother or I
Would find them.
When I feel confused, I return to them.
So I read them again today,
Since my mother just left to get a tattoo
Of the band Metallica."
Amanda paused and looked at Mara Jade before she continued.
"Another mom.
Wouldn't wear tight jeans and wedge herself
In the middle of my friend's conversations.

I look at the beginning of the document,
So formal and British like,
The Magna Carta from history class.

I've read the papers so many times; they're familiar to me,
But I go back for something more,
In case I'll find something to explain what
Turned my life inside out."

"Thank you, Amanda." Mizbie was surprised by her candor. "That had to be hard to write."

Rashmi entered the room, followed by the scent of curry. All eyes were on her brilliant orange sari. The intricate designs imitated the henna tattoos on her hands and forearms. A sparkling trail of beads wove its way into the long braid down her back. It swayed and shimmered. She took her seat.

"You look amazing, Rashmi. How was the student council meeting?" Mizbie asked.

"We are making plans for the homecoming dance. And today's my birthday."

"Oh! Snap your fingers, everyone. What's your favorite thing to do?" The class finger snapped a rhythm, a birthday routine Mizbie knew would put off any class work, but no one in the room would care.

"Probably it would be . . . doing Sudoku puzzles."

"One . . . two . . . one, two, ready go.

Rashmi is her name and Sudoku is her game.
You can catch her playing Sudoku in the sun and the rain.
She'll Sudoku high, Sudoku low,
She'll Sudoku Sudoku wherever she goes.
So if you're looking for a friend,
And you don't know what to do,
Just count on Rashmi,
And she'll help you!"

"Woo . . . happy birthday," they cheered and clapped.

"So what kind of birthday cake will you have?" Mizbie asked.

"No cake, just my grandmother's mango smoothie. It is my favorite. Can I tell about my outfit?"

"Listen, everyone," Mizbie looked at the back corner guys. Her traffic cop hand wasn't needed.

"This is from the Cahndni Chowk Bazaar, a market in New Delhi. My aunt chose it and sent it to my mother for my fifteenth birthday. It is one of the most-prized styles, made of Banarasi silk. It is hand woven. A sari takes the weaver about two weeks to make. It is one long piece of fabric about six yards long, and my mother had it starched and ironed to make it look just right."

Rashmi was sitting with her back away from the seat, probably to avoid wrinkles in the silk, or maybe just out of excitement.

"So, Rawsh, ya gonna dress like this every day?"

"Oh no," she smiled and answered Robin politely. "I prefer blue jeans. But for special occasions, it is fun to honor old traditions."

"Yeah, old traditions," Robin repeated. He was ready with a joke but caught Mizbie's eye, and thought better of it.

"Have fun celebrating your birthday today, Rashmi. I hope you get some new Sudoku puzzles," Mizbie said. "Any other birthdays today?"

Desmin raised his hand. "I wrote this pome on my birthday. It was Sunday and my dad called. I don't see him much no more, but he always calls on my birthday from wherever he is."

"Go ahead, Desmin," Never had Desmin offered to read before. Mizbie tried to remain calm.

"I had a confetti cake with white frosting birthday –"
Desmin interrupted his own poem. "–I had to start that way 'cause Miz Baxter – she always ax what kinda cake we have on our birthdays."
"– After I blew out candles and wished,
Dad called from Hope, Arkansas.
He ax how I was.
I say Dad, I hurtin'–
A hurt that don't go away.
He say that hurt is too much for him to handle and
Talk to you next year.

Next year?

41

I tell him I'm takin' driver's trainin',
Got a part-time job at Kenny's Market,
And my girlfriend's name is Shawnelle. (Genevieve whooped at that one.)
Next year I'll have a confetti cake with white frosting birthday
And hurt inside."

The room was quiet until Genevieve snapped her fingers in respect, and the others followed.

Robin changed the subject, revealing he had been homeschooled last year.

"What was it like?" Genevieve asked.

"You can take all the time you want on one subject," he said. "It was hard coming here at first. I had to get used to the bells, and I felt like there wasn't enough time."

This was the most serious conversation Robin had ever had.

"Our moms got a group of us together once a month, so we wouldn't feel so isolated. Hogwarts school science experiments at Halloween, a *Wicked* train trip to Chicago, figuring the trajectory of the train, Meijer Gardens for art appreciation, researching the Diaspora of Jews to Israel for world history, stuff like that. We had enough home-school people to get together a softball team in the spring."

"Softball for guys?" Justin said. "That's just weird."

"A diaspora. That's a great idea," Mizbie countered. "Imagine some-day when you all graduate and create a diaspora of your own in the world, spreading your worldview everywhere you go." She looked at Robin, who had told her he had an adopted Korean sister. Her Korean grandmother had told her that eight was an auspicious number, and she should marry on a day with an eight in it, probably on August, the eighth month. Robin had shown Mizbie a celadon turtle that his sister had made herself from clay that her grandmother bought on the Internet from South Korea.

The glaze's watery jade green was like the green of his adoptive mother's eyes, he said. Back in the 12th century, it was said to resemble the gray-green of the ocean surrounding Korea. Mizbie wanted to say that she hoped by the end of the year, the students might have been influenced a shade, just because she had the privilege of teaching them. She wanted to tell them how much she learned from them. But she knew what she'd already said sounded sappy enough, so she kept that part to herself.

Everyone appeared to be thinking about softball and the diaspora, except Edward in the back, who was reading another book about wolves. His bookmark was a picture he had drawn of a wolf. Mizbie had to seat him alone in the back corner because whomever she tried to seat him next to would end up in the counselor's office. Edward complained that students looked at him and spoke to him, and it made him want to kill himself. Edward occasionally mumbled something unintelligible. He had been seeing a counselor for more than a year according to his grandmother. Mizbie would speak to him during her walks around the room and once in awhile he would turn in part of an assignment on a scrap of paper, surrounded by drawings of wolf faces with piercing eyes.

Earlier she had seen him by his locker where he downed much of a two-liter Mountain Dew. "What's with the hand?" His right hand was red and swollen.

"I messed it up hitting the TV," he grimaced. "I was playing Drag Racer, and I wiped out my car."

"This is a video game?"

"Yeah, a Superbox game. So I wiped out my car, and I was so mad I walked up to the screen and popped it one."

"Edward, you – did your grandmother get mad about the TV?"

"No, it was my dad's. It's just a little crack in the screen. He thought it was funny. But it's my right hand. His face brightened. I can't write my quiz today."

"You're in luck! The quiz is on computer. All you have to do is press the key." She spoke to the class. "So remember our penny collection for hurricane victims. Tomorrow's the last day."

She took the picture that Edward had been sketching with his swollen hand, and slapped it on the white board with a magnet. Its piercing wolf eyes stared at her and a chill crept up her back.

Nick walked in and slunk to his seat. "Where have you been?" Mizbie asked. "We're half way through class." Classmates turned around to look at him and quickly turned back, avoiding his lightning-rod stare.

"I don't wanna talk about that duckweed Krahler," he growled.

In Mizbie's school mail that day she found a note from Nick's mother excusing his eight tardies. For all the make-up work Mizbie had given Nick, he couldn't seem to get it turned in except for a character essay on "The Pit and the Pendulum." Three quarters of it was in handwriting other than his own.

"Get those eyes off my paper, Nick." Izzy's papers were skillfully edited and she bristled at students who resented her work.

Nick mumbled something about the word gray.

"What 'chu mean I'm gray? You tryin' to act black? I get in your face when you get in mine? Why not just you be you, and me be me?" Izzy scowled at him.

"Okay, Socrates discussion question. Our question today is based on a quote from *Don Quixote,* thought to be the first European novel, by the Spanish author Cervantes, from the early 1600s. 'Facts are the enemy of truth.' So let's take the idea a step further. Can fiction ever be more honest than truth? Izzy, what do you think?"

"I think the Anne Frank diary proves that truth is important. Look at the impact that book had. I read it last year, and I still think about it. It wouldn't mean anything if –"

"Sorry the PA is down," a secretary walked in. "Robin, they want you in the office."

"Which one?" Robin asked.

"Blue pass. The guidance office."

"Well, I think it means sometimes facts can get in the way of the real point," Robin stood up from his seat. "Like Saturday, I was two hours late getting home and Dad was hot. That was a fact. But when he cooled down, I told him my aunt asked me to mow the lawn because she just got out of the hospital. That was the truth. He got mad for nothing." He left with his blue pass.

"It wouldn't mean anything if it was all made up," Izzy continued. "It's only powerful because it's true. Anybody who thinks the Holocaust never happened, they should just read this. Then they'll know."

"Desmin, you're looking like you don't agree," Mizbie said.

"Yeah, I mean just because a book is true doesn't make it something people can get into and walk around in, you know? I mean, look at *Catch 22*. It's not true, but it could be. The sh . . . the stuff that happens to Yossarian and stuff he thinks about . . . and that scene where the ball turret gunner's entrails are just hanging there . . . man! I'm sure that stuff happened, but he made it all up. He was in a war. He knew what combat was like. It's like he –"

Another secretary came in with a pass. "Izzy, they want you in the office."

"Ooh . . . orange pass . . . Izzy's in trouble!" Desmin said.

"It's like he used his memories to make something bigger than the memory. He wanted people to think, SO THAT'S what it's really like. If he had just written down the memory, it wouldn't a hit me that way. Those stories from your life are always better if you kick 'em up." Desmin slapped his hands on the desk. "Oh jeez –"

The first secretary returned. "I'm sorry. I hope this is the last. Edward, report to the science lab. Take your project draft with you."

"Yeah . . . I forgot," Edward said, gathering his books. He followed Izzy and the two secretaries out the door.

Mizbie tried to hold the thread of thought. "Oola, what do you think about truth and fiction?" She had raised a tentative hand, the first time in weeks. Mizbie could see she needed time to gather her thoughts, and translate them.

"I think . . . well it's so . . ." she halted and rearranged her words. "I think of *Hunger Games* book. What Katniss goes through is alternate world, but her family and her friends are very real." Oola pronounced her "R's" like revving motors. "Like my friends in Ukraine, I may never see again. I email and Skype them, but I miss them. Friendship is different at home. There are not pecking, pecking like chickens that we have here. Friends compete, then they encourage, then they hope, like in book, I think.

"I remember picnics in Ukraine with my grandmother and friends on top of hill over the Black Sea. Grandmother told about shipwrecks in sea, and sometimes we'd see bottle-nosed dolphin playing in waves. The breezes blew across our faces, through our hair. We ate pickled eggs and herring, and Grandmother talked about when she was my age, spitting three times over left shoulder and sitting on luggage before taking a trip."

"Superstitions?" Mizbie asked.

"Yes, superstitions. My mother has superstitions too. Never have an even number of flowers in a glass, or it will cause death. Odd numbers only. We talk and laugh. We work hard, but there is time. Here there is no time. Everything is rush, rush. My mother brings me here because there is not future for me there. She marries American, so she can come to this country to practice medicine and give me future. I have said too much."

A secretary walked in, braced for more protests. "I need Rashmi Kapoor, Sean Flanagan, Nick Huntsman, Mohammed Satr, and Rip Helthaller in the Career Lab."

"Do you have to take them *now*?" Mizbie voiced impatience.

"The state wanted this by yesterday." The secretary looked furtively, waiting for Mizbie to explode.

"Go ahead, Oola," Mizbie ignored her.

Oola's eyes darted from one student to another. "The book, *Hunger Games,* makes me think of friendship."

"I saw the movie. Did I tell y'all I got apple-smoked bacon for my birthday? It's my favorite," Desmin said.

"C'n I say something about special ed?"

"Sure. What is it, Corwin?" Mizbie was surprised they'd stayed with the subject as long as they had.

"Well," he paused, lifting his head covered with hair like brown shaved steel. "People have to relax about what's normal. The truth is I'm in Algebra II, and it's easy. But writing is hard. People think if

Give or Take

you're special ed, you're dumb, but the truth is there are lots of kinds of normal."

"Good point, Corwin. We can't assign people to categories, give them a label, and expect less from them. Go on?"

"Yeah . . . the Lansing Lugnuts rock! I went to the game last night and Shelton pitched a no-hitter, 3-0!" Corwin wasn't known for staying with one subject for long.

"A few final reminders before we head down to the computer lab. It might sound strange because you think facts and truth . . .well . . . facts lead to truth. But not everyone sees truth the same way. Each side has its own facts and its own idea of the truth. In Chekov's story, 'The Bet,' see how far the characters take the 'enemy of truth.'" It was too late. The teachable moment was gone.

"Remember to answer all questions carefully as you continue in your adaptive learning program, otherwise it doesn't help you. Any questions?" On the way to the computer lab, Mizbie tried to talk to Oola but ran out of time. Shortly after everyone had logged in, the third and fifth rows of computers went black. Genevieve groaned. "I lost my questions 24 to 38."

"Vampire death screen. It's a takeover," Robin said to Corwin.

Students hit keys and clicked the mouse, expecting something to happen.

Mizbie crawled on hands and knees to check the connections. If student volunteers were still allowed to work in the office, they wouldn't have this problem.

"Watch your feet," she checked foot placement near plugs. The school had to hire an additional secretary, so that meant the computer lab tech had to go.

"Any heavy books on the cords? Anybody look at their screen funny?" She crawled under the last row of computer desks and followed the cords to the back. Nothing appeared loose. If only the federal funds that paid for the adaptive learning program could pay tech support to fix glitches. On the floor before her appeared two brown wing tips. She stood up face to face with Krahler.

"Ms Baxter, I expect to see you act in a more professional manner in front of students." He turned and left.

∾

On an after-dinner walk in the park behind her apartment, Mizbie happened on Heuster. Still angry over Krahler's comment, she wanted to ignore Heuster, but he was carrying a tiny electronic device, pointing it up at the trees.

She stopped. "Spying in your spare time?" He still wore his shorts and gym shoes.

"You following me, Baxter?" He took a step back for an elderly couple who strolled by. "Damn you, woman," he raised his voice. "I told you I'd send the child support. Get off my back!"

The couple looked back at Mizbie. "He's a downright, absolute, inviolable, unequivocal liar." She tossed up her hands and they kept walking.

"Wait," Heuster looked at the device. A tiny red dot turned green and he turned a dial. The device chirped.

Heuster's face looked like a first-place winner.

Chirp, click, click, click, click, click, click.

Mizbie stood closer and listened.

"It's echolocation. That's the sound bats make when they're hunting for food. See right there." He pointed up.

Mizbie looked up at the tree overhead. A tiny black bat swooped down between the trees in the dusky sky. "Heuster, you have a secret life. You're a batman."

"Last summer I hiked Carlsbad Canyon and saw the Brazilian free-tailed bats. I was hooked. This echo locator is fresh out of the box today, and I thought I'd try it out," he handed it to her. "You know in a day these guys can eat their own weight in mosquitoes, and their spit might be used in heart operations because when they bite, which is rare, the blood doesn't coagulate."

She remembered something and handed it back. "Let me tell you a story about my friend, Jess, and me up at Interlochen."

"What's Interlochen?"

"Oh Heuster, Heuster, you've been in the locker room too long." Her finger poked at his forehead. "Those ammonia fumes are eating away at those leetle gray cells. On July third, my friend, Jess, and I were working our second week as camp counselors at Interlochen. It was the summer of our sophomore year. Spending the summer there was like living in a universe where – all day – the sounds of piano, brass, woodwinds, violins, and voices emanated from practice cabins under the pines.

"We were each in charge of a girls' cabin, and we took them each night to the outdoor concert shell or bowl, where students were required to attend concerts of faculty members and big-name professional musicians who guest-taught in the morning and spent afternoons relaxing in the woodsy air. We'd kayak with the kids on Duck Lake or hike the sand dunes with them. At concert's end, we'd shepherd our girls back to their respective cabins.

"It took some work herding teenage girls past the trail when it broke off in a Y. The boys' cabins were on the opposite side of camp. The couples stopped at the fork called 'Harmony Junction' for holding hands, kissing, and the occasional grope if the counselors' flashlights missed the furtive race of a boy's hand to a breast or nether region."

"Nether region? Are we talkin' nuns here?" Heuster sat on the grass.

"Who's telling this story?" Mizbie sat cross-legged in front of him. "Jess's campers were in bathrobes brushing their teeth, preparing to hop into bunks, when they heard a ruffling of wings from the rafters over the cabin toilet. Little Kayia, a bassoon player sitting on the 'Interlochen Bowl' at the time, emitted a scream that split the air. Someone yelled 'bats' and mayhem erupted with girls throwing pillows, scrambling like cats, and swatting the air with brooms.

"'Turn off the lights!' Jess motioned. 'Turn them off now!' The girls grew silent and turned the cabin lights off.

"'Now grab your flashlights and come to the front of the cabin.' Jess shined the light in her own face. Following her lead, they flashed the lights on their own faces. Wide eyed, they huddled close.

"After a silent wait, all eyes focused on the open cabin door where two little brown sets of wings swooped and dodged toward the light and into the trees. The girls hugged and cheered and ran back into the cabin, latching the wooden screen door behind them."

"So you were a counselor at some music camp?" Heuster saw another bat and turned his device up.

"Later that night, Jess decided to escape for more adult company. When she was sure the girls were asleep, she sneaked next door to my cabin, number 8. Quietly gathering counselors as we went, we ended up fitting seven into Arno's old –"

"Wait." Heuster looked up from the dials. "Who's Arno?"

Mizbie crossed her eyes and made fish lips. "Grand Valley senior who drove up."

Heuster made a condescending grunt and went back to his dials.

"Seven of us crammed into his Volvo wagon and made our way into town for a few beers."

"Seven isn't so bad. Unless they're all weightlifters," Heuster flexed a hefty arm muscle.

"Yes, we were the Interlochen Weightlifters and Flutists Society, but there was only one seat in his van, and Arno was sitting on it."

"Until you got to the bar."

"Astute, aren't you?" Mizbie told about the bar and the trip home, during which the counselors decided to do something special for the campers when they woke on the fourth of July.

As soon as we got back, we raided the supply cabin and got dozens of rolls of TP, draping the tissue from trees, cabins, the dining hall, fire pit, and canoe shed.

At 7:00 the next morning, instead of reveille calling campers out, the camp speakers crackled with the Doors, *Light My Fire*. Campers wandered out of their cabins to a dizzy array of dew-dampened tissue. Pine trees were spiraled in white. Picnic tables were wrapped with bows. Practice rooms had doorknobs and porches festooned in streams of tissue.

"The Doors? I'd go with Alice Cooper's *House of Fire* or Bad Company's *Walk through Fire*."

Mizbie ignored him. "Within days, the camp experienced a severe TP shortage, requiring a testy supply coordinator to make an emergency run into town. 'C'mon baby, light my fire – '" Mizbie sang.

Homework waited back at her apartment. It felt good to leave it behind, and when she returned after dark, she found another reason to procrastinate.

Jesspin9
to Mbax20
5:00 p.m.
September 28

Hey Miz,

I've been here in Amsterdam for a couple of days now. I found a good sturdy bike yesterday, so today I decided to take my first ride. I saddled the panniers on the back with my two jackets, extra water, notebook, and fresh, chewy baguette from the hostel where I'm staying. It's not far from the Van Gogh Museum. The lady who runs it has goats and makes her own cheese, and the cook brings fresh eggs from her farm each morning. The bread is chewy outside and the inside is gleaming and springy.

Anyway, after cycling a mile, the pannier flew off. Last night I had just completed ten pages of draft copy, and it hadn't been sent yet. I yelled a few choice words. The notebook would be ruined, and it wouldn't be the first one. (I dropped one over the side of a tour boat in Chicago last summer.) I walked back to retrieve the dusty lump at the side of the road, shaking it gently. There was no sound of broken glass or metal. I gingerly opened the Velcro flap and to my astonishment, the notebook was intact! If the makers of that pannier were here, I'd kiss each one of them for the sturdy construction of their saddlebag. I'll send them a most obsequious thank-you email, and I'll double-check the connecting straps next time.

You know how drivers treat cyclists in the states –, like they want to throw sand in our gears. I haven't been sideswiped once since I came to Amsterdam. This has got to be the bike-friendliest city anywhere. No one cuts me off or swears at me as if I'm usurping their space when I'm in my own bike lane. Drivers are so use to bikes here, and they don't hate us. Most drivers ride bikes every day, too. We're welcome to our part of the road like part of the mainstream, not a subculture. I wish we could rewire American drivers' brains to be like Amsterdamers.

How's Daphne? I miss my kitty. I hope you don't get in trouble for having a cat in your apartment. At least she's quiet. If you want to give her treats, the salmon-flavored ones are her favorites.

That was a hoot, the teacher across the hall taking a look at your homeroom kids and saying she almost quit when she had some of them last year. Does your Principal Krahler have it in for you or something? I know you'll handle it. Either that or you'll scare 'em to death someday when you get mad at them.

So you've rekindled your feelings for Carl. I remember when you lost your parents and Carl the same year. You weren't so resilient back then. I know Ben was mean calling Carl Dubiously Gay Carl. I think Ben was just a dork. But, Miz, I still think Carl is wrong for you, even though he's gorgeous with that grin and those Sean Connery eyes.

Tomorrow I have an 82-mile ride, part in granny gear of course, up some pretty impressive hillsides. I seriously think I will call Dr. Christiaan Barnard back from the grave and ask him for a full heart – lung transplant. I think I'll pick Florence Griffith Joyner's body. That'd be a good one on the uphill, I bet. I'll travel with a bunch of students on a school bus to the base of a mountain. I didn't realize we were so close to the Alps.

Jess

Mizbie read her friend's message and proceeded to drink a topped-off glass of wine. Daphne walked in perpetual motion, her silky tortoise fur brushing against Mizbie's legs. She saved the email to a file, with the intent of giving all of the emails back to Jess when she returned to the States.

There was a bigger reason Jess had felt the need to escape. Months earlier Mizbie had told Jess to wear neutral polish with her black strappy heels on the regional TV talk show, but Jess didn't listen. She called Mizbie from the green room, pacing the floor, wearing her carefully chosen neutral gauchos and cashmere sweater, just as the director suggested, with these painted toes sticking out like Red Hot candies. The wait was interminable. Every muscle poised for her first TV appearance, she waited to talk about her first book for which she had been given her first small advance. Readers bought this slightly altered version of her own life. The alterations turned it from autobiography to novel. Just by the change of minor physical details, ages, and circumstances, not much really, she altered it with reckless freedom.

Her fiancé, Ben, didn't even mind their story being turned into a book. She told him after she was half-way through writing it, after, heart pounding, she ripped open the letter about the book deal. Before dinner, they lounged and stretched on the couch with glasses of Prosecco, while she read a selected chapter to him. He laughed at the recreation of a shared memory, a simple pleasure, wondering how she could entwine her feelings and memories, like two naked bodies, into words.

She believed in him this time, not wanting a repeat of feelings left unsaid and strongly held beliefs half-spoken. After five years of marriage and five spent divorced, she was again his fiancé, his treasure, with the betrayals mostly buried and the wonderful season of their tempestuous affair and marriage returning like spring from bud to bloom. This second time, this lovelier, wiser romance had made the big WHAT IF question a Cinderella dream, not exactly with Prince Charming, but not with the Dread Pirate Ben either.

Jess stared down at her toes, then at the clock, when she saw his letter beneath the flowers he'd sent to congratulate her success.

My Dear Jess,

Love is to be treasured, if it is real. Its passion brings me pain and feelings of losing control. It's messy and unpredictable. But it weaves a tapestry of brilliant color and depth into my life, taking it from meaningless to extraordinary. I found some of that in a greeting card, but you know what I mean.

You know I'm not a writer like you are, so I got my friend, Art, to help. Then he got his girlfriend to look at it. See, I wanted this to be a positive thing for both of us. You know I'm not good at confrontation, and I can't stand to see you upset. You've been so happy lately with the book and the TV thing, I thought the best time to tell you would be when you were happiest, and that's today. Art disagreed with this, but I think I know you by now, right?

You won't want to hear this. I didn't have the guts to tell you when you saw me off at the airport yesterday. You know I'll always love you in my way. Remember when you told me that Chinese proverb about how things happen in your life and how they don't matter? That what really matters is what you do with it, how you use it to shape the person you are? This thing just happened. Neither of us planned it. You remember Minna and how hard we've worked. You were so trusting, and I loved you for it after what I'd put you through the last time. Again, we didn't plan it. We've just shared so much these last six months and with the Abidjan deal, you remember how hard that was and all the time it took; we really leaned on each other. She's been amazing.

Minna's getting a divorce. It will be final on Thursday, and we're getting married Friday. You'll always mean the world to me; Minna knows that. Jess, just about everyone we know has seen Minna and me together. You're so trusting, and people didn't want to tell you or hurt your feelings, but they know. It's a small town. So many times I've wanted to tell you, but I cared too much to hurt you.

I wish you good luck in your book deal. It'll still be okay, because it's fiction, right? That means people expect it to be fake? I shouldn't have put off telling you, but before you go on TV, I wanted you to know, to protect you so you wouldn't get hurt. Maybe you can say something on TV that will make it not so bad. I want you to be happy. I'm in crazy stupid love. Be happy for me.

    Always,

    Ben

Mizbie had watched Jess's TV interview. Jess appeared shaken. Mizbie could see why her friend wanted so badly to take this assignment in Europe. She was one of the few people who knew Jess's motive for leaving. Jess had told everyone she knew about her upcoming television interview and couldn't tolerate sad looks or comforting voices from pitying friends. The embarrassment forced her to call her publisher uncle in Chicago and beg for anything they had. In Europe she could escape the looks, the whispers that stopped when she approached. She was free from the recurring reminders of Ben's rerun of deceit.

Mizbie stepped onto the balcony to water the few flowers that hadn't been killed by an early frost. The young married family that lived next door had moved out. She was sorry to see them go, thinking about the cookouts they had shared on her deck. But that's the way it was in this complex, young families moving on to their first homes. Now because of the PharmaTek expansion, Ukrainian and Indian families were the norm. The Indian family on the other side of her was vegetarian, and she identified the smell of curry and a possible variation of *garam massala* in their cooking.

When her sliding door was open, the aromatic Middle Eastern dishes made Mizbie long to look inside the spice cabinet in their kitchen. The young man and his wife were polite, but refused her offer of a cookout, perhaps fearing meat would be served, despite her promise to cook without it. She closed the sliding door and the inside of her apartment seemed small. Longing to see in the neighbor's spice cabinet wasn't enough. Friends and neighbors had been to Europe, Ukraine, or

India and where had she been? Mizbie decided she had to get out of Astor.

∾

By mid-October, Mara Jade dressed like every day was Halloween. She stopped Mizbie on her way into class, smiling and draping her spider web vest across her face. "It's Moon Year 5,773 and we're having a party tonight at the tattoo shop to celebrate. Wanna come, Miz B?" Thick, black, eye makeup ringed her jewel green eyes.

"Sure, if I can bring a few friends," Mizbie answered. "We were going to try a few new songs. We could test them out at your party."

"They should be weird songs. Make them your weirdest songs," she twirled dramatically to her seat.

Mizbie marveled at the layers of Mara Jade, her fearless sense of fashion agnosticism, her dabbling in voodoo mythologies, her compassion and soldier-like defense of a friend. "It starts at seven," she zipped her notebook out.

Ever since the gris-gris incident, Mara Jade had stopped trying to climb out the window and channeled some of her creative energy into her role as Hecate in the upcoming class presentation of the Three Witches act from *Macbeth*, volunteering to provide the cauldron, dry ice, and flowing witch garb.

A few weeks ago, Mara Jade's friend, Mia, had tearfully taken her by the arm to the girl's bathroom where she rolled up her sleeve to reveal a bruise the size of a baseball. Mara Jade listened to Mia, whose boyfriend didn't believe her when she said there were only girls at the sleepover birthday party the weekend before. He demanded to be with her any time she saw her friends. A toilet flushed in a stall, but Mia was beyond caring if anyone heard her.

"Don't let him do this to you. Bad juju." Mara Jade reached in her book bag and took out a small cotton bag with a string tie. "Take this gris-gris and keep it in your left pocket whenever you're with him," Mara Jade hugged her friend.

Mara Jade's parents used to own a tattoo shop on Canal Street in New Orleans that had also featured voodoo charms. Her parents still sold Cajun and Creole charms in Astor, but they kept them in the back of the shop and only offered them when people asked, because the moral compass of Mara Jade and her family was a bit left of center for the Midwestern values of St. Bartholomew's parents. Most Astorians, even soldiers, weren't comfortable seeing gris-gris and little shrunken alligator claw key chains while they were getting inked. Mara Jade's friend trusted her and the gris-gris, the bag of special herbs, to keep her safe.

Minutes later, Mara Jade was called to Mr. Krahler's office and told to empty her pockets. In a locker search, they found a few more gris-gris, with tags labeled "good luck" or "curse," and a white scarf with a jagged black trim, like sacred ibis wings, hung from a hook inside. A makeup bag, a journal, a thick Gothic novel, tall black boots, and one black lace glove were all removed for evidence.

After class, Mizbie walked into Krahler's office where Mara Jade with her blue-green peacock headband sat with her parents, a willowy couple, both in jeans and bulky sweaters, sharing looks of worry and confusion.

"I can tell you right now, Mara Jade is not dealing drugs," Mizbie said, sizing up the situation with the gris-gris "evidence" strewn across Krahler's desk.

"We appreciate your concern, Ms Baxter, but the evidence is right here. And we found these in her locker," Krahler said, motioning to the little round bags tied with bright string on his desk.

"We've tried to talk to him," said Mara Jade's father.

With great impatience and many hand gestures, Mizbie explained gris-gris, how it was only carried, not consumed, and that there was nothing in the bag that could not be mixed in a biscuit, baked, and served with fried chicken to a preacher on a Sunday afternoon. She went on to say she had one herself, and then regretted it. But since she had started, she kept going about the spring break in college with Jess when they went to New Orleans and came across a voodoo shop, picking up gris-gris themselves. "In fact," she added to confirm how harmless it was, "the gris-gris was currently in a drawer of her bedside table."

"What kind of gris-gris did you choose?" Mara Jade asked, caught up in the story.

"It was . . ." Mizbie thought, how bizarre to say this in front of her principal, her student, – the student's parents. "It was for – love."

After a pause, someone sighed, and Krahler shifted in his leather chair. "Well, I don't suppose we'll have to have this tested."

Mara Jade's father assured Principal Krahler that she would never bring gris-gris to school again, and thanked him for understanding. Her mother thanked Mizbie and very reasonably told her, "You know, gris-gris power is weakened in time. Come to the shop, and we'll get you a new one."

Down the hall, Mara Jade felt her peacock headband grabbed, her hair pulled. She turned around to face Noel the Queen Bee and the throng of girls who surrounded her. "You aren't going anywhere yet," Noel said.

Mara Jade looked behind them and smiled. "You've got to be kidding." She snatched the headband and turned her back on them.

"If I were you, I wouldn't follow her, ladies," Mr. Heuster said from behind them.

That Monday, after Mara Jade's party, Mizbie saw Heuster walking in her direction. She thought of telling him about the dream she'd had of a chorus of voodoo priestesses with blue green peacock headbands circling a boiling pot, like Macbeth's three witches, tossing in rabbit droppings and dead possums, but changed her mind.

"I didn't know you were in a band," Heuster said Monday morning.

"I didn't think you'd get a tattoo," Mizbie answered.

"I haven't yet. Not too many competitive weightlifters in my class do tats. I'm thinking about it. Mara Jade's dad had some Gila monsters that looked pretty good. That martial arts demo was awesome."

They watched Seth walk down the hallway, not with his violin case, but with another pineapple carried like a football under his arm. It must be someone's birthday. Whenever a friend had a birthday, guy or girl, Seth brought them a pineapple as a gift. He'd even gotten Mizbie one last October. "I didn't get a pineapple for my birthday last year, and Seth was even on my cross-country team," Heuster said.

Mizbie returned to the subject of the party. She wanted to explain what had happened to her sound on Saturday night at the tattoo shop. It seemed her attitude, after a long week, played into her flute. Low note runs in and out of the guitar line did not sound as playful as they were supposed to, but squawked more like a scrappy wolverine. Everyone in her band had day jobs, so their practicing was hit and miss. Each gig sounded a bit different, depending on their emotional baggage.

Lenny, the bass guitar player, had penciled in the set list with a few changes scratched out. The notebook paper was taped to the side of the snare drum. Before the band warmed up, Mizbie decided to straighten out the cords from the pedals, amps, and mikes that snaked from their corner across to the middle of the wall by the door to the back storage room of the tattoo shop, duct taping them along the way, in case someone decided to dance over them and pull them out of the wall, killing their sound.

The door at the back of the storage room was open to the outside. A canvas yurt stretched around a circular metal frame. Wooden benches were placed around a portable fire pit that glowed in the middle. At the top was a metal ring the size of a dinner plate crossed with an intricate design of macramé knots that allowed smoke to escape. A couple of young men sat on the benches, their beards moving up and down reflecting an animated conversation in the firelight as they enjoyed a water pipe.

Once Lenny had tuned, Mizbie put her instrument together and tuned with him, allowing for the warm room, which would make the flute play with a sharp pitch. Mizbie would at times close her eyes and feel the frustration, tension, tenderness, or humor swirl through the instrument. Sometimes it worked into the song, but this time in the closeness of the tattoo shop, it happened to be tension. It must not have worked, and the vibes were all wrong, judging from the look the bass player gave her. After the band tried out their two new songs celebrating the Moon Year, Lenny and Mizbie stayed to listen to a tabla player.

The goat-skinned tabla was positioned in front of the player, but Mizbie noticed only hands pulsing, sliding from the heel of one hand to the palm. A flurry of blurred fingers erupted from the other hand with a contrast of loud raps and soft taps. Mizbie swayed into Lenny's shoulder, mesmerized in rhythm.

Last January, before Mara Jade was Mizbie's student, Lenny had gotten them their first gig at the tattoo shop to celebrate the Chinese New Year 4710. Mizbie watched Mara Jade, her brother, and his friends lined up underneath a lengthy paper dragon. They hopped and lunged to a drum-beat, carrying the dragon over them around the tattoo shop, its colorful feathers swaying, its eyelids and jaw opening wide, its tail wagging like a happy puppy. Mizbie was amazed by Lenny's knowledge of the auspicious dragon and the food.

A whole Asian carp took up most of the table in the middle of the room. The baked fish couldn't be served cut, because it only represented togetherness and abundance if it was whole. There was no tofu, because anything white would be bad luck. A plate of black moss seaweed surrounded brown rice and avocado. Lenny couldn't remember what it was for. The dried bean curd represented happiness, and long noodles represented long life. Hanging from the ceiling were rubber chickens, representing completeness.

"The band ended up staying through Mara Jade's little brother and his Kung Fu line dance, right up to the firecrackers at the end." She made a Kung Fu dance motion with her arms.

"You talk to me like I know something about music, and I don't," Heuster said. "That's okay. I like to hear you talk."

❧

On Monday, Singer shared his own gig story with Mizbie. Singer's band wanted an authentic album cover, so they decided to have a picture taken in black and white in front of the old Palace Theater where most of the album was recorded and where they were the opening band that evening. They took the shot at dusk, after a long recording session when they were all tired and the marquee lights had just come on. Behind them, the marquee read *Escanaba in da Moonlight.* Singer's brother, who taught him to ride a motorcycle, had his girlfriend use her secondhand store camera that took pictures where light escaped into the frame in unexpected ways. They took five shots in hope that one would have just the right effect.

"I didn't want to cement our music so it would never change, but the guys wanted the CD, so we made one." Singer told her. "We made our eyes look like this," he said, mirroring the guarded stony expression of other bands on other CD covers, eyebrows drawn together. The band had recently metamorphosed from garage grunge to include alt roots with the addition of a new drummer to replace the obsessive-compulsive one, who was too difficult to endure on tour in the close quarters of the van. Changing the makeup of the band wasn't taken lightly, but Harley the new drummer was a good fit for the group. Singer liked his easy-going nature, and he could actually drum with different dynamics, not just loud. "I guess it's all worth it to get our music out there," Singer regretted the dark way the camera picked up their facial foolery.

Before their last song at the end of the set, Singer grabbed one of the halves of the Marshall half-stack, and turned it to the right of center. The set list fell from his pocket and he assumed his position in front of the band. The snare drum snapped, and the bass line vibrated through the floor. Singer's lyrics crept up the backs of the concert goers, and the crowd grew more intense. Each riff pushed forward with a force defying convention and expectation. After exploring every angle of the song, he bent close to the mike to sing the last phrase, when a Converse All-Starred foot slammed into the stand. The windscreen smashed into Singer's teeth.

"Oh, man, oh, dude!" The boy dropped to the floor and his buds uprighted him on the floor. He stared at Singer and waited.

The last twelve-bar drum solo was shortened to four, the band looking at Singer and then at the audience, not wanting to lose the momentum they'd built. "That's okay," Singer said. At least he'd got the whole song out before the pain hit. His lip was cut, and he felt around for his front teeth with his tongue. They were still there, but the left front tooth felt rough. The coursing adrenalin overcame everything. He felt ragged-toothed and carnivorous, like the thundering dinosaur in the Dinosaurs on the Loose exhibit his little sister had dragged him to the day before. He was Tyrannosaurus Rex, the biggest, the most powerful, ready to eat up the audience, savoring every last morsel of yelling, dancing, and fists punching the air.

Chapter 4

Overheard outside math class –

Great. So I'm part of your life-defining moment. I don't know what mine is yet. Let me think about it.

They had walked three miles, with only four more to go, on the Saturday morning cancer walk route. Leaves of crimson and faded yellow crackled under their running shoes. T-shirts of every hue covered the backs of walkers, who dodged puddles, waiting for the next downpour. Mizbie could see Renee calm down, the music of Brahms flowing from a nearby speaker placed on a corner. Her face was looking less pinched. "I am frazzled down to my last nerve, which Rob Harris just trod on with cleats. It's like riding the bipolar express. Do you have Rob?"

Mizbie shook her head.

Renee's eyebrows shot up. "He's not the kind of kid who likes school."

Mizbie nodded. "The word makes him mischievous. Time in the Responsibility Room?"

"They installed a revolving door for him. I can imagine him sitting there—"

"With Davin's droning voice reading school rules. An assistant principal should know that isn't going to work." Mizbie rubbed a little stitch in her side.

Renee threw both arms up and walked backward to face Mizbie. "When I get him back, his smoldering temper fires up to a conflagration—"

Renee and Mizbie dodged a pothole. Women behind them spoke about pot roast, babysitters, and cross-trainers.

"My heart was thumping after the antics with the Taser, I'll tell you." Renee squared her shoulders, gaining composure. She sighed, having vented about Rob's yell as he retrieved a Taser from his pocket, brandishing it above his head and slowly lowering it, aiming for a freshman trying to open a stuck locker. "Just as he zeroed in on his random target, I knocked his arm and the Taser flew out of his hand." Renee demonstrated with her elbow.

"Krahler didn't let him off, did he?" Mizbie stopped walking.

"A senior picked up the Taser and handed it to me." She walked behind Mizbie and pushed her forward again. "Krahler has Rob out of school pending an investigation. What more is there to probe into? I'm going to have a shot of Jack Daniels before dinner."

"You still have the Taser?" Mizbie remembered there might be parents nearby and changed the subject. "Rashmi told me about her home in India the other day."

"Rashmi – gotta love her."

"It seems her parents decorated both homes the same way so they wouldn't miss their home in India. Her India room has the same chartreuse walls with white four-poster bed and white carpeting. The dens in both homes have a wall of similar books in English and Hindi opposite a wall of the same family pictures in the same frames, placed the same way." Mizbie described a mosquito net ring canopy over every family member's bed. Outside the front door, in place of landscaping beneath the front porches of both homes were colorful plastic and silk flowers. "Then she told me about a Persian story she's writing," Mizbie said. "The parents' love is so powerful, they eat up their children. What do you make of that?"

"I'd like to see her eat up some of the girls, like Noel, with their stares and stings. I've talked to Noel and reported her to the office. Nothing happens."

They turned another corner where they waved to a couple of students playing guitars with small amplifiers. "You know, Mizbie, your comment about my husband yesterday cut close to the bone. I might forgive you, but I'll remember it forever."

"I know. How about if I bake you cookies?" Mizbie had tossed out an angry remark about Renee's husband, Dirk, and his control of her. Dirk strained Renee's relationship with her children. No one else was going to tell Renee, and she needed to hear it. Then again, Mizbie's outbursts had cost her more friends than she could remember. She didn't want to lose Renee, too. "But you really needed to hear –"

"You're forgiven. How about some of your homemade granola?" Renee said. The guitar guys started singing a cover song from the nineties. "I heard you. I really did."

Mizbie changed the subject. She made Renee laugh as they walked the course, laying out a litany of summer jobs and part-time jobs she'd held before finishing her teaching degree. She had entertained her students with the list, letting them know what was in store if they didn't continue with school. She had stuck stickers on apples, washed hospital laundry, delivered telephone books, picked morel mushrooms (if only she could remember where she found them), polished chocolate for a local chocolate company, played flute in costume at a summer Renaissance festival, reenacted the ax-wielding Carrie Nation at the Carrie Nation festival, taken notes for blind college students, assisted a manager for an organic foods co-op, telemarketed for cemetery plots, and answered phones for a porta-potty company. She felt each job added to her character and gave her a background most teachers didn't have.

Perhaps one of the more memorable jobs was a summer gig touring with a roots/blues band in the Midwest. At first, it was exciting, playing in a new town each night, meeting local people, especially those who wanted their CDs signed after seeing the band profile on a social network site. But sleeping in or on the roof of a crowded van night after night dulled the glow.

Renee agreed that their jobs now involved Emo, pimples, current events, sex, drugs, ADHD, bullying, mind reading, A grades, and E grades. With her teaching salary, Mizbie talked about trying to fund a champagne glass life with a Dixie cup's worth of investment. So far, her investments into the teacher's retirement account were greater than their worth, but she hoped that ignoring them for a few years would reverse the trend.

After the Cancer Walk, Renee and Mizbie wandered into the air-conditioned Astor Art Museum, where they paused in front of a painting the size of a picture window. Mizbie felt transported to this stand of dappled birches with the hint of a breeze stirring the silvery leaves. She continued to stand in front of it after Renee had moved on, when she heard a grumble behind her. An older man with wild steely eyebrows and a riveting gaze loomed. Although they were the only two people in the room, it was clear that he wanted her to move.

She turned back to the painting and popped a peppered pecan in her mouth. Her students were selling them at the end of the Cancer Walk as a fund-raiser. Usually the pizzas, candles, and chocolate she bought from her students weren't the best, but these pecans were. She and Carl had made candied pecans a few times, tossing them in a big bowl, mixing in the sugar, butter, and pepper, waiting for the oven timer as the aroma of sweet nuttiness filled the room. Waiting in line at the oven was like waiting in line for the Dragster at Cedar Point, the latest Spiderman movie, or Macy's on Black Friday.

Swallowing another pecan, she moved on to the next painting, this one, a field of wild flowers, with a lake and farmhouse barely visible in the distance. The scene looked familiar, but she couldn't place where she had seen it. She looked at the artist's name in the corner. "Can you tell me about this artist?" she asked the docent.

"She's a local," the docent said. "Both of these are by Fran Bartner. Her family has a farm east of town. Been there for years. She takes her time with her work. Likes the oil paints and nature scenes. Sometimes takes her a couple years to finish one, because she paints a spot for two springs or two summers in case there's something new to add to catch plants that don't flower every year."

She thanked the docent and left to find Renee next to a sculpture made from rubber tires.

⌘

Mizbie hummed to the jazz strains of "Channel Swimmer." She prepared a loaf of bread to it now, grabbing the sticky dough that slipped through her floured fingers. A round loaf took shape between two tea towels, and she set the timer for a two-hour rise. The crust would be crisp, but she'd dust it with cornmeal to give it some outer texture and butter it for shine as soon as it came out of the oven. When the bread was warm from the oven, she would join Renee and Dirk for drinks and dinner. She'd cut it into bite-sized wedges (because it was round, they wouldn't fight over who got the heel of the bread) and pour a pool of Tuscan herb olive oil in a dipping bowl. The savory oil would pair well with Renee's sweet Moscato.

⌘

"Here's the sign-up list for tonight's call campaign. Elections are next week, so we have to get the vote out!" Clarisse announced at the end the October staff meeting. Clarisse had never had such an interest in politics until Hugh Roberts ran for governor. She described him as "wicked handsome" and "hot," not like the what's-his-name incumbent governor.

"But didn't he want to send the Indians back to India because they were taking too many jobs?" Renee said.

"They're taking all the top spots at our universities too, spots that should go to our students." Clarisse handed her pen to Heuster who was eager to leave.

Renee said, "Isn't Roberts the one who tied up his girlfriend at a party and has a paternity suit against him?"

"Oh, you're so picky," Clarisse giggled. "So he had some youthful indiscretions. That was probably a long time ago. Does that make him a bad politician? He's ahead in the polls."

"Yeah, so I hear," Renee said. "You coming to the Pussycat PJ Party on Friday?"

"After last year, I wouldn't miss it," Clarisse looked at her sign-up sheet with only two signatures. "No husbands, no boyfriends, no kids. We talk about anything we want, and I mean anything."

Renee's house was a logical place to get together because her three sons and husband Dirk had taken off up north deer hunting. Numerous activities took place the first weekend of deer hunting season, especially for wives of hunters, including two-for-one Margarita night at the Tikki Cove. Most offers revolved around shopping sales events, spas, and the ubiquitous Hunky Frenchmen dancers. But the women teachers at St. Bartholomew's were converging on Renee's house Friday night with their own mission in mind: to drink too much beer and wine, and tell stories they knew would never leave the house.

Mizbie brought a bottle of Number 8 Zinfandel. She carried a plate of apple slices fresh from a local orchard, each half covered with dark ganache. As she dipped them in the creamy chocolate, after school that day, she made a few taste testers for herself. They tasted so good, she could've easily eaten them all.

Corky brought her favorite Belgian beer. "When I told my husband we were meeting here, he said, 'what will I have for dinner?' I told him, 'Make it yourself.' My kids are going to the dance at school tonight. Jake will have to pick them up." Corky offered a bottle to Joanna, who declined.

"We just moved into a new condo, and Tom thought I was going to help him paint the living room tonight. Surprise! So what about Pam and Bill?" Joanna said

There was a pause while Renee and Corky shared a look. "The way they look at each other!" Corky said. "And they're both married with kids. I caught them in a lip lock in the third floor teachers' lounge. I was speechless, but they both just smiled and walked away. Really! You know they're moving in together."

Renee ripped open the top of some buttery popcorn she had just taken from the microwave and emptied it into a yellow plastic bowl. "Imagine their four kids living with them, and facing their friends at school." Renee continued. "What are Bill and Pam thinking?" She picked up a Jell-O shot and passed the popcorn to Joanna.

Mizbie and Corky moved to the kitchen to replenish their glasses. "I never knew all that craziness about Pam. How do people find out all this stuff?" Mizbie said.

"Where have you been? Oh, I forgot. You spend your lunch hour working on the school paper, don't you? You are such a hermit, Miz! You need to get out more," Corky said. The stories from the living room drew them to the arched kitchen doorway.

Women in loungewear and fuzzy slippers gathered around the coffee table in front of the gas log fireplace. A collection of Dirk's big game trophies included an elk from Wyoming, a tiger and antelope from Kenya, and in the archway between the great room and dining room, a whole stuffed brown bear from Alaska, baring its very white teeth. When the women said they felt like they weren't alone, Renee explained it was a trade-off. For every new animal head on the wall, she redecorated another room. She explained that the Kenya trip wasn't so bad. She spent two weeks helping out at a local Doctors without Borders station as a lactation consultant. She'd found it so rewarding, she continued to volunteer once a month at the Women's Teaching Hospital.

Renee's head was telling her to cut back on smoking, drinking, and eating. Her lungs were caught outside the sliding glass door, sneaking a smoke on her back deck. Her liver was hanging out in a bottle of Chardonnay. Her body was a far cry from her college hippie years with her long straight hair, no bra, a Boones Farm bottle in her hand, and free love in her heart. If that damned Mizbie would quit bringing those cream puffs and Texas fudge to school, she'd be pounds lighter.

"Okay, Ouija brain," Renee said to Clarisse. She blew the last breath of smoke outside before closing the door. Dirk could always tell when she'd smoked in the house. Clarisse had teased her about her May/December marriage to Dirk. "Older men have advantages. Their frontal lobes are mature, so they think about consequences for their actions.

Their emotions even out somewhat. Dirk's nine years older than I am, and he's even patient now when the restaurant host takes his time getting a table."

Her Yorkie, Smitty, hopped in her lap. She snuggled Smitty, picked up a paw and sniffed it. "I love the smell of dog feet!" She smiled, giving another foot a sniff. "I love my little dog. She is so much like me, and the parts that aren't like me I can ignore, not like people. Look at her."

The dog looked adoringly at her and the women around the coffee table. "How can I not love that face?" Renee cooed in Smitty's ear.

"Now Dirk's an older man, who has lived more, has more stories to tell, even if they are foggier stories and less immediate, but he still remembers the point." What she didn't mention was Dirk didn't believe in having a TV in the house and didn't own a smart phone. Only recently had he accepted dial-up Internet. Much to Renee's agnostic chagrin, he spent his evenings reading the Bible, which she referred to as his big Rorschach book, one he interpreted not by a religious belief, but any way he wanted.

"Last weekend I had a girls' weekend in Traverse City with my old St. James Catholic high school buddies," Renee said.

"Really? I never thought of you as going to Catholic school. I've heard about those schools!" Clarisse said.

"They've changed so much. My nieces go to Catholic elementary school, and their uniforms are khaki pants and a blue shirt. We had navy blue skirts with 36 pleats."

"You counted them?" Clarisse said.

"I ironed them. They had to stay neat. And we had to sit up straight. If we didn't, the nuns would put yardsticks down our backs. I remember Sister Martha tapping her yardstick up and down the rows while we worked. We didn't dare look up. If we even looked like we were going to turn around and talk, we'd get rapped across the knuckles with a ruler, so we only looked down or looked at Sister."

"How did you put up with that?" Joanna said.

"Everybody did. It was a really good school. Some of the nuns were excellent teachers. That's why I decided to become a teacher," Renee said, as she recalled the memory with a smile. "And we never crossed our legs. Only prostitutes crossed their legs."

A universal moan rolled around the coffee table.

"I did rebel, though," Renee giggled. "I often crossed my feet at the ankles. And once I was sent home because my skirt didn't touch the floor when I was kneeling for prayers; I had a growth spurt and my legs just became too long. So, I asked my mom for some red bias seam binding. I let down my skirt, pressed it, and re-hemmed the navy blue skirt with the red tape. Girls whispered and talked about the demerits I'd get, and how at that rate I'd probably be pregnant before I was 16. But I knew they were mad 'cause they hadn't thought of it first." Renee smiled. "Those were some great memories."

"Yeah," Clarisse looked around. "You were quite the rebel in Catholic school."

"Speaking of rebellion," said Joanna, shifting uncomfortably in her cross-legged position on the floor, "I'm conflicted. I was so glad to see Tom go up north with his buddies. I just want to be free of everything, just free to get away. You wouldn't believe how much I was looking forward to tonight, just to get out of the house to be with you all." She pushed her long hair behind her ear. "I could take a sabbatical, couldn't I? Maybe I could teach history in the Dominican Republic or Hong Kong, someplace different."

"How often do you two have sex?" Renee asked.

"Oh, it's not that. I can't remember the last time, I guess. And I don't care; isn't that awful? I just need a change before I go crazy." She sipped her wine. "And there's Sophie. If I go to the Dominican Republic, I'd take her. It didn't matter that she was bi-racial in elementary school, but now she doesn't feel like she fits in with the white kids at her school or the Hispanic ones. She's somewhere in between. Maybe she'd feel a part of a group there. She needs that."

"Hey, I hear you," Clarisse said, "about getting away. Every day I think, 'tomorrow is the day I'll walk out on Eddie. Then he'll do something so sweet, and I'll think, not today; I'll leave tomorrow. I've been saying that to myself for 15 years." She looked down at the bottom of her glass. "And then I try to imagine a life without him, and I can't do it."

Sonia gripped her glass of sangria. Her furtive glance around the group made them think she had something to say, but didn't know how it would spill out. "Last weekend Chrissy came home from college to ride in the Ionia County Fair with me. She wanted to ride Pete, who can be a handful, but she's ridden for years, and it was her choice. We were riding around the ring when Pete saw something, we don't know what exactly, but he suddenly reared up, and Chrissy wasn't expecting it. She fell off, her hat went flying, and when she fell, Pete fell and landed on top of her bad leg, the one she had pins in from her high school basketball regional injury. I tell you, I was scared to death."

"Oh, you must've been terrified," Mizbie said. "Even in freshman English, Chrissy lived for basketball and horses."

"But that's not the half of it. Arthur went ballistic, running out to the ring. He saw the whole thing and yelled at me for letting her ride. He said, how could I let this happen to his darling girl, and he was going to make me put the horse down. Make me put Pete down! Is he crazy?" Sonia's eyes became tearful and her hand shook the glass. "Chrissy's black and blue, but she's fine. She's ridden Pete for years, and tried to calm her dad. She walked away and had a doctor at the school infirmary check out her leg. She doesn't blame Pete or me. She understands horses. I've had Pete for 12 years. How can I put down a part of the family? Arthur and I aren't speaking right now. I'm giving him a week to cool down and realize he's being irrational."

"So Chrissy –" Corky said, but Sonia wasn't finished.

"Then there's Lilly with her piano lessons. I make her practice an hour a day, and we'll go for a week like that, but it's exhausting when she fights me after ten minutes. It's not like I don't have anything else to do," Sonia said, looking down at another pair of new shoes. Sonia's obsession with shoes had abruptly ended at income tax time when she stopped cold turkey. But by summer, she had relapsed with a trip to Shoe Depot. She hid the shoes and receipts from Arthur, convincing herself she could stop whenever she wanted to. She couldn't. "I'm a terrible mom. One day I'm so glad to be a mom; the next day I want to give Lilly away and never see her again. She's not motivated like Chrissy is. What if she doesn't want to go to college?"

"Exactly," said Edie. "Those of you who don't have kids, be glad you don't. And if you ever break up, you get a clean break. My ex and I fought for two years about custody of our son. We spent thousands and ended up with a six-day/eight-day split. That was nine years ago. Now that he's 16, he's so oppositional, neither of us wants him!" She sighed. "If only they'd stay babies. You don't have to pay for their braces, bail them out of jail, listen to their disrespect, and if they whine, it's not half as annoying as a teenager's whine."

"You think he's oppositional at home, try teaching him biology!" Clarisse piped up.

Sonia poured another sangria. "It's not just about Chrissy and Lilly." She took a drink. "Arthur and I knew each other three years before we married and had the girls. We went through counseling to make sure we'd be strong enough to handle a second marriage. I didn't want to fall in love with a white man, but color didn't matter with Arthur. It was a nonissue, or so I thought."

Renee shook her head and gave Smitty a pat.

"We shared so much. We could talk until three in the morning and still have so much to say. He even liked my peanut butter and cucumber sandwiches! I'd meet him at the hospital and see a husband or wife hug him and thank him for the bypass surgery that saved their loved one's life, and I'd be so proud. I'd think, I married such a good man. Then I saw the sent message."

Sonia brushed the corner of her eye with her hand. "How long was he going to go on before he would tell me to my face?" She took a few breaths while everyone waited. "He called his ex 'dear mouse' and said he was heartsick about leaving her and all he could think of at the time was hurting her in the worst way possible, which was to marry the 'black bitch.'" Sonia's fingers wiped at the mascara on her cheek. "So he married me 19 years ago and had two beautiful daughters with me for revenge? I mean, I thought he was my soul, my other half. My baby. No one could love him more than I did."

Renee brought a box of tissues from the kitchen, and Sonia picked out a handful. "Now that he's living with her, she found a key to the house, came in when I was at school, and slashed the family portrait over the fireplace. There are long cuts through the girls' and my faces. When I showed him the portrait and the threatening messages she's left, he denies that it could have been her. I'm so scared, I bought a camera for the front of the house. I need to prove to him what she's doing. She's threatened to hurt our girls." She drew another tissue from the box. "I didn't mean to unload all of this on you . . ." Sonia said.

"Of all the crazy, personality disordered . . ." Joanna said. "He doesn't deserve you, Sonia. He's never gonna be happy with anybody. Trust me. You deserve better." She walked over the legs and slippered feet to the couch and gave Sonia a hug. A tension hung in the air.

"Okay, how about a story? How about first dates?" Renee said. "Miz, you have a good first-date story. Let's hear it. How old were you?"

"I was 17." Mizbie was reluctant to talk, but looked at Sonia and saw that she welcomed a change of subject.

"That old? What happened?" Joanna asked.

"That's not so old," Mizbie built a defense. She brought up a mental cavalcade of college boyfriends. There was Joel from freshman year, a determined music major, who specialized in baritone performance. He would've looked just like Jon Bon Jovi if he lost his brother's dog tags that he wore around his neck, a memorial from the Gulf War.

Sophomore year was the agribusiness major Lars, a transfer student from Utrecht, Holland. Lars was tall, lanky, and laid back, a good listener, not too emotionally available but loyal like a Labrador. When he shook hands goodbye, he was good to his word, sending Mizbie's mother 100 tulip bulbs from his father's farm back home. There were far too many bulbs to plant in the sandy soil around the house, so her mother ended up giving many of them away.

Junior year was a waste. Senior year Mizbie dated a hockey player from Canada with good teeth. He sat on the bench a lot, but Mizbie never missed one of his home games. He visited her once before practice with his suit in a bag, and she practiced suiting him up. They found it so exciting, she then unsuited him again.

Further back was her first date ever. "So I grew up isolated on the lake; I was a late bloomer," she said. "There was this gawking grasshopper of a guy who asked me out junior year of high school. I found him dull. We had nothing in common, but I figured for a first date, he would be perfect because I was nervous and would learn what dating was like. I wouldn't be as nervous as I would've been with my secret crush, Lymon Dodge."

She sipped her wine and got into her story. "My date's name was Jerry, and we had been in a seventh-grade musical together four years before. It was a play that took place in a lumberjack camp. I had just come back to the camp after a long absence and Jerry's character, the flapjack cook, heard my voice and came charging out of the log cabin. He ran so fast that he tripped and fell flat on his ass. The audience roared, thinking it was part of the play and his face turned bright red in the stage lights.

"He drove us to the movie in his Volkswagen Beetle, and we stopped for fish and chips after. During dinner, he confided that he had loved me since that seventh grade play."

"Aww," Clarisse said.

"Get to the point," Renee was impatient.

"He had this earnest voice that cracked as all of this unrequited emotion tumbled out. I was so surprised trying to think of what to say, I couldn't listen to half of it. I felt so responsible and guilty that I couldn't return the feelings, guilty for using him for a first date. I reached across the table and grabbed his hand, squeezing it. He looked so hopeful. The best I could do was mumble something about being confused, not far from the truth, and ask him to give me time to think about it. Meanwhile, I'd have time to figure out what to say to him that wouldn't be too mean, but would still be honest."

"Oh, c'mon, Miz. You're way too concerned about people's feelings. You should've laughed in his face and told the jerk to buzz off," Renee laughed.

"There was this sensation of finding it hard to breathe, and looking for an escape. I don't know why. I just wanted to get out of there and get away from him. I told him I had a headache, and he took me home."

"Did he kiss you?" Joanna asked.

"That was my first date. Of course! I had to practice. It was a horrible, fishy kiss, and I could only yearn for Lymon Dodge. Jerry hadn't shaved and his prickly chin scraped mine. But after that date, I figured I could handle anything."

Mizbie was going to vent about her latest dustup with Carl, but this was one time when she filtered first for Sonia's sake, before bursting out with something offensive, one of the few times. Grateful that her offend-a-friend filter worked this time, she looked at Sonia, who was eating an apple slice and didn't speak, but had thrown away the handful of tissues.

From experience, the women knew that after Mizbie let loose on them, she'd feel remorse and head for the kitchen. Most of them had accepted her apology in the form of a loaded chocolate chip cookie, trail mix, or for greater feelings of remorse, such as when she told Clarisse that her voice sounded like a cackling witch and that's why so many of her students came to class with ear buds, a jar of her homemade strawberry-peach jam.

"I've always been attracted to geeky bookish types." Mizbie stood up with her wine glass held in a dramatic pose. "Here's my online dating profile: Mindless drones need not apply. If you could spend a weekend on a couch with a blanket, a James Bond movie, a good book, or a cup of tea, then I'm the girl for you. Thick round glasses are a plus." There were snickers as some women didn't know if Mizbie was teasing or serious. "Getting lost in a spirited game of chess, a computer program, or a science museum turns me on." She sipped the wine and returned the glass to its Statue of Liberty pose. "If you are more comfortable in navy blue turtlenecks, classic tweed with elbow patches, or pants belted like Urkel—" Mizbie pulled up the front of her yoga pants. Clarisse erupted in cackles.

"You look like my Uncle Bud," Renee said.

"Oh, Cork, did you get your hot air balloon license this summer?" Mizbie moved to a spot next to Sonia and sat cross-legged by the fireplace.

"Only three more classes and I take the exam. It'll have to wait until next summer now," Corky said.

"I'll bring the champagne, if I get the first ride," Mizbie said, moving to the beat of "Poker Face" playing on the tiny iPod speakers.

"Have you ever tried to get a baby stroller into the Bean and Leaf for a cup of coffee?" Clarisse asked. "It's impossible. I was meeting my sister last Saturday morning with Eddie Junior and Sasha in their oversize stroller. The woman in front yelled at me for hitting her in the ankles. I didn't, she just backed into me. I tell you, this happens all the time. They should make coffee shops bigger for strollers."

Corky poured another beer, resting a leveling finger on the top of the glass to stop the foam from overflowing to the coffee table. "Where'd you learn that?" Renee asked.

"I used to bar-tend on weekends when I went to U of M. Good tips. It paid for books," Corky said.

"Last Friday, my mother-in-law called to say she'd take the kids so we could have some time for ourselves," Clarisse said. "She's a dear, I tell you. So I surprised Ed with a candlelight dinner, fish tacos, his favorite." The women protested. "I know, but he likes the way I fix them. I wore the black negligee he gave me for Christmas. He was so surprised, and we were laughing, drinking rum and Coke. There was so much antici- pation, you know? Things felt electric, and we're alone so seldom with- out the kids, we had to take advantage of it, and Ed was being so darned romantic. He brought squeeze chocolate to bed and started decorating my boobs when –"

"Stop! I can't listen to any more of this! If that happened at my house, you know what I'd get? Pureed vegetables, that's what," Joanna said.

"Yeah, well, by the time we got in bed, we were exhausted. Ed gave me this long kiss and said, 'Do you mind if we just spoon? I'm beat.' I was relieved he didn't have the energy. We really don't have the energy very much anymore." She tossed a handful of popcorn in her mouth. "Ooh," she stamped her feet just thinking about it. "My pussycat's on fire! Where is he now?"

"Hon, have you seen Leila Baker, the counselor?" Renee asked.

"Yeah, go see Leila," said Sonia. "She's like visiting an old friend. It'll all become clear if you go visit Leila. Most of us have seen her, haven't we?"

Many women nodded readily. "Maybe she could help me get rid of my horrible dreams," Mizbie said.

"For dreams you need to see Ryder," Corky said.

"Ryder with the alligator boots? Are you kidding?" Mizbie was surprised.

The laughter and conversations wound down to the bottoms of glasses of wine and beer. In the quiet, they heard a few drops of rain plunk on the roof from an oak tree that towered over the back of the house. "Just a little tinkle from God's cosmic bladder," Renee said. She clicked the garage door opener down and closed the blinds. By two o'clock, most everyone was asleep.

❧

The bell rang and Mizbie walked down the hall to Renee's room. She looked old his morning, but it could've been her mood, changeable as the weather.

"What happened to you?" Mizbie asked.

Renee's voice was not her own. Dirk had gotten bad news about the treatments that were supposed to control his prostate cancer. They weren't working. "Depression has its ugly cloven hoof stuck in our front door. I tried to dislodge it with a croquet mallet but the damned thing won't go."

"C'mon with me," Mizbie said. She opened her hand to reveal a red jock strap.

"What are you doing with that?" Renee said.

It's a conspiracy and now you're a part of it so you can't tell,"

They walked down to the counseling office where May June, a counselor who was hired in the same time as Mizbie, was on break. May June was annoyingly happy. She would look at Mizbie, taking quick looks at the earrings she wore, same ones as yesterday, checking her lipstick that needed refreshing, not commenting on it, just judging and filing the information in her evaluation of Mizbie mental file. Mizbie remembered their last confrontation about Nick, a student who, Mizbie swore, could see through her clothes to her Marilyn's Closet lingerie. He knew her tipping points.

Nick would volunteer to read his essays that were peppered with innuendos just short of punishable, yet hilariously entertaining to a student audience. When she ordered him to sit down halfway through his last reading, he feigned innocence, flashing his smarmy smile. The class wanted to hear the ending. Mizbie took the essay to May June, who found nothing derogatory and handed Mizbie a New Age self-help book on finding the positive person within.

Yesterday May June had rushed up to her. "How *is* Nick doing, Mizbie?"

"He told a girl he wanted to suck her fingers yesterday," Mizbie looked her in the eyes, daring May June to respond.

"Oh, it must've been after lunch. It must've been the chicken nuggets. Maybe she had some on her fingers!" May June skittered away.

Mizbie thought about May June and people who took life's lemons to make sickeningly sweet lemonade. She had a sudden desire to provoke May June. There had to be something that would piss her off. She could put a quarter of Camembert de Normandie cheese in back of her desk drawer. She could plant a porn magazine among the weekly file folders meant for Krahler, those folders that always sat at the left back corner of her maddeningly neat desk. Or, she could toss the red jock strap –, the one Nick wore on his head this morning when he came tardy to class – on her desk. The one he wore, he said when told to remove it, because it proved to his girlfriend that "he cared."

It was a rare moment when no one was in the counseling office. "Here we go," Mizbie said, tossing the jock strap in the middle of the desk. It lay there in a crumpled figure eight shape.

On their way out, they passed May June's husband who was a speech pathologist and must've been working in the building. Mizbie grabbed Renee's arm to keep from laughing. They wanted to stay and listen to the conversation when May June returned from her break to face a red jock strap and her husband, but decided the conversation they imagined was probably better.

"I don't know if this was such a good idea," Renee said, trying to keep from laughing.

"May June needs a wake-up call," Mizbie replied.

"I know what you mean, but I'm thinking about her daughter, Stephanie."

"What about her? Stephanie's history class and my poetry class are working on a unit together. The students love her. I do too."

"Yeah, well, I'm keeping secrets on both sides here," Renee confided. "Remember May June's 45th birthday, her annual poisoning of self-pity?"

"You mean the black balloons and crepe paper all over her office? I remember."

"Even the counselor needs to talk to someone, and she dumped on me." Renee said. "She was tearful that day." They walked into Renee's room and she closed the door. "May June talked about how she'd tried and tried with Stephanie, and how much she loves her daughter."

"Oh, no." Mizbie sat at a student desk. "She was torn when her church told her Stephanie couldn't be a member if she didn't renounce her 'lifestyle.' She called her church a 'non-judgmental haven of moral solace.' It convinces people that dinosaurs and Christ walked the earth at the same time and evolution is only a theory. These members hate the sin and love the sinner and they would gladly accept Stephanie back if she would just quit living with her partner."

Mizbie had heard one more reason to be dumbfounded with The World according to May June. "So Stephanie has to endure this from her mother. Maybe we can send May June over to negotiate with the Taliban."

"May June called Stephanie selfish for putting her through this," said Renee. "She thought it was such a little thing to ask. Then she went on to describe how each boy-friend-less year she had steeled her resolve to fix her daughter. Because May June and her husband were completely normal people, Stephanie should be too. She just needed some encouragement. She had found a new young man to invite to dinner and thought this one might be the one to 'turn' her."

"She loves Stephanie. If Stephanie's happy with her partner, that should be all that matters," Mizbie said. "I'm wondering how May June decided to be a counselor. She's not one to ask questions if answers would put voice to the distance between them. The poor woman is dialed out of her bandwidth."

"It's complicated. Her belief in this religion is powerful. Then there's Stephanie's side. She was talking about a rock-climbing weekend she'd had with her partner, Rose. They've attended friends' weddings together and Rose's parents have accepted them. Stephanie's part of their family. She couldn't count the number of times she's tried to have the discussion with her mother, but May June won't hear of it."

Renee erased her white board. "I wanted to ask her, 'What's more important, your religion or your daughter? Where is your compassion?' Then I could hear my Jewish mother from her grave reminding me, 'This is your mitzvah, to keep them from turning their backs on each other.' If May June was my mother, I'd have turned my back on her already."

"When Stephanie was hired, she told the director of personnel about her personal life. She told her classes each fall, though most of them knew and couldn't care less" Mizbie grabbed the sides of the student desktop. "And she even reminded her softball and volleyball teams to tell parents in case they were uncomfortable. In four years, two of them removed their daughters from teams. Only two!" She sighed. "Stephanie couldn't get through to her mom."

Invariably, after Stephanie tried to talk to her mother, there would be an invitation to dinner with some hapless son of a friend's aunt sitting beside her at the table. One young man was gay. His mother was probably trying to turn him too, they agreed. He walked Stephanie to her car after dessert.

Chapter 5

A quiet moment in yoga class:
I'd of cut his legs off.
He didn't show up and she was screaming, then they made up and they're going to Vegas to get married this weekend. She's only known him two weeks. She's got a one-year-old.
Yeah, but when you know it's right, why wait?

Jesspin9
to Mbax20
11:30 PM
October 12

Hey Miz,
This is from my blog. I know you never read my blog, so I'm emailing it to you.
If I ever write an essay called "Pure Pleasure," it would include today's excursion on the Grand St. Bernard Pass. For you geography buffs, it's in southwest Switzerland, on the way to Brig in the country's fruit basket, also known for its wine. The air is thin at 2,000 meters up, but the last five meters at the top offer up an amazing view. I'm not sure if my eyes are tearing from the wind or the beauty. I'm riding up with a peloton, which makes it much easier. These are some of the steepest climbs I've had since I got here. It's raining a little and we track the spine of the road, venture off into some scenic switchbacks, then plummet down three times faster, loose gravel hitting us like rock bullets.

I drain my Camelback by mid-afternoon, but fortunately we reach Brig, so I can refill. On one switch back it rains and the road is reduced from two tracks to one narrow goat track in the alpine grasses. We round the hill and come face to face with a family of red deer, standing stock still, staring at us. We stop and stare back, playing the deer version of chicken, each of us wanting not to be the first to move and scare the other. The darling spotted fawn finally loses interest and turns away from us up the hillside.

One of the guys from the peloton has been to Brig and directs us to a small out-of-the-way establishment with good Belgian beer. We got to talking about author Michael Chabon's idea of pleasure, how it's an ambiguous gift, unreliable and transient, easily faked, mass produced, and how we mistrust it and its benefits do not endure. The ideas may apply to pleasures we buy, but not to what we experience today. So is it worth a grueling day of cycling in the heat and rain for the pleasure of seeing those red deer and the view from the top of the Pass? Definitely.

Jess

Mizbie rode in Corky's van to Chippewa Springs as she had many times during the summer, with friends from school. They aired up the tires and headed out past a meadow down a meandering bike path into a wooded area. She faced a sky free of clouds, the sun's unseasonable warmth cooled by the breeze through her hair that trailed in a wheat-colored banner. Mizbie felt like a part of the earth when she rode, powered by her own imaginary chimera created from an eagle, a cheetah, a gazelle and maybe the drummer from the *Caravanserai* album winding its musical way through her ear buds. Everything in her collective reservoir of consciousness placed her in this moment, her senses tuned to the hum of the trail under her wheels.

A lone cloud rolled above her powered by a few wind wisps above. She and Sarah, her childhood friend back in Alabaster, would stretch out on the beach in front of her childhood house on Lake Huron. On towels they'd burrow themselves comfortably in the sand and cloud watch through sun glasses. While the lake ran lazy laps to the shore, they identified rhinos and elephants, Saint Bernards and cows as well as a rasher of bacon parading by for their approval. Focusing her mind only on the clouds, Mizbie felt their motion as if she was floating along with them, light and free from the silent tension inside the house. Even now, the thought of cloud watching with Sarah was a meditation, a spiritual physical mind meld, a delight of her innermost being.

When she and Sarah were 12, they spent a long weekend at Sleeping Bear Dunes. While Mom waited with a thermos of iced tea, under a shade tree, Mizbie, Sarah and her dad scaled the hot dunes in beach shoes, falling back a pace for every three steps they took going up. Mizbie and Sarah reached the top first, turning to admire the rolling landscape of farms, roads small as ribbons, and the harbor, sparkling in morning sun. The girls started back, but Dad wouldn't hear of it. "Let's find the lake. You've never waded in Lake Michigan before. C'mon, it's just over that next dune." Sarah and Mizbie looked over the next dune and started walking. But at the top of the next dune, was another and then another. The girls complained of being tired and hot. They hadn't brought any water with them. Dad was unmoved. "Just one more. Quit whining."

Over the last dune, they looked up expecting another sandy, grassy expanse, only to find the wide open blue of Lake Michigan. Mizbie and Sarah squealed and ran to the water's edge, kicked off their shoes and balanced on pebbles through numbing cold water up to their knees, until they finally reached sandy bottom, where they splashed and dipped in the waves.

∾

As her bike cleared a curve, a wheelchair cycler cut her off, a racer in a muscle shirt who just missed her front wheel had she not crossed to the left at that moment. Mizbie yelled her favorite curses and he shot ahead of her so fast, she felt like she was pedaling a stationary bike. He waved and disappeared around a bend. Who did he think he was cutting people off riding that fast? Mizbie had seen him before with his damned broad shoulders and his tousled hair. She geared up to catch him and cycled beside him for awhile, but she lost him at a hill when she slowed down; he didn't.

Ahead she saw White Lake and felt a welcome puff of breeze. She dodged acorns from the woods beside the lake. Along the shore were docks for paddle boats and kayaks, some moored making barely audible plashes, others out on the lake piloted by kids and parents making their own waves. A watershed flowed under a covered bridge with weathered boards that felt like wooden corduroy under her tires. On the other side of the watershed that led to the lake, was a children's park with a castle that echoed with young voices. Her handle grips felt hot through her padded gloves and she shifted her hands in the humidity, swinging her arms beside her, losing her annoyance at the paracycler.

Stretching forward into the speed of acceleration on a straightaway, she greeted a family with children on training wheels. Curving away from the lake, the trail became a long downward coast through heavy woods, a cool contrast to the sun. A chipmunk zipped across her path, nearly missing her front tire. Corky and Heuster came up behind her. Corky had a stuck gear that Heuster fixed a few miles back. They breathed in the cool scent of woods, relaxed their pace, and watched the few patches of sun filter down.

The group biked 20 miles and took a break. Mizbie felt the heat of the day without the wind to cool her. Drops of perspiration glistened on her back. In the shade of the pavilion, the cyclists rehydrated and passed around packages of trail mix and grapes. She saw the wheelchair racer with his nerve and his toothpaste-ad smile, slow down and make his way to her.

"I'm Mizbie," she turned to him, swallowing some grapes. "I've seen you around before. Are you training?" She offered the grape container to him.

"Yeah." He popped a few in his mouth. "I was just messin' with ya. Most people see the bike and give me a pass, but not you."

"So how'd you do in your last race?"

He looked at her reddened face. "Respectable," he said. He snapped the top off a water bottle. "Look, this probably sounds weird, but I have to ask you, do you know Fran Bartner?" When she didn't answer he said, "The local artist?" He gulped his water. "You look just like her."

"Fran Bartner. Nature scenes, right?" She looked at him, wondering if he was going to ask her out. And if he did, she wondered if she would accept. "I teach here, but I didn't grow up here." She caught his puzzled look. "Don't think anything of it. People say I have a familiar face."

"That you do. Fran is my neighbor, the best anyone could have. Well, there's my ride. I'll see you around." When he said his name, Orlando, Mizbie knew she'd remember it. Orlando wheeled himself to the van that had just pulled into the parking lot. Mizbie watched an athletic blond step out to help him. He didn't require much help.

❧

After work and her customary caffeine fix from the Leaf and Bean, Mizbie opened the door at the Fit For U Center. Her yoga class was already putting out the mats.

"Take a cleansing breath." Julie said. "And downward dog"

Mizbie hadn't considered yoga before this group, but it was strongly suggested as a condition of her probation for road rage, in addition to losing her driver's license for a year. Three years later, not only did she have no thought of buying another car, but she continued with yoga. She credited it with preserving her current friendships. Even so, she often grew impatient with the slowness of the positions, finding it difficult to breathe and stretch when there were issues crowding her thoughts.

Mizbie stretched into the pose, looking upside down at the EXIT sign over the back door, a fluorescent orange beacon reminding her of Carl's Houdini escapes from her life.

"Full sun salutation. Think of opening up," Julie instructed.

Mizbie arched her back up, facing the orange sign right side up, willing herself to concentrate on breathing. An exit from the snoring, the clean freak mentality, and the moodiness.

"Mountain pose. Navel to the spine. Chin straight. The blue green chakra is emanating from your head. Find that balance."

Carl had called Mizbie's reactions excessive. But that was only because he was so high-maintenance himself. She had lit lavender candles, found some classic Sun Ra music and slipped into the bathtub with Carl. They talked over the bubbles. "Are those sweet nothings you're whispering? she said.

Carl breathed in and whispered in her ear, "Nanoparticles."

"Ooh."

"Higgs Boson...quarks...photons..." he continued.

"Mmmm."

His soap slippery hands made long smoothing strokes, over her shoulders. "Eye of newt." She turned bringing him into her. They kissed in a sliding rush, the roughness of his stubby beard heightening her excitement as they pressed so closely into one another, losing themselves in their selfish shared delight.

She lay curled into his chest as he scooped bubbles around them both. "Oh, Miz," Carl gave her a slippery hug. "I was playing this probability game on the New York Times site. Monty Hall gives you one door. Say he gives you door #3. Are your chances better switching doors or keeping your original choice?"

"Oh no!" Mizbie laughed, hugging his arms. "I'd have to say it doesn't matter."

"But it does matter! If you change your door, your chances are one in two instead of one in three that you'll get the right door. It works. I tried it. So do you ever think about moving in with me?"

Her hand dipped below the water. "But you're place is so far away," she said. "How would I get to school? I'd have to get a car." She knew it was the wrong thing to say as soon as it was out of her mouth. He wasn't serious, but couldn't she have just played along for the moment and said yes? Would that have been so hard? "Wait a minute, Carl. Let me – "

But Carl was already standing up. He showered, dressed, and left without a word.

She looked at the closed door, and back at Daphne, curled up, comforting as a pillow mint, asleep by her bed. Why did her love for Carl make her so miserable?

Daphne stretched. Cats lived in the present. They couldn't tell lies, weren't weighed down by mistakes and didn't worry about the future. "Daphne, I can take a lesson from you," she said.

"Superman, plank, high lunge."

Mizbie knew the fresh soap and water smell of Carl's neck when she hugged him, and the bump in his nose from a childhood fight with his cousin. She knew his favorite dessert was his grandmother's Boston cream pie recipe with caramel chocolate frosting, a recipe she made for his birthday. His favorite musical was *The Lion King*, and he had a birthmark on his leg they named Pumba. She knew he loved running the engine of the *Mistress* flat out on a calm Lake Michigan day, and one day, he confessed, he'd be content to die there. Mizbie leaned into the high lunge.

She relaxed her shoulders, focusing more on breathing and movement. Julie spritzed herbal fragrance in the air. The Eastern Indian music drowned out the sound of treadmills and ellipticals on the other side of the fitness center.

"Breathe deep...chin to chest, circle left to the shoulder...exhale, chin down... right arm stretch..."

Mizbie thought of a comment she had made to Brent, the class president who refused to complete his self-reflection essay. "I'm just goin' with the flow," he told her, stretching out in his seat. A low snicker infected the class.

"Only dead fish go with the flow," Mizbie answered.

She knew he understood. She also knew he'd put his own twist on her comment to his lawyer father and Principal Krahler would get another call about her.

"Table top...downward facing dog."

Mizbie stood up stretching her back, inching her heels to the floor, backside in the air, palms on the floor.

"Shoulders back, find that stretch." Julie said.

Mizbie inhaled, relaxing into the stretch, blood rushing to her head, wondering about the backlash of her words to Brent. What would happen when there was one letter too many in the principal's file? Mizbie had slogged through a lot of jobs, but hoped to keep this one.

"Cow face pose"

She sat, stretching her legs up and out in front of her, stacking her knees before her.

She had scored a point at lunch in the cafeteria. "Mara Jade, you have your surveys?" She asked. "Robin, did you bring the poster and pencils? Okay, let's find a place to sit where we can get students fired up." Mizbie looked around.

"Muffin top, hey you, sitting by yourself," Noel said. The girls she called friends, laughed. Every round cafeteria table was filled except for Amanda's, where she sat alone.

"It's Muffin Top! BMI 30! Baby fat!" Noel shouted.

Mizbie walked next to Noel and glared at her, dispensing a look that registered pangs of her mother.

"Amanda," Mizbie turned to the big empty table. "Can we sit here?"

Amanda looked up from her carrot sticks where she stared half way into the vacant wasteland between yum and disappointment. Mizbie reminded herself that she could have easily become Amanda if she hadn't taken up cycling.

"Okay," Amanda said. Her table was soon filled by the newspaper club, their papers and babble suddenly drowning out anything Noel could say.

"Give me one," Mara Jade asked her friend who was passing out questionnaires. She had the instincts of a boarder collie. "Amanda, would you answer this for our survey? What do you think of the jokes disrespectful of women on social networking sites?"

"I'll take one of those," Amanda reached out over her celery and peanut butter.

"Deep breath...forward bend."

Mizbie opened her eyes with her hands on the mat and looked upside down through her legs beneath the frosted window glass of the fitness center. Some boys were skateboarding back and forth on the sidewalk. At first it was all legs and knees, then one of them slowly rolled by crouching low, his face peering under the frosted glass at the women on ellipticals and then right at Mizbie's behind. Justin! He smiled and waved in surprise, wobbling on his board before the boys skated away.

She wanted Julie the yoga instructor to hurry up.

∾

Mizbie asked Renee how many pumpkin pies she should bring for Thanksgiving dinner.

"Two... make it three," Renee said. She began to lament that her sons were bringing their fiancées to Thanksgiving this year. Each twin tried to outdo the other. "And their fiancées are just as bad. I'm the one who makes this huge dinner and they completely talk over me. It's like I've been relegated to the side dish of their lives. I want to be the main course again. I'm not the refried beans, I'm the hot taco with spicy salsa."

Mizbie anticipated a few days off. "Justin had a day today. It started first hour when he rushed into the room explaining his grandmother's car and his sister's car wouldn't start. They finally siphoned gas into his brother's car and got Justin to school.

"See? Smell my hand," he said sticking his gas-smelling hand in front of her nose. "So that's why I'm late. It's not my fault. My grandma was going into the hospital this morning too. I picked up my sister's back pack, so I don't have my homework. Tomorrow I'll get organized. I'm gonna pass this class. I'll buy a new book too. The one I had got lost somewheres. I'll get a new journal and write all those journal writes I owe you. I did the first seven, but they got lost somewheres. They're probably at my sister's house."

When we were in the library minutes before the bell rang, he couldn't hold it together any more. He burped and asked, "Why aren't bones floppy? Why do spiders make webs?" I was counting the minutes. Then he said, "You won't answer any of my questions!"

"It's a full moon, you know." Renee said. "That's why these kids are acting this way."

"There's more," Mizbie said. "Seconds before the bell, he stood up, took off his shoes, unzipped his jeans and pulled them down to his knees. The class just walked around him when the bell rang. I spouted off something to him and he just stood there in his shorts."

"I had to make an adjustment, see. If I went to the bathroom, I'd be late for science." He wriggled and pulled and zipped. "Why won't you answer my questions?"

"You forgot your meds today, didn't you? Didn't you tell me sitting in class was like itching all over and you wanted a zipper so you could slip out of your skin? Those pills would get rid of that feeling. You could concentrate, Justin!"

"I pretend to take it. When Grandma turns around, I put it in a ball of plastic wrap. A guy on the bus buys 'em for $2. I'm saving for a new game. I've almost got enough money. I'll see ya tomorrow. I'll be better tomorrow." Justin said.

"I called Grandma and that's the end of that." Mizbie said.

"Floppy bones," Renee laughed. "After Thanksgiving, my mother would give me the leg bones from the turkey. They earned a place on the bottom shelf of my bookcase, the shelf under the *World Book Encyclopedia*. When the bones dried, I lined them up and played them against each other like bamboo chimes. Each bone had its own sound."

∾

Brent pulled up a chair and stared into the eyes of the doe-eyed Linda, the student library volunteer. Linda was bi-lingual. Her professor father raised her speaking only French, her psychologist mother, only English. As a high school freshman, she was dually enrolled in college algebra. "Hey," Brent said, locking eyes. Linda saw his smile and smiled back. "Aren't you supposed to be in Ms. Baxter's class?

"She gave me a pass to work on my research project. I thought maybe you could help me."

After class, Brent looked in on Mizbie offering a convoluted excuse. In her hands were the class papers. "Whose responsibility was it to turn your paper in on time?" She asked.

"You bitch. You don't listen to anybody!" He spit, red faced. "I want to call my mom. You can't give me a late grade. I was in the office. You can't do this to me."

"So tell me. We've been working on this project in class now for three weeks. How much do you have finished?"

"Finished? You haven't even given me enough time to start it yet. What are you talking about?"

"Brent. You'll have lunch with me today and you can call your mom. Then you can have lunch with me every day until your final copy is perfect. If you forget, I'll pull you from your cafeteria table. I know who you eat with. This could take awhile. Get going!" She saw the surprised look on his face.

Mr. Krahler read the end of the day announcements. "...and for president of the freshman class, Brent Price."

When the system was turned off, he said to the secretary, "President? Him? He won't even run a lap around the gym. How can he run the freshman class? Am I missing something?"

Just yesterday Krahler called Brent to the office for threatening a friend at lunch. Brent spent too much time in Krahler's office, offering wild excuses. Krahler shook his head, usually giving him a break.

Mizbie couldn't understand why Brent got off with so many warnings. He probably reminded Krahler of himself when he was in school. Once after he took back a day of school detention he told her, "He's just suffering from Senioritis, even though he's only a freshman."

❧

"Here Ms. B., Lexi said, quietly walking in before class. "Read this during homeroom, but don't tell anyone about it. It's a poem I wrote.

Lexi loved to write. Mizbie remembered a character assignment that Lexi had volunteered to share a few days ago. "I chose an imaginary pet instead of a human character, one that can sense the emotions of its owners and send its thoughts and needs into its family's mind. The family calls it Dobro."

"Dobro skittered across the slippery kitchen floor rubbing his furry wrinkled back along Sarah's ankles," she read. "She reached down to give his ears a scratch. 'Dobro, you little stinker,' she said. That's my dialogue."

He warmed to her touch, leaning his flat head against her leg. His fur, stuck out like electrified hair, and tickled her. He began to hum. It was the only audible sound he was able to make for his entire short life, but Sarah knew what he meant. She knew that out of everyone in the family, he was most worried about her."

Krahler gave a particularly long morning announcement, so Mizbie had time to read Lexi's latest poem. In verse that was more like performance poetry, she wrote about her father who hadn't lived with her for a number of years. He lived a few blocks away with a house full of teens and drugs. He died, probably from the drugs, the poem didn't say. The housemates didn't know what to do, so they carried him to the curb in front of the house. A jogger found him in boxer shorts. She missed her dad. Mizbie looked up from the paper and caught Lexi's eye when she finished, motioning her to the hallway.

"Oh, Lexi, Alexandra, what can I do?" Mizbie held the poem in her hands.

"It's okay, Miz B. I'm okay, really. She backed away. I just wanted you to know. We're not having a funeral, but the family's getting together Thursday, so I won't be here.

"I'm so sorry."

"I hadn't seen him in three years. He had problems and my mom didn't want my sister and me around him"

"What will you do now?"

"I'm gonna help Grandpa. It's pretty hard for him. I'll spend some time with him after school. Don't worry about me."

"Lexi...you should talk to the counselor."

"I don't need that."

"Maybe not now. I'll ask you again soon."

"C'n I go back in now?"

"Yes you can go back to class. Talk to me any time. Come back later if you want." Mizbie tried to widen a safety net for her.

Lexi was on her mind at the end of the day so she called the mother to say she'd be looking out for her daughter.

"What? What are you talking about?" Lexi's mother said. "It sounds like Alexandra's been telling stories again. She does it at home too. I think she does it for attention." Her mother called to someone else in the house. "Good or bad, she doesn't care, as long as there's lots of drama involved. Look, I know you mean well, but trust me, her dad is just fine."

Mizbie heard her voice call to someone in the room, "Talk to her, hon, this is Lexi's teacher."

"Hello? How can I help you?" a man's voice asked Mizbie.

"It's...never mind. Let's just forget this ever happened."

Chapter 6

Penciled sign over the mailboxes in the teachers' work room –
Ludington Ice Fishing and Bowling weekend. It's the Big LaWalleyeski
XVI! Be there or else! Sign up with Heuster.

"I've got an idea for the newspaper," Singer said, slipping in front of Seth as if his news couldn't wait. "I'm doing an interview. I've got 10 people so far. My headline is 'How Has Climate Change Affected Your Family?' On our motorcycle trip we met this guy whose house in Colorado burned from a wildfire. Amanda's grandma in Mississippi lost her house in a flood, where there had never been a flood before."

"That's a start, Singer. Remember to check the name spellings." He grinned. "It looks like you have your smile back since that microphone hit you," she said. Mizbie had hoped for a moment of down time to talk to Renee after school, but that wasn't going to happen.

"Yeah, I got it fixed. I'll try Han. His dad got back from Australia and the drought is so bad there that some lake dried up."

"Get the name of the lake, Singer. You're fired up about this! Remember to get it in the newspaper web file by 4:00. The lab closes early today."

Seth stood before her with a paper in his hand. He had patience; he waited well. Some teachers liked patient people, but Mizbie didn't see this as any virtue, waiting around for something to happen. She was unable to understand patience and found it an annoying quality.

"I had a concert last night." Seth's voice was dull. She waited. "All right, I just didn't get it done." He looked down and, instead of leaving, walked to the window and began pacing back and forth, waiting to say something.

Mizbie thought of all the other things she should be doing, and Seth often seemed about to say something that wouldn't spill out.

"My dad talks to everybody the same, except when he talked to my mom, he had this special tone of voice. He only used it when he talked to her. I know it sounds weird, but Dad could say her name and I could hear the love in it."

"That's not so strange when people care about each other," Mizbie answered, trying to imagine that voice and the sound of it. Her eyes followed Seth as he paced.

"When she got sick, Dad cared for her every day and got a nurse when things got bad at the end. It was hard keeping up the farm and taking care of her. I helped a little but I was at school when . . . I mean, he never complained. He said Mom had given him so many wonderful years, this was the least he could do for her."

Mizbie could feel the loss in his voice. She went to the door and quietly closed it, in case someone came barging in before Seth finished what he wanted to say.

"He told me it was once in a lifetime that you found someone you could love like that, and if I ever found someone, I shouldn't let anything stand in my way." He looked at the floor. "Before the cancer when they would argue sometimes, they'd argue loud, but they wouldn't cut each other down. They'd just say stupid stuff and I never felt scared about it. In the morning before she left for work, they'd look at each other and smile. They'd kiss this long sloppy kiss and I'd make a face and say, "Don't do that," and they'd laugh. I want a girl to look at me some day the way my mom looked at my dad in the morning before work." He stood in front of her desk again. "So that's why my essay's late."

Mizbie stood and walked around the desk facing him.

"It was two years ago yesterday that my mom died." He took a big breath. "And I'm afraid that I'm going to forget what she looked like. I don't mean from the pictures of all of us, but when I think of her cheering at my T-ball games or yelling at me to clean my room, her face isn't as clear anymore. I'm afraid. I don't want to lose her."

"Seth, your mom would have been so proud of you." Mizbie grabbed his wrist and squeezed too hard, caught up in his worry. She thought of memories of her own parents. "You will always carry those memories with you." His eyes brimmed and she thought he was going to throw his arms around her and cry. Instead, he put his paper on her desk. "I think it's a good one," he said. "Thanks for ... listening."

ა

"I'll see you, Renee. I'm really leaving this time," Mizbie sensed something going on in her own room before she heard the voices. "What – ?"

Her room had been usurped, seized, and overturned by her students, metamorphosed into something else entirely. The ceiling was festooned with strings of white Christmas lights woven through the suspended ceiling, hundreds of tiny orbs dangled above their heads like suspended confetti. Strings of lights were masking-taped in corners where they tumbled down walls, angled into designs of Christmas trees and gingerbread men and women. Lights framed her desk, the white board, and each window. Mizbie walked around the room and felt the warm glow, so much more inviting than the cold compact fluorescent energy-saving room lights. She wanted to keep these lights up forever.

They watched her to see if she was surprised or if they had ignited her temper. In the planning, they realized it could go either way.

"No –" Mizbie couldn't get the words out, turning to look at the wonderland of light.

Mara Jade laughed. "We planned it three days ago, Shannon, Stella and me. Izzy had some extra lights and we asked Corwin to help, then Robin 'cause he's so tall."

"Yeah, but we would get on chairs too, so it wasn't so hard," Corwin said.

"Look at this!" Shannon said, holding Mizbie by the shoulders and turning her around to see the wall over the bookcase.

"You didn't!" Mizbie laughed.

"I told 'em." Izzy said, "Don't go putting up her name in no lights like no hootchie, but uh, uh, they did it anyway."

There it was, MS BAXTER glowed on the wall. "I'm famous," Mizbie said.

"Mr. Krahler say we couldn't put up no tree, but he didn't say nothing about lights." Izzy grinned. "Leastways, we didn't ask him about lights."

"How sneaky is that! What did you do –, tell Mrs. Auger to keep me in her room all that time?"

"That was the easy part," Robin said. "You guys are always talking anyway. Now since it's all decorated," Robin walked backward using his fingers to frame the room like a high honcho auteur, sizing up the scene, "I think we should have a party tomorrow."

"We can celebrate Emily Dickinson's birthday. Tomorrow is December 10th. She was born in 1830. Let's throw a birthday party for her! I'll make a gummy-worm cake!" Mizbie was getting excited. "We'll look at her poem, 'A Bird Came Down the Walk.' Emily Dickinson. That's perfect."

Silence. An Emily Dickinson party was not what they had in mind. "Robin, you can come up with a dance to teach us, can't you?"

"I'll do The Worm," he demonstrated. His chest flopped to the floor and he pushed back up with a back that curved and sprung like a Slinky.

Singer walked in. "Miz B, I finished the article. Got it in before the deadline. Hey what's with the –"

"Shannon and I can do a line dance," Stella said.

"Bring music too." Mizbie reached for her camera phone.

"I saw Mr. Krahler walking this way," said Singer. "He looked mad about something."

"Lights off! Lights off!" Robin raced for one outlet and Izzy another until the lights were unplugged and the room became dark. In silence, they stood still and watched the hallway through the glass in the door.

After a few minutes with no sign of Krahler, smiles returned. "Lockdown practice successful," Robin plugged the lights in again. "Remember your stations in case we have to do this tomorrow." Before they left, Mizbie took pictures of them under her lit up name, in addition to one of the ceiling where Robin and Singer reattached a fallen drape of lights. She sent pictures to Jess. Europe wasn't the only place with surprises.

> Jesspin9
> to Mbax20
> 12:30 a.m.
> December 3

Hey Miz,

I was mad at you because I hadn't heard from you and then your email came. Love the pics of your classroom and your name in lights! Your students wouldn't do that for just anybody.

I was remembering my Canadian grandmother and how we'd planned that I'd cook for her in her Cuban condo over Christmas. She'd always have Christmas dinners when I was growing up. I'd put her china away in the cupboard, still warm from the scalding rinse water. So many of the dozen plates were chipped through the pattern on the gold edge, even though she rarely used them. When I asked Granny how they got chipped, she just lowered her head and turned back to the dishpan.

Later my uncle told me that when she was first married, the wealth of Grandpa's family at the book editors confused her. She came from a hardscrabble life during the Depression, plucking chickens after school for a few pennies. Her dad held one job after another –, lumberjack, milkman, knife sharpener, cabinet maker. Her mother was the neighborhood midwife. As a new wife with a fine home and comfortable life, Granny felt guilty and undeserving, so she smashed the edges of her china as a way of making them worth less. She could live with less-than-perfect china and it wouldn't appear that she was showing off if she used it.

Thinking about her makes me feel out of place and time. I've been here since October and I have this gnawing feeling I won't be able to afford a trip to Chicago to see my uncle for Christmas, let alone Cuba. Then my brother, Hank, called. His bank has him in Barcelona for six weeks, including Christmas. Elle and the kids are with him too. It's in the Gracia neighborhood, two connected flats, and they invited me to stay for Christmas week. Miz, I'll have my own room with drawers for my stuff. I am so looking forward to sleeping in a bed in a room by myself instead of a hostel with snoring, whirling dervishes.

I had dinner with them last night; Elle's always been a good cook. I have a couple week's work to do nearby in Sant Cugat, but I'll be back here for Christmas week. Kit and Leo are so adorable; it's going to be fun to be with my niece and nephew for a week, taking them to puppet shows and parks. And I can ditch this damned backpack for a week! Oh, I'll bring you some saffron from Barcelona if you want. The city market there has lots of it.

Here's my other holiday surprise. Early this morning I opened this tall, wood door of an old pastry shop. Terrazzo tiles spelled Cafe Jardin under my feet. I breathed in the chocolat and buerre, passed over the baguettes and little soucées covered in buttercream frosting. I zeroed in on an espresso tart. The young woman behind the counter described it having a chocolate cookie crust with a layer of ganache espresso mousse in the middle, and caramel drizzled on top. Between her limited English and my limited French, we struck up a conversation and she handed me an old, two-sided key over the counter. She motioned me around to the back of the shop. I could see the counter stretched clear across the entire place, separating customers from bakers. I paid and took the key around back with its flour-covered circle of wood chained to it.

When I jiggled the key in the lock, the door opened and I looked down a long narrow stairway and one tall angry baker with an oversized rolling pin. He glared up at me. I surrendered the key and he motioned me in. We were in a cramped kitchen under the patisserie, but there was a gleaming stainless steel table before me, so I sat right down. Three bakers gathered around with forks, spoons, my espresso tart and two other desserts for me to try. They were speaking such fast French to each other, using *expressive gestures, I couldn't understand much, but I think they wanted to see whose pastry was best.*

"Look at you," I said in my best French. "You are so thin. How can you work here and be thin?" I used the word fluet, which I hope they figured meant thin.

They didn't smile and didn't answer, just passed around spoons and forks, each with a pastry of their own, different from mine.

I knew better than to wolf them down, although I wanted to, Miz. That first bite of the espresso tart sent me over the edge. My eyes looked up to heaven and I just moaned. I tried to find a word to tell them, but the best I could do was point to the tart and say, "Vous êtes doux . . . vous êtes comme ciel"

The young woman who gave me the key seemed to get it and translated for the others. They nodded, slowly eating their own confections.

The last two desserts were thankfully small, but I was ready to dig in. One was a round, flaky pastry with buttery layers cradling a scoop of triple cream or mascarpone, I believe my translator told me. In the cream were freckles of dark chocolate and swirled raspberry coulee. At this one, I whinnied like a horse. Saying "très très bon" just wasn't enough, but it's all I had.

But the last one, let me tell you, had a tart sweetness I'll always remember. It was a little key-lime allumette layered with almond marzipan and the raspberry coulee swirl again. I ran out of French and just started babbling in English, faster than my young translator could muster, but the other bakers nodded, so I imagine they understood.

Eating those last flakes of pastry from each plate and smiling at all of them, I hoped they understood these were the most primo sweets I had tasted in a very long time. Of course, they probably thought I was a crazy American, but I think I saw a hint of a smile on my translator.

I stood to go and when they stood, I hugged them all for their kindness. My translator gave me a business card for my book.

Getting on my bike and slowly peddling back to the hostel, I felt like I had the best job in the world.
    Love, Jess

∾

It was the annual staff ski weekend at Nubbs Knob. Mizbie begged off last year, but this year she couldn't wait to get away. She left the ungraded essays at home and threw her backpack in Corky's van, jammed with seven other teachers. They arrived Friday night, just as snow began to filter down on the ski trails. Dusk brought lights, their soft glow falling over the undulating ski runs dotted with snowboarders and skiers.

Gliding into position at the top of the hill, Mizbie peered through fog and snowflakes, barely able to see the slope. Trusting to her memory of the run from a few years ago, she sped down the hill into a wonderland. The whoosh of snow under skis and the building puffs on pine branches floated past in a panorama of light and shadow. Gliding through white powder heightened Mizbie's senses, as if she was skiing for the first time. Corky and Heuster alternated S curves with her, threading themselves down the slope in a loose braid of exhilaration. Competitive spirit kicked in and they schussed in a race to the bottom of the hollow.

Cool darkness fell and the fog dissipated to a crisp clarity, changing the mood from a surreal fantasy to cold reality. Minus the fog, the wonderland became once more a ski hill under lights at night. After several more runs, she heard Guy Heuster's familiar voice. "Hey, let's go hit the lounge." Fingers and toes stiff with cold, bodies radiating heat, they headed for the sounds of laughter and a cover band, a rustic bar, and a warming stone fireplace.

On the long drive home at the end of the weekend, Mizbie was excited and more than a bit envious as she told the skiers of her friend Jess's upcoming Paris assignment. As the van passed the Interlochen exit, Heuster said, "Hey, Miz, it's Interlochen. Tell 'em your bat story."

Mizbie launched into her Interlochen memories and others that she and Jess shared. "Come on baby, light my fire –" Mizbie sang.

"Try to set the night on fire," Heuster continued in a voice like gravel.

"Ahhwooooo! Werewolves of London," Joanna tried to carry the tune. The skiers howled along.

Chapter 7

Chinese proverb on a door poster –
What happens to you in your life doesn't matter – it's what you do
with it that shapes who you are and makes all the difference. Someday
something good will come out of this. It could be the knowledge never to
do this again.

Jesspin9
to MBax20
10:00 a.m.
January 27

Hey Miz,
I'm sitting here staring at the big white envelope and my cell
phone. I'll tell you because you're about the only one who would
care. I've gone through all the pages three times and spoken with
my brother; there's no mistake. Noreen sold everything from the
Apple stock to the McDonalds stock, a small fortune that Dad had
purchased at $2 a share, and up until recently, totaled well into
six figures.
They put in so many long days at their small business, City
Fuel Company. All those years, Ma would come home early and
fix dinner, Dad would come home exhausted around 7:00. I'd
set the table, and we'd eat dinner, deciding what to do with Mrs.
Turnipseed who ordered 100 gallons of #1 fuel oil but could only
pay for 50. They'd put her on a budget plan and give her credit

when no one else would. Dad would look at Ma with a lop-sided grin. She'd look back and arch an eyebrow.

After dinner I'd follow him out to the garage, handing him tools while he fixed the garage window, hammering on it a little harder than necessary. Dad would say, "I don't know what I did to deserve your mother, but there musta been something."

Forty years of shared love and hard work are reduced to 23 pages of paper I'm holding, with names of stocks and bonds followed by the words, "no longer held."

I just talked to Noreen's daughter, Rona. "I know. Half that money was mine," she said. After Ma's death, Dad married Noreen, a waitress he met at the Jupiter Coney Island. She lived in an apartment by the strip mall. Of course, there was no need for her to work once they were married. Where Ma's eyes were playful, Noreen's were shrewd. Where Ma's hands squeezed Dad's, Noreen's weren't to be touched, in case her manicure got smudged. Where Ma cooked home-style fare, Noreen insisted on eating out and having Dad pull out her chair for her at each meal, kissing her cheek like a trained seal.

Rona told me at the wedding that her mother always got what she wanted. I didn't catch the meaning then. My dad, always gentle, acquiesced when Noreen questioned a prenuptial agreement claiming no one else but she could be trusted to be an executor of his will. He agreed, calling me from Walgreens to tell me. Walgreens calls were our means of communication, along with a couple of stolen games of golf on afternoons when Noreen had her hair and nails done. I'd ask him if he was okay and if she made him happy. He said she did, and that was what was most important.

So many business associates and golf buddies shook my hand at his funeral. His accountant called Dad the most honest man he had ever known. I'll always remember that. I remember the graveside murmurs and Noreen with her daughter seated before the casket dabbing at their eyes as if they had been family forever, not just family for two years. There was no chair left, so my *brother and I stood behind them while the pastor spoke, my legs shaking, at the sight of dirt being shoveled over a body that had been my dad for 23 years. I wondered how he could breathe under all that dirt, that's how my thoughts ran, not making any sense.*

Now, a decade later, Noreen is well into her nineties and calls the shots on a large sum of money. The pages of paper said that my parents' years of saving had been reduced to $21.00. Rona explained, "It's online poker." Her voice was flat. "I caught her doing it a few times, but I thought it was harmless. I could have called the accountant, I guess." She paused, trying to find words, I suppose. "Oh, I wish I knew she carried on that far. This is terrible. Just awful. I didn't realize anyone could go through all that money so fast."

Rona complained about how she now had to find her mother a more economical assisted-living facility, but I couldn't listen to the rest, cutting the call short, my clammy hands shaking. This won't change my life, Miz, and certainly not Hank's. I know it won't change anything, really. But there was the accounting of my father's life on my lap. A life invested in hard work and devotion spent in a heartbeat by an old lady playing poker.

Jess

Krahler had brought his notebook to Mizbie's class a few times for her evaluations this year. "I just can't place what it is," he said. "I don't know why, but you're not connecting with these kids. Look at you. Did you ever do modeling before you came here?"

A strange question, but Mizbie answered, "I modeled once for a college benefit show."

"That's it. You walk as if you're a machine. Like an automaton. You don't move like a person. These kids get caught up in watching you, and they aren't listening to what you say . . . what you teach. They're just not getting you. Be more casual. Slump a little."

With their recent conversation in mind, Mizbie sat on the front of her desk looking at her expectant class. She tried rounding her shoulders.

"What's wrong with you?" Desmin asked.

"You're sitting funny," Mara Jade said.

Mizbie soon forgot about posture. "So what do you think of Thoreau's quote, 'Some men lead lives of quiet desperation.' Can you give me an example?" Mizbie asked.

"Yeah . . . like when you're in a tense situation on the football field, the coach yells for you to get out there, but he doesn't understand the tailback for the Kingston team just nailed your best defensive lineman and he's not talking," Brandon said. "Lack of communication. Disaster from silence."

"That's desperate . . . Kim, add to that?"

"When my grandmother visits from Japan, our house is turned upside down. We do everything the old way. Shoes by the door, slippers for the bathroom, chopsticks with all meals. But you can't say anything because she's grandmother. It is truly quiet desperation."

"Nathan?"

"It's like a fight between Spiderman and the Sandman."

"Oh, no . . . not Spiderman again," said Justin.

"Yeah . . . Sandman is the only one who has the power to pour like water or have the strength of a solid. Kind of like the Brazil nuts in a can of mixed nuts? You'd think the heavy nuts would sink to the bottom of the can, but they stay on top."

"Okay, Nathan, you're making me quietly desperate here. Seth?"

"It's like on the farm when the cow is gonna calf and she might be breech and it's 4:00 in the morning and you have a big math test first hour. You can't leave her, but ya really need sleep. The cow just takes over your life for that time, and all you can do is wait and be desperate."

"My half-sister is older and she froze embryos when she got divorced," Noel interrupted. "Then she decided she didn't want them, so she tried to give them away for research. She was desperate and called three places, but no one would take them. She asked the fertility clinic what they would do with them. They said they'd throw them away. They said they threw away embryos every day once people couldn't afford the storage fees anymore."

"That's better to throw them away than to have them born into some kind of Frankenstein."

"My sister's embryos wouldn't have been Frankensteins!"

"Couldn't they put out a message to let stem-cell scientists know they were available before they trashed the embryos?" Seth asked.

"No! It doesn't matter what some scientist says. It's better to trash them than to have them turned into zombies!"

"But what about cures for diabetes or Parkinson's? My uncle used to be a boxer and he has Parkinson's disease. With enough stem cells to work with –"

"We've got some great ideas here," Mizbie said. "Stem cells, voting age, the Middle East War or –"

"Ms Baxter, can animals they use for research be quiet desperation?"

"Sure, Corwin."

Justin leaned back. "How about brains, I mean, guys have more brain ability." A groan circulated around the class. "I mean, girls are better at writing and stuff. Guys are better at math and problem solving and taking risks."

"Don't you think some of the girls here are going to pull you apart when you leave today, Justin?" Mizbie said.

"Sure, but so what? It's the truth. I read it on the Internet."

"Miz B, my dad finally got a job in Georgia. He was desperate for a job. He's working at a chopstick factory. They make 40 million chopsticks a day and send 'em to China, Korea, and Japan. It's so weird. The Chinese took his old job, now he's taking theirs."

"Hi, Miz B," Zoe walked in, stopping abruptly to stand in front of the class. "Guess where I've been?" Not waiting for an answer, she said, "Mr. Krahler's office. Me and my friend hacked into the school computer system. Really private school stuff. It was soo awesome. But now we aren't allowed to use computers for the rest of the year, so any time we do research in your class, I don't have to do it!"

"Wait, Zoe, what do you mean you hacked into the school system?"

"Just like that. We pushed a few keys, just to see if we could do it y'know? And we did it like that. But Mr. Krahler was mad. He called my mom but she won't care. Anyway, now I don't have to do the research project."

"Yes . . . you do have to do the project, just on your own time."

"But what will I do when everyone else is working on theirs?" She smiled, bouncing up on her toes.

"We'll work it out. Sit down," Mizbie said.

Zoe lost her smile, furrowed her eyebrows and stomped to her seat, slamming her books down, standing in the middle of the room. "I'm tired of sitting. I need to stand up."

"Fine. You need to use the restroom too? Here's a pass. Go use the restroom, then you can stand in the back if you don't talk to anyone."

"No, I don't need to go pee. I need to stand here, not in the back. How can I write if I'm standing in the back without my stuff?"

"You have a lot of questions today, Zoe. Step out in the hallway a minute."

"No! I want to –"

"C'mon, Zoe, give it up," Robin said.

Mizbie told the class to get out their journals and write down their opinions of Thoreau's quote. With noise and mumbling, Zoe stomped to the hallway. "You are so mean. You embarrassed me in front of the class."

"Your talk with Mr. Krahler wasn't a good way to start out the morning, was it?"

"That was nothing. You're the problem!"

"Here's your journal. You can do your work out here standing up, and you'll have all your materials with you. When you feel like you can sit down, you're welcome to come back in."

"Don't yell at me! You are so mean!"

Mizbie closed the door. "Okay, class, review your notes for tomorrow's quiz. Remember the Sugar Beet Fest starts tomorrow. Jerry Caswell's sister is running for Miss Sugar Beet, so be sure to cheer for her. Good music and good food. You might find something to write about in your journal for Monday."

∞

Mizbie took an alternate route down a road where two of her students lived. The first house had no vehicle parked in the drive. The front screen door had been broken out and what was once the only window in the front of the house now had plywood nailed over it. She took the letter she had prepared, in case no one was home, and placed it far inside the mailbox, its useless door hanging below, like a broken jaw. Because Lilac and her sisters were with their father this weekend, Mizbie hoped this message wouldn't be hijacked, like all the phone messages and emails she'd tried to leave. Mizbie had Lilac's sisters, Daisy and Lilly, and a half sister, Aurora, in previous years, but Lilac was the youngest and brightest.

She kept riding her bike down the road until it grew narrow and ran from pavement to potholes. After the fourth phone call home, and Rip's dramatic back-stabbing incident, Mizbie wasn't going to accept his laconic, "I guess my mom got your message," any more.

"Mrs. Helthaller is furious, to put it mildly," Principal Krahler said. "She wants to pull Rip out of your class. You're picking on him."

"Darn right I am. I'm not going to quit picking on him either. I'll keep telling him to bring his book, get out his pencil, do his homework, quit grabbing the girl's bra next to him, and pull up his pants so we can't see his underwear. He is able to pass my class, and I'll keep picking on him to make sure he does."

The meeting with Rip and his mother was scheduled for Friday. Mizbie wanted to see what didn't add up, so she decided to stop by the house the day before. Dodging cracks in the cement drive, she looked up to see Rip's tidy house, green siding with purple shutters. On the lawn in back of an overgrown iris bed was parked a 1995 Impala. Mizbie parked her bike on the sidewalk and greeted an elderly man walking toward her. "Is Rip Helthaller's mother available?" She identified herself and explained tomorrow's meeting.

"Over there in the car," the man pointed. Mizbie saw a woman in the driver's seat, flailing her arms. The driver's window was down, despite a brisk fall afternoon, and her sleeveless arm moved in and out. She appeared to be talking to someone, but no one was there.

"Are you Rip's mom?" Mizbie introduced herself.

"That would be me. Get in. We'll go for a ride," she said.

Mizbie noticed there were no tires on the car, just cement blocks holding it off the lawn. She walked around to the passenger door.

"No, no . . . get in back!" The woman motioned behind her.

Mizbie stepped back, opening the rear door. An overpowering smell of cabbage assailed her. Rip's mom gripped the steering wheel with manicured hands. "Y'see, Miz Baxter, Rip's my hope . . . my good child. His older brothers, one's in prison up north and the other got a dishonorable from the Navy and who knows where he run off to. But Rip, he's my pride. Except for that one time I caught him masturbating in the bathroom. I put the fear of God in him that time, I tell you. He'll never do that again. So when he comes home and tells me you do him wrong, picking on him and yelling at him, why, it's time to talk to that principal."

"I see," Mizbie said. Mrs. Hellthaller glared at her in the rear-view mirror. Above her shaved off eyebrows were penciled eyebrows redrawn in perpetual surprise.

"Have you seen Rip's report card? Did you see the Es in science and history?

"What Es? He's got Bs and Cs in everything except your class," Mrs. Helthaller answered, gesturing with her hand and jangling her many bracelets.

"If you look closely, those Bs might have been changed, Mrs. Helthaller. Our school records show Es in science and history, and also in my class. Let's see if we can work together to get Rip back on track. I'd like to –"

"You'd like to help, like hell! You're not doin' nothin'! We're driving up to that school and I'm telling that principal what you done to my boy, my good child. It's your fault he's got a E. All them other grades are Bs and Cs. You lie. We're almost there now. Just let me fix my hair before we go in."

Mrs. Helthaller ran her hand through her brittle brown hair. She pulled a red lipstick tube from the ashtray. Mizbie could see from the reflection in the visor mirror that only part of the lipstick made it to her lips. It reminded her of a child trying to color in the lines.

Mizbie stepped out of the back seat. "I'll see you at school, Mrs. Helthaller."

"You bet you will, Miz Baxter. I'll be right in. Just let me get my lipstick on." She ran the lipstick tube over her lips again, checking and smiling in the mirror. As Mizbie walked back to her bike, she glanced at the front door where Rip stood, watching. She waited a moment, making eye contact in case he wanted to say something, but he hung his head and shut the door.

ༀ

Mizbie looked back on a whack-a-mole week in school, listening to the song "Larry" to even out her mood. Renee's TGIF was just what Mizbie needed. She looked through the fridge trying to decide what to bring. There was some Leelanau raclette she could melt in a fondue pot with a little cherry brandy. That would be quick. She could pick up Italian bread for dipping. Finally, she decided on an Italian burrata or buffalo mozzarella because it was at its peak of flavor. She grabbed a focaccia round from the freezer, some cherry tomatoes, and basil. Renee would have the microwave for warming and olive oil for drizzling.

While the focaccia thawed, she poured a glass of Sixth Sense, a Shiraz, and looked out over her back deck at the park. She thought about a retirement party she'd gone to with Carl. He was getting to know everyone well, drinking way past the point she had seen him drink before. The next morning he woke with a terrible hangover and she watched him searching through her refrigerator for a cure. He brought out a coconut and wrapped it in a dishtowel, eyes up. From her tool drawer he grabbed a screwdriver and hammer. Slamming the screwdriver down into a coconut eye, and then pulling it out, he tipped the coconut over his mouth and gulped the water down to the last drips. As Mizbie's mother would say, his eyes looked like two burnt holes in a blanket. He sighed. "You know, when you and everyone else wake up, that's the best you'll feel all day. But for me, after that coconut water, I'll just keep feeling better and better."

The evening after Renee's TGIF was the Celebrate Art fund-raiser. It wasn't the type of gathering Mizbie and Carl were usually invited to, but she decided to dress the part. Carl, hoping to impress prospective clients, bought a new tux. Mizbie did not spend much time or money on clothing. She tended toward a few mix-and-match classics and wore them until they frayed at the seams or folds. She felt compelled to shop for the same clothing rather than try something new. It was frustrating when they didn't make the clothes she wanted anymore.

Finding nothing in her closet for such an event, Mizbie checked out the resale designer shop racks, grabbed three dresses and pulled the tie-dyed curtain on the fitting room. Pulling on a long black jersey dress that reminded her of Morticia from the Addams Family, she overheard giggles in the fitting room next to her. It must've been larger, if there were three women in it. "It's wonderful, dearie. That jacket's a perfect fit," one said.

The other chimed in, "It's just right, praise the Lord."

There were a few more oohs and aahs. They sounded as if they were eating chocolate. "My my . . . You know it's because you tithe, that's why we found this suit. That's why it looks so good on you."

Mizbie was losing patience when she tried on the third dress. Although they were all the same size, each one fit differently. She assessed herself in the mirror and knew this was the one. She couldn't wait for Carl to see it. The black dress accented the good curves, not the bad ones. One shoulder was bare. She had a silver pendant on a black silk rope that she felt would give it a classic look.

When Carl came to pick her up, she replaced the Depeche Mode concert ticket she kept as a souvenir bookmark from a concert in Chicago, setting the book on a table. They had taken his boat, *Mistress*, docked at Navy Pier, and taxied to the concert, returning that night to rock the boat before racing home over the choppy waves Sunday morning.

Carl couldn't speak when she opened the door; her transformation from the usual jeans and T-shirt was that stunning. Mizbie replied, "You look smashing, yourself."

He walked around her. "You look amazing, Miz." He enfolded her in his arms, feeling the sleek fabric of the dress and her body beneath. "I have to warn you," he said. "This is going to be so boring compared to the way you look." She laughed.

Tonight her bond with Carl felt far away from a bargain-basement, rock-bottom remainder to an elevated top floor love. As they drove, she glimpsed his face between street-lights, wanting to walk around inside his mind, to inhabit the little corners she couldn't access. The mind that made him successful and alpha, made him annoyingly off-putting with meticulous attention to detail, but magnetic for the same reason. She suspected a bit of ruthlessness in his business dealings but replaced those thoughts with reminders of his philanthropic contributions to Celebrate Art and other charities. The strength of men of his ilk didn't occur often in Astor. Even the robber barons Carnegie, Stanford, Rockefeller, and Duke ended up creating foundations and universities that exist today, long after their monopolies, exploitations, and quasi plutocracy passed. She saw Carl as they were: daring, brilliant – and he wanted her.

The fundraiser was held on the top floor of an old warehouse that had been turned into the tony Holden Towers loft apartments. With champagne in hand, Carl and Mizbie stood by the window looking over the Grand Rapids skyline at night, far removed from their usual Saturday night life.

Her eyes scanned the guests reflected in the window and she noticed they had decided not to "dress down" to fit in. From their sparkly gems to sky-high shoes, she checked her own gently worn designer dress, straightening the single shoulder seam, and deciding it was a good fit in every sense of the word. Even the men, mostly older, were showing attention to detail in their hair color and creative face work, black silk ties, bowed and straight, and shoes she would never see in Astor. These men and women of indeterminate age appreciated beauty and were willing to pay handsomely to surround themselves with it.

Sipping champagne and nibbling canapés, she floated from one conversation to the next, curious about these area movers and start-up donors who afforded a life of plenty, yet searched out worthy causes for giving their money away. "It's all about international securities," she heard Carl say to a group of other men. "I've sworn off stocks, except maybe water stocks. It's the new oil."

The donors' motives could have been guilt about all the jobs they sent abroad, or a tax write-off, but Mizbie suspected for most, it wasn't so far off from her reasons for teaching. She might have been loud and short-tempered with students sometimes, but she had an instinct for filling those empty parts of her charges. Outside of needing a paycheck, she taught high school kids for the satisfaction it gave her. These folks wrote checks instead of receiving them, and they could find and refill coffers, helping a lot more people than she could, but she guessed they felt that sense of satisfaction too.

"The conversation hasn't been that bad so far," Mizbie told Carl, as they danced. "We've discussed Joseph Campbell, Bill Bryson, and Nutella." Carl changed her focus, telling her that her eyes looked transcendentally violet, and her smile made him feel powerless. He wasn't a man who was use to feeling powerless.

After the song, their hostess rushed up and Carl excused himself. "I have to say your dress is absolutely lovely," she smiled. Mizbie could tell this was a woman who had created many of these good-will gatherings. With one necklace or any one of her diamond rings, she could have funded Celebrate Art herself. "And what a catch your Carl is."

They watched as Carl walked over to a group of men who opened their conversational group for him to join. There was something about the stature of his presence and the warmth of his voice that seemed to fill the room. Now that he was apart from Mizbie, two attractive women joined him. One must've said something clever, because all the men began to smile and laugh.

"You'll want to keep your eye on him," the hostess said.

Mizbie knew he was talking about business, which she'd heard before. She was drawn to a mixed group of legislators, passionate about their causes, but backed away when she saw them listening to Rich Burns, one of Celebrate Art's biggest donors. Burns was well-known for donating millions to campaigns around the country to help defeat Roe v. Wade. He donated millions to local and national legislators' campaigns, if they would support the Burns' view with their votes. His political blocking made it easier for many hospitals and pharmacies to deny morning-after pills due to religious beliefs.

Due to his efforts, food assistance for the needy was drastically cut, even though half the recipients of food aid were children. When legislators approached him about hungry children, he threatened to spread information that would not only ruin the legislators' reputations, but he would withdraw all monetary support and find someone who would vote to support his causes, not the good of the needy.

Occasionally Mizbie caught a glimpse of Carl, finding one of the women clinging to his arm like an indelible stain. As he spoke, he gave little away, a flicker of recognition in his eyes, or maybe just the sparkle of light from the chandeliers.

Turning at the sound of a hearty laugh, she was startled at the sight of the Comptons. She hadn't seen them since last summer. Rand Compton had been doing business with Carl since they met for a weekend at the Phoenix Lake Resort in August to seal a deal. The resort had kayaking, wind surfing, volleyball, jogging paths, and lounge chairs for relaxing around an infinity pool, all clothing optional.

Mizbie and Carl had never visited a nudist resort before and noticed right off, everyone carried around beach towels. Comments of, "Like your towel," and "Let's hang out" were considered resort humor whether meeting at the pool or the miniature golf course. Golf carts playing country music or summer beach tunes traversed the resort, carrying bronzed couples with no tan lines. Joggers had nothing to hide, sporting the occasional fanny pack and Nikes. Mizbie and Carl skinny-dipped in the cool water of Phoenix Lake with bass swimming and nibbling around their bodies. A blue heron swooped near and scooped up a fish.

Chantilly and Rand purposely chose a Harley and Yoga Weekend at the resort, so Carl borrowed his friend's candy apple red and silver Harley Sportster for the occasion. With many motorcycle events scheduled, Mizbie and Carl chose a familiar one, the Bite the Weenie contest. On the hot, cloudless Saturday after lining up to maneuver a circle obstacle course of orange cones, the couples or spouses passed slowly under a swinging hot dog covered in spray whipped cream. The partner on the back of the motorcycle tried to bite the hot dog, which wasn't as easy as it looked. Mizbie and Carl were allowed three passes. The first and second times, Mizbie steadied her arms around Carl, tipped her head back and bit, but the elusive dog popped out in a slippery slide before her teeth could sink into it. On the third pass, she succeeded with a small bite, her mouth dripping in a whipped cream goatee that soon melted down the front of her body where it ended up in a small sticky pool on the hot black Harley seat under them. The crowd gave encouraging hoots and applause with Chantilly and Rand bouncing up and down, patting their sun-reddened backs.

By the end of the weekend, Mizbie and Chantilly had joined in a few yoga groups with so many fronts and behinds of every shape and size, Mizbie had become numb to them. With the sound of motorcycle engines revving up to leave on Sunday night, Mizbie and Carl said their goodbyes and put clothes on to return home, surprised at how free and relaxed they felt. Even so, Mizbie didn't feel drawn back to Phoenix Lake any time soon.

It was too late. Chantilly had spotted her and sidled up. "Mizbie, I'm delighted to *see* you!" she gushed, patting her arm. Where was Carl? Mizbie pictured Rand and Chantilly recounting their weekend together, someone taking a cell phone picture, and having the whole story get back to St. Bartholomew's. Offended parents had wreaked havoc on teachers' careers before, but this time it might be hers. She could see the headlines in the *Astor Index* now: "Cavorting Teacher Nabbed Nude." Worse yet, if Rich Burns heard of it, his private cadre of yellow journalists would end her career in short order. Teachers were even lower on his hit list than hungry babies were. Even if her career survived, people in a small town never forgot these things.

On the way home, Carl smiled when he told Mizbie what Rand Compton had said about her. "'Like Chantilly and me,'" he said, "'most of the people at Phoenix Lake have been coming here for years. Time and gravity have done their work. But Mizbie, she's a mighty perky girl there, Carl.' That's what he said, 'mighty perky.'"

Mizbie groaned and Carl laughed. "We could've won the Bite the Weenie contest, if you'd just steered a little bit to the left," she said.

"Yeah, I was surprised they gave Chantilly and Rand Best Bite. Remember Chantilly falling off the back of the bike with the weenie in her mouth?"

Sunday night Carl had flown to Dallas for a Monday morning meeting. Mark Norcross, the science teacher down the hall, called and asked her if she wanted to join him at Tikki Cove to watch the Pistons game. Talking to Mark was like talking to a girlfriend from high school or a favorite brother, even though Mizbie had known him for only a few years. Renee asked if Mark was her "work husband" but Mizbie didn't care. She'd only met his wife, Margaret, once, but wondered what his wife thought about their friendship. Margaret had nothing to be jealous about, but Mizbie wondered what married people thought about opposite-sex friends. Maybe there was a bit of jealousy, but Mark never hinted at it. They ordered beers and wings. He said Margaret had taken her mother to bingo at the Catholic church that night, and was happy for him to have something that got him out of the house.

It wasn't long after Mizbie shared the story of running into Chantilly that their talk turned to school. "You have Margo, don't you?" Mizbie said. She knew Mark did. Margo actually liked geology and astronomy; she never passed up an opportunity to ask Mizbie why her class couldn't be fun like Mr. Norcross' class. "Her poetry is brilliant. There should be a place for kids like this, kids whose bright rebellion blocks them from 'play the game' of the raised hand, the fill-in-the-blank, and the multiple-guess quiz." Margo loved archery and was an excellent markswoman; a crossword puzzler; a sketcher of haunted, troubled faces; a writer of short novels; a collector of new words. She was so far beyond the Es, that Mizbie had to enter after her name in the grade book.

"I told her, 'Margo, if you won't do this assignment, make up one for yourself. Write something about the Hudson Bay writers or the mysteries surrounding Edgar Allen Poe's death. What will it be? What would you really like to find out about?'"

"'Nothing.'"

"'Google a topic from our time period that interests you. Trace your family tree back to the time of Emily Dickinson. Let me know what you decide.'"

"A few minutes later, I checked back with her to see that her computer screen was tuned to anime cartoon figures. She looked up with defiant eyes, one dark blue and one chestnut brown."

"'This is a crock. School is a crock. I can't do this.'"

"'Margo, you choose not to do this. Imagine what you'll find.'"

"'I don't care about grades or anything in this stupid school. I just want to read vampire stuff. I read the *Historian* and all of Ann Rice's vampire books.'"

'Okay, then how about Transylvania? How about something from eastern Europe?'"

"'School sucks. It blows.'"

"'Let's be politically correct,' I said. 'Say, school inhales.'.

"She looked at me, about to say something, but didn't.'"

Mark nodded. "Did she show you the Moon poem she wrote? We were talking about how Americans ignored Soviet contributions to space. The far-side geography of the Moon has Russian names. They were first to send living beings into space, they invented the first space suit, and if you look at the name cosmonaut, it can derive from the Greek word chaos, yet it also has to do with the study of an orderly, harmonious, systematic universe. Margo completely got it. Ask her about the poem."

Mizbie grumbled and dipped her wing deep into spicy barbecue sauce.

∾

Rico's grandmother cornered Mizbie in the hallway as the bell rang for class. "Jeez, there's so many kids," she said, swatting with her good arm. "I've been trying to help Rico with this dang work, but my arm's in a sling, as you can see, so I can't go to work and I can't help him as much as I'd like to." *You mean you can't write his papers for him,* Mizbie thought.

"So I want to know, what is this 'un? What does 'un' mean? How do you expect me to help him, when you don't explain in the directions?

"Oh, we talked about that in class, Ms Broom. UN stands for United Nations. It's an essay about peace and –"

"Well, let me tell you what happened with my arm." She looked down at her right arm bandaged and in a sling. "You see it happened Wednesday morning. I was letting the dog out when –"

"Ms Broom, I have a class to teach now. Please make an appointment with the office and we'll talk later. Thanks for coming." She closed the door.

Ms Broom yelled, "Don't get uppity with me, missy. I'm going to the office all right. I'm going to tell that principal you slammed this door in my face."

"Don't mind Grandma," Rico said quietly. "She talks like that to everybody. She won't really do nothin'."

"Okay, let's hear your alliteration. Robin?"

"An amalgam of amorphous aardvarks amble amiable around."

"Good. Julie?"

"A lost, lonely llama lumbered longingly, looking for a lime lollipop."

"Okay, Justin?"

"My most miserable makeshift Mazda morosely moped through muddy muck."

Mizbie smiled. "I like the morose Mazda. Gilbert?"

"Seven slippery serpents snaked silently through a slit in my sock."

"A sock! Amanda?"

"Earth to Amanda . . . are you star gazing or navel gazing?" Robin asked.

"Robin, see me later." Mizbie gave him the look.

"Can I read my poem now?" Gilbert asked. "First, I want to talk about Saturday," he said, not waiting for an answer. "We raise canaries and Saturday's the annual American Birdsong contest over in Chelsea. We came in sixth last year with Bubba. He likes to sing to Mozart, so we play it for him a lot. He comes from Hilda and Garth, who was a real screecher, but it worked out 'cause he learned his dad's loud voice and his mom's melody. Yup . . . Bubba's got a good chance of winning this year. Well, my poem's called 'Potatoes.'"

Potatoes mashed with sour cream,
A whole bunch of baked garlic, salt and pepper,
Don't even need butter,
They are that good.
They're soft like a blanket on my tongue;
They slip down my throat in a warm hug,
Filling me up,
Singing a song in my heart.
Their fresh-smelling ingredients tickle me.
I'd drive all the way to Arkansas and walk over burning clay
For my Aunt Cissie's mashed potatoes.
Just don't ask me to use her outhouse. It's nasty.

"Okay, Gilbert. Good luck on Saturday. Izzy?"
"It's called 'Skin.'" She adjusted her paper closer, then farther away.

"Something I'm curious about – skin.
The dimple over each finger of my baby niece,
A dozen wrinkles around my grandma's eyes when she laughs,
The bags under my dad's eyes he calls money bags,
Uncle Tracy's shiny shaved head,
Hirsute skinned men at the beach. See, I used a new word!
Desmin, who is called black when his skin is coffee brown,
Miles of skin, oceans of skin,
Holding us in and showing others shades of who we are."

"Hey," said Desmin. "I'm in your poem. I like it. You okay, Izzy."
"I like the way you look at something familiar in a whole new way, Izzy. Mara Jade?
"I'm still working on it. It's called "'Friday Is Sky Blue."'"
"What do you mean, Mara Jade?"

"It's hard to explain and write about. When I hear the word Friday, I see sky blue. It's synesthesia. I hear and see the colors." She shifted uneasily. It was a risk for her to talk about something that made her even stranger. "I'm not crazy or anything. My grandpa in New Orleans sees the colors too. His parents thought he was crazy and tried to keep him in the house so the neighbors wouldn't notice, but he ran away and joined the Navy. He'd talk about the sounds on the ship having their own colors. We don't see the same colors, though. When I hear drums, I see fiery orange flames. Grandpa sees a blood red color at the sound of sea waves."

"What color are canaries singing?" asked Gilbert. "Yellow?"

"I can't think of a color for that kind of bird sound, but robins and jays sound like purple to me. Concerts are my favorite thing because of the colors. When the music plays, it's like there's a giant screen in front of me and I can see the band, but there is sky blue at the top and these splashing waves of color constantly move through. That's what my poem's about. A concert. The music makes bright, strong colors for the loud parts and softer calmer colors like purple and pink for the slower, quieter parts. The color is the music. I've looked it up. Some famous musicians and artists are synesthetic. There's Duke Ellington and Leonard Bernstein. Tori Amos is synesthetic."

"Who's Duke Ellington?" Gilbert said.

"He was a famous jazz musician," Izzy answered.

"Not everybody who has it has the same kind. Some kinds turn months into personalities, like May is friendly. I don't have that. Some people taste the words, like the word Florida might taste like coffee. I don't have that either. I like seeing colors when I hear things. I can't think of my life without seeing them."

"That explains some of your journal poems, Mara Jade. I hope you'll read 'Friday Is Sky Blue' when it's finished."

"Noel?"

"I call it 'Sacred Space.'"

"Is this a religious poem?" Corwin asked.

"No, it's just a title," Noel answered.

"Astor—Deer Park means memories
To those who proposed marriage there,
Took their kids to feed the deer
Or played their guitars and protested war
Back in the hippie days.
But attachments collide over time
With reality borne of possibilities
Of shopping in a new Mega Mart
Of cement and steel sprouting
Where trees were.
Change over time is reality.
Deal with it.

"Poems are stupid. We use Deer Park to hang out in all the time. Who wants to meet in a Mega Mart parking lot? You just want the Mega Mart store 'cause your dad owns a cement company and that whole store is built out of cement," Justin said.

Noel turned to him and looked down. "Get real. The deer are inbred anyway. Hunters should just go in there and kill them all. Why do you need a place to hang out when you can go shopping?"

"Yeah, like you'd ever shop there," Mara Jade said.

"Okay, let's get into our research groups now," Mizbie said.

Carl had invited Mizbie over for dinner Friday night. He told her it was just casual, but he had something else in mind. He set the table with cloth napkins and a candle. His pilot buddy had flown in fresh lobster from Maine. He toweled the wine glasses for water-marks and set hers down next to the small satin covered box. Watching her place at the table, he rehearsed what he would say.

He grew impatient with the time and the waiting for her. Then he remembered the earlier message he hadn't retrieved because he was on another call. Mizbie's recorded voice came through the speaker, "Hi, love . . . sorry I gotta cancel tonight. Our band gets to open for – get this – Transgression!

Can you believe it? It seems somebody in the other band got sick today, so they needed a new band fast, and we're it! How could we refuse? There will probably be 150 people in the audience. I hope you didn't go to too much trouble for dinner. Talk to you tomorrow . . ."

It was late when she got back and Carl was gone. The gig was too exciting to allow sleep, so she pulled out the last few Michael Moore essays, forging ahead with a singleness of purpose, purple pen in hand, an English automaton with metaphors of Kmart, GM, Smith & Wesson, health care, and terrorism flitting before her mind's eye like an iPod play-list. There were cursory flybys, struggling plods of effort, brilliant fireworks of effortless thought, and careful well-planned A-seeking go-beyonds. With the turn of a page, Mizbie felt exasperated, entranced, captivated, furious, and energized. She even considered purposely hitting her head against the kitchen wall multiple times. Finally, she looked down at the last paper. With pen in hand, she debated correcting it later when her mind was fresh, or finishing it now, knowing everything was done when she went to bed.

Rashmi's papers were usually corrected last, so their quality wouldn't influence the other grades. Sure enough, from the first phrase, Rashmi hooked Mizbie into her thesis of Moore's wide pendulum swinging to draw attention to the issue. By the third page, the support built to a paragraph of depth and insight, which Mizbie read with incredulity, mentally cheering on her student who she tried so hard not to favor.

Then a word caught her eye. A phrase actually, that she'd remembered from a review she'd read and chosen not to use in class. It couldn't be. Mizbie checked her laptop and brought up the phrase on advanced search. It came up on the first try, not only the phrase, but the entire paragraph. Rashmi had lifted the paragraph and built her own reasoning around it. Mizbie re-read it to make sure it wasn't faulty paraphrasing, searching, hoping she was mistaken. Mizbie swallowed hard, slamming her pen on the table, feeling betrayed. This was corruption. But Rashmi? The pressure to be better than best? Pressure from her parents and even more from herself? What the hell? The trust was broken and Rashmi would never get it back.

Mizbie yelled curses, slamming drawers and doors, thinking of revenge. Specifically, the revenge of the grade book. Not only would Rashmi get a zero for the paper and a conference with Mom, she would fail the term. Mizbie rehearsed a scathing note to leave in Rashmi's permanent file, confiding that after all her extra books lent, extra vocabulary sessions, and encouragement, this is how she was repaid – with deceit, pretense, and fraud. She tossed ice cream, chocolate sauce, and a sprinkle of chili powder into the blender, drank the mixture out of the blender jar, and stomped off to bed.

Chapter 8

A girl shows her friend a text message: NO really means TRY IT. Cmon U R so hot.

"Love is like spaghetti," she told her friend. "You start at the beginning and nibble your way through in a ladylike way to the middle, and there you are surprised to find a tramp."

Jesspin9
to Mbax20
12:22 pm
April 12

Hey Miz,

Sorry about your star student cheating. So you went soft and let her rewrite the paper after all. So what? You did that One Forbidden Thing teachers aren't supposed to do and backed down. You didn't make her accountable. But it felt like the right thing.

I just got a surprise invite to the Rhein River in Switzerland for some white water rafting before I leave for Paris. These cyclists I met said it was a class III-IV, a little over 12 miles, starting in Llanz. Even a 12-year-old can do that. Let me tell you, the runoff from the glaciers was uber strong this year, and the ride was any-thing but class III –IV!

It's called the Swiss Grand Canyon even though the canyon walls are granite. The sheer cliffs are sprinkled with evergreens and the water is an icy (believe me) light aqua. But I couldn't even enjoy it. I was white-knuckling my paddle all the way. Each drop was steeper than the last. Our helmets clunked into each other constantly, the raft jolting us in every compass direction like one of those bistro broncs we used to ride on Friday night pub crawl.

I fell out of the raft three times before we'd even gone the first six miles. The third time was a huge surge and wave crest over the bow of the raft and I thought of the stuff in my apartment that would kill me if anybody saw after I drowned. My brother would not believe I would be capable of doing stuff like that, especially well, you know. Can you imagine? But here I am, alive to tell the story. So Miz, you've gotta promise me that if anything happens to me over here, you'll use the key I gave you and grab the evidence so no one else finds it. I know I can count on you.

The last mile was beautiful, though, almost calm, and we all cheered and patted each others' backs for surviving the other 11 miles. We rehashed the whole trip over Indian Pale Ale. All in all, a satisfying ride. I'm gonna turn in, but I wanted to thank you again for sending pictures of Daphne. When you said how she stretches on the couch with her face dangling off, watching you upside down, following your movements with her little black eyes, wriggling her nose, paw in the air, I remembered her doing that too. I sure miss you guys.

I just have to wait for the final okay from Herrod House, but I'm going to see the city that inspired Hemingway, Gertrude Stein, Ezra Pound, Scott and Zelda Fitzgerald, not to mention Baudelaire and Diderot before them! I can sing "Light My Fire" on Jim Morrison's grave! Remember Interlochen and the flea market? I can shop the Marche aux Puces flea market for costume jewelry on a Saturday afternoon.

The thought of the creperies and patisseries draws me like baked almonds. Imagine waking up in a little Paris flat, looking out the balcony window over the city street, finding a sidewalk cafe for some people watching, enduring the crabby Parisians who are sick of tourists.

They say once you've been to Paris it stays in your heart always. I'm making room for it now. Isn't that crazy to be so enamored of a city you've never seen? I can't remember ever being so excited to see a place in my life.
Jess

Mizbie cycled a final round through Indian Springs, darkness settling around her, stealing the last freshness, listening to the earthly quiet. Pangs of envy over Jess's trip to Paris became worry over her student Jenna who had some rough days since her sister Loni's death. Mizbie remembered the last time she had sat with Loni and listened. Loni spilled out a story of secret love with a senior boy, the absence of two periods, the panic, getting dumped. Her hand clutched her books as she fumbled for a tissue. Loni and Jenna's father was very strict, and they knew if he ever found out about Loni, he would throw her out of the house. She knew he would because he had already warned her about this boy, describing how she would come home from school one day and find her bed and clothes on the sidewalk if THAT happened.

Mizbie put her arm around Loni and hugged her. She was sorry... so sorry, but Mizbie's words seemed so feeble. She told Loni about safe houses where she could go for help. Her dad didn't need to know. Together they would figure things out. She didn't have to make the decision alone. As Mizbie told Loni to let her know what she decided to do, her next class walked in and Loni ran off. Now there was Jenna who needed her support.

At her apartment, she stared into the bathroom mirror, unsettled. Carl's call from Japan last weekend was unsettling too, but she refused to let it undo her. Actually, she appreciated his honesty. If human beings would be more honest, it would save a lot of time with wars, trials that dragged on, and politicians. Then again, it would be hard for people to trust themselves to be honest, to depend on themselves when they may as well leave it to chance and bet on a slot machine, lottery ticket or the stock market.

Carl's call began with small talk about his meeting in Tokyo and his amazement at the kindness and hospitality of the company people he met. Then he veered off into some tangent about the first English language teacher to land in Japan, named oddly enough, Ronald MacDonald. He landed on a volcanic island called Rishiri. When he landed, he thought he was seeing Japanese people, but they were really Ainu, the aborigines of northern Japan. They were quite hirsute, unlike most Japanese, and the women tattooed their upper lips. Miyo, he assured her, was not hirsute and did not tattoo her upper lip, but he wanted to date her and felt it would be only fair to tell Mizbie so she could date other men too. "Since I know you value honesty," he said, "I wanted to be upfront with you."

Mizbie met Grant online. He was a tech writer who composed manuals in Silicon Valley and Detroit. She rented a Zip car and drove an hour to meet him at a coffee shop between their two homes. She opened the coffee shop door and didn't see anyone who matched his picture, so she waited in line for coffee. A man cleared his throat behind her. Turning, she looked down to see a man her age, wearing stained sweats, a distressed leather jacket and a scowl. The top of his disheveled black hair didn't quite reach her chin. She bought a coffee as he left the shop.

Five minutes later, he returned and sat across from her. "You must be Mizbie. Buy me a coffee?" Grant said.

"That was you," Mizbie said. "I didn't recognize you from your picture."

"I had to go a... check on my dog," he stammered.

"You left it in the car?" Mizbie wondered why he would bring a dog.

"Left *her*. Yeah, she's like my wife. She goes with me everywhere," he said.

Cyril Pinkwater's internet profile said he was Mizbie's age. She was a bit suspicious about her second attempt to replace Carl when the lapels on the jacket in Cyril's picture looked very wide and polyester. After a few emails and calls, they met at the Tikki Cove for lunch. He was already seated and smiled broadly when Mizbie arrived. Searching his face, hoping she was mistaken, he spoke and removed all mystery. "You are lovely as your picture, my dear."

Cyril was old enough to be her grandfather. He laughed about his picture and admitted it was taken more than a few years ago. "But would you have come if you'd known I was older?" he said.

He turned out to be a fascinating lunch companion, in a curmudgeonly way. An architect, the son of an architect, he had traveled the world but was here temporarily to build the Burger Castle down the street. He had ridden a camel, discovered a 1300 year old sarcophagus on an archaeological dig, and organized the placement of community wells in Mozambique, saving villagers five miles of walking a day and insuring their health with fresh water. He railed against politicians who didn't support his desire to invest in third world projects. Over chocolate cake, they debated books they had both read. Alas, Mizbie admitted she had been born in the wrong generation. He smiled not unkindly and they said their goodbyes. Dating was so much more difficult than it was in college.

"My kids -" Jack was ready to unload the moment they were seated at the restaurant table. *Minus one point for her third date,* Mizbie thought. "-are 10 and 14. The ten-year-old never says anything and the fourteen-year-old is a pistol in school. ADHD. At home he never does anything but sit around and eat, read about wolves, or look on the internet for Civil War guns. He loves 'em. And will he do anything I tell him? I tell him he's gotta get interested in something. Something he can do for a job, but hell no! He sits there and stares at the TV. I give up. I don't know what to do with him. You're a teacher; what would you do?"

This man has known his child for fourteen years and he's asking me what to do with a boy I've never met. How sad. I wonder what Carl and Miyo are doing? "I'd find something positive. Something we had in common. You divorced a year ago. He has to get through that too. What are his good qualities? Can you build on those?" She tried to listen and feign interest.

"That's just it." Jack said. "He has no good qualities."

He said wolves. She thought of Edward. "This is pretty personal on a first date, but has he ever threatened to harm himself? Is his name Edward?"

Jack's barrage of words assaulted her and she tuned out, pretending to listen but praying not to feel so much like a referee. When the meal ended and he asked if she'd like to continue their talk over dessert or coffee, Mizbie said she was sorry. "I don't think I'm up to the challenge of children and I'm not the person you're looking for."

As she excused herself from the table, Jack launched into a speech about all women being alike and it wasn't his fault that he had problem kids and what was the idea with stupid women anyway. "You're a teacher for God sakes. Whaddya mean you aren't up to the challenge of children?"

People turned and stared. She thanked him for the dinner, touched his arm, wished him good luck, and walked away. *I hope he stays home for parent teacher conferences,* she thought.

∾

Mizbie woke to the refrain from a Joni Mitchell song, "We are stardust, we are golden...we are billion year old carbon..." played on the classic rock station, her morning alarm. Her consciousness began to clear, and a rerun of a heart-stopping night terror popped back into her mind. She forced it out, along with last night's dinner with Jack. Instead, she thought of a time weeks ago when she sliced open a bosque pear, scooping out the core, slathering it in Tupelo honey and sprinkling it with cinnamon. Picking up a quarter, she bit into its juicy sweetness, wiping a honey drip from her chin when Carl walked in. He touched his hand to her face, catching the last of the honey before he kissed her. They embraced and her arms brushed the smooth fabric of his new suit, probably from Japan. "You haven't come in days and I bet your nuts are bursting," she said.

She could feel Carl's ribs wriggling, trying to keep down a laugh. "You mean I'm ready to bust a nut," he said.

"Oh," she breathed, finding him disturbingly irresistible.

He picked up a pillow from the sofa and tossed it on the floor, drawing her down so that her back would arch upon it.

They welcomed each other in familiar ways and, Mizbie noticed, new positions, until they were spent and lay on the floor with his arm curved around her. He was geeked up about the idea of everyone being composed of stardust. He rambled about a star reaching the end of its life, then exploding from its core, releasing all these particles that traveled through the universe to become the genesis of new planets. Those elements became part of new life on the planet, and here we are.

From the recommendations by the Pussycat PJ Partygoers, Mizbie decided to ask Ryder about these night terrors that often woke her. Others spoke of him in low tones and said Ryder kept a dream diary, though no one ever saw it. Some called him a dream interpreter, others a dream guru. He rode a Harley and read palms. A man of indeterminate age and questionable character, he was still attractive despite multiple marriages. Like the matryoshka, the Russian nesting dolls, he had lives within lives, some known, some yet to be revealed. Teachers knew his fifth wife had divorced him and was living in New York. No men would admit that they secretly envied the excitement they believed his life held in a Richard Cory kind of way, making theirs seem pale by comparison.

Ryder couldn't see why anyone cared about his past, or why he had agreed to see Mizbie after school today. He had a pounding headache, so he drew the blinds down and clicked on instrumental music from a computer site, more for him than for her. Leaning back in his chair, he stretched out his legs and crossed one scuff-toed cowboy boot over the other. He thought of the papers he'd signed yesterday and sent back to New York, and further back to the first time he'd met Penelope. It was after a rodeo final in Tucson that he happened to win. He was elated, she was tipsy, and they married three days later. It only lasted a year, but a feeling like love grew in him. Penelope, like Ulysses wife, faithful and patient, beautiful and resourceful, virtuous and sexual.

His days on the circuit were numbered and here was this opportunity to teach. He weighed the regular hours and pay; he wasn't getting any younger, and he could exit on a high note. Here at St. Bartholomews he didn't speak much of his rodeo days, adapting to the pain free predictability of school life from the adrenaline charge of riding the circuit. Alas, Penelope, a former Playboy Bunny, was not about to live in a small town where the streets were empty by 10:00 at night. Then came the supporting role offered to her in a New York City soap opera. So they split, not unamicably, he to tiny Astor, she to the Big Apple, neat, clean, no strings attached.

His spirit, however agnostic it seemed, yearned for Penelope and the electric spring of their brief courtship and marriage. He had kept a journal, an Excel spreadsheet actually, of their couplings, all 237 of them over the course of the year. He read the spreadsheet occasionally, even though he hadn't seen her since August of 2012, reliving the serendipity of discovery like saddling up a new pony for that first wild ride. With Penelope, little surprises added to his fascination for her from her ticklish ear lobes to the way she sang when she had her way with him.

But along with the previous four wives, Penelope's coltish behavior became tiresome. Moving on was surely the best decision. Yet he returned to those spreadsheets, keeping alive the tiniest details of their brief life together, savoring the memory of her scent and the way her body responded to his.

Mizbie greeted Ryder, hoping her voice covered the loss of her last nerve before this relative stranger. "Okay, it usually starts with me in this heavy old blue car," she said turning to face him.

"Wait. Sit down here," Ryder motioned her to a chair. "Can I get you a soda?" he said in a voice that could've belonged to a late night radio host. From the back of the room he drew two bottles from a small refrigerator. "Let me make sure I know a bit about you first. You're unmarried...early thirties...you work out, am I right?" He watched her twist the cap, observing her like she was a painting in a museum, explaining that he drew the shades and put on the music because of his headache.

"I thought I recognized the tune." Mizbie had the flute CD at home. "It's Ian Anderson's *Divinities,* right?" Mizbie asked. "Are you sure we shouldn't do this another time?"

He assured her the ibuprofen was kicking in, the caffeine would help, and he sometimes played instrumentals to help calm and focus his students. "I know dreams..."

Was he convincing her or himself that he was a credible authority?

"Do you believe dreams tell stories about our subconscious? Our wishes or hopes?" He smiled looking past her at a triangular patch of light escaping from the side of the window blind to the floor. She explained that she'd had the night terrors for so long, and one in particular was haunting. "Go on," Ryder said.

"I'm driving this old blue car. It's so big I can hardly reach the pedals or see over the steering wheel, but I have to go fast because someone is chasing me. Then the road ahead turns into a bridge so steep, there is no top. The clouds turn gray and a wind like the Mistral comes up so the bridge is swaying under me. I push the gas harder but the car only goes slower and the bridge gets steeper, bouncing like a tightrope. This feeling of dread washes over me and I want to go back, but the car behind is closing on me. I push the pedal into the floor but the car feels heavier and slower like it will never make it over the top of the bridge no matter how hard I push. My heart races and I grip the steering wheel and look over the side – "

"So ...as you're driving, everything becomes darker and you're driving up the bridge. Can you see what's at the base of the bridge?"

"Yes, the water is far below, all choppy and murky gray, and black birds are flying in all directions. I know they're waiting for me to fall, waiting for me to die."

"And?"

"Through the windshield I see this monstrous train, some sort of old steam engine coming up the other side of the bridge on a collision course, billowing smoke. The tension is unbearable. I flirt with the idea of letting go and turning the car deliberately into the guardrail to end the terrifying – ”

Mizbie stopped and gulped the Coke, realizing her hands were clenched and hot. Ryder hadn't moved.

“I look out the side window and there is a man there staring at me, watching. He wears a smiling mask like Alice's Cheshire cat and he's holding out a gift box. I reach out my hands to take it and when I take the box, the car is gone and I'm falling toward the water and I can't breathe. I'm falling so fast, waiting to fall deep under the water, waiting to drown, then I gasp and wake up.”

Ryder felt her anxiety and waited for her take another sip before he spoke. He leaned forward in his chair and rubbed his stubbly chin. “Puzzling...and scary for you.” He stood up and walked to the windows, raising the blinds just enough to let in a little afternoon sun. “Some parts of your dream are universal. The car, for example, you're traveling through your psychic life, unable to control it, feeling it's too much for you to handle. Would you say things are stressful for you?”

Mizbie thought of Carl. “Not really,” she lied, wishing he'd just talk about the dream without her having to reveal more.

“And the blue of the car could be the wheel or energy center of your body. Do you practice yoga? It's a psychic center like the top spoke of the chakra wheel that is your brain and the crown of the head, clear thought, like a blue sky. But then your sky was gray. So you're trying to make sense of it, trying to harness the big unwieldy truth, when the car gets darker as if something is intruding into your search for the right road, your longing for self-knowledge. And that tall bridge straight up...like a mountain, your archetypal self, heroic, loving a challenge, yet uncertain, needing to confront feelings and issues to resolve them.”

Mizbie looked puzzled.

“Carl Jung discusses this myth/dream relationship from deep within. You said you've had these dreams for a long time; I'd believe they're archetypal. The energies of your body are in conflict, like the brain that heats up when you're trying to sleep, but instead it can't keep from rehashing the events of the day or planning for what you expect to be a conflict tomorrow. Our dream state magnifies these energies."

He paused in thought. "And your fear of falling into the water? Water represents the source of all...or it could be something magical. Or maybe something forgotten. But I'd go with the source of life." He held the cool drink in his hand, but hadn't opened it.

"My source of life...my parents? Then what about the car chasing me?"

"Being chased means having a need to face your fears, the unknown. And that face in the mask? He's a silent witness, an imbalance between your emotion and your intellect, one fighting to overpower the other; only you can decide. Could be work overpowering a personal life?" He gave Mizbie some time to think. "Somewhere lies an issue you need to confront." Ryder leaned forward toward her and stood, watching her reaction, seeming pleased with his interpretation and where it might lead.

Mizbie thought about the conjectures and how confusing they were. How could he know? She wasn't sure this explanation made the dreams any clearer than they were before, or if trying to understand them would make them stop. What emotional issue did she need to confront? "How can I confront what I don't know?"

He looked at the cold drink in his hands. "Is there something in your past you need to face? Estranged sisters? Parents? A lover?"

"I have no family anymore."

"Oh...I see...sorry...a persona of yourself, maybe? You know, like Eleanor Rigby, picks up the face that she keeps in a jar by the door? What's behind this lovely face?" He smiled in an effort to lighten the conversation and chucked her chin.

She sat back at his spontaneous touch. So many interpretations bombarded her. "I don't know; this is all so bizarre. That horrible train? The gift?"

He sat back down. "You described the train as monstrous. You may desire to return to what is small and secure as opposed to big and power-ful like your car and the steep bridge. And the gift...well...evil sometimes masquerades as good, concealing powers behind a smile, powers of the spirit, a loss of trust, a deception from someone you loved. A transformation, maybe, a loss from a stable foundation.

You know according to the NY Public Library, the word nightmare is an ancient superstition from the eighth century. In England it was believed that a female monster spirit or mare would sit upon a sleeper's chest. The sleeper would experience a suffocating feeling and try to free herself, sometimes waking because of it." *Where did that come from? It must've been something Penelope said.*

Mizbie wondered if he often talked like a textbook. There was the weighty feeling that came and went after these dreams. She thought of the feeling as anxiety, but now she would probably imagine a female monster looking down at her as she lay in bed. She thought of her childhood up north, her parents. "I haven't been back home in years," she said. "Do you think I'd find some answers just seeing the place again? Going back to the home I grew up in?"

"Could be...Cars are designed to catch the eye; dreams catch the mind. As years go by you have more memories to attach to dreams, fewer controls. The front of your brain that organizes thought is turned off when you sleep, so Lady Gaga theoretically could ravish the Pope. In your dream it would make perfect sense. Give it a try. See the house again. Take in the breeze coming in from the lake, you know. It might help you come to terms with whatever this is. It could lessen the frequency of the dreams or eliminate them.

Now I'm going to throw out some other ideas and you can see what makes sense to you. If you look at Joseph Campbell, he talks about the time you dream and how the permanent conditions in your psyche relate to what's happening in your life at the time. Dreams are never-ending sources of spiritual information, you know. Take the elements of your dream, for example the lake and the bridge, and associate with them. It is somehow significant enough to influence you, yes? If you think of a dream as a myth, the myth is the dream of a society. Dreams are your own private myths. Sometimes they exist in harmony, and then sometimes, like yours – "

"What happens if it's not in harmony?"

Ryder thought a moment. "According to Campbell, you're in trouble. Dig down deep into your psyche and work it through. I know I've thrown a lot out for you to think about. I'll go with you if you like and try to help sort through them. I'll bring a lunch...a bottle of wine...I'm damned good at picnics," he smiled.

Mizbie's mind was sputtering with questions about her foundation, confronting what? Chasing whom? "Thanks for...listening. You've given me so much to think about. I'll let you know," she said.

By the look on her face, Ryder thought he'd added more worries than not. He thought of one small step. "Try this. Close your eyes and imagine the dream. But change any of the troubling parts. Change them any way you want. Make a new dream. Take the old one, wad it up in your mind and throw it out the window."

Mizbie closed her eyes and imagined throwing out the old dream. She was in the car, but instead of riding up a formidable bridge, she was driving a sporty red Dodge Viper up a curvy road, a hill with a hiking path as beautiful as those Jess described in her notes from Europe. At the top, she stepped out of the car and looked out over a vista of small lakes, green hills and endless sky.

"Not everybody agrees with this dream change thing. Carl Jung would turn over in his grave, saying you'd be missing important messages the dream was trying to send. But hey, if the old dream tortures you, if you can't sleep, what kind of message is that? Get rid of it. Now whenever you have the nightmare, throw it out the window again and repeat this new dream to yourself. Add details like the scent of the air or the quake of leaves, but make it the same dream. You've had this nightmare so much, you've taught it to yourself like a habit. Now you have to unlearn it. You can change the plot"

"I can change the plot," said Mizbie.

Mizbie cycled home after yoga and drew a bath tossing in oil beads and lighting candles. She immersed herself feeling like a French fry in its basket descending into lovely hot oil. What had Ryder said about being unable to control her psychic life? She wasn't looking for a mind reader. And what about the search for a big unwieldy truth? There were no secrets lurking in her past that she knew of anyway. But like the freight train, her sheltered childhood id contrasted with the Big Unknown she was living each day. She was in her thirties and still didn't know each spring if her annual pink slip would end her teaching job by the fall. Daphne meowed, circling outside the tub. Mizbie reached over and sprinkled water drops on her whiskers, watching her bite at the drops. She sank back into the warmth of the bubbly water, wondering if she could ever take the kind of European junket Jess was having. She imagined walking down a cobble-stoned European street with lace curtains fluttering through Medieval windows or floating down the Rio di Palazzo under the Bridge of Sighs in Venice with a stripe-shirted gondolier singing a tune from an Italian opera.

∞

Mizbie opened Renee's front door for her. "C'mon in Sharon. Hi Ted."

They walked through Renee's living room with it's collection of big game heads and a new dragon kite hanging from the ceiling, to the dining room set with six mismatched wine glasses for each plate. The scent of basil, oregano and portabellas sauteed in butter and garlic wafted in. They sat with Heuster and the others at the table bursting with a melange of color – red peppers, purple Japanese eggplants, and yellow squash were printed on the tablecloth.

Clarisse sat with her bare arm against Ed, sipping her Gewurztraminer, a New Zealand vintage. "Yesterday was our anniversary!" she announced, like a kid finally allowed at the adult table. "Oh," she smacked her lips. "I like the buttery stuff." She turned to her husband with a grin and a wink. "I can't believe it's been a whole five years." Her look was like a kiss to Eddie and no one needed glasses to see the electricity between them.

"Miz, I thought you were bringing that new guy you met. Bob the well-spoken one?" Sonia asked. Arthur, her doctor husband was conspicuously absent.

Heuster, the newest member of the group, put a bread stick on his plate and looked up.

"He was pleasant enough. We talked over dinner for a few hours," Mizbie said. "The time flew by. He kept up his end of the conversation, but he was actually a good listener too. We both like to cycle, enjoy the same garage bands, but then his phone rang and he excused himself, saying he had to take it. It was his mother. I thought it spoke well of him that he'd be so solicitous of his mother, until I realized he's 35 and she wanted to know when he'd be home."

Clarisse crowed with her cackling laugh and Corky pounded the table.

"It wasn't just that." She had their attention. "The two of them kept talking. He'd listen and say aha and hmm. Then he'd reply and say something soothing to her, assuring her that he'd be home real soon." Mizbie's voice took on a tone of growing annoyance. "The check came for dinner, and when he reached for his wallet with his other hand, he showed me a picture of her. It might have just been a bad picture but she looked like a blow fish. They must've talked for a half hour. I lost all patience and excused myself. He waved goodbye and kept talking. Sonia, your mother-in-law lives with you. How's that working out?"

"Oh, don't get me started," Sonia said, tasting the second of six wines. Ryder had just circled the table, pouring for everyone.

"You two," Renee said, free of Dirk's reproach. "It's a good thing Dirk's not here to hear this or I'd take out a life insurance policy on him right now in case he died of boredom. He's playing poker tonight, but he asked you guys to save a cigar for him."

Ryder cleared his throat. "Hey, how about those Red Wings?" Ryder's black pullover shirt did little to hide his muscle. Renee reached around behind him and gave him a big hug before he sat down. "Where's that red-head you brought to wine club last month, Ryder. Wasn't she a nurse?" Renee asked.

"I don't want to talk about that, Renee." He answered. "Nurses are too much like mothers. Not like Sharon, here, eh Ted?" Ryder was thinking of Sharon's early retirement from her dot com start-up. She had left teaching to start her own app management company. Within a few years, she was bought out for a handsome sum.

Renee began passing around the fruits and cheeses, including the *la roule,* an herb-kissed French triple-creme cheese that was first to be devoured.

"Hm...this wine tastes like saddle leather...with butter in it," teased Corky.

"Oh...I taste moss with a hint of eucalyptus. It's just not arugula enough for me," Joanna added in an affected British accent, wrinkling her nose.

During the last wine club at Sharon and Ted's house, the guys had retired to smoke cigars on the back deck. This night Ryder showed Heuster a small humidor and invited Renee if she wanted to try one. "I'm going to eschew cigars tonight," Heuster told them. "I've just launched a health and wellness website. Trying to distance myself from the suffering of my prolonged adolescence of being a Postmodern male, spending too many hours on World of Warcraft."

Sharon complained about the smell of cigars. "I'm getting bored staying home day trading in front of CNBC. I could start a new company and Ted could get a job as a Megamart greeter or something," she said.

Sonia laughed at the thought. "Ted does not have the patience to greet people with a smile." She had to admit, Sharon and Ted looked more tired and worn than when they both worked 60-hour weeks.

Renee brought in the garlic sauteed portabella mushrooms from the kitchen as Heuster and Sonia oohed and aahed. She rubbed her hands, covered with artsy silver rings to distract from her arthritic fingers. "Every year I say this will be the last one. But it's still too much fun teaching with you guys. They haven't thrown me out for being too old yet. Besides, I don't have enough saved up to retire," she said.

"But look at the morale at St. Barts compared to what it was last year." She took a sip of the third Gavertz, the last white, before they began passing around the reds. "Remember how it was with Smithfield?"

"He was only here a few weeks in September, wasn't he?" Clarisse asked.

"You're still a baby aren't you?" Renee said. It was Clarisse's first year of teaching at the high school. "When he was principal, things were different. Nearly every teacher in the district wanted to work for him. He demanded our respect, and he earned it. He worked hard and we worked harder for him; his approval meant that much."

"Even the kids behaved better," Corky sighed. "Then he got called up by the Marines for a second tour of duty. That's when it all happened."

"His poor wife and kids, oh my," Sonia said. His girls were just in elementary school. Anyway, Clarisse, he put all his affairs in order before he left, got everything ready for the family and the day after he left – "

"Yeah, just one day after," Renee said.

"The day after he left, Superintendent Winchell terminated his contract. His family was left with nothing." Sonia said.

"Can you believe it? His wife asked everywhere, trying to figure what went wrong. Smithfield couldn't do a thing being a world away in the Middle East, and they knew it. She couldn't afford a lawyer," Corky added. "They lost the house and ended up moving to the Marine base."

"Could that woman cook. Remember the zabaglione she made for Christmas?" Mizbie said.

"With what that little family endured and all you think of is food?" Renee said. "So Superintendent Winchell hired Krahler, who happened to be an old friend of the family. The whole thing was fishy. But there I go, thinking again. Can you smell the circuits burning?"

"Welcome to Astor politics," Mizbie said, scooting over to clink her glass with Renee's.

Mizbie watched as the food she and Renee had prepared for two days, shopping for the ripest tomatoes, the freshest swordfish steaks, the most fragrant peaches, was slowly savored by friends who shared her love of food. They tossed the parsley garnishes at her if they happened to scoop one on their plates, knowing she actually liked fresh parsley. Mizbie picked them up and popped them into her mouth.

"Okay," Sharon brushed the shaggy brown hair from her eyes, "I've got an announcement." She stood. "Ted and I are moving to Charlevoix," The table was silent. Sharon and Ted were really leaving, the Megamart comment a mere hint. "We needed a change of scenery and this tech start-up offer kinda fell into my lap."

Heuster was the first to express his surprise. "What will wine club be without you guys?"

"We'll come back now and then, and you can come up and see us," Ted twirled the wine in his glass. The silence from the group was not exactly what he expected. Sharon talked about the home with five bedrooms and how welcome everyone was to stay with them. "We're even close to wine country," she said, looking hopefully around the table.

Voices grew more subdued, instead of the usual ramping up of satisfied good cheer. Sharon and Ted felt the change. "This one's a Molly Dooker Shiraz, "The Boxer". Corky read the descriptor from the bottle before she circled the table pouring her own glass last. All the wines were from Australia or New Zealand. Heuster forked the last swordfish from the platter, spooning a Cajun fruit fusion salsa on top.

Everyone agreed Renee and Mizbie had outdone themselves. The candles on the table lit up the friends' contented faces. After a last bottle of wine, a Leelanau dessert ice wine that Sharon and Ted had brought as a surprise from their newly adopted home, Mizbie returned from the kitchen carrying a tray of strawberry tortes drizzled in chocolate ganache she described as a "melody of flavor with major notes of cocoa." She nearly tripped on a rug, catching herself in time. To top the tortes, Mizbie brought out a chilled mixing bowl full of whipped cream. Despite groans and protests, Mizbie took the ladle and with a flourish, plopped a snow drift of whipped cream on top of each torte asking, "Is that enough?"

Circling the table she persevered through the bellyaching, ladling whipped cream until the mixing bowl was empty, watching them wade in with forks and spoons to find the tortes beneath. She tasted a bite herself, then sipped the ice wine, loving the taste of both, and already missing Sharon and Ted.

Chapter 9

In the locker room –

And I walked out of my apartment like I do every morning and I heard her again, her voice through my bedroom wall. I wonder what she looks like? I bet she's beautiful, long dark hair, dark eyes . . . It's torture. One night in my bed, I moaned back. Their bed quit hitting the wall. Yesterday I saw the guy across the hall picking up the newspaper. He stopped to listen too. I'm not the only one.

The night Carl told Mizbie he was to be married the next day, they lay in the dark on her bed, looked up at the luminescent stars painted on her ceiling, and listened to Miles Davis. Carl had surprised Mizbie with unaccustomed ferocity in their coupling. In one of those moments of raw sharing afterward, Carl revealed to her the qualifiers of Miyo, that woman in Japan, making her sound truly inferior, when she called Carl a "crafter of lies." Mizbie commiserated and trivialized Miyo, whispering in his ear that he was a storyteller or weaver of dreams, not a liar. She reached for a Michael Ondaatje poetry book on her night-stand, a book of passion and what-ifs, looking for the poem "The Cinnamon Peeler" to read to him.

"Remember the Woody Allen movie, *Manhattan*? We saw it at the art film series. Remember the part where he thinks about what made life worth living?" Carl turned to look at her, the picture of contentment.

"Um hm-." Mizbie turned pages. "I remember."

"We went to that old theater and heard the Holzt concert, "Mars" from *The Planets*. We saw the Chahuly glass that weekend too."

"All those organic blue and green sea creatures. You pretended you were a clam," she smiled.

"Summer at our favorite secluded bike path at Indian Springs, the picnic, my homemade Chambourd caramel sauce –" He sat up on his elbow.

Mizbie tossed the book and relaxed into the pleasurable images from which she had memorized tiny details. His expression resembled the barely graying male T-shirt model in a Sears Father's Day advert, handsome and true. As he moved and stretched himself out, she looked at him and thought of Michelangelo's Ufizzi marble come to life, where the male figure awakens and his muscles become taut, a classic body captured in stone.

"I'm getting married tomorrow at noon," Carl said, moving his fingers around her shoulder. "We're flying into Metro Airport, taking a limo to the boat in Monroe, then hitting her wide open on Lake Erie, heading for Put-in-Bay for some serious partying. Remember the T-shirt bar? And the thunderstorm that kicked up with me in my tux and you in your dress. It took us hours to get back, rolling in those 10 foot waves. When we docked back in Monroe, I remember you kissed the boat." Silence. "There's a big reception at the country club before we fly out to the boat. I was hoping you'd come," he said.

Mizbie was stunned, trying to make meaning out of this tumble of words. She sat up. "Did I hear what you just said? We've been together for three years, Carl. We're lying on my bed tonight and tomorrow you're marrying someone else? Not only that, but you think I'd want to be there at your wedding?"

Carl inched away, falling back down on the pillow and fixed his gaze on the ceiling.

"I don't go to bed with one man and tell him I'm marrying another one tomorrow." Her body tensed.

Carl tried a calm voice. "The marriage doesn't mean we have to quit seeing each other, Miz. I still love you." He tried reaching for her and she backed away. 'I love you, I've always loved you and I hate being in love with you. I thought if I could just cause a conflict that would break us up and allow me to blame it on you, I'd feel better. And ultimately, that's what it's all about, Epicurus' pursuit of pleasure."

Mizbie was silent.

"My father's had other women since he married Mom. We do business in a lot of different places. Having other partners, it's been common in Europe for centuries. C'mon, you're open-minded. I mean, look at the name on my boat. It's been an unspoken understanding. What did you think?"

Mizbie visualized the transom on the Outerlimits boat. It was, indeed, named *Mistress*. It was a common boat name. She ordered herself not to react like some scorned fury. Suddenly Carl wasn't worth her anger. "That's all this is about – the pursuit of pleasure? So does your fiance know about me?" Her face grew hot.

He didn't answer.

"I didn't think so. No, I'm not coming to your wedding reception, you bastard." *I can't let him know how this hurts.*

"Go," she said, pushing him off the warm bed toward the door. "I'm not going to be a part of your secret life, you narcissistic ass!" *No, not this Carl who knows me so well, this Carl who always wanted more.*

"Narcissistic? Me?" Carl's voice lost it. "You're the one who was never ready to move in with me. You don't know Scott –"

There it was. The name. Mizbie didn't want to know Scott's name, associate with anything having to do with Scott, have a student named Scott, or watch a movie where the name Scott was lovingly whispered in an ear, because the name made it real.

"Scott?"

"We met in Italy last year. Scott is –"

"You deceptive, deceitful, lying son of a bitch." She walked toward him and Carl backed away.

"Miz, you're coming uncorked."

"You prevaricating, dishonorable, double-tongued, fallacious –" Mizbie gathered his clothes and threw them out the door. He stood looking at her. She pushed Carl hard and he stumbled out into the hallway. In one fluid motion, she slammed the door and locked it behind him. "Don't ever come back." *Broken-winged, barbed-wire words. I can't fight this.*

The Murano glass orb he had brought from Italy sat on the end table. She grabbed it, opened the door, and threw it with all her strength. It hit the baseboard heater in the hallway and broke in two. Carl was already halfway down the stairs.

She closed the door and leaned against it, listening to the slam of the outside door, furious with his cavalier, offhanded suggestion that she become a concubine, and more furious with herself for ignoring the hints of his idiotic polyamorous arrangement. Mizbie grabbed a bottle of wine, but that wasn't what she wanted. Opening a kitchen cabinet, she didn't want to eat either.

She didn't want to marry Carl, yet the ache of loss grew in her. To hell with covenants and what-ifs. The brain's love chemicals had stopped smoothing over the provocations revealing sandpaper beneath. If she had said yes and legally contracted herself to a few years of together-ness, what then? A lifetime of enduring anger and excuses? She had sewn and stuffed her feelings into a few years of relative happiness, but now that issues were tearing away at the fabric, it was time to cut them loose.

She donned a shirt and stood out on the deck to cool her burning cheeks. The red taillights of his sports car disappeared. Weighted with loss, she stood in the chilled breeze. She heard a meow and felt Daphne's fur sail past her leg. She had forgotten to close the sliding door. Daphne leapt off the deck into the darkness below. "Daphne!"

Mizbie scaled the deck railing and jumped down onto the neighbor's patio below, scraping her knee. Through the trees, she ran barefoot and called to the cat. She tugged her shirt down and sobbed. Her knee throbbing at each step, she limped behind one tree and another. There was the traveling. When Carl came home, they were too much in each other's way. It must've always been this way, but she didn't see it until now. Renee had always said, "People don't change. We just finally realize who they are."

Once she had met Jess's brother and his wife at a Christmas party. It was hard for her to understand married people who were loud and hung their marital laundry out on the line in front of everyone. Marrying Carl might have been that way without the breaks they had from his intensity and her temper. Besides, Carl had his own quirks to rival Ben's crocheted jock straps. There was Carl's vast collection of science-fiction comics and the fact that he preferred briefs to boxers. She could have used one of his magic decoder rings right now.

"Daphne." She saw the flick of a tail in the shadows. Daphne purred when Mizbie patted her to check for pain. "Oh, kitty, you scared the hell out of me." With her face nuzzled into the soft fur, she hugged and sighed, "You're okay, you're okay." Then she laughed. *"Mistress."* She told Daphne, "Imagine Carl taking this Scott guy to Put-in-Bay on the *Mistress.* Imagine Scott's reaction when he sees the name of the boat!"

After she stumbled back to bed, she stretched herself across it, something she couldn't do when Carl was in it. Instead of luxuriating in the space, it felt as if the bed was stained. The years with Carl weren't just about being loved. She could let loose and indulge in silliness so embarrassing she could never imagine revealing herself to anyone else that way. But Carl had endured that and more, except for some of the worst night terrors and outbursts.

She sighed. There was a peace in the absence of that love. Something had been missing. Certainly there would be women or men who would find that love gratifying, as she had at the time, but now that it was gone, she felt repelled by it. She looked down at the ugly jagged edges on her knee. She cleaned and patched it as best she could, but the scar would be a reminder of this night. Whatever she felt was missing, what she really wanted was as elusive as the cause of the night terrors and their headaches afterward.

Jesspin9
to MBax20
9:00 a.m.
April 30

Hi Miz,
I can see now what Hemingway meant when he called Paris a "moveable feast." After being here a week, this place feels like a part of me. The natives look straight-faced through tourists as if

we weren't here. Everywhere is pricey, but it's Paris! I've done all the required museums and now I'm exploring the quartier perdus, those less gentrified places where local cafes and fruit markets have survived for generations. Earlier I devoured a thick-crusted white bread slathered in herb-flavored goat cheese with pepper sprinkled on top. It was still warm from the oven.

I see what Papa Hem means. I sat out on the lawn with people I'd just met, a bottle and a baguette, waiting for the sun to go down and the Tour Eiffel lights to put on their show. I typed chapters from the Bateau Bus while cruising down the Seine for hours around the Île de la Cité and under bridges.

I share an apartment with another cyclist and her Australian girlfriend. We're between the Musée d'Orsay and the Tour Eiffel in a five-story walk up. Our room is about the size of our old dorm room at college and the bathroom is down the hall. I bought an air mattress and sleep on the floor. There is no air conditioning, but we keep the windows open for the breeze at night. On our only window is a filigree iron grating.

Peering out over trees, motorbikes and yarmulke'ed pedestrian men below, we can see a street vendor selling falafel. I've had more than a few meals at street vendors. Yesterday I found a tasty white bean soup with a small turkey leg. I've found a couple of crepe stands where I've gone back for seconds. Down the street from the crepe stand I happened by the Shakespeare Book Store. I was standing where James Joyce and Sylvia Beach had their talks about publishing Ulysses. Before I leave Paris, I'll pick out a book just for you.

Jess

Mizbie refused to think of Carl on his honeymoon with Scott. She tried not to think of Jess exploring Paris while she taught school. Instead, she had arranged for a Zipcar for next weekend's trip to Alabaster. As Ryder had suggested, she was ready to confront or uncover whatever she could find. But first came one of her most irritating weeks when her students confronted or uncovered possible vocations for Career Week. Noel walked up, her face like a brunette Barbie with a petulant streak.

"Can I have scissors?" Noel popped her gum twice.

Mizbie directed her to the plastic basket in the corner where student supplies were kept. Students were moving desks into groups. She gave the scissors to her friend Char. They cried and giggled as Char slit a hole in the knee of Noel's new jeans. When groups convened, Noel couldn't consider working with her group. "Look, I can't go through school looking like this!" Her eyes welled with tears.

"Didn't you give Char the scissors to cut your jeans?"

"Yes, but I didn't think they'd look like *this*! I have to call home. My therapist says I'm not supposed to get upset. Mom has to bring me a new pair."

"You have other jeans with holes in the knees. Now you have another pair," Mizbie said, motioning Noel to her seat.

She rolled her eyes and stomped her foot. You don't understand. These . . . the hole . . . it's too . . . *look*." She held up her knee for effect. The difference between the offending hole and any other was impossible to figure.

"Go call your mom," Mizbie said, knowing Noel would not concentrate on any work until Mom was called.

Noel often called Mrs. Sharpe, and any attempt to curb the calls was met with another conference with Principal Krahler. Any time Noel received a grade on a paper less than she felt was fair, Noel's mom would speak first with the principal, then the teacher. Mrs. Sharpe came to school often. On Noel's last comparison/contrast paper, Mrs. Sharpe told Mizbie, "Noel deserves at least an A-. I spent three hours working with her."

When Mizbie suggested that maybe she was helping Noel too much and Noel should experience her own successes and failures, Mrs. Sharpe's voice became a controlled clip. "I'm taking this to the superintendent," she said. Mizbie hadn't dealt with Mrs. Sharpe in awhile, but heard she argued with the office about Noel's failure to follow the school dress code. Whether it was the height of a hemline, a bare midriff, or a revealing neckline from her daughter's extensive wardrobe,

Mrs. Sharpe was there to support her daughter's freedom to express herself fashionably. Rarely would the scowls on their faces relax, except on the occasion of wearing down Principal Krahler after a dress code kerfuffle.

For her mock career interview, Noel brought a brown paper bag and asked to change in the restroom, because she would be embarrassed beyond belief to wear interview clothes all day, as most freshmen did this time of year. Returning to class in orange soccer shorts, a T-shirt, and gym shoes, she took the long way around the room to make sure most everyone had seen her, then stopped by her seat, waiting for Mizbie's reaction before she sat.

"I have no comment on your attire," Mizbie deadpanned.

Noel let out a high-pitched giggle and frowned, annoyed at everyone's lack of attention.

As Mizbie walked among students, she noticed Brent had stopped work on his resume. At 14, he had no work experience.

"Haven't you ever raked leaves or shoveled a neighbor's sidewalk in winter?" Mizbie asked.

"No."

"Okay, Brent, what do you do around the house? Have you ever washed the car? Cleaned a closet?"

"No."

"Set the table?"

"No."

"Made your bed?"

"No."

"Incredible. I'm calling your parents. You need some responsibility."

"Just because I don't have experience, you can't mark me down for that part."

"I can't write a cover letter for a job. I don't know what I want to be," said Oola.

"We've been working on this for two weeks. Yesterday you wanted to teach elementary school."

"No, you told me I wanted to teach elementary school."

"You had "teacher" written on your paper."

No, I said on my resume that all subjects applied to a job and you said that sounded like an elementary teacher, so I wrote elementary down."

"Think of a career path you've been studying. What interests you?"

"Pink. I like pink. I want to do something pink." Oola glared through her swagged curtain of hair. "You're not going to get me to read that," she said about a "Top Careers in the Midwest" handout Mizbie dropped on her desk. "Yes, I want to be an educated person." She broke her pencil in half. "I know that the harder I work now, the more choices I'll have to get that great job I really want, yadda, yadda." She pulled off the eraser. "You've told us that over and over. I'm sick of hearing it. I'm not reading it and there's nothing you can do about it. Nothing."

"Did you know, Oola, that Edison came up with our greeting 'hello' when we answer a phone?" Mizbie said, disregarding the complaint. "His friend, Alexander Graham Bell, wanted to say, 'Hoy, hoy.'"

For Izzy's mock interview, she was going to practice for her real interview with *Sports Illustrated* next month. As a 90 pound freshman wrestler, she could nearly bench press her weight and the guys often milled around to talk with her after her many wins, asking her about times and moves. Izzy was comfortable around them and had more in common with them, having had nine older brothers with whom she'd wrestled most of her life. Joining the boy's team this year was merely a matter of learning the rules of the game. She soon attracted college scouts and the magazine. Because the wrestling team had a meet tonight, the guys were dressed in shirts and ties, while Izzy wore her swingy little dress, timely for the wrestling meet and her mock interview.

"Izzy, you're squinting. Have you had your eyes checked lately?" Mizbie asked.

Izzy squirmed, as usual, because it was hard for her to sit still. She spoke so only Mizbie could hear. "I had 'em checked last year, but," she paused, "glasses are expensive."

"I think I know someone who can help you out," Mizbie whispered.

After class, Izzy noticed Noel and the group she called friends, cornering Mara Jade in the hallway. She decided to duck into a doorway and listen, in case Mara Jade needed her.

"So what does it feel like to be *you*?" Noel edged closer, the girls she called her friends blocking the view of passersby.

"What do you mean? What does it feel like not to go to church? That doesn't mean I don't have beliefs."

The girls were not here for a philosophical discussion, but Mara Jade continued.

"When Mr. Ryder talked about Joseph Campbell and the meaning of life, that's a belief system too. We can't say what the meaning of life is; it's like asking, What is the meaning of a rock or a tree? Meaning is awareness of each moment and feeling the rapture of living it. Remember? It's like that."

Noel was about to say something but Mara Jade cut her off. "It's like Chief Seattle said in 1852, every part of the earth is sacred. How can one person or one country own the freshness of the air or the sparkle of the water? We all belong to the same family, share the same water, and breathe the same air."

Mara Jade looked from one face to the next and took a breath. "What we do to one another and the earth, we do to ourselves, so that's why we love the earth and love one another. When we love everybody and all our cool different beliefs, we are also loving ourselves. See what I'm saying?" She searched their faces through eyes that were pleas of passion. She remembered Izzy who described these girls as nasty, heat-seeking missiles. Was any of this sinking in? When she first read Seattle's letter, it suddenly became so clear to her; she felt it answered her life question about the "Way Things Were." Didn't they understand? Chief Seattle knew this even way back then.

"I believe all religions are cool and interesting because they tell what's important to people. I'm curious about all of 'em. So tell me about yours. I'd like to know, really."

"You said *cool*. Nobody says *cool*," Noel sniffed and walked away.

After school, Izzy caught up with Mara Jade in the library. She had just returned carrying her current protest sign from the front of the school, "If you think poverty of the body is bad, poverty of the mind is worse."

"Let's make some more signs for tomorrow," Mara Jade said, spreading new poster paper on a table. She convinced Mizbie that she needed the paper for part of a Career Week visual aid. Mizbie knew it would end up as a picket sign, but gave her the paper anyway. Mara Jade got out her markers and suggested to Izzy that they make a sign protesting the ill-treatment of artist Cho Honan on a human rights issue. Another promoted motorcycle helmets – BRAIN BUCKETS SAVE LIVES. Their next sign promoted universal background checks for guns because a bank teller hostage was killed in California. The gun, homemade nearby in Mayville, had been purchased over the Internet. Together they propped up the protest signs they had used outside after school today, placing them in the corner with their book bags, but Cindy the new assistant librarian wouldn't have it.

"The library is not a place of controversy. What is this?" she said, pointing at the signs as if they were dead fish.

"I'm done with them," Mara Jade told her. "You can recycle them now if you want to. I'm going to do some research." Mara Jade and Izzy conducted their research incognito past the watchful eye of Cindy. Singer found them there after asking friends by the front door where they were headed. His offers of friendship with Izzy had withered and faded so far, but he persevered, hanging around the tattoo shop asking Mara Jade for some female guidance in the fine art of wooing a girl.

Tiptoeing behind the American history stacks, a tendril of an idea spiraled through Mara Jade's mind as she searched titles. She opened a neglected book in a corner where only a booklover would look, a universe of possibility, worlds away from Cindy. As the three of them talked, Mara Jade and Izzy told Singer how much they missed Ms Pepper, St. Bartholomew's single real librarian, banished last year due to budget cuts. Ms Pepper remembered every child's name who walked through the door of the elementary, middle school or high school libraries. She seemed to be in all buildings at once, the encourager, the open-minded listener, and the grant writer.

Under assistant Cindy's guidance, the library became more a place of penitence than a haven where Ms Pepper would draw them into conversation. Gone were the young people who would amble in to spend a few hours in spirited banter while they escaped an empty home with both parents at work. In her defense, Cindy had a superior record for the return of late library books, hounding her students' households with robo calls until the books were returned. Now, at the end of a school day, the library was a quiet, orderly place with hardly any backpacks piled by the door. Instead of debates about cell phones and driving, or discussions about the cleaning of Ms Pepper's giant fish tank, which she dismantled and took with her she left, the library was devoid of controversy, perfectly appropriate.

∾

At the end of the study, when students had explored a career path that fit their aptitudes and inclinations, including early bloomers, late bloomers, and those in the early bud stage, Mizbie took her class to a nearby GM assembly plant that made trucks. Their tour guide was Charlie Buell, a wise veteran of the plant, now in the position of quality control. He walked with Mizbie and the class, warning them to stay within the green lines; watch for forklifts buzzing by; and listen as giant clanging robotic arms bolted, lifted, spray painted, and fitted truck parts. The occasional worker waved to the students and yelled, "Stay in school. Don't end up here!"

When he paused in his narrative, Mizbie asked, "How many new employees do you hire every year, Charlie?"

He stopped and turned to her. "We haven't hired anyone off the street in 18 years. When people retire, we just replace 'em with workers from other plants that have shut down."

They followed Charlie through the gargantuan factory plant, walking between the green lines so they wouldn't be run down by a speeding fork-lift-truck. Workers adjusted squishy moldings around truck doors to soundproof them. Others grabbed gorilla-sized drive trains and expertly placed them on a chassis that slowly coasted down the ever-moving assembly line. Around a corner, the students watched amazed to see a chassis float up from the basement and a cab float down over it. From a parallel line, a trunk fell into place fitting perfectly behind the cab, and then robots dropped a front end in place. All the parts were welded identically, just like the other 599 trucks that came off the line that day would be, choreographed as gracefully as a New York City ballet. At the end of the line, a man got in the truck, started the engine, and drove it away to be tested.

"What if they don't work?" Mizbie asked.

"That rarely happens. But if it does, they put it here," Charlie pointed to a garage-like area. "This man can fix anything that is wrong with any truck."

The class turned their eyes to the truck doctor. Mizbie could see that it was important to have a worker there who could fix anything at the end of the assembly line. But to pay someone much more than she made with six years of college to stand there for days with nothing to do but wait for a mistake? Quality was that important to car companies.

Chapter 10

Overheard before St. Bartholomew's Show Choir practice –
Girl – I love Shakespeare. Hamlet's my fave. I've read it three times.
Ophelia is so lost and tortured.
Boy – Yeah . . . me too. I like his poem about the big black bird that
says, "'Nevermore.'"
Girl – "The Raven"? Yeah . . . I like that too."

Mizbie was on the computer when a student came up behind her.
"Miz B, about my paper –"

"Hi, Edward, I – oh, Desmin! You sounded just like Edward."

He smiled. "My aunt always said I could fool anybody with my voice. I fooled you."

"You did." Mizbie thought. "Can you do a British accent?"

With a straight face, Desmin straightened, rubbing his chin. "Well I – might find it a bit of a challenge – a sticky wicket you might say."

"Desmin!" Mizbie laughed. "I can't believe it. You have to try out for *Hamlet.*"

"Say what! You sh . . . you kiddin' me."

"I am not kidding." She slapped his shoulder that towered over her. "Think about it."

He frowned at her, shook his head, and took his seat.

Margo came up to the desk. "We talked about my paper yesterday. You know I know the stuff. Can't you just give me a grade?"

"Margo, I can't give you credit for just saying it. Maybe you have a good idea, but you say it and it's just noise. People say, 'Ya know what I'm sayin'?' and we don't always. Somebody didn't carry the thought through and care enough about it to write it down. Show me you think. Care enough to get it on paper!"

She glared at Mizbie and sat down.

"I've mixed up your seat assignments for the new unit," Mizbie said. "You'll be working with different students in groups."

"Who's that?" Seth said. "We have a new student!"

He was looking at Kelsey, her white-blonde hair touched by the sun streaming in the window and framing her face instead of being controlled in its usual ponytail. "Seth, Kelsey sat a few seats behind you all last marking period," Mizbie said.

"No, she didn't," Seth said. "Who's Kelsey?"

The class groaned as Kelsey turned to him and lowered her newly contact-lensed eyes, half smiling.

"Kelsey," Mizbie patiently answered, "I think Seth is noticing you."

"Oooh . . ." the class said.

"Hey," Seth shifted in his seat. "How would I know? She was behind me." He shrugged and mumbled, "uh uh . . . I'm not gonna skin *that* cat."

"Okay, we talked about the Renaissance or rebirth of curiosity in literature, art, architecture, and music in the 1300s. Now who remembers Donatello, Michelangelo, Leonardo, and Raphael?" Mizbie said, running a Power Point of art on the board behind her.

"In my humble opinion –, and whether I mean it or not, I'm always humble –, the Ninja Turtles," said Robin.

"And Renaissance artists, goofball," said Izzy.

"You're both right minus the name-calling. Now at that time in England, there was a famous playwright whose plays today are still performed and translated into more languages than any other book except the Bible. Who was that?"

"Who's that lady who wrote Harry Potter?" said Corwin.

"Actually, she's still living near Edinburgh, Scotland, Corwin," Mizbie said.

"Shakespeare." Jessica said.

"Exactly. Two truths and a lie. Tell me which 'fact' is not true. (1) Shakespeare had twins named Judith and Hamnet. (2) During times of plague, he wrote sonnets to earn a living, because the theatres were closed down, or (3) The movie *Shakespeare in Love* was nonfiction.

"They're all true," said Noel.

"Nah, that movie was a fake," Desmin said.

"Right you are, Desmin! Now back to the twins. Some scholars believe Judith became the character Juliet in *Romeo and Juliet,* those star-crossed lovers who taught their parents what?"

"That hate destroys and love is more powerful," Rashmi said.

"And Hamnet became the prince of Denmark, the Melancholy Dane, Hamlet. What do you think?"

"I think Shakespeare plays are about the dumbest things they is. Ya can't understand 'em. We don't talk that way no more. They stupid." Desmin said.

With Desmin, Mizbie had to target his learning. But it still seemed as accurate as buckshot, hit and miss. "Well, picture this, Desmin. A college guy is called home from school. His father has just died, so he's depressed. He's dressed in black."

"A Goth," said Oola.

"Well, not exactly, but when he gets home, he finds his mother is preparing to marry his uncle, his father's brother. So his uncle is now going to be his stepfather."

"Eww . . . that's nasty," said Desmin.

"That's *Hamlet,*" said Mizbie.

"I had an aunt that did that. My cousins were piss . . . really mad. So what happens next?" said Izzy.

"Take these copies of the play and we'll find out. Let's have some class tryouts for parts. *Hamlet* will be the school play this year. Ladies, check pages 42 and 64 for the parts of Ophelia and the queen, respectively. Look over the lines and I'll call you up to try out. Class votes for the winner."

Mizbie wrote criteria for voting on the board. "When you listen to your classmates try out, remember to vote carefully. Who do you want to be listening to for the next few days of class? Make sure they use a voice that has energy in it. Make sure they express the feeling of the character in their faces, and their understanding of the character in their actions."

"Miz B, you're left-handed!" Gilbert chirped. "So am I!"

"Duh," Mara Jade replied. "You haven't noticed since September?"

"You're right, Gilbert. You know what you can say when people ask you if it's weird being left-handed? Just say all creative people are left-handed. Michelangelo was. And don't forget Alexander the Great, James Baldwin, Jimi Hendrix, Paul McCartney, Angelina Jolie, Larry Bird, Babe Ruth, and Bart Simpson."

"Okay . . . Who was after Alexander the Great?" Gilbert asked.

"So was Shakespeare left-handed?" Mara Jade asked.

"Of the few pictures we have of Shakespeare, some show his clothing as having two left sides. That symbolized his playing a central part of a tradition promoting cryptic, concealed ideas, called the Rosicrucian movement. But he was still right-handed," Mizbie said.

"Next we'll have Hamlet, Laertes, and the despicable lying traitorous King Claudius. You guys have pages 46, 77, and 48 respectively."

"Can guys try out for girls' parts?" Robin asked.

"Suit yourself," Mizbie answered. The class thumbed through pages, checked out parts, and practiced aloud with partners.

The window was opening wide and Noel was securing her gladiator-sandaled foot on the window-sill, ready to climb out.

"Stop what you're doing. Close the window," Mizbie said.

"My pencil dropped out the window. I'm going out to get it," Noel explained.

"The pencil stays. You stay."

"Hey, look at this, Miz B," Brent stuck out his wrist. He had secured a large safety pin through it. "What d'ya think, huh?" he repeated, holding the reddening wrist under her eyes, waiting for a reaction.

"Read your script," Mizbie said. At least he had arrived on time today. Brent had eight tardies, for which he had conned the assistant principal into one measly lunch detention.

"Ooh, it's all red, Miz B. D'ya think it's infected? I should go to the clinic."

"You're still sitting up. You can talk. Can you still think?" she asked.

"Yeah ... I guess so."

"Good. Amanda, Izzy, Jessica, Margo, let's hear your voices for Ophelia."

After several tryouts, tension grew palpable. "Okay, here is our last major character. We'll volunteer for smaller parts tomorrow. The king is a character in the play who many professional actors enjoy because he is so purely vile, underhanded, and conniving. If you're not sure what some of those words mean, you'll soon find out. This is the character the audience loves to hate. King actors, come on up."

No one raised a hand. Mizbie waited. Edward slowly walked forward. Students watched the boy, who seldom spoke except to make a disparaging remark. He hadn't raised his hand all year. No one else volunteered.

"Okay, Edward, because no one else volunteered, you get the part. But let's hear you say the lines anyway." Mizbie was sure he would need all the practice he could get.

He began by staring into their faces with his dark, deep-set eyes and a sneer on his face that transformed him into a much older, meaner man. Mizbie almost expected a wolf's growl. His over-the-top exaggeration of the part mesmerized the class. They couldn't help but applaud and cheer when he finished. Walking back to his seat, Mizbie caught a hint of smile on his face.

Jesspin9
to MBax20
11:00 p.m.
May 5

Hey Miz,

Well, it happened. This feckless man, the one I've seen for the last three cities, took off. If you'll remember, he was the British carpenter, Cecil. Can you hear me hissing his name between my teeth? I asked him why he was leaving when we were having such a good time. He replied, "My father always said the more you drill on a piece of wood, the lighter it gets." I mean, what kind of an answer is that?

I thought about what you said, your concern for your newspaper students who were on the cusp of becoming academic eccentrics, all bookish and how you could relate. I can too. The looks we get from the corners of people's eyes, like my mother's eyes, a mixture of exhaustion and resentment that I recognized when I was old enough to know she'd always wished I'd been a boy. My brother was so much easier. Unlike Chinese parents, she couldn't kill me as an infant. After she realized I wasn't going to just disappear, my mother decided I had to be endured. We had an understanding. I didn't talk to her or demand anything of her and she ignored me.

When I was seven, my neighbor, who was a valedictorian, took me to the library while she studied for hours, letting me loose in the children's literature department. I grounded myself in Caddie Woodlawn and Laura Ingalls Wilder – beguiling, fearless, girls.

I'm going to be more like you – so busy that I don't have time to form real relationships. If you don't have a relationship, you can't lose one.

That sounds catty, doesn't it? I don't mean it that way. After all, you have me. But you have a full life, Miz, and it doesn't allow you time to feel sorry for yourself over Carl, like I'm feeling right now. That's what I want.

Cecil was a vegetarian anyway. Can you imagine being in Parma and not eating prosciutto? He was so disagreeable, that smug vegetarian. As we ambled down that vague landscape somewhere between friends and dating, he said my idea of him had become diminished, and, you know, he was right. He was headstrong, which is what initially drew me to him. But when I saw how strong and decisive he was, I thought less of him. What do I want, one of Hemingway's bullfighters? Who knows?

I had a cappuccino in a cafe yesterday with the most charming older man on his way home to his wife. He recounted some trips they had taken and recalled a trip to India along the Ganges

River. He told this heartbreaking story as he had watched it, and I could just picture it – piles of wood stacked along the river's edge, bathing the deceased husband in the river, then cremating the body along the shore. The men complete this ritual and the women stay at home, or sometimes the widows throw themselves on the funeral pyre. Fire, water, air, earth. Forget it! I could never give up my life like that.

See? I feel better just writing this to you. Probably the worst thing Cecil said was right before he hugged me goodbye. He said, "I loved you." Hearing those words made me feel like I'd sipped warm, flat champagne, but his voice had such tones of finality to it like the words THE END after the last scene of an old movie. Definitely the worst "I loved you" I've ever heard.

I am now retreating further into my cocoon of singledom. I need someone to fill up my empty spaces. I'll be okay. I'm off to Tours. There should be lots of fun-loving people there, right? The food is supposed to be a bargain and eclectic too. By the way, I got a tattoo of a cat on my neck, just a small one. It reminded me of Daphne and I miss her. Hope you're both okay. Carl was a jerk.

Jess

Mizbie read the message, dwelling not on Jess's loss but looking into the mirror of their friendship. Daphne was pacing on her little feet, purring. Was Mizbie's busy life an excuse for avoiding the possible pain of another relationship? "You're my buddy, aren't you, Daphne?" Mizbie said, as she scratched the cat behind the ears. Daphne hopped on her lap, walked in circles and plunked down with her paws on Mizbie's knees.

After the fracture with Carl, she carried on as though their years-long partnership was still rock solid. The loss was beyond her control, but maybe she could control the collateral damage. It would be awhile before she could casually tell anyone but Jess that he had left. Maybe it was the identity of being part of a couple that she wasn't ready to give up. Or was it the desire of wanting those who cared about her to believe she knew how to balance her man and a time-sucking job? Most likely, it was the consoling words she didn't want to hear, those words that would inevitably follow the news that she was spending nights and weekends with a cat for company.

One morning when she and Carl were still together, Carl pounded a fist on the bed they shared. "After three years, the fire still burns." He squeezed her hand. "Maybe it's just a pilot light sometimes, but dammit, it's still burning."

Time had helped, and she liked the feeling of forgetting, as it made the betrayal and rejection feel less like a good drubbing when their song played on the radio. Like a song she'd practiced on her flute until it surrendered itself, she realized the limits of power in these memories. Gone was the idea of the two of them claiming each other as a treasured gift. Looking to a future without Carl in it didn't hurt so much.

She poured coffee into a mug, spooned in homemade caramel, then half-and-half, stirring the coffee to melt the caramel, stirring and stirring. She was impatient with the time it took to melt the caramel off the spoon. Taking that first hot sip, she found it didn't taste as good as she'd hoped it would. She held the mug, warming her hands. She had been holding on to Carl for too long. There were papers to grade and the *Hamlet* performance to prepare. But she would definitely explore Jess's idea later, when she had time to devote to it.

Pencil in hand, she began to block out the play. Seth was doing well with the lights, but she'd have to remind him about the spot for Hamlet's soliloquy. Because Hamlet moved, the spot had to move too. Jenna helped him and the play seemed to help her with the loss of her sister. She thought of Edward playing the king, a role that surprisingly fit. He stalked and ranted, even managed to lift one eyebrow when he called Hamlet his "cousin." Was it her imagination or did he seem to be scowling less lately? She didn't think he'd had an evil word with another classmate all week.

There was a knock at the door. "Hi, Ms Baxter. Would you like to buy some candles for our church basketball team?" Dori, the third grader next door, asked, holding up a colorful brochure.

"Sure, Dori. Let's see what you have." She made her purchase and wished Dori good luck. Mizbie microwaved popcorn, corrected a few essays, and went to bed. Her life was a Zeno's paradox: she always seemed to be chasing something that had a head start on her, and even though she moved fast, she couldn't seem to catch up yet.

Chapter 11

Overheard –
'To thine own self be true.'
Where'd you get that?
I copied it off a mug at the Bean and Leaf.

After only a few days of play practice, Mizbie was in the copy room making script copies to replace those already lost by her actors.

"So you had an uncle there?" Renee asked Krahler.

"Yeah, My dad's brother. We'd visit him a couple of times a year. He worked in the upholstery shop, I think. That place was huge."

Renee and Dirk had spent a weekend by the lake in a refurbished condo. "It's hard to believe they'd turn an old state mental hospital into condos, restaurants, and gourmet wine and cheese shops. All those ghosts."

"What do you mean?" Krahler walked up to her.

"Just going there and walking down the halls, it felt like friggin' frozen hair follicles standing up on my head and creeping down my back. See, I came from a small Catholic family and we lived near the mental hospital. There were seven of us kids and our family was one of the smallest. Most parents had a dozen kids. My parents were looked down on for not having more kids, so my dad, feeling the weight of Catholic guilt on him, volunteered on spring weekends at the mental hospital, and he'd take my friend, Mary, and me with him. Because he grew up on a farm, he helped the patients learn farming. The hospital was completely self-sustaining then, you know. All the patients learned a trade, like your uncle learned upholstery."

"Yeah. We'd go see him and I counted the hours until we could leave."

"When my dad was in the fields, Mary and I would watch the patients through the open windows, their hair askew, arms flailing, voices yelling. The staff didn't have much medication for them in those days, other than sedatives, to keep them from hurting themselves. We'd go up and down the hallways passing out packs of cigarettes to them."

"Your dad let you do that?"

"He thought nothing of it. I can still see the smoke and smell that hallway as they lit up. Funny my dad would let us loose at the mental hospital, but I couldn't date until I was 17, and then I could never date a guy with a van. Go figure."

"That's not what I heard," Mizbie teased. "How about that hippie in the Dodge with flames on it?"

"Oh, Darin?" Renee smiled. "I'd meet him around the corner where my dad couldn't see the van."

Out the front window of the copy room, Mizbie could see Mara Jade and Nick squaring off. On the left side of the sidewalk stood Mara Jade in striped leggings, carrying her picket sign with some long quote condemning semi-automatic weapons. On the right side was Nick whose sign read "Down with big goverment gun laws." Once the crowded sidewalk began to clear, Mara Jade directed her comments to Nick, rather than the students eager to leave. "What does your sign mean? I'm curious. Do you think regular people need semi-automatic weapons that shoot 40 rounds a minute?

"You don't know nothin'," he answered. "Ya gotta pull the trigger for each round."

"I see, but I still can't figure this out. Hunters wouldn't need a gun like that to shoot deer. There'd be no meat left. So what would people shoot at with 40 rounds a minute?"

"The gover'ment, stupid! Don't you know nothin'?"

"I know government has an 'n' there," she said, pointing to the misspelled sign.

"So what. I was in a hurry," he said.

"You mean they need to shoot at government buildings? Legislators? How would this help?" Mara Jade asked.

"Jesus, you are stupid. Figure it out. The gover'ment's too big and too strong. We gotta get the power back to the people where it belongs."

"Oh, you mean like states' rights, the way it was in the South before the Civil War?

"Yeah, like back then. Things were better back then."

❧

That night after *Hamlet* practice ran late, Mizbie needed a computer. She was relieved to see Guy Heuster at the locker room door. "Am I glad to see you! They're using my room for driver's ed and the office is locked. May I use your computer for a sec?"

"Sure. I'll unlock my office for you." He told Mizbie about the Mayville baseball game they had won by one run. "Just lock it from inside before you go."

Opening the door, Mizbie was assailed by the smell of sweat and body spray. The janitors had been there, but after years of use, that smell couldn't be vanquished short of fumigation. She turned on the light in Heuster's office and saw his wall décor held by thumbtacks – a shirt of weightlifter Ronnie Coleman with the original sweat stains. She felt around the back of the computer for the switch, and heard a noise from the girl's side of the locker room. Annoyed, she opened the door, passed the first bank of lockers and turned on the light. One of Heuster's base-ball players probably stayed behind to sneak around to the girl's side. She yelled, "Are you still – Stella! What are you doing here?"

"Hi, Miz. B. I'm just hanging out waiting for Mom to pick me up."

"Why not wait by the door? How will you know when she comes?"

"Oh, she got held up and she said she'd be another couple hours, so I thought I'd wait here so the custodians don't keep bugging me to move."

Something wasn't right. A coat and pillow were spread out in the corner and a zipper bag of make-up beside it. Stella, you're not telling me the truth. You're living here, aren't you."

"No, really, my mom –"

But her voice lacked conviction. Mizbie caught a quaver in it and saw her nervous fingers flutter over homework spread out on the locker room bench before her. Stella's pencil dropped to the floor. Mizbie sat on the bench across from her, held her hand, and waited.

She sighed. "Okay, Mom's not coming." Stella straightened her pillow. "Mom and I lived in this dinky apartment and they were going to evict us. I came home from school and our stuff was in the street. The landlord gave me a message that Mom was coming back for me, so I waited for hours with our stuff. She never came." Stella shifted on the bench, her body on edge like her voice.

"Your mom didn't come for you?"

Stella didn't answer, but gave her a half smile. "Back when we had the house, I had a big sleepover in seventh grade." Stella's voice lost its edge. "Girls used to come over all the time. Everybody liked Mom. Anyway, we had pizza and Mom had made this cake for us. It was a joke. It looked like cat litter in a cat litter box and she scooped it out on paper plates with a cat litter scoop. My friends looked at the cake, then at me, then at my cat and went "Eeww!" Nobody wanted to eat it, and I could see my mom felt bad, so I grabbed a plate and started eating, since she made weird foods a lot, and they were mostly good. It had green pudding, cake and some kind of whipped cream.

What grossed us out was the Tootsie Rolls on top. They really looked like something my cat left in her litter box. Then my friends started eating it and laughing, and Mom was laughing. It was so much fun. They talked about it in school afterward."

Mizbie watched Stella's expression as the memory replayed in her mind. She was reminded of a cat litter cake one of the band members brought in for them, also with a litter scoop, and Mizbie's friends reacted the same way.

"And when kids came over, she'd just stick around long enough to let them know she was glad they were there, but not long enough like she was trying to be one of us or anything. They'd say they wished they had my mom. I used to be happy she was my mom. Then they outsourced her job. So she got another job and was laid off. We had to sell the house and lots of stuff, and we moved to one apartment, then another.

"We both needed someone to lean on, but we couldn't lean on each other. Mom went to a support group for a while. We lost so much, Miz B. During school, I got free breakfast and lunch. I sneaked extra food for the weekend, but by Monday, I was really hungry. I never saw Mom drink and I never smelled alcohol, but I'd find bottles stashed around the house, vodka in the overhead kitchen light or behind the bathroom towels. I'd always dump it down the toilet and she never mentioned it, but then I'd find more."

"Stella, I'm so sorry."

Stella bristled at those words. "I don't want anyone to know. You can't tell them. I couldn't stand it if my friends knew. Please! Promise you won't tell."

"Okay, so your mom's gone. What about your dad?"

"He was some religious person. I never knew him. Mom said she loved him, but he couldn't marry. He wanted her to get an abortion, but she didn't, then she lost track of him. When the bad times came, I found his address at some Franciscan Order. I wrote him letters for months. Eventually someone there sent a letter saying he had been placed in another parish, but they wouldn't tell me where he was. I lost him."

Mizbie looked at Stella seated on the locker room bench, her fingers combing through her wavy brown hair, reaching for her pillow and hugging it with clenched fists.

"You can't stay here. Let me call Protective Services and get you a place to stay until your mom – "

"No! No Protective Services. I stayed in a foster home for six weeks last year when they took me away from Mom. They had a foster boy and he would come into my room at night. He said he'd kill my mother if I told. Finally Mom was okay again, and I went back to live with her. I never told. I've already said too much. You understand, I can't go to a foster home." Her eyes darted around the room and her jaw tightened. "If you call them, I'll run. I don't know where I'll go, but I'll leave – "

"Oh, Stella." Mizbie watched her, wild-eyed and agitated. "I'll tell you what. You come home with me tonight. We'll fix dinner. No cat litter cake for dessert, though. We'll figure out something in the morning. Grab your stuff. Let's go."

"You don't have to do this. I've gotten along here. Nobody hassles me." Stella's shoulders relaxed.

"Stella, I have to be the bad guy here." Was this happening? She was beginning to sound like a parent. "It's not safe for you here. It's not healthy. You can't keep staying here."

"I found some jobs on craigslist. I can get a part-time job after school." Stella opened a folded paper from her jeans pocket. "Here's one for plastic etching. Or a loss control inspector, but I need a camera for that. Maybe I could borrow a camera from the library. Or I could be a house sitter to take care of horses, but that only lasts two weeks."

"Do you think I could get to sleep tonight knowing you're here alone sleeping on your coat on the floor? I don't think so. C'mon, Stella," she said. She began picking up the pillow and backpack, despite Stella's protests, and they walked out of the locker room. Mizbie knew her decision was incredibly wrong. There was probably something illegal about taking a homeless student home with her. But she wasn't ready to risk being the cause of more trauma in Stella's life. Stella was ready to escape, that free will that seemed to be hard-wired in, a part of kids' DNA. "It's all right," she said automatically, like a parent. She touched her circle necklace with one hand and gave Stella's shoulder an encouraging squeeze with the other. "It's going to be all right." She felt an intuition of hope, ingrained in Mizbie by her parents, one following in the slipstream of the other.

Together they unpacked Stella's few belongings and arranged her pillow and a quilt on the couch in the apartment. Mizbie worked with Stella on dinner. She slapped a chunk of butter in the saute pan, plopped in a couple of oversized portabellas, sprinkled some hot chili oil in the gills, mounded the mushrooms up with smoked Gouda and leftover prosciutto shreds and roasted red peppers, then broiled them in the oven until the top of the cheese became golden. She gave one to Stella.

"This is good. It needs a little pepper," Stella said.

Mizbie watched Stella grind the pepper over her mushroom, turning it nearly black.

"You have so many books. I had picture books when I was little, but then we moved so much that we couldn't keep them. I see *Lord of the Flies.* I liked that one in eighth grade –. *1984* too. I checked them out of the library. I spent a lot of time in the library after school and on Saturdays, so I ended up reading a lot of books." She ate the last bite of mushroom. "Do you have anything sweet to eat?"

"Let's see. I don't usually have desserts around just for myself, or I'd look like a bus." Mizbie opened the fridge and found some Greek yogurt, blueberries, and strawberries. She alternated them with her homemade maple-syrup granola, confecting a parfait in a glass.

Stella savored each spoonful. "Books were my water park, my beach, my vacation away from home. They kept me from going insane, I think."

"We have to let your mom know you're here," Mizbie said.

"I don't know where she is. I don't know how to contact her."

"Did she know you were living at school?"

"We have a post office box. I left her a letter and she picked it up." Stella finished the last bit of granola and stretched like a contented cat. "It's safe here," she said. "I haven't felt like this for a long time. I don't need someone to look out for me, but that's what you're doing, I guess." She leaned forward with her elbows on the table. "Thanks, Miz B."

Mizbie felt the full weight of this safety, and the guilt of wondering if she was doing the best thing for Stella. "That's okay, but tomorrow, we tell the counselor at school what you've been doing. We have to find your mom."

"Can we please wait, please? If you tell the counselor, she'll tell Protective Services. My mom might come back any time now. I'll keep checking the mailbox. Just a few more weeks?"

Mizbie watched Stella's shoulders that sagged from exhaustion or fear, she couldn't tell which.

"Let's go out on the deck for a minute," Mizbie said. They opened the sliding glass door and stepped out into the cooling evening air. The scent of fabric softener wafted up from the laundry room beneath Mizbie's apartment. She liked the view and the close proximity to the laundry, but that also meant hearing neighbors washing clothes at odd hours.

"You have a good view of the park from here," Stella said.

"Hear the crickets? They're singing."

Stella listened and looked out over the park, then with a sigh, walked back to the couch, curled up with her blankets and closed her eyes. Mizbie slid the door closed, looking at Stella, a wisp, a feather on a sea of uncertainty, wrapped in blankets on her couch. Daphne purred next to her on the floor. Close to sleep, Stella scratched Daphne behind the ears. As Mizbie watched, Daphne hopped up, curling herself under Stella's chin. "Just push her away if you don't want her there," Mizbie said.

"She's okay. I kinda like her there," Stella said in a drowsy voice.

Returning to the deck, Mizbie looked out over the park. Now she could add kidnapper to the list of offenses in her school file. With no one else in Stella's life, Mizbie had never experienced the profound feeling of another life so dependent on her before, this weight of responsibility.

She looked back at Stella, already asleep on the couch, the lines between her eyebrows now relaxed. She looked younger than her 17 years. Now was not a time to wallow. Stella was a survivor, an independent soul who had gotten along before Mizbie discovered her. Stella was not a fragile, defenseless child and she didn't deserve Mizbie thinking of her in this way. She deserved respect and a safe sofa to sleep on, that's all.

～

"Remember to turn in your permission slips for the Romeo and Juliet field trip." Mizbie tried to ignore her anger bubbling from one travesty piling on top of another that morning. "Now think about earth, air, fire, and water. What do they have to do with Shakespeare?"

"Their theatres burned down a lot," Robin said.

"That's true, but these were considered to be the four elements that made up all substances. Now we know there are more than100 elements, but back then, Elizabethans believed there were only four. It was thought that even people had to possess all four elements in their bodies to have a healthy spirit, or to be 'good humored'."

"So what's Desmin missing 'cause he's in a bad mood?" Gilbert asked.

"What you sayin'? Watch it you little –" Desmin's eyes flashed.

"Okay, both of you. When the body was thought to be deprived of air and fire, it was thought to slip into melancholy. Hamlet was morose about the death of his father, so he was called the Melancholy Dane. So, Edward, how were Hamlet's thoughts different in the beginning than at the end?

"I don't know."

It was hard for her to believe Edward had aced the SAT in eighth grade and was taking honors physics as a freshman. "Think about it, Edward. Hamlet is resentful. His father's death is possibly a murder committed by his uncle/stepfather's hand. What changes took place?"

"I'm thinking in 150 years or so no one on Earth will know us. We'll all be replaced and not one of us here will be known by anybody except as an old picture on a computer somewhere. My great-great nephew will point to my picture and say. 'Who's he?' and his mom will say, 'Some old guy.'"

"Could be, but what if you write books or compose songs? People might still know you. You know Shakespeare, and he lived more than 400 years ago. So what could Hamlet be thinking?"

"He's superstitious because he believes in ghosts."

"Go on."

"He might think he has to avenge his father's foul and unnatural murder, so his father's restless soul can rest in peace. I know I'd sure want my restless soul to rest in peace."

Desmin and Gilbert laughed at that.

"And why does Hamlet wait when the king is praying? He has the chance but he doesn't kill him."

Izzy's hand shot up. "Hamlet's looking at the king to see how he reacts. If his face turns pale, Hamlet knows he's guilty. He can't kill him when he's praying or his soul will go to heaven, and he doesn't want that."

"Right." Mizbie was surprised at Izzy's quick response. She made it a point to tell Izzy how good her new glasses looked. What a difference it made after one optometrist donated his services.

"Now that we've finished our class presentation of *Hamlet*, you've heard the thoughtful, earnest Hamlet searching for the truth, passionate for it. You've heard Ophelia's crazy songs from a young woman mourning her father's death and confused about her boyfriend who murdered him. You felt emotions juxtaposed, like passion/pain and love/loss, and watched them communicated through the lyric iambic pentameter that is Shakespeare. So what do you think now? What makes a man a man and a woman a woman?"

"Ooooh," Izzy said.

"Oh yeah . . ." Robin said.

"You know what I mean! Noel, your pencil is sharp enough. Sit down. Think of what we've read, listened to, and watched. How do you know when adolescents become men and women?"

"Well, I think of Romeo," said Rico. "He was a teenager, probably, and he acted without thinking."

"Yeah, like Chyna at that party last Friday!" said Desmin.

"Shut up!" said Chyna's friend, Keyana.

"Desmin, can you add to Rico's idea about acting without thinking?" Mizbie said.

"Well, when Romeo killed Juliet's brother, he wasn't thinking, like Rico said. He said, 'Oh, I am fortune's foe.' Not like Hamlet, who thought way too much before he did anything. Then when he thought he ran the king through with a sword, he really ended up killing his girlfriend's father. They were both screwed. But Hamlet thought before acting, and that's more like an adult. Even though the man makes mistakes, he thinks about it first –, then he's less likely to mess up."

"Good example. Margo, add to that?"

"Women have it different, especially back then. If they acted up, they had to do it quietly because they were expected to stay in the background and they couldn't get jobs or do much to make decisions in their own lives. Their lives were pretty much set when they married and it was hard to change. Abigail Adams had some ideas about women's rights and later Virginia Woolf when she wrote 'If Shakespeare Had a Sister,' but . . ."

"Let's get back to what makes a woman a woman."

"Yeah, I'm getting to that. In the 1800s, Sojourner Truth talked back to the minister in 'Ain't I a Woman?' about how she had 13 kids and they were all sold off as slaves and didn't she have the rights of any man, and shouldn't things be more equal? So I guess it means you're a woman when you know you are capable of knowing your own thoughts and acting on your own, being responsible for your own life."

"Yeah, like getting your license and driving wherever you want," said Rip.

Mr. Krahler silently motioned Mizbie to the hallway. "I didn't want to embarrass you in front of the students, but I've been listening outside the door and you've been off task for seven minutes now. Remember the main thing is the main thing. Let's get back to the course outline for today. Oh, I nearly forgot; I need to talk to you after school about Nick's grade. Superintendent Winchell will not get another call from Nick's mom, so that means you will figure out a way to pass him with a 38 percent. Be prepared to defend the grade in my office," he said.

"Defend from what? You want me to pass him for the semester with a 38 percent?"

"Mom says you didn't give him a chance. He's so afraid of you, he can't work at school or at home. He can't make the team if his grades don't improve. Do you want to be the reason why he can't make the team? Look through your grades and see where allowances can be made."

"This is all about his being eligible for basketball?"

Like a safe cracker with a practiced hand, Krahler circled his index finger at her face. It's up to you. It's on your shoulders." He turned and walked off.

That was it. The day began with the loose bike chain this morning, making her late for school, moved on to the angry parent who waited for her, swearing he never received the last seven messages about his daughter's failing grades; she gritted her teeth. Renee had volunteered her to represent the department at the emergency staff meeting tonight. When Shannon walked up delivering 10 days worth of wrinkled, ripped, late work into Mizbie's hands, asking what her grades were now that she turned it in, she held it together. But Krahler's order to pass Nick with a 38 percent was too much to bear.

Her shoes clicked across the floor and her voice shot loud, vile epithets that busted the pledge she'd made in her anger management class last year. She faced the students and her arms flailed. She fired words at them that she hadn't bantered around since her Brit Lit class at the university, words like pilock, wazzock, and twonk. The students in her college study group pitched the words regularly, words that become permanent parts of their vocabulary, a kind of code that few others recognized, but worked for them as a freeing release.

Last year she'd even sold her '04 Mazda Miata after the anger class to eliminate the chance of another outburst ending in a road-rage incident. Her voice in full default, Brit Lit mode, she railed on with wanker, bloody bugger, and her favorite, numpty –, a curse that was usually a catharsis for her. With energy spent, she returned her attention to the stunned class who stared back at her, expressions glued for all the wrong reasons. Recognizing they weren't the target of her fabulous outburst, they waited for whatever came next. Mizbie apologized. "Don't take it personally. I've had a bad day. A really bad day." She sighed. It was only first hour.

Desmin responded like a sinewy sapling blown over by a gale wind and righted again, "Hey, man, that's cool"

After school, Mizbie had her defense ready with copies of emails to Mom, missed dates of offered lunch make-ups that wouldn't interfere with practice, second and third chances for extra credit, and talks with Nick's coach. She'd say, "I did everything according to the book and more, Mr. Krahler. Nick had every opportunity to pass. Mom knew all along. Look at these email responses. She even tried doing some of his work for him."

When the PA called her to the office, she wasn't sure if it was for Nick or her outburst. Krahler took the copies of emails to Nick's mother.

"Oh, by the way," Krahler said, as her hand was on the door. His voice was surprisingly neutral.

Mizbie looked back, her face contrite, ready to face retribution, her punishment, her Golgotha.

Krahler was thoughtful. "I got a call from Superintendent Winchell this afternoon. His talk with me was similar to my talk with you this morning. We have to keep Mrs. Huntsman from harassing him again."

"What is she thinking? Is she helping Nick by fighting to get him out of his work? How could he ever pass college classes if he can't pass high school? He has to do the work."

"Winchell's tired; I'm tired. I'll set up a meeting for you and Winchell for Monday. Just show him what you have."

"You mean I might have to pass him anyway? That goes against every bone in my being. What is Winchell thinking by wanting to pass him along?" Mizbie snapped, her fist clenched.

"I'll let you know about the meeting. And . . . I want you to be here from 6 to 9, Wednesday and Thursday, to supervise the science fair open house for parents."

"That's not my department. What about John Wilbur? They're his kids."

His wife had her baby today, and he has to accompany the students to the science fair in Lansing on Saturday. Thanks, Mizbie. I knew I could count on you."

Ryder caught up with her and they left the building. She vented about Mrs. Huntsman and Superintendent Winchell. "Can they fire me for refusing to change Nick's grade?"

"Dunno," Ryder said. "But last year at East High, those two football players got sprung from jail for armed robbery so they could play football. Caused a stink in the local papers, but they did it anyway. They were let out for practice and games, and then returned to jail at night. The Powers That Be have their own set of values, looks like."

Jesspin9
toMBax20
12:30 p.m.
May 14

Hey Miz,

I'm in Spain on Costa Brava, scarfing down a falafel and tak-ing notes about this place. Guess who strikes up a conversation with me? An urbane Spaniard. It seems his date was indisposed and he had these reservations for a year to Ferimez's restaurant, El Toro. So he asked if I'd join him. I laughed and assured him that after what I'd been eating for the past six weeks, this would be pure heaven.

We started with seafood bisque, the waiter said, with Basque and Catalan influences. Next came spider crab, heavy on the garlic, with a txakoli wine. Then gooseneck barnacles with fava beans served with a peppery Rioja. The entrée was lamb with a hint of lemon. Dessert was traditional fruit, a fresh pear but with a walnut-size, hazelnut chocolate ball, very creamy with cocoa. I was in love.

Afterward, I felt like Jabba the Hutt in Star Wars. Jobim was a prince; really he was an international banker like my brother, but he could curse in four languages, except Welsh, of course. When he took me to his apartment and opened the door for me, the truth came out. There was a pile of unwrapped wedding gifts in the middle of the living room floor. It seems the "date" who was indisposed was his fiancé who took off with a local politician the day before the wedding. The next morning, he unearthed a brand new toaster from the box, plucked from the depths of the pile of gifts, and he is toasting the first slices of bread as I type this. I'll never be able to write this in my food book, but I can tell you.

By the way, a fellow writer at Herrod House just sold 1,000 copies of her book of crafts! Things made from dryer lint, every- thing from hats to Christmas stockings. It looks like boiled wool. Go figure.

Good luck on your play –

Jess

In the kitchen, Mizbie recalled her meeting with Superintendent Winchell as she splayed chicken breasts between sheets of waxed paper and began to pound them. The flesh fell away from the bone and she hammered harder. It seemed Krahler had taken her side when he made the appointment for her to visit Winchell, but Winchell refused to accept her documentation, intimating her refusal to comply could jeopardize her job. She swallowed the knot in her throat and contin- ued to whack harder than she should have, until the chicken splayed beyond butterflied to become translucent. Just before she was about to pound a hole in it, she started in on the celery, bludgeoned the spine, and threw it on top. How would it look to the rest of the kids who earned their grades with hard work? Mizbie couldn't even entertain the thought of passing Nick, a decision neither fair nor ethical, just an easy way out.

"If you want the grade changed, you have the authority. You can change it yourself," she said out loud, "but I won't do it." Whack, whack – she slapped the leaves of spinach on the chicken breasts, slathered them with goat cheese and then stirred the pine nuts toasting in garlic and olive oil. She thought of her ability to support herself hanging over her head like the Sword of Damocles, but Nick and his mom needed to know they couldn't manipulate the system on this one, and she was going to be the one to tell them.

She scooped the pine nuts on top of the chicken breasts, rolled and tied them with string, and drizzled the remaining garlic olive oil over the top. The oven was hot and ready. She was too. Since she had cycled home from Winchell's office, she sensed a falling away, as if her stub- born will had not proven her sense of fairness at all. Would her refusal be remembered and filed away to shadow her later? Renee had told her she should let it go and just get along because that's the way things were done in Astor, but somebody needed to take a stand.

∾

As days drew near to the *Hamlet* opening night, cast and crew members developed a camaraderie so close that they also knew which of each others' buttons to push, creating occasional dust-ups. After an argument with Jenna and Seth over lighting, Justin confided to Mizbie that when he was four, he had fallen out of a tree and landed on his head. To be fair, he was less focused than a Jackson Pollock painting, but when he steered his tangible energy toward hammering and nailing sets of the castle and the play-within-a-play throne room for the scene of the king's poisoning, he was all business: the business of carpentry.

Corwin helped as Justin patiently told him where to nail, even letting him cut a few studs for the 10 foot castle wall. They worked as a team enjoying the progress of the castle as it took shape, listening to the actors' "oooh" and "look at this!" Gertrude and Ophelia walked in and out of the castle doors and up on the platforms around their sets smiling and shouting out favorite lines.

As practice ended and most actors had left, Mizbie picked up left-behind scripts and props from the floor, when two purple canvas shoes and striped socks stopped in front of her. "Mara Jade. You're back. I thought our costume mistress had to take time off because your parents were taking you to the Wolf Trap Camp, was that it?"

"Oh, the Wolf Trap Psychic Fair. No, we ended up not going."

"What is it?"

"I came to say goodbye, Miz B." She touched her tongue to the corner of her mouth and tried to smile. "Today is my last day. We're moving back to New Orleans."

Scripts dropped from Mizbie's hands. Not now, when the costumes were nearly finished. And not Mara Jade, of all students. "You're leaving? When did all this happen?"

"It all happened really fast, actually. I'm okay, though. I have my old friends in New Orleans. Really, I have more friends there than I do here.

My parents say it'll be good there." She balanced back and forth on her feet, so that Mizbie watched her like a clock pendulum.

"Oh, Mara Jade," Mizbie reached out without thinking and threw her arms around the girl. Mara Jade hugged back. They stood balancing back and forth, a tear in the corner of Mizbie's eye. She could think of a half dozen students she wished would move away, but not Mara Jade.

"I wanted to say thanks for, you know, being my teacher. Thanks for what you did with the gris-gris and all. I'm going to keep writing because of you." She looked down at her feet that had become still, and remembered something. "I went to your room and took my journal." She held it out in front of her. "Is it okay if I take it with me?"

"It's yours," Mizbie said, grabbing a tissue from the makeup table, turning her back for a moment. Besides no more picket signs, there would be no more grand entrances with feathers and beads, no more avant-garde poetry. Her class was losing this girl who searched out underdogs on the verge of a crisis and provided a listening ear, because she had been there and knew how to survive. There would be no one leaving anonymous gris-gris on her desk for "Love" and "Peace." Surely Mara Jade would no sooner arrive in New Orleans than she'd seek a new drum to beat. Mizbie grabbed another tissue and sniffed before she turned back around. "Mara Jade, you know we will miss you. Who's going to use up my poster paper? Who's going to shake things up in the library?"

Mara Jade almost giggled at the thought.

"Remember to send me your address as soon as you get settled. "I'll send you copies of the school paper so you can keep up with what's happening here, if that's okay."

Mara Jade nodded and gripped her journal. She looked up at Mizbie with a tight-lipped grin that nearly masked her trembling chin. She disappeared out the door, her tie-dyed scarf trailing behind her.

Days before the performance, Mizbie had to shorten play practice for parent-teacher conferences. She mentally kicked herself because there was no one to blame for the scheduling but herself. Teachers waited for hours with empty tables, even after calling and inviting parents they really wanted to see. In the spring, few parents came.

Renee stopped by her table. "I just talked with Nick Huntsman's mom. I guess she was part of a partnership that bought the building across the street from Mara Jade's. Her company spent some time there fixing it up to lease out. I think she ate up more time spying on the tatoo shop. She complained that their apartment upstairs never had the drapes closed, so how could she help but notice they had no TV and a wall full of books when neither of them had been to college? How does she know this? She said she resented the way their tattoo shop attracted riff-raff military types. Like the National Guard armory across the street was a haven for 'riff-raff.'

"She said when Luke and Mara Jade came to her door with a 'silly' survey, trying to gather signatures to keep Canadian trash out of our landfills, she refused to sign any survey they proposed. Then Mara Jade asked her if she drank coffee. When she responded that she did, Mara Jade told her about the free-trade Arabica at the tattoo shop and that she should stop by. Mrs. Huntsman sounded agitated. 'Imagine if my bridge club saw me going into that evil place. The Chamber of Commerce should close it down. They're probably Democrats, I'm almost sure of it.'"

Renee and Mizbie looked around for waiting parents. Renee continued, "Then Mrs. Huntsman told me, 'Yet the other day at the Mega Mart, I caught myself reaching for the Folgers with a twinge of guilt. I did look over at the more socially responsible coffee on the next shelf, but it was too expensive.'"

As Renee was leaving the table, Shannon's mother stopped by, not so much to hear how Shannon was doing, but to vent about the school coaches who kept asking if she played basketball, which she didn't. Shannon was the kind of tall that guys looked up to, but not in a good way. "I have to re-introduce her to friends who haven't seen her in a couple years," she laughed. "I tell them I'm going to put her in a shrinking machine."

After an hour with no parents, Rashmi's mother floated to her table, a light scent of jasmine and patchouli following her. A remarkable woman wearing a sari that captured the glow of an apricot sunset, it was rumored that she had spent more than $3,000 at a perfumery in New York to recreate the fragrance of her courtyard garden in India. If this was the scent, this whiff of olfactory bliss, Mizbie could see why. A reflective essence with a subtext of honey and wild animal was a match for this vision who turned heads as she walked. She sat down and signed her name with impeccable penmanship. "How is Rashmi doing?" Her smile was brilliant.

"Rashmi is a delight, Mrs. Kapoor." The Michael Moore plagiarism was resolved and all but forgotten. "She does more than I ask for and still challenges herself. Have you seen the play she's writing?"

"Ah yes, the play. She was working on it while waiting for her piano lessons." Mrs. Kapoor's bracelets jangled beneath the sleeves of her colorful sari. "I am pleased that you think Rashmi is doing well, but 94 percent is not acceptable to her father and me. Can you please tell me where she lost her way? What can we do to help her see her errors and improve for the next report?"

Mizbie explained, wondering if this effort was for Rashmi or the honor of her family. She thought of the copied paper and couldn't imagine the pressure she was facing at home in addition to the "thousand natural shocks" every-day at school.

"I am also concerned with this *Hamlet* play. She spends so much time on the lines just to help the others. She takes her role as prompter so seriously, I am concerned it is interfering with her real school work."

"Rashmi is a tremendous help to me and the student actors," Mizbie said. "I don't know what I'd do without her." From the expression on her mother's face, she didn't believe Mrs. Kapoor felt it was a wise use of Rashmi's time.

"Thank you. She enjoys your class," Mrs. Kapoor said, after exchanging polite pleasantries. She rose from the cafeteria seat as if it were a throne and glided across the floor.

Justin's jean-jacketed grandfather sat down before her. His craggy but clean-shaven face searched hers. He held out his hand and pointed to a dime-sized scab on the back. Looking from the scab to her, he asked, "Is this for identification?"

Mizbie could tell he was waiting for a response, so she looked at his hand with its crinkled veins and worn gold band, pausing before saying, "Sure it is. You know, Justin is quite an interesting young man. He questions everything and doesn't take anything at face value."

"You know the value of water. We got it stored in our storm shelter, 600 gallons of it. In 2018 all the water's gonna dry up, but we're gonna store enough water to stay alive for a good ten years until the rains come. That and beans. We got a ton a canned beans. We'll do okay, Justin and me."

"Yes, I just want to remind you about the incident with Justin's pants. He has to be reminded to take his meds and keep his pants on."

"Just 'cause three quarters of the earth is covered with water now, don't think it's always gonna be that way. Remember I warned you." He shook his finger at Mizbie. Remember 2018 and be prepared!"

"Okay, now I'd like to talk about Justin's grade." She offered a paper to him. "The essay was supposed to be five paragraphs on one topic. Justin has three paragraphs on many topics. The sentences run on without punctuation. I know he has a better understanding than this."

"English teachers. Who needs 'em?" Grandpa was listening now. "My grandson can take apart and put together a truck engine in a weekend. Who cares where he puts a damn question mark? He doesn't want to think that hard for that long!" Grandpa slapped his hands on the table, glaring at the window through bushy eyebrows. "Ya know, I've been a temp worker for PharmaTek for 12 years since the transmission factory closed. They got a government subsidy so they could hire temp employees. If they work us under 30 hours a week, they don't have to pay benefits. By the time the temp agency takes their cut, we make under minimum wage. There are hundreds more like me, workin' side by side for years, workin' different hours but bein' available all the time, like we was full-time. If folks ain't available or sick one day, boom. They get fired. That's it. I ain't missed a day in 12 years. Why do I stay? I'm old. Who else would hire me?" He straightened to his full height. "Looks like it's puckerin' up to rain. Dark as a pocket. Gotta git home and take the clothes off the line."

Sonia, at the next table, asked, "You have Justin too?"

185

Mizbie sighed. "His grandfather is preparing for the water shortage. He wanted someone to listen."

"I hear you," Sonia said, walking to Mizbie's table. "I called Grandma the other day," she said in a softer voice. "I told her Justin started singing in the middle of an exam. It seems she can barely look at Justin anymore. She said his mannerisms, his voice when he comes into a room, the way he combs his hair, all look just like his father who's in prison. She says that every day Justin looks more and more like the man who killed her daughter and it scares her."

"Oh, he's not so bad, really," Mizbie said, talking about Justin's work on *Hamlet*. He was strikingly different from his brother Lance. "He just needs to remember to take his meds."

"Yes, it's easy to tell when he needs them. He can't remember what you said five seconds before, and he says he feels like ants are crawling over him," Sonia said.

A thin, nervous man sat down and introduced himself as Jim's father. "He's my youngest and I guess I kinda give up on him. After 10 kids, the last one I just kinda let the bigger kids raise after Ma died. I guess his brothers give him the bad ideas, ya know. I don't know; what should I do?"

"Mr. Johnson, I've only had Jim for one day. Mine was the third English class he's been transferred to in four days. So far, he has not made a positive impression. He won't sit down. He touches the girls' arms and makes suggestive comments. The counselor and I have talked with him about appropriate behavior. I don't know what his old school, Hillbridge, allowed him to do, but his behavior has to change at St. Bartholomew's. Do you have consequences for him when he misbehaves? Could you take away his computer privileges? Television?"

"We ain't got no computer. TV he don't watch. When I try takin' away his cell phone, he gets real mad. I can't do that."

"Maybe it's time to risk the anger to help him. He needs discipline, Mr. Johnson. He wants to push you to see what you'll let him get away with."

"Yeah, I've heard that from teachers before. I'll see what I can do, Ms Baxter. I sure want Jim to graduate, not drop out like his brothers and sisters when they got to 16. Ya know there's not a lot for a kid to do anymore when they drop out."

"That's right," Mizbie said. Maybe there was hope if Dad realized that Jim needed to graduate. "Jim needs our guidance and support."

Gilbert's father, who raised canaries, signed in. "His mother and I can't do anything with him, and believe me, we've tried everything. He's shut down. He's never been like this. His sisters and brother always do their work, but he's the oldest and we're afraid he's setting a bad example for them. His grades are taking a nosedive. We've even made him stay in his room for Friday family video night. Any suggestions?"

"You know about Zo – a girl in his class? He can tell you her name." Mizbie stopped before she revealed more than state law allowed.

"A girl? Gilbert has a girlfriend? So that's it. He won't tell us anything."

"He's a freshman boy. Freshmen boys don't talk to parents so much. Here's what you do. Use this to your advantage. Set the oven timer for ten minutes . . ." Mizbie went through the recommendations for parents that she had already suggested that evening, trying to make it sound like she was saying it for the first time. "You can get a lot of leverage out of this!"

Gilbert's dad smiled. "A girlfriend." He shook his head and walked away.

The three-hour conference allowed time for Mizbie to correct a few papers. Only once, with Rico's grandmother, did she have to concentrate on her breathing, when she realized she couldn't bring his grandmother around to talking about Rico. Like the anguish of the uninvited guest who doesn't know when to leave, Grandma gave the history of Rico's mother, who was uninvolved in California, and all of her chronic illnesses. Mizbie attended to her with assurance, without trying to change her situation, enduring it, letting it pass without rumination, and having compassion for herself for doing so. She saw 10 parents or grandparents, a better turnout than last year, before it was time to go home.

Cycling home, she stopped in front of Mara Jade's building, wondering about Noel's builder father and his plans. She figured the gentrification of the tattoo shop to maybe a gourmet deli or an art gallery. Like the big bad wolf licking his chops at a little pig, she pictured him investing minimal drywall, maybe some paving bricks in front and a trendy sign with a bit of grit to it, in keeping with the neighborhood.

What he and Mrs. Huntsman didn't realize was that the growing popularity of the neighborhood real estate was due in large part to the tattoo shop, not despite it. Mara Jade and her family organized food drives, sponsored walk-a-thons, hosted barbecued rib cook-offs and open mic nights that brought a sense of community to an otherwise lackluster corner.

She looked up and saw a hawk glide across the sky, then lazily spiral up. Another joined it in a similar spiral until both became mere dots lost in a cloud. When Mrs. Huntsman bought Mara Jade's building and hiked their lease payment, forcing them out, she lost the only thing that made her new investment valuable. It would take a few months to realize his mistake, but not one to be left with a worthless hovel of old brick and cement, he would let the bank take the building. Mizbie wasn't the only one who wondered about Mara Jade and her family's move back to New Orleans, as she stared in the vacant windows, thinking of the Chinese New Year's party. The many pots of wave petunias and tall red oats that would've been bursting with color by now, were already withered and brown without the attention of Mara Jade and her mother's green thumb. The neighborhood was quiet since they were gone. People who had clucked their tongues at their arrival from New Orleans, now felt like something was missing.

During the dress rehearsal, tensions began to build. Rashmi had given Desmin several lines and they were losing patience with each other. Mizbie had just chastised him for making fun of Rashmi.

"And by a sleep to say we end the heartache and the thousand natural shocks that flesh is heir to –"

"Desmin, try that line again," Mizbie said.

"No!" Rashmi stood and walked to Desmin, her long braid swinging down her back, looking into his scarred face. "This line – 'the thousand natural shocks' – it's what we go through every day here, you and I. All those slights and snide comments, whispers and smiles every single day and you know the next day will be the same, and the day after that."

Mizbie had never heard Rashmi speak with such force.

"You know it and endure it and move on with it. Say it like you've lived it. Say it like this is our inheritance." Rashmi's voice rose and Desmin looked at her without glaring.

"Yeah . . ." he nodded, looking at her like he'd never seen her before in his life. "I get it."

"Let's pick it up at, 'O my prophetic soul,' Desmin. Expression!" Mizbie said.

"O my prophetic soul!"

"Did you step in something?"

"O my . . . prophetic soul!"

"Desmin, you just confirmed that your stepfather/uncle, that serpent, has murdered your father. You are so honorable and ethical, you make a promise to your ghost/father to get his tortured soul out of purgatory and avenge his foul murder. Feel it, Desmin, feel it!"

Desmin took a breath and spoke in the depths of a low rumble, "O . . . my . . . prophetic soul!"

No one said anything. "Well, how 'zat? Can I keep goin' now?"

"You got it, Desmin. Do it just like that," Mizbie said.

"It's about time. I feel cobwebs crawlin' up my a – ankles."

"Don't mumble. Keep going." Mizbie felt a hand on her arm. "Stella, what is it?"

"We don't have enough stage makeup and Ophelia just quit. She has an ACT test on Saturday morning." Yet another cast member had dropped out, joining a handful of others. Mizbie had run out of substitutes. But this was Ophelia.

The skull Desmin had picked up for the graveyard scene nearly rolled off a table. Mizbie raced to catch it before it shattered on the floor. She didn't want to know where he'd found it. "Just keep her another half hour, Stella. Can you do that? I'll talk to her."

The final dress rehearsal ran over and Ophelia left before Mizbie had a chance to convince her to stay. The first performance was tomorrow and there was no Ophelia and no understudy. She had only enough money from last year's play to pay the custodians and rent the stage, not enough for more stage makeup. Every year Mizbie swore the spring play would be her last, but this year topped everything. "Rashmi, we need to talk," she said.

∾

Every seat in the auditorium was filled. The audience members chattered and fanned themselves with their programs. Mizbie had just let loose with a string of unbridled language, like roiled spring waters converging in a river delta. Students knew not to take it personally. It was unseasonably warm, and, without air conditioning, large fans were brought in to cool the audience. Justin had been hopping like a water bug from prop to set making last-minute checks. It unsettled her to watch him, so she sent him out to buy another case of bottled water for the cast and crew.

Mizbie told the actors they would have to speak louder to be heard over the fans, since she had not yet been able to convince the administration to use some of the play profits to purchase a sound system. An outside door at the back of the stage was left open in hopes that as the sun set, cooler air would find its way to the heavily costumed actors, laboring under the hot stage lights.

By Scene II, the stage was radiating with heat. Stage right actors stood in their places for the play-within-a-play, and stage left actors were seated as the royal family. Actors' faces glistened through heavy stage makeup. Desmin was enjoying Rashmi's discomfort with Ophelia's lines that she knew too well. "Lady, shall I lie in your lap?" He stretched himself out at her feet looking up at her with a coy smile.

Rashmi looked down at him automatically clutching the costume to her breast. It was not revealing by American standards, but it displayed more of her than she had ever shown in public before. At her feet she saw Desmin with that same look he had when she had spouted off at him during dress rehearsal, except his acting makeup, which Mizbie had just purchased that afternoon, completely covered his scars. He was actually quite handsome. "No, my lord." She said in a prim solemn tone.

"I mean, my head upon your lap?" Desmin said, sitting up.

"Ay, my lord," With her consent, Desmin gently rested his head in her lap. Rashmi felt strange, as if she were burning up from the inside out.

"Do you think I meant country matters?" he said, looking up at her. What he saw stunned him. She wasn't surveying his face perusing the scars but looking into him. He could feel Rashmi's warm, brown eyes searching his. What was this feeling? He didn't feel the need to lash out at her in defense. He swallowed hard, wanting more of this feeling, like an unquenchable thirst.

Rashmi forgot her line. The more she tried to remember, the more fearful she became. The pause in their timing seemed interminable. "I think . . . I think . . ." Desmin whispered to her.

"I think nothing, my lord," she said, over the hum of the fans. Desmin saved her.

After the play, the applause, and the bows, parents congratulated the actors and took pictures. Even Margo, who had been in the audience, walked up to Mizbie and swung her hair to the side, looking directly at her without blinking. With a scowl, she said, "I don't always hate you."

No one stayed long, hurrying out to escape the heat of the auditorium. Actors rushed to the back room to return costumes. Looking forward to one more performance, they had mixed feelings that after tomorrow and the cast party, everything would come to an end.

Desmin turned to Rashmi. "That was good. Really good. You comin' to the cast party tomorrow?" He unlaced the vest from his costume to let in cooling air.

"Oh, we did it. I was so scared, Desmin. Thank you for giving me the line. Thank you." She fanned herself with a program.

"Yeah, sure, so will you come to the party?"

"Maybe. My parents don't let me attend school parties. I hope they will make an exception this time." Rashmi smiled.

∾

Shortly before the Monday morning bell rang, Mizbie's phone buzzed. "This is Mrs. Kapoor, Rashmi's mother," said the terse voice. "Rashmi's father and I were not pleased with the performance of the Shakespeare play. We were not pleased that Rashmi was put in an exposed position in front of everyone. And with that boy. We have decided you are not to seat Rashmi and that boy together in class. He is a bad influence. They are not to participate in any class activity or anything that might place them together."

"Mrs. Kapoor, Desmin . . ."

"Rashmi must not speak to that boy!" Mrs. Kapoor's controlled alarm traveled through the phone to the pit of Mizbie's stomach. She could picture the steely resolve in Mrs. Kapoor's eyes. "I do not want to remove her from your class this late in the school year, but I will if you cannot keep them apart. We need your cooperation, Ms Baxter."

Chapter 12

A student approaches Mizbie before class –

– I couldn't do homework, Miz B; I got three bonuses on Countryville and I just had to keep going. After my friend sent me supplies, I had to use them. Then when I looked up at the clock by my bed, it was 2:00 in the morning, so I had to get some sleep for school. Give me a break.

You played from after school until 2:00 in the morning and didn't notice the time? What's the problem here?

Now you sound like my mom.

Jesspin9
to MBax20
10:00 p.m.
April 30

Hey Miz,

I'm on the beach at San Sebastian. Yesterday I cycled with a group on the Monte Igueldo trail, nearly 20 miles, mostly right by the beach with some turns through hills and a breathtaking view of the sea. A Spanish local from the group invited us to join her at home for an event that night. There were several wines brought out throughout the evening, including a Sine Qua Non Eleven Confessions Grenache 2003. You know how I love Grenache! Uniformed waiters served never-ending tapas.

She had her name engraved on a plaque in some Egyptian museum, thanks to a collection of some small makeup jars she had purchased at auctions over the years and donated to the museum. They were very old, handmade glass, different sizes, shapes, and colors. Apparently some of them had been stolen a century ago. She bought them with the idea of returning them to their rightful place. She made a short speech that included the possibility that maybe these jars had been touched by Cleopatra or her handmaidens, and everyone applauded her generosity.

Later when I was walking around behind her spiral staircase looking for the powder room, I saw three amphorae in an alcove. Remember when we saw those amphorae in a history museum in Ann Arbor? These were on a stand with no special support and no lighting on them. Other works of art were lit up around the house. How suspicious is that? Miz, I'm no art expert, but they had to be 2,000 years old or more. When I asked her if she was sending these back too, we exchanged a look. "A diver friend gave them to me," she said. "They were a gift. I'm keeping them."

What do you make of that? Tomorrow our group is cycling farther inland on the Aranzazu trail, more than 50 miles.

Remember when we drove all night to NYC for the winter Jazzfest at Greenwich Village? We stayed in that asparagus green hovel two blocks off Bleeker Street and heard jazz at the Poisson Rouge that made you gag? But there was that one group, Havana Salsa, that you really liked. They're playing right here tonight in San Sebastian. I'm going. Have fun in Alabaster.

Jess

∾

"I don't like fiction, Miz B. It's fake, pretend, lies," said Robin.

The class looked at her for a response. She sensed a moment. "But squeezed in between the lies are truths from the writer's life, Robin, spun like spider webs, sewn in many colors like a patchwork quilt, turned inside out like a shirt." Mizbie walked toward his seat, speaking faster. "The writer has his own view of life, unlike yours or mine or anyone's." Her hands gesticulated. "He can capture that for us in characters and show us parts of ourselves in ways we never thought possible. Life can be seen through lenses that are aging or ageless, depending on the whim, or the reader's light that filters through them."

"Yeah, whatever. But it's fake light!" Robin said.

Rashmi had just called Desmin "baboo," an Indian courtesy that he took as an endearment. "Oh, yeah, Miz B. I was gonna ask, what about Kafka? I heard Rashmi say Kafkaesque and I didn't know what that was," Desmin asked. His newly minted relationship with Rashmi was creating interest and paying dividends.

Mizbie knew Desmin was stalling to prevent her from passing out the quiz in her hand, but she couldn't resist answering. She talked briefly of dark existential themes, surreal images, and alienation, until she saw his attention wane. So she changed it up a bit, "You know, that reminds me, a friend of mine recently visited Prague and talked about pausing on the Charles Bridge where Kafka walked. Did you know that some of his letters are yet to be found? Then that same friend went to San Sebastian, a beach resort town in northern Spain. She and some cycling friends met an American there they called Harvard Mike, who graduated from Harvard a few years back. He had a math degree and went to San Sebastian to live. You think he started a business and did well? No. He sold tickets at the bus station and wrote concert reviews for local music. That's all –, Harvard to bus station."

Where was she going with that? She felt out of focus, like the night of her 30th birthday, after a night at Tikki Cove with the girls, when she went home to eat a whole jar of Nutella before losing it all in the porcelain bus.

∞

Turning the junction from I-69 to I-75 in her Zipcar, Mizbie felt the caffeine from her oversized travel mug; these highways that drew her away, were now taking her back home to Alabaster, past corn, winter wheat, alfalfa, and soybean fields tinged in spring green.

Last night she had sat bolt upright in bed, strangling her pillow, panic so real, it took a number of seconds to understand it was not reality and her life was not over. The night terrors seemed to run in a series, like obsessive images of old horror films –, the steep fog-drenched bridge, the sound of the old steam engine, and the terror of falling to her death – that clawed at her as she fought to overcome them. Her nightmare was a Siamese twin with one shared heart, impossible to separate from her waking life.

Gasping in huge breaths of air, she calmed herself and thought back over the familiar death flash, seeing something that had always been there, staring her in the face. While the refrigerator made sounds like a ghost cricket, she groped for a pad of paper and a pencil, flipped on the bathroom light and returned to stretch out on the bed, scribbling a cobwebbed outline in the semi-darkness. She didn't want to believe the images that had reappeared night after night, making less sense on paper than in the dream, but she decided to take the paper with her to Alabaster.

She turned off M-57 for the first time since her parents died. The narrow road, which had been made of pebble-sized pieces of white alabaster, was now widened and paved in black asphalt. The name of her road was changed from Johnson Road to Lakeview Drive. Private driveways elbowed each other, splaying from the once solitary narrow pass. Her eyes searched for the old tree stump that she used to jump from, pretending she was Superman. Now it had been replaced with a sunshine dappled lawn and a gable-roofed house.

Mizbie drove to the place where she thought the house should be. The wood-stained log house had metamorphosed to white. A second-story A-frame loft with tinted windows had been added, dwarfing the original structure. Near the front walkway where the cherry tree used to be, a wind chime sent out its deep harmony from a puff of breeze. Compared to this, what was once her haven nestled in trees would now look like an afterthought, an old unloved but tolerated relative. The shed where her father worked on the lawnmower or fixed table legs had turned into a three-car garage.

Two marks remained on the long branch that extended from the oak tree in front of the garage. No one would notice the knots in the branch, unless they had seen the rope swing there years ago. The memory etched a smile, revealing itself in a crinkle in the corner of her eye. The ropes were so long that even when she was very young, she could will her bare feet backward in the sand, then point her toes heavenward for a breath-catching arc that swooped up almost to the leaves. As she got older and was able to swing higher, she could even see over the roof of the cottage to the lake. Of course the A-frame would block that view now.

She stretched on her toes at the end of the drive, not ready to approach the house. Beyond the house, Lake Huron sparkled in morning sun. It had rained and the air had the familiar weighty scent of leaves and fish. A seagull swooped with wings stretched, caw-cawing and diving.

Before breakfast, she watched her dad start up the old white Sea Ray fishing boat and waited for the sound of the waking engine. "First fish gets a dime, biggest fish gets a quarter," Dad said. They had their favorite spot halfway between Charity Island and the old Alabaster crib. The crib hadn't docked a freighter in years, but made a perfect landmark. Dad sang old jazz tunes, not very well, but they were recognizable and familiar. His songs didn't seem to scare away the fish. When the cagey perch ate her bait and swam off, she'd reach her hand in the minnow bucket, looking for the liveliest specimen.

It wasn't until she was older that she would bait her own hook, overlooking the physical pain to the minnow. Early on, Dad would hook the minnow clean through the backbone, teasing her for her tenderhearted cowardice. It wasn't long before the familiar tug-tug on the line made her heart race and her hand spin the reel, bringing up a plump yellowbelly. The trick was to unhook the lip of the fish, being careful to put her hands over the fins, which could give a nasty cut if she grabbed them fin up. The two of them caught thirty perch in less than an hour. "It's about time," her father said. "I'm sure your mother has the fry pan heated on the stove."

At those words, she brought up the anchor line, and Dad turned the boat to shore while the fish flopped and jumped in the carrier.

It looked so easy, the way Dad filleted the perch, ignoring the pungent fishy smell. "Take these in to your mother and I'll finish the rest."

Mizbie ran into the kitchen with the first half of the fish sliding on the plate, ready for a good rinse. Mom already had the butter and oil nearly bubbling. First the egg bath, then a dip of flour mix, salt and pepper, and the perch were ready for frying. By the time Mizbie returned to the chopping block for the last fish, her father had buried the heads and fins in the sand. As they opened the back screen door, there was the first platter of fish on the table, golden, warm, and ready to eat.

Playmates around the lake were few, but every summer, Joey came to visit his aunt, who lived one house down on the wooded side of the road. Mrs. Crowley's backyard was a maze of tangled tree limbs, a childhood delight. Mizbie's backyard was sand, little stones, and a cold lake, so she welcomed the chance to take her empty mayonnaise jar to Joey's backyard. At dusk they punched holes, with a hammer and nail from the garage, in the screw caps of their jars. Grabbing a few handfuls of grass to place in the bottom for food, they lurked, tiptoeing around the side of the garage under the cottonwoods, birches, and soft-needled white pines. A lightning bug glowed, and they both lurched at it, collided, and ended up on their behinds.

"Quiet, Joey," she said. "We'll scare them away." Quick and sharp-eyed, Joey caught 12 fireflies in the time it took Mizbie to collect 5. As dusk turned to dark in the woods, they stretched out in the middle of the soft grass and watched the jars light up. At the end of summer, Mizbie missed Joey when he left to go home.

Bringing her thoughts to the present, Mizbie looked past the swing, and saw the familiar grapevine seat set in a shelter of birch trees. Its weathered, web of vines looked like it grew there, instead of being crafted by her dad. With its heart-shaped back just big enough for two, she pictured her parents sitting together with their after-dinner mugs of tea, watching her child-self swing higher before them. Even though her home was no longer hers, she couldn't help but sit down on the grapevine seat, resting her back into the curve of deceptively strong vines, looking up at the leafy canopy above her, remembering. She pulled the paper from her jeans pocket, looking at her sketch of this grapevine seat. It couldn't be anything else. She waited for some epiphany, some aha moment, but nothing came.

Peeking in the window at the side of the garage, she saw two-by-fours along the back wall. The furniture grade wood – beautiful mahogany, red cedar, and bird's-eye maple – had been in the old shed. Her father worked for Shirkey's Lumber Company in Tawas and purchased some of the best pieces of wood for himself, heading out to the garage right after supper to make a table or lamp base. He gave most of his creations away, although Mom thought he should set up a booth at the flea market and sell them.

The pieces were beautiful, especially the bird's-eye maple table that had been the family kitchen table as long as she could remember. Her mother would rub mineral oil on it each week to keep the iridescence of the wood. Playing solitaire on the table in the afternoon, patches of sunlight would make the bird's-eyes shine between the cards. The table legs were curved with lion's feet that rested on the green and brown tile of the cottage floor, a floor terminally sand-covered in summer from trips to the beach.

Occasionally her dad would take her for a visit to the lumberyard. To the side of the yard was a miniature village with a train that Mr. Shirkey would fire up for children who visited. It wove its way through a train crossing, past a library, general store, a row of tree-shaded houses no taller than her waist, wagons, and horses, arriving at a miniature Shirkey's Lumber Company. Dad had to drag her away and lift her up into the truck when it was time to leave.

After her graduation, she overheard an argument between her parents. Arguing was so rare that she couldn't concentrate on the words through her bedroom door, only the fear she felt. Many times she had relived the argument but could not recall its content, only the sound of toppled furniture, a scream, and her mother wearing long sleeves afterward to cover up deep purple bruises down her left arm.

The argument was followed by a silent hostility between her parents that lasted through the rest of their lives. She walked in on a few conversations, overhearing words like "going back" and "divorce," conversations that would stop as soon as they saw her. Even though each parent treated her with kindness and love, their marriage became more of a marathon of endurance that Mizbie was in no hurry to emulate.

On one of the last fishing trips she had taken before going to college, Mizbie drove the boat after her dad set the trim tabs for her to see out of the windshield. She grabbed the steering wheel with both hands, angling the bow away from Charity Island toward home, while Dad secured fish hooks into cork pole handles. "Just like driving the boat, Mizbie," he said. "Set your trim tabs at the university and head yourself in the right direction." She remembered the look he gave her, as if he'd already lost her, resigned to her return from college as a woman with secrets he would never know.

As time grew closer to her venture into university life, the tension between her parents grew more palpable with each day she crossed off her calendar. When they were at the kitchen table or in the same room, she could see it in their movements and glances, feel it without a word being said. She would excuse herself, boil a mug of water for tea, and retreat to her room with one of a dozen books she'd checked out of the library, chosen carefully from the college freshman recommended reading list.

A tactic her parents had used when she was young, sending her to her room for a temper outburst, she began to use herself as a retreat. It was the summer of the annotated *Pride and Prejudice;* Anaya's *Bless Me, Ultima;* Atwood's *The Handmaid's Tale;* Chopin's *The Awakening;* Walker's *The Color Purple;* and Dostoyevsky's wrist slitter, *Crime and Punishment.* She immersed herself in the poetic storytelling of Morrison's *Beloved,* opened herself to spiritual philosophy in *Siddhartha,* and felt dazed with incredulous satire in Heller's *Catch-22.* She looked for something she knew was there, but couldn't quite grasp in the lives of the heroes and heroines, an answer to unvoiced questions. Having the books in her room provided a comfort that was gone when they were returned to the library. She read their titles one last time, remembering the emotional upheavals they created as she slipped her self inside their covers. The literary escape helped her pass the days wondering less about what would happen to her parents when she left.

Mizbie thought about the life she led at St. Bartholomew's, empty spots where Carl used to be that she filled up with work. She couldn't decide if it was a good idea, seeing this place again. These strangers living here never knew anything of the swing or the grapevine seat. A sense of sorrow swept over her as she remembered the day of her parents' funeral, the gathering of people watching her sit alone on the church pew. She wished the world would just stop for a while so she could make sense of it. She scooped up some pebbles from the driveway, threw down a few plain ones and pocketed the rest before she knocked on the door.

Before her hand made a sound, the door opened. An older man peered out at her, jarring her out of her reverie. He introduced himself and his wife, Bob and Ruth, then asked how they could help her.

"I used to live here, grew up in this house, actually." Mizbie introduced herself. "My father made that grapevine seat. He and my mom used to sit there in the summer." *Does he believe me?* she wondered.

She was surprised to find them excited to see her. They invited her in to see the improvements they had made to the cottage, adding central heating (instead of depending on the stone fireplace), a new roof, and a big bay window overlooking the lake. Mizbie talked about the fishing and her mother's cooking. She thanked them for satisfying her curiosity and walked toward her car, having learned more than she thought she would.

"Wait a minute!" Ruth called to her. "Bob, remember that picture? Where did we put that thing?"

Bob paused a moment and walked away. She could hear cabinet doors opening and closing. He returned with a thick manila envelope, handing it to Mizbie. "We found this tucked away over a rafter in the shed when we tore it down. Lucky we saw it before it got destroyed. We thought we'd save it in case any family ever came looking for it." He looked at Ruth. "And here you are."

Mizbie opened the envelope. Inside was a snapshot in a birch bark frame. "They're so young. And that must be me," she said to Ruth, pointing to her parents holding a baby. Bob and Ruth were pleased to have kept the picture and delighted to give it to her. She looked at her parents' picture in her hands, seeing them smile into the camera. Mom and

Dad weren't ones to take pictures and she couldn't remember a camera in the house. It wasn't until college that she bought a camera for herself. She rubbed her fingers on the powdery birch wood that framed it. Dad had probably made the frame, carefully mitering corners for a look that was both natural and meticulous. She thanked Bob and Ruth for hanging on to the picture.

Driving home, she wondered about the other woman in the picture, probably a neighbor, standing in a yard with her parents. Maybe her husband was the man taking the picture. All she could see of him was his shadow.

She heard the whir of her tires as she crossed the Singing Bridge, kindling a memory that compelled her to make a quick turn into the Singing Bridge Cafe. She wasn't so full of regrets that she couldn't resist a visit and a salty strip of deer jerky. Instead of pickup trucks in the parking lot, SUVs and Priuses took their places.

When he heard the bell ring over the weathered door, Lar's round apron-covered belly preceded him through the swinging double doors from the kitchen. He wiped his hands on the white apron that had fresh, red meat stains. Without a word, he looked at her and brought out a strip of jerky from the meat case. Lars concentrated on her face for a while until a slow smile spread above his many chins. "Audra and Dylan's girl, all grown up, looks like."

Mizbie was carried back to the days of after-school walks and girl gossip, biting off a chunk of salty, chewy goodness. Thank God he hadn't changed the recipe. They exchanged small talk and what a shame it was about Audra and Dylan. "Do you know if they still have fishing trips down at Green's Marina?" she asked.

"Green's Marina?" the gray-haired Lars repeated. "That's been gone a few years. Not much good fishing around here now – just a few wall-eyes now and then. Old man Green sold it to that developer fella."

They talked as Mizbie paid him, and Lars wrapped up a few extra strips of jerky for her ride home. "You can play miniature golf and rent jet skis there, where the old marina was. It's Bohunk Pete's now," Lars said. "A teacher. Imagine that. Don't be a stranger around here, will ya?"

Mizbie drove farther and made another turn down a short drive of crushed alabaster rock. She stopped before the white clapboard Alabaster Community Church. The door of the little chapel was unlocked, and she walked up the aisle, sitting in the same seat she sat in for her parents' memorial service. It was so quiet, she could hear herself breathe. Watching the afternoon light filter through the windows casting alternate shadows and sunbeams, she began to remember the day in pieces. The fabric on the draperies had faded from red to rose, the sun and the reflection from the lake speeding the fading process.

On that day, the portly pastor with thinning red hair and a beard that moved up and down as he sang, provided the homily and the guitar music. His seafaring songs echoed off the wooden floor and hardwood pews.

A small flock of parishioners sat on pews behind her, but she sat alone without grandparents, aunts, uncles, cousins, or siblings. She could feel their eyes on her back, observing her. That's what people do at funerals and she had done it herself. She hoped to remember some of them afterward and thank them for coming. Her parents' deaths were so sudden and she was unable to fathom all the protocol, like trying to play marbles on a tipping ship. The family members of the murderer were conspicuously absent.

After the conviction of the drunk driver who killed her parents, her friends at home in Astor told her that the trial brought justice or at least closure. Sitting in the courtroom, she listened to the story of his 40th birthday and how he never drank, but the guys from work talked him into having a drink before going home and he never had before, but heck, he didn't turn 40 every day. So he had the drink and then a few more before he got behind the wheel to go home to his wife and three school-aged kids, who were waiting for him with homemade birthday cards and chocolate cake. He was sentenced to 15 years in an Upper Peninsula penitentiary for manslaughter, while his wife could rarely afford the time to visit him because she was trying to hold down two jobs. Lives lost.

After the verdict, Mizbie wanted to shout. But she looked at the family huddled and crying as their beloved husband and father, who never had a speeding ticket, was taken away, and she was robbed of motive for her blame, helpless to assign fault. Instead she felt only more grief for their loss and her own. It wasn't the way things should work. Justice ought to bring closure. A murderer is supposed to be a scroungy lout, not an Eagle Scout. He's supposed to be deceitful and uncooperative, not honest and open. Things didn't work out the way they should have. Both his wife and Mizbie suffered, deprived of even a compromise of their grief.

Mizbie continued her reverie. The pastor's last guitar notes ended. She looked up to see that his beard had stopped moving and looked around to see what she was supposed to do. The service was over and a man who looked like Uncle Sam in a black suit, motioned for her to stand and walk with him past all those pairs of eyes.

Walking down the aisle of the little church, she thought of pie making. Her mother never allowed Mizbie to cook, only set the table and watch. The kitchen was set up well for this, with a snack bar and two wooden stools separating the kitchen from the living room. Mizbie sat on a stool while her mother rolled out homemade French pastry, working on the kitchen side of the snack bar. The heavy, wooden rolling pin, which was now in Mizbie's kitchen, clunked and rolled on top of the wooden snack bar, as the crust achieved its near-perfect shape.

One of the few kitchen tasks Mizbie was allowed to help with was pitting the sour cherries. As they pinched cherry after cherry, the juice spattered over the sink and landed on their aprons, sometimes stinging their eyes. The pie crust was non-negotiable, so Mizbie watched her mother tuck the dough into the glass pie plate, heap in the cherries with a bit of tapioca, and top them with chunks of butter. The cinnamon tickled her nose and made her sneeze. The top crust was crimped into place with a practiced thumb, a few holes for escaping steam made a snowflake design on top, and the pie was ready for the oven. She wished she could watch her mother make the pie one more time, only this time Mizbie would be in the kitchen with her, getting the feel of the dough in her hands, not just watching.

Jesspin9
toMBax20
12:30 a.m.
May 19

Hey Miz,

That had to be tough, dredging up all those memories about your parents in Alabaster. Did you get some answers about the nightmares?

My brother and Elle stopped by with the kids. They were going to spend a few days, but cut the visit short because he is so bull-headed. "Look at you. You're stuck in muddleheaded adolescence. You're indulging yourself, unconditionally affirming yourself with pseudo-self-love." His cheeks and ears turned pink, like they used to when he spouted off about who was best at the video game Duck Hunt. We'd had this argument before about philosopher Sam Keen's views of self-love vs. positive thinking. It didn't go over any better today than it did then.

I thought about when your parents died in the car accident. Remember that night we spent on your couch, watching old Audrey Hepburn movies with a box of Kleenex and a bottle of Chianti? You were disoriented and angry and blanketed with memories. That's how I felt when my brother and his family took off last night, only I didn't have you here to listen to my ranting.

Hank was pushing my buttons about traveling and dredged up all the responsibility he shouldered with Mom and Dad and their hospice care. He said I should get a real job but instead I escaped family responsibilities, like I was still in high school, and he wondered when I was going to settle down.

Elle, just sat there, pregnant and tired, and didn't even take my side. She's been like a real sister since the day they became engaged, and she didn't even say a word of support! I told him I did have a real job and if he had a problem with it, he could take it up with Uncle Claud and the publisher.

He was relentless, Miz. He said journalism is tangential, dying. I couldn't do this for the rest of my life. I needed a real job where I could make a living and save for the future, like computer software designing or something. One thing led to another and I told him I never wanted to see him again. So he left. He took my Elle, now a traitor, and my niece and my nephew. I looked at Elle one last time as if I was looking at her reflection sinking through water, misshapen and dark. I imagined her swollen feet, sinking in murky sand. God, I hate my brother. I'm getting a bottle of Montepulciano, a box of Kleenex, and some Hepburn movies for tonight.

Yesterday I rode hard from Montpellier to Carcassone along the old Roman Road trying to forget about my brother. I found a local bouchon. An old man and his wife served the same menu the chevaliers ate 800 years ago – crusty bread, sausage, white goat cheese, green olives in thick oil, and an earthy red local wine. We ate table d'hôte style, one long table where strangers ate together. There was a big plum tree out back, where his wife picked a few plums, wiped them on her apron, and brought them into the kitchen. After the meal, the plums on the plate were still warm from the sun. I left my quittance, a measly two Euro, and she left the change on the plate. It's funny how they never put the change in your hand.

Even though I'm still mad at Hank, I think I'm finally over my old boyfriend, Ben. You won't believe how it happened. I was cycling near this fruit stand, and I was getting hungry. My Herrod House writing stipend doesn't come until next week, so I'm conserving money. I happened to remember I had the last of Ben's crocheted jock straps in my backpack. DON'T lecture me about why I brought a jock strap to Europe when part of the reason why I'm here is to forget about him!

Back before our big blowout, Ben and I used to crochet together when we got tired of the karaoke bars. Ben felt funny about it and asked me not to tell anyone, but I'd crochet kitchen washcloths and he'd make bookmarks. Then I made a halter top and he made a jock strap. We kept making them and then we'd wear them in front of each other. It got to be a contest. He had made about seven jock straps in fluorescent colors. My halter tops took longer, so I didn't have as many. Later he began to obsess about the jock straps and made a big deal of me promising never to tell anyone he had crocheted them. I guess it was that macho anxiety of his. One day he came to my apartment scowling and said he'd burned them all. Actually, he hadn't burned them all; I had one in the bottom of my lingerie drawer.

Anyway, since I was hungry, I figured I'd try to barter with the fruit vendor, so in my sketchy French I asked him what I could get for a "banana hammock." He looked puzzled, so I pulled out the shocking purple jockstrap – yes, it was clean – and cradled a banana in it, swinging it back and forth. The vendor looked to be a college guy on vacances d'été. He watched the swinging banana, then looked at me and broke out laughing. He made giant circles with his arms and said, "Prenez ce que vous voulez" – take whatever you want.

I filled my hands with fresh peaches and a few plums, but not before I took a picture of him smiling, swinging the banana in the jock strap. Immediately I sent the picture of him to Ben. Imagine the look on Ben's face when he sees it . . . priceless. Then I said, "Merci beaucoup," and meant it. Standing up, the fruit vendor stacked the banana on top of my fruit, tossed the strap up, and caught it. I just closed a door behind me, Miz, and the other side is looking good.

Jess

Jesspin9
toMBax20
3:10 p.m.
May 22

Oh, Miz,

I'm writing this from jail, although I'm not writing on the back of a grocery sack like M. L. King did in Birmingham. I bet he didn't feel sorry for himself, either, but one thing we have in common, we're both innocent. I'm in this Spanish Basque border town of Lugar de Cria de Cerdos, which means place of pig breeding, and this cupcake baker was a pig. I was just getting a breakfast cupcake at a shop where I got the same cupcake yesterday. It had cappuccino caramel frosting with cinnamon on top, and they had one left. When I asked for it, the baker said it cost €0.50 more than yesterday. I yelled at him and the people behind heard me. Suddenly 20 people were pushing and shoving in the street. When la policia came and asked who started it, everyone pointed at me.

I see the judge in an hour. I'm sure we'll get it straightened out, and I'm not going to call my brother, even though he could catch a train easily and make it here in a few hours. I'm still so mad at him; I could put ants in his bed or push him out of a tree. I did those things when we were little. I'm so mad at him, Miz, but maybe he's right. Maybe I should get a real job. I just don't like it when things aren't right between Hank and me.

Jess

∼

Cooking for herself usually encompassed a Mediterranean diet. Cooking with Stella involved compromise with Stella's favorite cuisine: Southwest. With a recording of Mumford & Sons harmonizing over bubbling pots and sizzling pans, Stella tolerated Mizbie's musical choices, humming along as they chopped onions, spinach, and garlic for a frittata. Mizbie rummaged for spatulas and spoons, slamming drawers and yelling the occasional "damn," or "Curse this stove!"

Stella's knife cut vegetables to the rhythm of the music, focusing on the immediate, secure in the knowledge that she didn't have to concern herself with hunger, a bed to sleep in, or getting found by the wrong people. Her past and future were consciously kicked out of her mind.

"You know, this really doesn't go with frittata, but," Mizbie paused, measuring some chipotle and adobo sauce, "I feel like some pasta. Let's make some."

She took her kitchen shears to the basil plants growing by the sliding glass door, and snipped the fragrant leaves. Washing and patting the leaves dry, she rolled and cut them for minimal bruising, kneaded them with a mixture of flour and egg, rolled out the dough, and cut it into wide noodle pasta. They ate the fresh-cooked pasta with drizzled olive oil and stuffed, roasted red peppers with sausage and rice inside. As they ate, Mizbie told Stella about her parents, leaving out the worrisome memories from her childhood that she had relived in Alabaster.

"That's different, going fishing with your dad," Stella said, as if fishing happened in another universe. Then she scooped another stuffed red pepper on her plate. She told Mizbie about swimming in a lake with her parents when she was younger, recalling details as if she wanted to secure them in her mind so she would never lose them.

That night Mizbie took the snapshot from its manila envelope and placed it on the marble-topped library table her dad had made. She scooped the pebbles from the pocket of her jeans, wiping off the sand, and placed them in front of the picture.

"What's that?" Stella asked.

Mizbie told her about the couple who lived in her house and how they had saved this picture. She pointed out her parents in the photo and the birch frame her father had probably made.

"You had a pretty normal family," Stella said.

"I guess so," Mizbie said. "I didn't see it at the time, but I guess we were." She stood up. "I'm going downstairs for a while."

Then she took the flashlight and made her way to the basement storage room, unlocking the chicken-wire mesh door and pulling out the one milk crate she brought back after the yard sale of her parents' belongings. Until now, she couldn't get herself to look at the things she had jammed in it, but tonight, she was curious.

There was a box of costume jewelry she remembered playing with, the woodworking tools she remembered her dad using, their handles dark and smooth with use, and a dozen worn album covers stacked in the back, ranging from, Guns 'N' Roses to The Clash. It wasn't so bad, remembering.

Chapter 13

During a break in baseball practice, a lanky player slips beside the only spectator on the bleachers, a girl pondering calculus homework. He takes out her earbud and whispers – music is like the ocean. The deeper you swim into it, the further away the other shore gets. Ya wanna go swimming with me?

Her legs grew heavy. She willed them to move faster, but they responded like columns of stone. In water up to her neck, she searched through fog for a sign of land anywhere. A slippery stone beneath her feet began to move and knock her off balance, first shifting right, then left, as she searched for a landmark. Her mind felt as foggy as the air. The moving stone kept sabotaging her balance, when through the fog she saw a spot far off on the horizon. The stone slipped away, and she was forced to swim for the spot, hand over hand, countless strokes, but the island never appeared any closer. Mizbie grew exhausted, slowing her stroke to a crawl. Breathing didn't seem to matter anymore. It was so much easier to give up breathing and swimming, to let herself sink, allowing the water to envelop her.

She awoke paralyzed in panic, struggling to move even a finger. The pressure on her chest seemed to push her back into a never ending hole. When she was aware enough to realize the haunting physical force was a dream, she forced herself remake it, as she had that afternoon in Ryder's room.

∾

Last year Jess and Mizbie chose a theme of foods with the letter P in them. Food lovers brought pomegranate smoothies, pineapple with pork, homemade kosher dill pickles, poi that tasted like wallpaper paste, chili rellenos (peppers), Philly cheesesteak, tandoori chicken with peanut sauce, pepperoni pizza from John's pizza (somebody ran out of time on that one), tabouleh (with parsley), pot stickers, pulled pork with heavenly smoky barbecue sauce, pork rinds from a wild boar hunt (a bit tough), and pink pickled eggs. Missing Jess's help this year, Mizbie emailed her food-loving friends to choose foods with a bit of the color red in them.

Hungry people and their food began to arrive shortly after six o'clock in the park behind Mizbie's apartment. They brought spoons, forks, or chopsticks and a dish to share for Mizbie's Second Annual Food Fest. By seven, the clink of serving spoons and the sound of chatter brought Mizbie's neighbors, who had ignored the invitation, to their balconies to see what the aromas drifting up from the park were all about. Park grills sizzled and bowls were passed from picnic table to person and back, their delectable contents picked at until bite by bite, they disappeared and new ones took their places.

A bowl of matzo balls crisscrossed linguine and clam sauce, tandoori chicken again (with red pepper this time), grilled kielbasa, and a spicy cold shredded mango salad. Up from the back grill came lemon and red pepper catfish, then mac and cheese. There was crunchy red-skin potato salad with paprika and green beans smothered with Vidalia onions and bacon, which the cook mentioned was red before it was fried.

Wearing Mizbie's clothes, Stella wove her way through the gathering. With her hair tucked in a baseball cap, she offered her tomato zucchini frittata, which Mizbie had taught her to make. Mizbie made a rough count as she walked around with her own plate and fork, estimating about a third more cooks this year. She didn't recognize everyone with a plate or dish, probably because some friends brought other food-loving pals along. A howl made Mizbie turn to see Guy Heuster eating a habanera pepper, seeds and all. "Damn, that's good!" He grinned.

As it got dark, dishes were emptied, some licked clean. Mizbie climbed the stairs to her apartment and took out a huge bowl of strawberry granita from the freezer. It had taken two days to make, letting the granita set, roughing it up with a fork, then refreezing. On her way out of the kitchen, she grabbed a half-empty bottle of crème de cassis for pouring over the top. By the time she held the dessert out for her stuffed-to-bursting food festees to dive into, her fingers felt frozen.

"Here, dear, let me take that off your hands," Renee smiled, taking the first big scoop. Others then took the bowl, passing it so quickly that, Mizbie had to sprint to pour on the crème. In a few short minutes, the bowl was empty. The group grew smaller, moving like sloths in the dark, looking for their bowls to take home. Mizbie sighed and smiled with satisfaction and a full stomach of her own, oblivious to a man in khaki, finding his way to a plain white van down the block.

After the food fest, Mizbie woke three times before getting up. Her mind raced, dreaming and thinking. She would wake after five minutes, thinking it was an hour, then wake again in a few minutes. Stella seemed to enjoy herself and no one was the wiser. But how long before someone discovered her? She fell back on her pillow. When she awoke again, it was noon and she felt groggy instead of rested, curious about the unreal sense of time in her brain that had tricked her into feeling like she'd fallen asleep for only a few minutes more. She pulled herself out of bed and rushed out to the sofa to see if Stella was still there, but the sheets and quilt were tousled and empty.

"Morning, Miz B. I made you some coffee," Stella said, already sipping her own cup.

Relieved, Mizbie told Stella about the dream. "You were painting a room so big, it never seemed to end. I was helping out, rolling a shade of lavender paint on the wall. Just when we could finally see the wall at the end of the room, a woman came at us screaming. I reached for the paint to throw it at her and then I woke up. Weird, huh?"

Jesspin9
toMBax20
7:00 a.m.
May 25

Hey Miz,

Sorry I missed the Second Annual Food Fest in red. Anybody bring dragon fruit? You might be right about my brother. You said he's probably feeling tied down. He's in Europe with a family to consider and I can go wherever the spirit and my editor moves me. You know how to buck me up. Yes, I got out of jail after a talk with the judge and a €15 fine. He told me to leave town and not to buy any more cupcakes.

You know people who seem completely normal but in their real life they do some pretty wacky insane stuff? How about climbing on the roof with a lucky talisman and singing into the wind to keep evil spirits away from the house? Someone just told me that one. Anyway, I'm reminding you that you weren't crazy to escape your parents' tension with library books. And you know stuff about me but you're sworn to secrecy, right? No one will ever know about that letter I opened before the book interview, especially my brother, Hank.

So here's another story to keep quiet. I know, email isn't safe, but I have to tell you. When I came to Europe, Herrod House didn't provide me with much advance money, so when a woman approached me at the airport and gave me a clear plastic package of drug store cosmetics – all of three ounces – to deliver to Charles de Gaulle Airport, I wasn't that concerned. She looked like a pulled-together businesswoman and she was so grateful. All I had to do was put the bag in my carry-on. I was hardly off the plane when a smiling Frenchwoman in a dark suit approached me for the bag. Shaking my hand while putting a thousand Euros in it, she then disappeared. Then again the French don't smile, so that should've been suspicious. Was it really makeup? Not one of my better decisions. It's been on my mind for months and I had to tell you.

Yesterday on my way to Chamonix near the Swiss border, I stopped at the side of the trail, (packed dirt), to fix a chain, when a snake bit me. I didn't know if it was poisonous or not. It was a brown snake with black diamonds on its back, about medium sized. Minutes later, this Dutch cyclist stopped and helped me with the chain. I told him about the snake, and he reached into his backpack and pulled out some crème de cassis, you know, that liqueur made from currants? I laughed, but he was serious.

"Really. This has been used as a cure for snakebite since the Roman times. Take a drink." he said.

I looked at my heel. Achilles never had it so good! Maybe it was a bit red. I took a swig. The warm, sweet tartness swirled down my throat, leaving a spicy taste. He smiled at me.

"A votre santé!" He said, returning the bottle to his pack and cycling off. I never even caught his name. Why would a cyclist happen to carry that in his pack? I'll never know.

I rode a mile past sunflowers not yet blooming, and there was a raspberry patch. It was mid-morning and the dew was just evaporating from the plants. I chose a berry, checked for bugs, and popped it in my mouth. Such tart pleasure! The lime in the soil must have something to do with the difference in flavor from our raspberries at home, just like wine. Our raspberries are a solo or duet of flavor. These are a chamber orchestra. I tried to identify the flavors, like we would at a wine tasting, Mizbie. I detected lime, lemon, plum, and even green grapes. Looking at each of the little globes of juice just ready to burst in my mouth made me reach in all directions, grabbing berry after berry, stuffing my mouth full, tasting past the little seeds ooh-ing in orgiastic pleasure.

I took my helmet off and felt the breeze. It was one of those simple moments, Miz, that life presents to us if we recognize and take advantage of them. What I didn't see was a farm truck pulling up a one-lane rut, heading right toward me. I turned, berry half-way to my open mouth, when I heard an angry voice. "Allez, allez! Zut alors!"

The berries were irresistible, I explained in my apology. I'm writing a book. I trespassed. I ate. He was not amused or forgiving. The farmer, I later found to be Tristiane, decided to have me work off my debt. He tossed my bike in the back of his truck, strong-armed me into the seat beside him, threw it in reverse straight back – to other raspberry pickers. No, I know you're wondering; I wasn't afraid. This guy had to be 70 and I knew I could flatten him if I needed to. With more fist waving and yelling French too fast to translate, he gave me a basket and ordered me to pick.

I spoke to other pickers, "bonjour, eh bien," mostly high school students and immigrants, maybe illegals. They said, "Don't bruise the berries," and returned to picking silently. I spent the next four hours in hot sun that way. Four hours for a handful of framboise! I mentally figured the cost of those berries in Euros.

A distant cowbell-like ring made everyone stop picking. We placed our baskets in a shaded shed and a truck came to take them. I followed the other workers, still silent, up a curved, rutted path to the farmhouse backyard. In the middle of the yard was a long table, shaded by orange, blooming, trumpet vines. We sat down; there must've been 25 of us at the table covered with a white plastic cloth. At various intervals along the table were carafes of water, wine, and bottles of olive oil with herbs inside.

Two women came from inside the main house with armloads of baguettes, putting them on the table and chatting with the workers, who chatted back after completely guzzling down the water, and then starting in on the wine. The wine had been mixed with water, as they would mix it for children. You can't have tipsy workers picking raspberries, but contented ones are okay. Workers tore off pieces of baguette, drizzled them with olive oil and ate one small piece at a time. I tasted first and then tore off bigger pieces, figuring I'd earned it.

An older woman with a few baguettes left in her arms announced behind me, "And this is the one who was stealing raspberries, ha ha! I think your work has more than paid off your debt, jeune fille." Her voice changed the conversation and everyone began talking at once.

"Keep her all afternoon!"

"Make her also pay off her meal," another followed.

"Non, non . . . if she writes her book, we want her to say good things about our berries." The woman who was Augustine, old Tristiane the truck driver's wife, said. "The Paris bourgeoisie give the rest of us French a snobby reputation. Let her show the real French people in her book." It was agreed. These were the real French in many colors, from pale blonde hair to darkest brown skin, who enjoyed their food and good conversation after work.

After the bread came trays of pears and cheeses, then bowls of Swiss chard and rutabaga. The rutabaga earned groans from the workers, but it was actually tasty, seasoned with nutmeg. I asked Mata, a native Moroccan next to me, why he didn't like it. He answered in passable English. "Eet goes back to World War II," he explained. "Peeple associate rutabaga with the food shortages, when rutabaga was all they had to eat. Eet is a poor man's food. The distaste for eet has been passed down from parent to child to this day."

We ended the petit dejeuner with light vanilla custard, topped with framboise. I couldn't have ordered a better lunch. The Moroccans told stories about their families at home and their dreams to make enough money in France to build a big house for their extended families at home.

Mata had a large family with a wife and seven children, the youngest being two, and a mother-in-law also living with them. That was one reason he was happy to be in France. He loved his homeland though. When I asked him what he missed most, he said it was like trying to explain the Mediterranean Sea with a raindrop. He missed his wife and worried about his son, Karim.

"He is ready to take his weekend journey into manhood this summer. The journey includes survival for 48 hours with nothing but a spear and a canteen of water. I will not be there to greet him when he returns," he said with regret. For his own right-of-manhood journey, Mata killed a wild pig before it killed him, but broke an arm in the process.

Mata was a great storyteller and easily held the attention of everyone at the table as he told about respect for the wild animal and the cunning required for the kill-or-be-killed journey. A celebration ceremony always followed the journey and Mata was torn between missing the rite of manhood and the need to provide support for his family.

Morocco sounded beautiful, the people lively and intense. It became less mysterious than I had imagined. Maybe there's a Morocco book in my future. I heard an engine behind me and there was Tristiane pulling up in the old truck. He brought out my bike for me, chuckling. I thanked him for "kidnapping" me and providing another story to write about. Looking at my watch, I found we'd been eating and storytelling for three hours. Tristiane explained that framboise do not like being picked during the hottest part of the day, so a long lunch for us was best for the berries.

"Here is a handful of berries for the road," he said, pouring out the red globes from a small container. Augustine unzipped a flap on my backpack and slipped in a half baguette, "for your travels," she said. I started pedaling and looked back. Augustine stood there waving goodbye.

Jess

Chapter 14

Overheard on the bus –
You shaved your head bald.
Yeah . . . it's aerodynamic.
The back of your head is bumpy. It looks funny.

M izbie grabbed her little black dress, the default fashion she wore
to weddings and funerals. There was something about the dress
that made her comfortable whenever she wore it. She thought about
the teachers gathered for coffee on Monday mornings before school
started, wearing their black pants, sweaters or turtlenecks. Black was
the color of comfort when looking forward to a whole week from the
vantage point of Monday. Black was the color of defense when confronting 33 faces that wanted to be somewhere else.

From a peg, Mizbie took a black and gray geometric scarf with
wisps of red and draped it to the point of the V neck in front of the dress.
When the *New York Times* fashion page would tout a different color as
"The New Black," that would cause department stores to prominently
carry that color in a seasonal sea of purple or gray. But the women in
Mizbie's world returned to reliable black. She checked the mirror and
adjusted the scarf before heading out the door.

The bride's family told her that Gramma Louise was a safe driver.
Unfortunately, Mizbie didn't pick up on their grins when they said it.
Renee, who had been in Gladwin since the day before, had called to
say her mother, Louise, would be there in a few minutes to pick Mizbie
up for her niece's wedding. Renee thanked her profusely for providing the flute music. Gramma Louise arrived in her turn-of-the-century,

vintage Buick LeSabre. The car looked like it had just been driven off the showroom floor, except for a faded bumper sticker on the back that said, "Believe."

Gramma rolled down her window and peered at Mizbie. Mizbie leaned in and said, "Don't you think this is a bit early? It only takes about an hour to get to Gladwin."

She thought awhile and replied, "This is my only granddaughter. I don't want to miss a thing."

Mizbie plunked her flute case and music on the back seat and sat next to Gramma in front. She began to be suspicious of the early departure time when they hit I-75 and Gramma's top speed was 45 mph. She watched the dashboard light go on as Gramma set the cruise control. That's when she knew she should have rented a Zipcar and driven to the wedding gig herself.

Renee had said the rehearsal for the wedding took place the day before at the home of the bride's friend. Only the humanist wedding officiant was present, but she seemed to know what she was doing. Outside of a concern about black roses and a bridesmaid's shoe that could not be found, it looked like the event would go off smoothly. The groom, a potato farmer, was Jewish, and the rabbi that the family had known for years would also assist. Beforehand, Lucy and the groom had decided which parts of the ceremony would be in the humanist mindset and which parts would be in the Jewish tradition.

Mizbie asked Gramma Louise what her favorite memories were with her granddaughter. "When my Lucy was little, I'd take her to yard sales with me. She was quite the little shopper, always looking for art books and pictures of landscapes," she said. "Lucy's always had an eye for beauty."

Mizbie's feet tapped as she looked out the window at flat farmland. Her band had a gig at Magic Mans tonight, but she turned it down for Renee's niece.

"My Lucy marrying a potato farmer. What will she do so far away from Ann Arbor and her art museum?" Gramma Louise wailed. "She was curator for the U of M, you know."

Mizbie could hear the pride in Gramma's voice. They drove by a lone tractor crossing a field and Mizbie wondered if Lucy's potato farmer knew about landscapes in oil or watercolor. She thought about Corky who was having a Molly Ringwald DVD marathon tonight, while Mizbie would probably do the chicken dance to a DJ's music and eat wedding cake with white icing.

Two hours later, they arrived, very safely, at the county park south of Gladwin. When the motor died, she swung open the door and breathed in the fresh country air, stepping away from Gramma and the cloud of Estée Lauder perfume that had permeated her lungs for the past hours.

Mizbie changed clothes in the park restroom, tuned her flute, and found Renee dressed in black and purple challis. "How's everything?" she asked.

"Oh, the usual family drama," Renee replied. "We were up early this morning. Dirk helped install the huppa, with great difficulty for Chrissakes. I'm glad I'm an athiest." It seems the groom had locked his knees and fainted during the rehearsal, but Mizbie saw him talking to the rabbi, and he looked upright and willing now.

"My niece is insanely happy," Renee said. "Her new life is going to be a change." She shook her head at the thought. "I went to her wedding shower a few months ago in Ann Arbor. We pub hopped from a limousine and scavenger hunted with single men drinking champagne from glasses propped between the bridesmaids' breasts. Weeks later was the shower from the groom's side of the family up here. We played a game called Name That Tool. There were a dozen tools lined up on a table and we had to write down the names of them. I swear, I was completely baffled after the C clamp and the needle-nose pliers.

"These women have their own vocabulary revolving around farming and goat cheesemaking. They flavor the cheese with whatever they have. The ones I sampled were varied in flavor, surprisingly mild and really tasty. I'm thrilled that Lucy found her farmer." Renee almost said maybe there was someone out there for Mizbie too, but stopped in time, knowing her friend would bristle at that. "I'm taking lots of pictures," she said with a Canon in her hand. "Years from now, the camera memories are the ones that stay with us."

Mizbie looked around. Fifty white chairs were situated with an aisle down the middle. An arrangement of calla lilies stood at each side of the huppa. Trees provided a lacy canopy, protection from the sun.

Guests and the wedding party took their places as Mizbie began the bride's processional, Pachelbel's Canon. Mizbie played from memory, watching the faces of Gramma Louise and Renee light up as Lucy placed one slippered foot in front of the other down the aisle. The humanist officiant spoke of the mystery of life and the rabbi spoke a Hebrew prayer before Gramma Louise and the groom's grandmother slowly walked to the huppa to light two candles. Mizbie held the flute, preparing to play Fauré's *Pavane* as the bride and groom solemnly gathered under the huppa, took the two lit candles from their holders and lit the single candle in front of the rabbi.

Mizbie's tension grew as she barely heard the officiant's liturgy of extinguishing two flames and joining them as one. What she envisioned was a wild bird beating its wings against the cage. She stared at the single flickering flame, a barrage of mixed metaphors coming to mind: Don't extinguish yourself. Guard against the pain of the covenant that forces two different people to stay together for their entire lives, even after they grow apart, seething from resentment of lost desire and freedom to live lives of wooden sameness. No matter how much you love them, this is your last chance. If you walk away now, then it won't hurt as much as drifting apart later with all the baggage and lifetime memories. Go now while your electric wires have all their insulation, not later when the wires are frayed, brittle, and volatile.

It was too late. The single flame burned with a steady glow. All eyes were on Mizbie as she realized she was next in the ceremony. Her notes were true, but she couldn't smooth the telltale edge from the tone of her flute. She knew the audience could feel it when they began wincing in their seats. Instead of smiling at her when she finished, the pianist looked at her silently, betraying a fellow musician with his eyes piercing hers from narrow slits.

The rabbi had the bride and groom drink wine from one glass. He wrapped it in linen, and placed it on the grass where the groom smashed it beneath his foot, two souls split and reunited at a higher, deeper level. Mazel Tov! All in all, it was a lovely service, unique as it was. Mizbie did not look forward to leaving. Gramma was not staying for the reception because of the long drive. Mizbie asked around to see if anyone else was leaving early, but unfortunately Renee wasn't leaving until tomorrow and no one "gave a fiddle" as Gramma Louise said, for Mizbie's plight.

Waking up in her own bed the next morning, Mizbie wondered about Lucy, the art curator, giving up her devotion to art for devotion to her potato farmer.

∾

Mizbie hadn't cycled out this far on the rail trail for awhile, but her mood and her singing leg muscles kept telling her just one more hill; *Let's see what's on the other side.* Nature sounds and the smooth trail were forgotten when she was distracted by the scent of fresh basil. She squeezed the hand brakes to scan the horizon and saw a few dozen greenhouses with windows open. Turning her nose west, the scent of the air reminded her of a poem the class read about Zephyrus, the god of the west wind and harbinger of summer breezes. She'd have to find out where that farm was and buy enough basil to line her balcony garden. Her balcony had never yielded enough basil for pesto or shrimp salad, but this summer would be different.

She stopped for a water break at a pond where a white egret picked its way across a fallen log, its mirror image rippling in the water. A blue heron swooped toward her, then changed its mind, unfurling its wings in mid-flight and disappearing in the opposite direction toward the woods beyond.

Weeks ago, one of the last few days of late spring when winter's last rout discouraged spring shoots, Mizbie biked, wearing layers of fleece. It was at the point where the heron was lost from view that she walked that day. Past patches of blood root, she stopped to look at the trillium, ready to bloom. The sound of a shovel in earth made her turn. She found a woman with a paper bag, digging up shovels full of the protected plant. "What are you doing?" Mizbie yelled.

"What does it look like? These don't belong to anybody."

Mizbie stood waiting. The woman gave up, dropped the bag and stomped past her, shovel in hand.

Lifting the nearly full bag, Mizbie tried to find the pock marks where the trillium had been. She found homes for a few and tamped them back in the damp soil. The rest she invented new homes for, parting leaves and squashing the roots of the plants into soil. Nearby she found a clump of ramps. She cut a pinch of the greens with a pocket knife without disturbing the bulbs or roots. They would taste good in potato soup.

Riding over a patch of gravel, Mizbie was suddenly aware of a hissing sound as her bike slowed to a crawl. She hadn't had a flat in a while. Scanning the meadow for shade, perspiration crawled down the center of her back. The breeze had given way to hot, humid, unrelenting sun. "Son of a bitch!" she yelled alone in the open field. "Shithelldamn!" Mumbling similar strings of profanity, she rolled her way up a grassy hill to the shade of a lone pin oak tree.

Leaning the bike against it, she removed a spare tube from the seat pack and flipped the bike upside down to rest on the handlebars. She cursed the tire for being a rear tire, thus harder to change. A milk snake slithered close, its white and red stripes inching closer until it bit the toe of her shoe. "Get the hell off, you bonehead," she yelled, kicking her foot until the snake finally dislodged itself and went flying. Loosening the derailleur, she pulled the tire from the rim, gingerly extracting the tube, pumping it up with her portable pump just enough to detect what happened. A thorn as long as the tire width had broken off inside.

She took the new tube from its box in the bike zipper pocket and fit it into the tire with the air stem in the right place, pumping it up just enough to seat it on the rim. Her hands were slippery with sweat, dust, and grease, but she hadn't thought to bring a towel. Looking around, she pulled a handful of oak leaves, wiping her hands and fingers, then returned to the tire, checking the bead before pumping it full of air.

Without a tire gauge, she'd have to guess at the pressure. A robin sang "Julia-tealeaf" overhead as Mizbie's frustration abated. If she could just get the tire back on without a problem, she could soon cool off with a 15-mile-an-hour breeze. Stretching the slippery derailleur, she eased the wheel in place, snapping the lever tight. The derailleur would not catch the chain. She stretched the chain once more, feeling the grit and grease cling to her fingers and her bike shorts. Finally it clicked in place. She spun the sprocket around with her hand, listening to the satisfying click, then righted the bike.

Grabbing one last handful of leaves to wipe her hands, she looked up into their deep healthy green. Cheek by jowl, this leafy canopy wouldn't miss a few stolen leaves, now littering the grass, with their forgiving dense community.

With each push of the tire pump she repeated, "cheek by jowl," creating a rhythm. Sarah, her childhood friend, used the phrase to justify her move to Glen Arbor. Sarah, now a writer and weaver, made the move when she and her new husband, a folk art carver and painter of wooden crows, decided southwest Michigan didn't quench their artistic thirsts. So they moved to Glen Arbor where, evidently, like-minded artists and writers resided cheek by jowl. Mizbie hadn't heard from Sarah since the move, and missed her renegade shock of brown hair springing like a menace from her forehead, her handmade sweaters, and her biting commentary, told as if every word was spoken to her best friend.

Parking her bike at the edge of town, Mizbie grabbed her water bottle and ducked into the air conditioning of the first commercial building on Front Street, an art co-op. The small shop hummed with energy for a Saturday afternoon and as she stood admiring a handmade paper sculpture, she turned at the sound of a familiar phrase, "It's cheek by jowl in here!"

"Sarah!" Mizbie blurted, open armed, seeing her wiry friend turn and return the hug so strong they could feel each other's ribs.

"Eew! Shower much?" She grinned. Mizbie regretted hugging Sarah's vest with her greasy hands. It was probably handwoven.

Mizbie explained about the flat and they walked across the street to the Tikki Cove for a Belgian beer, Sarah's drink of choice. The outside tables at Tikki Cove were more of an open gazebo with a small raised platform where bands played on weekends. When the weather was warm, everyone ate outside. They walked past the sign that said, "No parrots, elephants, or dogs" and chose a table under a paddle fan. Their table was opposite the guitar player on the platform, but next to a man, in unlaced high tops, slurping crab bisque with a messenger bag beside him. He looked up at Mizbie in recognition, but she didn't connect with him except for his shirt that said "Freebird." She had seen the shirt before.

"So how do you feel about your move to Glen Arbor, Sarah?"

"Like I never want to come back. I'm just here visiting relatives for a few days. Glen Arbor is a place I've had in the back of my mind come to life. Remember when you said you always wanted siblings when you were growing up in Alabaster? That's the way I feel in Glen Arbor with the artist community." Sarah was also an only child. "It's a mecca for people like Val and me. Instead of feeling like we have three heads, we're at home there. People visit from Chicago and locals want organically grown wool without unnatural dyes, and a surprising number of people buy black wooden crows for their porches or dens. It gets a little quiet in winter, but friends become family."

"What an unusual necklace," Mizbie said, noticing the ceramic spirals strung on black leather.

"I picked it up on a trip to Santa Fe with Val. We might spend a few months there next winter after the season's over in Glen Arbor. Anyway, we were on Canyon Road and I found a friend of a friend's gallery and walked in the front door. I heard a voice. 'Come around to the back.' There he was, a Geppetto with a potter's wheel, caressing this blob of clay. 'You're welcome to watch,' he said, not looking up or taking his attention from the project. He pulled the blob up and out until it became something, somewhere between a plate and a bowl, perfectly round. With a wire, he loosed it from the wheel, then he hacked off a quarter of the edge. I gasped and he laughed. 'This is how collectors know it is mine,' he said.

"He reached behind him, peeled back a towel and picked up a delicate clay insert to fill the hacked-off part. It looked like worms crawling through lace. I'd never seen anything like it. He worked quickly, attaching the worm ends to the plate bowl, occasionally adding slip and spraying the whole thing with water so it wouldn't dry too soon. Right then I knew this was where I wanted to work.

"I took out a few pieces I'd brought with me and showed him photos of more of my work. He agreed to show a half dozen of my pieces a year, and directed me to a small space where I could work in back. Val and I can live there too. After a year, we'll see how things go and renegotiate. It's a *milagro*, a miracle, as they say."

She took the necklace off and put it around Mizbie's neck. "It's an ancient Pueblo symbol for the life force, the migration of native peoples. Now it's yours."

"Oh, Sarah. It's the most meaningful piece of jewelry I've ever had." Mizbie touched the swirl in the hand-crafted glaze. Mizbie had nothing to give her friend, but had a sudden impulse to spill her secret. She had nearly revealed it by accident a dozen times that week. Each time, her frontal cortex kicked in to stop her. To reveal the secret in school could end her career. Stella had agreed it was best not to tell anyone, especially students or staff at school. If they could just make it until the end of the school year, some arrangement could be made during the summer, and no one would have to know. But the longer Mizbie kept the secret, the stronger her desire became to profess it. Holding it was stressful. Letting it out, getting rid of it would provide relief. Just having one person know would make it bearable. "Now I have something to tell you."

Mizbie reasoned if she told Sarah, who was going home to Glen Arbor soon, no one else would find out. Sarah was a woman she could trust. She relayed the plight of Stella, how she couldn't imagine her living in a school locker room for months, and how much Stella needed the routine in a stable household that Mizbie took for granted. "We can't let anyone know at school or they'll have to call the authorities. Stella was in the foster care system for awhile and has nightmares, so I'm her mentor now. Her grades are excellent and she's applied for a few college scholarships. Sarah, you should see her curled up sleeping on my couch. She woke up from a nightmare. She was terrified, so vulnerable and alone. I can only imagine what her life was like before."

"That's a big secret. I don't know what to say, Miz, but knowing you, I can see why you didn't turn her in. Let me check into a few of the summer camps by Glen Arbor and see if they need counselors. That might be a way for her to earn some extra money and escape prying eyes."

Sylvia, the owner of Tikki Cove, zigzagged between tables to serve them, a growler of beer in her hand. It seemed that Sylvia was always in the kitchen or on the patio, picking at the waitstaff, washing dishes, then chatting up the customers from noon to close, her swaying gray hair and jangly beads always in motion. At night she would return to her home on a cul-de-sac to play with her dogs, meditate, and cogitate on a disagreement with one of the youngest of her customers who dismissed the idea of blocking off the main artery of town in an antiwar protest in favor of flash mobbing the department store to sing, "This Song's for You." As if that would change the world.

Sylvia had been widowed for years and Tikki Cove was her retirement income. Her only son worked for a multinational company and uprooted his wife and two kids every three years for another European country, climbing the ladder, but what was the point? They had two years to go in Luxembourg, where they had a country club membership in the same club as their second grader's teacher. During Sylvia's visit last summer, while they were sunning by the pool, Lindsay said, "Grandma, here's my teacher."

There she was, all right, half naked, the top half. Sylvia watched her son, who had a hard time keeping his eyes on the conversation. Two years, and two more Christmases, until she'd see them again. If she didn't call them once a week, she'd hardly hear from them at all. Lindsay and Liam sent pictures, though. Her refrigerator was covered with them. When new ones replaced old ones, they were carefully placed in a folder. Sylvia had planned to put them in scrapbooks to give to the grandchildren when they graduated.

Sarah offered Mizbie a tissue for the grease streak on her cheek. Mizbie spied someone out of the corner of her eye. "Don't go away," Mizbie said. She sprang out of her chair and ran across the street. There stood her student, Brandon, barely able to hold up his head. She took Brandon's hand and put it around her shoulder, helping him walk back to their table. He needed a shower more than she did, and he leaned heavily on her – each slow step was an effort. He looked like he hadn't slept in a week.

"Brandon. We missed you in class. Where have you been?" Mizbie asked

"I don't know, Miz B. I'm here. How'd I get here?" He looked around and plunked himself in a chair. Mizbie noticed his shirt was buttoned wrong. Under the shirt was white tape rolled around his ribs.

"You've been gone three days. And look how sunburned you are." Puzzled, Mizbie looked at his red arms and face. Brandon usually didn't get out in the sun much.

"Three days? I – can't remember. The last I remember, I was playing video games –"

"What happened to you, son?" Sylvia came to the table. "You look like a dug-up sweet potato. Let me get you a cool cloth."

Mizbie grew anxious as he tried unsuccessfully to piece together the last few days that had escaped him. "Brandon, something's wrong. We've got to get you to a doctor."

"Wait . . . I remember a guy in a blue shirt. He gave me shots." He opened his wrists and the three of them looked at a series of tiny holes, the kind from inoculations in his arm.

"Brandon, what have you done?"

"It's not drugs. I don't do drugs. It's that blue-shirt guy. I don't know!" He grew more agitated, glancing from side to side and back to Mizbie. "Help, Miz B. What's wrong with me? Why can't I remember?"

"I don't trust just anybody," Mizbie said, covering the tiny holes with her hand, calming the tension in her voice. "So if I trust you, you must be telling the truth. Do you remember anything else besides the blue-shirt guy?"

He squinted his eyes as if he was trying to remember tectonic plates or an answer for a quiz. "I remember it was really hot and my hand was taped. There was something really heavy in my hand. I could hardly lift it up."

Brandon lived with his older brother, whom Mizbie remembered from parent-teacher conferences. Their parents had died two years ago, but his brother said, "I'm responsible and I want what's best for Brandon." Even so, his job kept him away most nights.

"Let's get a hold of your brother." Mizbie reached for her phone.

"I can't remember the number." He reached for his own phone. "My phone's gone. I don't know what my brother does or where he goes. He tells me not to ask questions, so I don't anymore."

Sarah and Mizbie looked at each other. "C'mon and get in my car," Sarah said. "Let's find this brother of yours."

After checking Brandon's home, a neat, modest bungalow, they left a note for his brother and took Brandon to a nearby clinic.

On Monday, Mizbie relayed the experience to Renee, including the confrontation with Brandon's brother and his feigned innocence. "Renee, Brandon's brother knows something. If they ever try to hurt Brandon again, they'll be in a world of trouble and I told him so. You wouldn't have believed the look on Brandon's face. He was completely lost. He couldn't remember a thing." The story tumbled out of Mizbie as she expressed her relief that Sarah was there to help. She imagined Stella in such a situation and shuddered.

"How badly was he hurt?"

"The doctor said he had two cracked ribs and he'll have headaches, but he should recover completely. While we were in the doctor's office, Brandon remembered something. The doctor heard it too. Brandon said there was a bunch of guys in a farmer's field. The crop had been cut and he remembered the stubble was cutting his hands and face. Something heavy was taped to his hand, and the guys were laughing, telling him to point the heavy thing at something that moved in the field. Then he came out of it."

"What do you think it was?"

"What do *you* think? That's when Brandon's brother came in. He hugged Brandon, nearly cracking another rib it seemed, and I could tell he was alarmed. I mentioned that our next stop was the police and he said he'd take care of everything. But what if Brandon was drugged and what if he shot someone? Is a person who committed a crime while under the influence of drugs guilty of murder?"

"Miz, how do you get involved in these things?" Renee said. "Let the police figure it out."

"I was obsessing about it Sunday, so I called Desmin's aunt, Ms Gray – she works for the prison system. She said 20 percent of crimes are drug related, but he's a minor and a first-time offender. He wouldn't be incarcerated with adults and he'd get schooling in prison."

"What if they don't find a body? Don't they have to find a body?" Renee said.

"Not always," Mizbie said. "Back in the 1600s in England there was a case where they hanged a man for a girl's disappearance. After the hanging, she showed up a few days later."

"Poor Brandon," Renee said.

"Ms Gray said she's seen these things before. They probably grabbed Brandon for fun or to get his brother's attention. Maybe he was trying to get out of whatever he's involved with. She doubted they would actually have Brandon murder a rival and bring attention to themselves. These groups weren't usually that over-the-radar. I hope they really went to the police. Sylvia, from the Tikki Cove, is going to look in on Brandon for the next few days and bring him food from the restaurant. I think I'll check the police this afternoon to see if –"

"Miz, you can't save every student. You've done what you can. Let it go," Renee put her arm around Mizbie.

Mizbie looked at her friend and bristled at the phrase. Did Renee know that Stella was living with her? If Renee knew, that meant everyone knew. She changed the subject. "So how are the newlyweds?"

"They sent a picture from Poland yesterday." She reached for her phone to find the picture. "Lucy's husband was asked to go there and talk to a group of farmers, like the grange of Poland or something, so they combined their honeymoon with his work."

Mizbie looked at the serious young couple standing on a bridge. "Somehow, Lucy doesn't seem like the potato-farmer wife type."

"I can't see it either, but all you need is love, right?"

"That's what they say."

Heuster walked up as Mizbie unlocked her bike after school. Mizbie looked him over. "You're looking good today. Did you win your competition over the weekend?"

"I came in second. The guy who beat me, I tell ya, had to be working out eight hours a day. He was a powerhouse. Ya just can't keep that up."

"Second isn't bad."

"Yeah," he scratched himself. "I was okay with it. I think it's the yak urine. I got these capsules online. It's supposed to be Tibetan yak, but the capsules are from China. I take a couple a day. It's supposed to enhance your overall well-being. You know, Gandhi drank his own urine every morning."

"I didn't know that," Mizbie said absently. "I want to ask you something, Heuster. This guy in a white van seems to be following me. He's everywhere I bike. I see him in different places every day when I leave from school, even if I leave at different times." Her voice lowered. "He doesn't follow closely, but if I end up at the Fit for U or Bean and Leaf, there he is watching from around the corner or at the end of the block."

Mizbie's voice grew more exasperated. "I want to go nose to nose with the guy and tell him to bug off before I call the police. But now I'm thinking you might be a more fearsome option. What do you think?"

Heuster smiled, crossing his muscled arms. "I bench pressed 250 last night. Let me know when you're doing the nose to nose and I'll stand right beside you. Just like this. He looked down at Mizbie with a scowl. His gripping gaze poked holes through her. If she didn't know him, she'd swear he was about to do a job for the mob, or at least act as a bodyguard in an action film.

"You can be one scary guy," she said, smiling. "You're hired."

He laughed, hitting her on the arm. She was sure he thought it was a playful tap, but she'd probably have a small bruise tomorrow. Perfect, she thought.

"If you feel like you're being followed, don't run, but walk like hell to a public place and bury yourself in a crowd. This is unless I'm there.

In that case, just point him out to me and I'll take care of him for you. Seriously," Heuster said.

She cycled back to her apartment, but didn't see the man or his white van. She pulled open her sliding door and looked over the balcony at the park, where a group of jugglers practiced, alternating balls and clubs, one woman juggling with two young men, laughing when one of them dropped a club. She told Stella to put on a baseball cap and watch with her. A freshman she recognized from school, not hers, was juggling balls with sparkly insides. Farther back in a clearing past the trees, a larger group of young men practiced Dagorhir, which means "battle lords," a role-playing competition dreamed up from *Lord of the Rings* that Carl had once explained. This unit practiced every Tuesday afternoon, spring through fall, with full weaponry and equipment, and protective armor. Mizbie sometimes watched their animated crusades as they swung padded swords, launched padded arrows, and hacked away at one another with padded axes while their girlfriends, wives, and children watched from under the trees with picnics on blankets.

Stella retreated to her homework, but Mizbie decided it was too lovely a day to be inside. She grabbed her papers to correct and headed for a park table. As she sat, putting papers in order and drinking an ice-cold tea, her eyes scanned the streets for the white van. There he was, pulling away from the hardware store parking lot on the adjacent block, out of her sight.

Jesspin9
toMBax20
8:00 a.m.
April 13

Hey Miz,

I read your email about your flat and had to tell you I nearly face planted myself on a chip-and-seal road yesterday. Those roads are anathema on road bikes, but they're not so good on mountain bikes for long distance either. True, back tires are a bear to fix with the derailleur, but a flat front tire can flip you right over if you have any speed going into it.

My train from Montbéliard leaves tomorrow. I'm in an Irish pub, the Hungry Eye, in Pascalville just south of town, and as you can see they have free Wi-Fi. Every town I've been to in France has at least one Irish pub with its heavy dark wood, brass bars, and some stained glass in front. I'm listening to the issues of the world being discussed, like the ebb and flow of the garbage water that breathes in and out on the banks of the River Liffey in Ireland. Flotsam and jetsam of life's travails, never pauses long enough to regain bearings before moving on. There is one local politician bellying up to the bar next to me. He's talking too fast for me to understand, but he's boiling over about some bridge-repair issue. The heartbeat of a neighborhood pulses through the neighborhood pub.

Out of the corner of my eye I'm watching a guy and, I would guess, his girlfriend. I could write a bodice ripper about them some day. Here's how the scene will go: he'll reach for her hand, then slowly look up, catching sparkles of understanding in her eyes. All the illnesses and depression (there has to be depression), all the friction with relatives, and all the misunderstood conversations clear away like fog at dawn. She finally understands what this was all about. He has rediscovered her; their insights mesh at last.

What do you think? I'll name them Anais and Maxime.

Actually, I've been sitting here for two hours, my chapter sent to Herrod House minutes ago. I've already heard the town "story." Pascalville, a one traffic-circle village, sleepy with grain elevators and farm markets, is ripe with social networking – the old fash-ioned way with rumor. According to the pensioner playing chess behind me, the town's first murder occurred last year, jarring the little village into suspicion and worry about those still alive who deserved to be victims themselves. Jon Couson, a local farm owner, had a respected opinion about goings-on at the cemetery before the death occurred. The cemetery was a meeting place for gravestone tracers, high school Goths, and photographers looking for orbs. It seems Hertha, the victim whose body was still unaccounted for, frequented the gravestones with her camera.

Hertha's pictures were an extension of her personality and ended up around town in odd places –, on community posters, at the local college, and on the backs of the petrol station bathroom doors, men's and women's. One picture, taken when Hertha was fresh out of high school, was from a canoe trip up the Anjou. She set the auto shutter and joined three bedraggled canoe mates as they uprighted their soggy vessel.

Now it seems new evidence has been unearthed at the sight of that canoeing picture; her bracelet with the phrase"plus ca change" on it. I guess that's short for "the more things change, the more they remain the same." How intriguing! The waitress here was one of Hertha's friends. This along with Anais and Maxime over in the corner might make a great short story. I'm taking notes.

But enough of conjecture, on to a bit of perspective here. When I stepped off the night train in Montbéliard (almost Germany) a few days ago, it felt like stepping back in time to the triple digits, around 985 actually, or back in the "Roman times" as they say. In the 11th century it became part of the German Empire, then after the French Revolution, it became part of France, one of the few Protestant/Lutheran bastions from all that old German influence, you know. The Württemburg family from German times left their mark on architecture and the local castle, with its coat of arms: two jumping fishes under a palm tree. Don't you think that would be a colorful word picture for my book? My book with my name on the cover, my book that will surely outlive me, like a child. My book IS my child, Miz.

When I wheeled my bike off the train, I noticed the brake was loose. C'est le fin de la vericottes, as they say, that's the way it goes, the end of the beans. I walked my bike to the first breakfast place I saw, Vela –, named for a sail-shaped constellation, even though Montbéliard is landlocked, ha ha. I'm standing there surrounded by bikes, getting out my tool kit when a guy walks up. "How about a Segway ride. Thirty Euros for two hours? I'll show you the Hotel

De la Balinée, les halles (shopping), everything you want to see."
Thirty Euros was a bit steep, but I've always wanted to ride one of
these things, so I said okay.

I explained that I just needed to fix my brakes and have breakfast. "Let me treat you to breakfast. I will tell you about our city, things you would not find out from anyone else. Then you come ride with me, eh?"

Where have I heard that before? Then he flashed his smile and I couldn't refuse. We had savory croque monsieur hollandaise with crabmeat, and he explained how he'd lost his job at the Peugeot factory where he'd worked for seven years. His father had worked there and he expected that would be his life too. We walked a few doors down, past hanging baskets of flowers and a fruit seller under an umbrella, to his Segway shop. He locked up my bike in his shop and gave me some time to practice the balance of the Segway; he held the handlebars while I stepped on. "Where's the brake?"

"There isn't one," he laughed. "Just move the handlebar toward you when you want to slow down. But don't move too far back or you'll fall off."

It didn't take much practice in the courtyard behind his shop before we were zipping around Montbéliard's sidewalks at 12 kph, turning on a dime at hotels and castles, and even the old Peugeot factory with its green dome.

Our tour ended up being 2 ½ hours and Leon, my guide, indeed did show me places I wouldn't have searched out on my own. "This doesn't seem like the dour serious Calvinist town I expected at all," I told him.

"I'm glad to break from the mold of your thinking," he said, which means insights, I hope, rather than moldy thoughts.

"You can fix your brake here," he said, wheeling it into the courtyard for me. He then brought out his tools and nearly did all the fixing himself. "Just give me a good review on your American travel website. Five stars, yes?" he said. "Remember if you take your bike on Mayard Street," he pointed around the corner, "it is all cobblestone; it could jar your teeth out of your head."

I like Montbéliard. Maybe I'll return someday. Before I catch my train tomorrow, I may have to stop by Vela for one more crab croque monsieur!

A demain –

Jess

Chapter 15

Overheard in the hallway –
– Oooh, fight.
Where?
In the gym.
Worst place.
Yeah . . . my mom says fight at home. As long as no blood's drawn, she
doesn't care.

Jesspin9
to MBax20
8:00 a.m.
May 26

Hey Miz,
I'm with a group of cyclists for a couple of days, just outside
of Monte Carlo. The country of Monaco is less than a square mile,
so it's easy to traverse the border and back. Workers who live
in France or Italy arrive every day. The whole place looks like a
James Bond movie from the '60s. They let us in the lobby of the
casino, but we weren't dressed enough to actually see the casino
itself. The place is electric with the Grand Prix starting tomorrow.
Unfortunately, we have to leave this afternoon, but there are piles
of tire barricades for safety and crowd control. The hairpin turns
have to be seen to be believed.
Yesterday was Sunday and we treated ourselves to brunch at
the Fairmount Hotel at the base of the most extreme hairpin curve,

238

right by the Mediterranean. The fresh vegetables and fruits, local seafoods, and breads were beautifully presented on curving island tables and the desserts were works of art. They tasted as luscious as they looked. Our umbrella-covered table on a patio overlooked miles of sandy coastline and mountains. We watched a small ship pull up to the dock of the hotel.

Yesterday we walked our bikes up the 50 steps on the northern side of the city to see an ancient monastery with a gorgeous view of the ocean. On the other side of the street was France. For dinner we found a little bouchon called Tip Top. I ordered a spicy tomato dish with local mussels and little octopi, their formule or special for the day. Alexandre, our waiter, said he could take a break after my meal and offered to drive me around the Grand Prix route on his motorcycle if I wanted. Of course I said yes, I didn't realize he meant to go around the track at the speed of light. Jeez! I was hanging on to him so tight, I think neither of us could breathe, but I could hear him laughing. Tomorrow I'm off to Italy.

Jess

❧

Singer couldn't wait for his senior year to end, along with the attention he never wanted. His gigs with the band, his position on the track team, even casual overheard words with friends were both worshiped and demonized by classmates behaving like paparazzi in a virtual tabloid. A raised eyebrow or a simple comment could be taken out of context, twisted, hyperbolized, mocked, checked for sexual ambiguity, and texted beyond recognition. He was a fish jumping to escape from the bowl.

The Monday after his gig, he wore his brown leather jacket with a stand-up collar that had become part of his identity at school. It suited him. He found it after a late-night gig last summer, splayed across a picker bush behind their venue. It was just distressed enough to give it an edgy look and even the procurement story added a sense of mystery. People looked at him as if he was someone not to be messed with when he wore it, so it was an easy choice of attire.

He was surprised to see a handmade sign taped to his locker that said "Singer is the 1." Maybe the band had untapped potential, like the venue manager said. Maybe music was in his blood like Miz B kept telling him. The band decided to play his new song with the '90s track looped in the background, and might even decide to put it on the B side of their new seven inch. "To Infinity and Back" got a decent response from the crowd. He was thinking about a few chords to tweak the next time he played it. He wasn't suspicious of the side glances as he worked the numbers of the com.

When the combination clicked and he opened the locker door, his throat caught from an overpowering stench. He backed away. "Oh, man, what reeks?"

He looked down to see a brown paper bag of shit. Hadn't Seth just said yesterday how he hated the job of cleaning up after the pigs? But Seth wouldn't do this. Students began to gather around making gagging noises.

"Sucker punch, bro." Robin wasn't joking when he slapped Singer on the back.

He and Robin read the words written on the bag, printed in black marker, WAT YOUR WORTH, in capital letters. An anonymous sticky note on his history book said, "I loved you before you were hot. Now I hate you."

∾

"I know it was good writing, Miz B," Seth said. "None of us wants to read any more good writing. Give us some bad writing for a change. There's only so much good writing we can take."

"Why do we keep reading good writing?" she paused. "You can't take it anymore you say?" She heard a few groans. "Is it a waste of time to struggle with life's deepest and most eternal questions? Aren't we students of humanity, learning what it means to be human? How to conduct ourselves in the world?" She walked around the room.

"Even Michael Jackson searched for a way to achieve immortality. Like Michelangelo, he tried to bind his soul to his work. After he died, people all over the world danced together to his song, "Thriller." People everywhere made this tribute, this remembrance! Do you think that's a waste of time too?"

"Think about this." Mizbie wrote a quote across the board. "Who said, 'Loyalty to petrified opinion never broke a chain or freed a human soul?'

"Huh? What's petrified?" Justin said.

"You know man . . . like the trees. Stone that useta be wood a long time ago," Desmin said.

Justin laughed.

"What's funny about that?" Izzy said.

"Break free . . . that feel pretty good . . . like free you up," Desmin said.

"Chains from slavery," Izzy said.

"Okay . . . this dude is so Civil War." Justin moved his desk and scraped the floor.

"Who had petrified opinion?" Mizbie stood by Justin and raised her eyebrow.

"I wish Mara Jade was here . . . unchanging, unwieldy, stubbornness. That would be southern leaders. Jefferson Davis. Grant." Izzy said.

"What are you, some history book? That ain't funny, man," Desmin said.

"That's the way the northerners see it. I'm from Georgia. We wanted to preserve our way of life. Good southern folk don't want to be told what to do by some Yankee. It means we have to look beyond our own ideas; we have to be open to like, different opinions. Old opinions that don't change aren't going to do anything but give us the same stuff. Souls can't be chained to the past." Izzy adjusted her glasses.

"That's all 'Kum Ba Ya' stuff. Where's the funny in that?" Desmin said.

Mizbie explained that they were right about the time period, and the quote was from Mark Twain. "Imagine how Twain would respond to issues today? Terrorism in the Middle East?"

"Same thing," Izzy said.

"Social networking?"

"He'd be on it for hours every day, just like us." Justin dropped a book.

"Business-class flight?"

"Quicker than long ship voyages to speaking engagements, but he'd miss his cigars," said Edward.

"Teflon fabric?"

"He'd make all of his white suits out of it to keep them clean," said Rashmi.

Mizbie passed out *Lord of the Flies,* their last novel of the year. She expected a comment from Desmin, but saw him focused on his forearm and Rashmi's. They were talking about skin color. At least he wasn't interrupting class. "What's with you, Justin?" she asked as she passed his desk.

His head dropped to his hands.

"You look like you've been wallowing in the pit of despair. Pull yourself out of it."

Justin shot up out of his seat. "What do you know? You . . . just you don't talk to me." He pushed the rest of his books on the floor and stormed out.

"Man, don't you know nothin'? Din't you hear the news?" Desmin asked. "Justin's brother is missing."

"Lance? Missing from what?" Mizbie countered.

"He in some country in the Middle East doin' tech work. Some liberation tech thing."

"He's a liberation technologist," Izzy said. "He takes a backpack with Internet components and gives them to people in countries where the governments have taken away their Internet access to have more control over them. He was just moving to a new location and now he's disappeared."

"Lance," Mizbie's voice dropped. "was in my freshman English class. He used to be fascinated by computers, even then," she said. "I remember he worked with the school tech specialists during the summer. I have to tell Justin I didn't know. Everyone be kind to Justin today. I'm sure he's worried about his brother."

The bell rang and she walked to the hallway directly into a tsunami of punches between two muscular boys who towered over her. The crowd grew and she yelled, "Who's losing? Who's losing?"

"The kid in the black shirt," someone replied.

"Hey, black shirt! Black shirt, out NOW!" Mizbie yelled.

The smaller black-shirted boy tore himself away from the fight. She figured he was grateful. She took him by the arm to the office, and left the other fighter red faced with no one to hit. Although she didn't know the name of either boy, the other name would surely come out under the determined questioning of Mr. Krahler. "So, was it worth it?" she asked.

Black shirt rubbed his arm. "He looked at me funny," he answered.

Jesspin9
toMBax20
4:20 p.m.
May 20

Hi Miz,

I'm still here in San Gimignano outside Siena, Italy, longer than I expected to be. I finally got my stipend. I was flat out of money and my editor had amputated my whole chapter on Barcelona as trite and flat, so I was feeling down when I found a truck stop on my way south. I smelled fresh bread and paella. Not only did it smell good when I peeked in the cooker, it had fresh Mediterranean mussels and clams, and the tomatoes were local. I guess truck drivers know where to eat here, just like they do in the states. I asked if there was any day labor and the cook told me about the lavender farm down the road, so I took a job harvesting lavender with a bunch of tourists. It really wasn't bad. They gave us room and board, youth hostel style, work for five hours a day, and the rest of the day was our own.

Here's a quick study on lavender. I didn't realize there were so many kinds. Of course, the French think theirs is the best, but the English variety is more fragrant. The lavender here could hold its own against any of them I'll bet. The season can be a long one, up to nine months if you keep snipping the blossoms, so it wasn't hard to be here in "the season." The bushes are about five feet tall, so snipping off blossoms is actually pleasant. The owners dry the blooms and sell them in bunches as potpourri, or put them in something called sleep pillows. In a tag on the pillow, it claims if you sleep on the pillow, you'll dream of the lover you'll marry. I've worked the stand a couple of times and there have been young people stopping their bikes. They read the tag, smile, then buy a pillow. I had to restock a couple times. I have to admit, smelling all this lavender for about a week now has mellowed me out.

I've taken a few bike rides up through the hilly, cedar-lined paths to see the abbey with its one famous Annunciation painting that the people in town were talking about. If you take the steps down off the Appia Antica, there is a smaller version of the catacombs under Paris. Back in the early Christian days, they preferred to bury their dead instead of cremating, and they were too poor to buy land. They were persecuted then, but that isn't why they buried their dead here. The catacombs allowed them to bury their dead in communities rather than alone. After they were allowed to buy land, a wealthy landowner would open his area to others of the faith. It's not a gruesome as it sounds. It's actually peaceful, like its own meandering sanctuary.

They secretly celebrated the Eucharist there, celebrated anniversaries of the saints, but didn't use them as places to hide. The galleries or niches were cut out by fossores or gravediggers who put the rocky earth in baskets and carried it out. Light and air came in from skylights. It really didn't smell bad at all down there;

it just felt cool and quiet like a well-kept basement. There were a few tourists there with me, but I still felt at peace. I can see why believers would seek out these places for pilgrimage and renewal. With all the arrangements of flanges, femurs, and skulls in arches and circles, it's more a tribute to life than a memorial of death.

I wanted to talk to one of the monks, but the one who spoke English wasn't available for a few hours. The day ticked along as it does when you're waiting and all you want is to get on with your plans. I rode my bike down a nearby pedestrian walkway/alley and stopped to see some colorful ceramic earthenware, probably from Urbino. It seems pretty safe here, but I'm always aware of my passport, wallet, and room key in the linen zipper bag under my shirt. I found a street wagon and picked up a tomato and buffalo mozzarella salad in olive oil along with a sparkling Pellegrino for lunch before heading back to find my monk. A prelate silently motioned me through the gates, across a courtyard, through a front hall and back to a dark corner room lined with books that smelled of old leather. From a small narrow window, I spied an herb garden with flowers.

"Benvenuto! Welcome! You have some questions about the catacombs, no? Cripta under the earth. Our brethren are there. Centuries of monks, Christians from within and outside the city walls, saints, now fragments of lives. Most people come and pay the admittance, then leave a few minutes later. You stayed. You waited to come back and talk with me."

I leaned toward the monk in the robe the color of caramel latte, tall and wiry with a smile like the Dalai Lama. "The catacombs aren't as morbid as I thought. I can't explain it, but they're comforting . . ."

He chuckled. "We're on this earth a short time, a vacanza, a vacation. We are dead for eternity, a very long time."

He raised his hand and motioned to a picture on the wall opposite the reading table he probably used for a desk. I followed the direction and saw in the picture a child's face, radiant, calm, and hopeful.

"That child was one of the last to be buried in the cripta. He died of a fever a year after his picture was painted. Look at it closely."

I walked over and looked at the brushstrokes in the natural light. The artist's name was Lippi. Whether it was the kind smile of the monk or the strange comfort of the catacombs, it was a curious, memorable afternoon.

But how I happen to still be here is another story. When I got off the train and unloaded my bike, I discovered there was some horse race between Fiorenza and Siena, so there was absolutely no place to stay, let alone a place with a spare seat for dinner. Vittorio, a local man with a sack of garlic and Serrano peppers, good sign, offered to take me home to his place for dinner. He said I did not want to eat in the local restaurants anyway; he made the best food in town in his own kitchen and he had the best view too. All this and he didn't even know what I did for a living! How could I pass that up?

We walked the five blocks past lemon trees in courtyards and fragrant jasmine twined around an archway, up the stairs to his ordinary second-floor flat. He let me walk in the door first, and the smell immediately made me look for the bathroom. There with the door open was an old man with rubber gloves, standing over the toilet pushing something, through a sieve down into the bowl. He turned to me, smiled and waved with his yellow glove, "Bo journo."

"Papa, privacy!" Vittorio chided, closing the door. "That's my great-grandfather. He fought in the war, but now his mind isn't so good."

"What's he doing?"

"Oh, he's going through his poop looking for worms. It's something he has to do. You can't talk him out of it."

On a small patio was strung a clothesline, just like everyone else's. On the clothesline were three adult diapers, neatly clothespinned. "He does this too, Papa does."

Vittorio quickly unpinned them and put them in the trash. "He won't remember that I've thrown them away." Vittorio looked at me out of the corner of his eye for my reaction. I didn't know whether to be stunned or fascinated by my new companion's family. "Papa and I used to go fishing. He taught me how to make flys for fly fishing. He'd tell me stories about the war. A real storyteller he was. He's forgotten most of them now, of course, but I remember. I'll tell my son someday."

"So . . . let's start with dinner. You help? Look at these tomatoes. San Marzano. We'll make a sauce."

"Sure. I'll sauté the garlic," I told him.

"No, I think we'll bake it and squeeze it in later. About two heads will do," he said. We washed our hands with lemon soap, and he took a couple of chops with a forged blade knife on the butcher block, popping the heads of garlic in a ceramic dish and sliding them in the contemporary gas oven. "Now we'll bathe the tomatoes and peel –"

"Basta!" The door opened and slammed. In walked a girl with mascaraed raccoon eyes, pierced tongue, and a pink stripe down her long black hair. From my limited Italian I picked up something about "That *#! principal, that @! * teacher, that *!# Cici who said she was my friend, they all spoiled my birthday. When I find out who told, I'm gonna whip their –"

"Francesca, clean up your mouth. We have a guest," Vittorio barely raised his voice. "Say hello to Jess."

"Bo journo . . . and today's my birthday!" she continued. "Cici said I was the one who sent the naked breast picture and –"

"What picture?" Vittorio stopped his tomato trimming.

"A picture I sent to Raymond. He wasn't supposed to send it. He pushed the wrong button." She stomped her foot. "Basta! I'm suspended from school until Monday and it's not my fault!" She dropped her backpack on the floor, took a few long strides to her room, and slammed the door.

"Is that your sister?" I asked.

"No, my niece, my brother's girl. Her mom died giving birth to her and my brother has a time with her. He doesn't know about 14-year-old girls. She is turning into a feisty Italian woman, yes? But she has a good heart."

I chopped onions with Vittorio in his kitchen. I'd never seen anyone sauté chopped onions in olive oil over such low heat, for nearly half an hour. He looked at me and kept stirring with a practiced hand, saying it was for sapore dolce or sweetness. The onions cooked down to a caramel brown color before he added the fresh vegetables and herbs. We poured the tomato sauce over mustaccoli and added the fragrant roasted garlic. Vittorio made a cherry tomato and pecorinni salad with rosemary and olive oil, and poured wine from a dark Sicilian grape, nero d'avola, with pasta – dolce salato! Yum! For dessert, almond biscotti to dip in limoncello served with apricot bars. After dinner Francesca had calmed and we sang happy birthday to her –, Papa, Vittorio, her dad (Silvio), and me.

"What about the great view you mentioned?" I asked. You said it was the best in San Gimignano."

"Ah that view," Vittorio said. "Come here." He led me by the hand to the bathroom. I hesitated, but there were no remains left from Papa's earlier efforts. From the small bathroom window I could see the rooftops of town, punctuated with centuries-old towers, and a road that angled down to a valley of blue and green hills beyond. A yellow orange sun slipped behind the cedars and through shadowy fields of olive groves.

"Ooh . . ." I said without thinking. It was a view beyond words at that moment in the day.

He squeezed my hand. "I will leave you to your view," he said.

How strange that they would build an apartment like this with the best view from the bathroom. Then again, this building was clearly centuries old. It wouldn't have been a bathroom then, and the view would be quite different, in some respects, except for the olive groves. Maybe that's why Papa wanted to spend his time here with his sieve and rubber gloves.

Vittorio kept putting off my departure saying, "Before you go, there is just one more thing you must see." He led me down the steps, back to the cobble-stoned town square, down a narrow alley, past a ceramics shop with a dozen colorful plates of the shop owner's design, displayed outside on the wall.

"This is where you taste gelato," he said. "Don't go for the piled high fluffy stuff you see the tourists lining up for. This is real gelato."

I looked at the flavors, wine, hazelnut, tiramisu, and lemon. "Buona sera. Hazelnut and tiramisu mixed, per favore," I asked the girl behind the counter. Egg yolk, milk, fruit, and sugar made the perfect mix of tart and sweet. Vittorio laughed at my adulation.

"Just one more thing you have to see. You can go tomorrow," he said. And so three days later, I'm still here. I am due in Parma on Thursday to interview a cheesemaker, so I'll really have to leave. La vita bella! As they say three times here, ciao, ciao, ciao!

Jess

Chapter 16

Overheard in the bathroom –

– Hey, here's the deal. My brother likes the Army. He's doing his third or fourth tour over there. There's no job for him here, so he's stayin' in. The way I figure it, I'm sellin' the stuff that gives the insurgents the money to keep their side of the war goin'. If they didn't keep growin' those poppies, and those guys ran out of money to fight, my brother'd be out of a job. See what I'm sayin'?

"They pulled his scholarship to Stanford, for God sakes!" Mark charged into Mizbie's room after school. She hadn't seen him in weeks.

"Hey, good to see you too," she said.

"It's Jim Keating, you remember him. He was in honors college on a team doing experimental cholesterol drug research as an undergrad, no less! Everything was fine the first year of research. But this year things didn't add up. His team found the statistics they'd been given by PharmaTek didn't match the research. He was just being honest. When he started asking questions, they pulled his scholarship and told Stanford his work wasn't ethical. Jim Keating not ethical! To hell with academic freedom. It's PharmaTek that isn't ethical!" Mark shouted.

"What will he do now? Mizbie asked.

"How's he gonna find a new research university when Stanford's thrown him out? PharmaTek will make sure he never gets a research grant again.

Mizbie looked at him, trying to fathom her friend's anger and Jim Keating's loss. Mark's eyes needed sleep.

"Research has lost one of its brightest. I just can't figure this out," he said, staring at her desk.

"Here, have a box," Renee said, bursting in, tossing a banana box onto Mizbie's floor. "It's that time of year. Do you know anyone who didn't get pink slipped? No matter. We'll pack up as we do every year, then in August they'll hire us all back after they find out what the state will pay. What's with him?"

Mark left muttering something about Stanford. Mizbie explained.

"We're all a little edgy this time of year," Renee kicked the box to the wall. "I can just imagine the last minutes of class now. I'll have a few things to say to a few choice students. 'Congratulations, you are five of the most annoying students I've ever had. All year you've been competing with one another to be the most irritating. One of you scratched her metallic nails on the blackboard, a second whined like a broken record. Not to be outdone, a third craved attention handcuffing himself to his chair, then the fourth and fifth competed, dropping books on the floor during tests. You were all successful. I'd be hard pressed to say who was most annoying, most distracting, or most successful in getting the entire class off task, especially during directions or reviews. Decades hence when loved ones say final words over your dead bodies, you can all have the distinction of knowing you were supremely annoying, just as you wanted. For the rest of you, who actually possessed self-control and tried to learn something this year, I applaud you for your patience and perseverance. I'm sure your next social studies class will be more pleasant for you. You should never have to put up with their inane, insipid, mindless, thoughtless, brain filterless, wasteful, inconsiderate, childish, ridiculous, mind-numbing, intelligence blocking, reason leaving, and teacher-ignoring behavior ever again!' That's certainly what I'd like to say."

"Thanks," Mizbie said. "Banana boxes are the best." She grabbed one and started lining the bottom with paperbacks from her student bookshelf. "How's Brandon doing for you now that he's back?"

"Different. Quiet."

"He's lost his energy. He stayed after at the Tikki Cove the other day when I had my end-of-the-year alumni get-together. Sylvia sat down with us. She's really been taking care of him. He can't tell his friends what happened. He won't go to the counseling center. I don't know what May June could do anyway. He's afraid of getting arrested. His brother has been gone for four days and hasn't called. He's scared."

"You can't save 'em all, Miz."

"His cousin's family has a hardware store in Canada. I told him to go there as soon as school's out. He's better off out of here. Sylvia agreed. She's looking into train tickets for him."

"Did you hear they found Justin's brother, Lance?" Mizbie wanted to share better news. "Justin said he's in Tibet. Lance doesn't know how he got there. All his equipment was gone and he was pretty beat up. In the picture he sent, he looked to Justin like his face was bruised, but he'll be okay. He said the only thing Lance had on him besides his clothes was a folded copy of part of that Rumi poem that I taught his class:

Love is the mother We are her children.
She shines inside us,
visible-invisible, as we trust
or lose trust,
or feel it start to grow again.

"That explains a lot. Justin's been in detention more than he's been in class." Renee said.

Imagine," Mizbie said. "Justin looked pretty hopeful that his brother would be home in a couple of weeks."

Mizbie went home and soaked the pebbles surrounding the stalks of her bamboo plant. The more she thought about it, Canada seemed like the safest place for Brandon. And as for Justin, at least he could look forward to his brother coming home. She spotted a possible comeback, a healthy green leaf sprouting up from the base of the plant. Once the plant was returned to the sill, Daphne sprang up, grooming her whiskers on the stalks and curling up next to it for an afternoon sun bath.

MJade17
toMBax20
4:00 p.m.
June 2

Hi Miz B,
Thanks for sending the school paper. My parents found a shop at the edge of the French Quarter. We're going to fix it up and live on the second floor, like we did in Astor. School lets out earlier here, but before the end of the year I made a few protest signs about people needing to be more welcoming to the Creole community. A friend carried a sign with me. My mom said I'm like the honey bee that isn't designed to fly, but does anyway. I will soar!
Love,
Mara Jade

Jesspin9
to MBax20
11:30 p.m.
June 5

Hey Miz,

How's Daphne? Does she miss me? I hope she doesn't try to sleep on your face anymore. I never tried to break her of the habit and I should have.
I don't know if you remember Stephen, the marketing major I dated junior year? We kind of drifted apart, but I happened to be in this little taverna here in Italy looking out the window at the Alps and he sat down next to me. We ate souvlaki and talked. He spent a couple of years in Mumbai with its colorful street murals and world-class street food. He described sunsets at Chowpatty Beach and Bollywood movies. He said there's no place on earth

like it and wants to go back. Unfortunately, I had a deadline, so we went back to my room and he worked on his marketing, checking out collaborations on the Venice Biennale. Meanwhile I finished my chapter on the Tuesday Market Day here in Cuneo. We used to study together at college too.

At 2:00 a.m. I finally emailed my finished chapter and we made our way to my bed. He decided to celebrate our physical reunion standing up, but his feet were slipping on the bare floor. After a few attempts, he was afraid he was going to end up on the floor doing splits, so he said, "Wait a minute. I'm getting my shoes."

It was dark and I couldn't see, but just imagining this lovely naked man, clomping to my bedside in nothing but shoes, tickled me. I didn't want to ruin the moment, so I tried to swallow the laugh, but it just didn't work. I started snorting and gasping and Stephen started laughing too, although he had no idea why I was laughing. It was so incredibly silly and delightful to fall asleep, wrapped up in each other.

The next day I took a side trip with Stephen to the Venice Biennale, an art festival with works by artists from about 90 countries. We put up a colorful installation on a walking area next to the Arsenale, remember from Dante? Except back in his time, it was a huge shipyard where parts were mass produced like an ancient Ford factory. This art was anything but. Every color, texture, and shape juts out, all positioned to face the canal. After the major pieces were positioned, we had smaller, solid-glass blocks radiating from the center. Each had to be perfectly placed with levels. Connected to the glass blocks were rusty metal sheets secured in various positions, so visitors could walk through them – an eerie walk to be sure.

We stopped for lunch at an outdoor cafe with some other English speakers. Portuguese actors were practicing creative per-formance art outside. We overheard some art critics at the next table. One woman they called Pima, a Brit, stuck her finger down her throat to describe her evaluation. It was so bad. Each was more pedantically puffed up than the last, tripping over words so their critiques were meaningless, one more unreal than the last. Phrases such as "presumptuous rubble," a "lost effort at paradox," and a "missed stab at oxymoron."

When I coughed a clearly fake cough, they looked at us, but I don't believe they had a clue to the connection. The Biennalle is a celebration of energy, irony, and humor. I think they picked away and missed the whole experience. I'm off. Stephen has a ball of string, so we're going to make a huge spider web and attach it to each hand and toe of this lurching figure next to a blue plow. We're going to find a plastic spider to hook in it and name it Charlotte. The Venice Biennale reminds me of our Grand Rapids Celebrate Art, but it's had a 50-year head start growing and evolving. The Venice Grand Canal is breathtaking, but my bike isn't much good here. Oh well, my behind needs a break anyway.

Jess

∾

Mizbie looked for a message from Stella, as she did every day, hoping the internship was still a possibility. She was surprised with how much she missed Stella and their movie nights making popcorn and slathering it in Spanish smoked paprika butter, watching *Ferris Bueller's Day Off.*

Chapter 17

Overheard in the girls' bathroom –

So I'm like, what the heck? I sent that picture to him. I told Cam not to send it to anyone else and it was on her phone. Now everyone's gonna see my boobs.

They caught him in the girls' locker room with a camera. Cam's such a jerk. He was waiting for us to come in from the softball field. He only got a three-day suspension.

Cam Roberts is so hot. He's suspended for nine days for selling Vicodin in school, but it was really stool softener, whatever that is. He's so hot.

Jesspin9
toMBax20
8:30 a.m.
June 10

Hi Miz,

Stephen suggested I go to Vienna for the coffee. I hadn't con-sidered it, but I could squeeze in a few days before Florence, so I took the morning train from Venice. This was my first view of Austria, and I found Vienna bright, Baroque, and so clean. The subway took me from the opera house to St. Stephen's Cathedral in a flash. The Leopold Museum had a fair collection of Klimt paintings. I found shopping squares with chocolate shops and yes, Viennese coffee is bold and aromatic. Like Paris, the outdoor cafes are known for people watching. On a tree-lined street, I found one for an afternoon coffee break and watched as a brass band in red uniforms marched before me on their way to the Hapsburg Winter Palace two blocks up.

I tried to find a place to spend the night, but Vienna was too expensive, so I decided to stay in Bratislava across the Danube. I boarded the hydrofoil with my bike and realized it took 90 minutes. I thought it was closer and I was starved for dinner and tired for a place to stay. The view from the Russian vessel was worth it, though, a pleasant change of pace.

Bratislava was full of contrasts. The Czech Republic is part of the Eurozone, but it feels like stepping back decades in time. I could feel energy here, with old buildings being repaired and morphing into new beer gardens, pubs, and cell-phone stores. There is still some serious poverty, but the prices are much more reasonable than Vienna. Walking into the first local restaurant that looked clean, I found white tablecloths, cloth napkins, and waiters in tuxes. I felt so out of place in the biking gear I'd worn all day, but they greeted me in Slovak, completely incomprehensible, and ushered me to a seat, placing a napkin on my lap. They found an English menu for me. Perusing the offerings, I forgot my appearance. Miz, they had escargot, carpaccio crepes, and Italian ice lime, all for 15 Euro. It would've been three times the price across the Danube in Vienna. After eating way too much, a moonlit walk along the Danube after dinner made me think of how Stephen would've enjoyed this.

With only one more day, I decided to spend it in Bratislava instead of Vienna, especially since it happened to be part of the Spring Food Fest. Here I found just about every seafood imaginable. They have Italian, French, and Thai cuisine, mixed in with traditional Czech food. Endless tables and countless aromas of seasonings followed me as I ate my way through, finally finding a traditional dish, bryndzovéhaluşky. The cook, who was also server, handed me a plate that looked like potato dumpling pillows with crisp bacon on top. It was mild flavored with a surprising sharp tang from the sheep cheese, hearty and filling. I washed it down with a local beer; there were so many and each brewmaster was more proud than the next. I decided on a dark sweet ale that tasted like Dr Pepper combined with a Heath bar. It reminded me of your Food Fest in red that I missed this year! I ended up with reviews of three wonderful street food vendors, but the coffee wasn't quite as memorable as Vienna's coffee was.

I hesitate to put expats I've met in categories as I'm segueing to Italy here, but they seem to be married, gay, retired, or students. One of the most genuinely kind companions I've met, one who doesn't wonder what I want from her, one who isn't out to impress me by name dropping big destinations, and one who responds to what I'm saying as if she's actually been listening, not just waiting for a break in the conversation, is Coleen, a Canadian. We met over coffee at tables that were squeezed next to each other in a piazza by the old/new market Loggia del Mercato Nuovo, in Florence. This ancient market, from the 16th century, has a huge covered roof, sculptures in the corners, and a smiling brass hog or porcellino at the entrance. We patted his nose for good luck when we stepped through the arch.

Inside the market, Coleen and I found two scarves, black and gray with tiny blue dots, and we both wanted them. No other scarves looked like these, so we bartered with the saleswoman with our biggest gesticulations and most convincing voices. She agreed to half price.

Pleased with our bargains, we put on our scarves and decided to take the bus tour of a nearby ancient Roman ruin.

The ruin was a formidable fortress-like structure 2,000 years old, but rain, wind, and sun had done their work. Huge repairs were badly needed for the structures and drainage. A door lintel fell off a communal bath while we were standing there, and the tour guide said there just weren't funds to repair it. I'm going to find out where to send donations to keep it up, and see if UNESCO knows about it. There were rows of clay amphorae, their size determining their points of origin and contents, hundreds of amphorae brought here on sailing ships, like our container ships.

Archaeologists found something resembling wine in the bottom of one of the containers. Imagine wine that old! But the taste testers found only clay and mud. Coleen and I agreed it sounded like a little more "terroir" than we would like in a glass of wine. We part ways tomorrow, but it's been fun traveling with Coleen.

Love,

Jess

∾

Mizbie woke Saturday morning to an anguished cry. She was used to Stella's nightmares and could relate, but then she heard two voices. She reached for the door and then sat back on the bed to listen.

"Where have you been? How did you get here?"

"Oh, Stella baby, I picked up the letters you left in the post office box. I'm cleaned up now. I've got a place over the bakery. We can share a room for a while until I save up enough for a bigger place. I even got a job down at the Brights Auto Parts. I figure you can get a job this summer and we'll be okay. What do you say? Come home with me, Stella."

Mizbie could hear fear in the voice.

"Mom . . . you look great," Stella paused. "I'm glad you have a job and a place to live. I have something to tell you too. I have a scholarship to U of M for next year, and I have an internship at the pharmacy company in Kalamazoo for the summer. Miz B helped me –"

"No no . . . now that I've found you, we can be together. Do you make any money at the drug company?"

"Science is something I want to study. If they like me, they might hire me after college."

"Work for free? Not my girl. Uh, uh. Look, I'm sure you can get a job at Rube's Lounge or Saturn Coney Island. That's the kind of job for you. You get tips. You' can't go to college, not when I've just found you again. I forgive you. I forgive you, Stella, now let's go."

Mizbie couldn't take it any longer. She charged out of her bedroom in her sleep shirt and disheveled hair, wedging herself into their conversation. "Damnation! Forgive her? Forgive her for what? Putting up

Patricia Duffy

with your selfish addictions? Look at Stella. She was living in the girls' locker room when I found her. The only food she had came from the school cafeteria and she took showers there in the locker room. She slept on her coat on the concrete floor. Even through all this, she's graduating in the top 10 in her class." She could feel heat welling up inside and her hands balled into fists. She took a long breath to will the anger back down. "And now you come in here –"

"Mom, you don't have to forgive me," Stella said, as if Mizbie wasn't there.

"Listen to you, Stella. You're the victim here, but you don't have to be," said Mizbie. "We are the way we are, but you don't have to do this. You have a choice, right now, not to be the victim." She turned to Stella's mother. "You take off abandoning your daughter and just because you've cleaned up, what's to prevent the same thing from happening again? Then where will Stella be?" Mizbie looked from mother to daughter. "She'll be out of school with no home and no scholarship, no internship, because she gave it up for you. Just because you threw your life away, don't mess up Stella's! She's not going with you!"

"Who do you think you are, talkin' to me like that?" Her eyes darted from Mizbie to Stella. "I know you took Stella into your home and I'm grateful for that, but you are not her mother." She eyed Mizbie with keen calculation. "I know what's best for her. She's not the type to go to college; she's just like me. She'll go there and fail, and then where will she be? Crawling back to me. I'm gonna spare her that rejection."

"You're not even giving her a choice. You don't realize how strong Stella is. She wants this challenge. If you don't let her take this scholarship, Protective Services will –"

"No, Miz B. She's my mom," Stella's voice was soft and reasonable. "I want to go with her. She's the only family I have. Thanks for taking care of me when I needed it. Now I need to take care of my mom."

Stella's mother straightened and sighed. "Now you're talkin' girl. Let's get out of here."

"Just let me get my things, Mom."

260

"Stella, think this through," Mizbie's ears were burning, but she used her controlled teacher voice. "You can still live with your mom and do the internship this summer. You can still go to college."

"I've decided." Instead of the hopeful lilt in her voice that Mizbie heard when they talked about her scholarship and life in the dorms at U of M, Stella's voice was now a resignation. "I'll get my things. It won't take long."

Stella withdrew to the bathroom. Breaking a painful silence, Mizbie said, "You're making a hell of a mistake, you egotistical, narcissistic, self-serving excuse for a mother. Quit thinking only of yourself."

"I've been called worse," she said. You're just a teacher, Miz B. You've never been a mother. You don't know what it's like." Her shoulders drooped. "You don't have a clue what I've been through. It's hell out there not knowing where you're goin' to get a meal or . . . or knowin' who's around the next corner waitin' to take your stuff. You don't know what I went through to get myself together, to get her back. I deserve to have some help and Stella's going to be there for me. That's what daughters are for."

Stella returned with her backpack and a grocery bag. "I'm ready." She looked dragged down by the weight of it. "I hear you, Miz B, but you can't tell me how I feel. Thanks for everything you did for me. It would've been great going to college. But I can't leave my mom. Now that I have her back, I just can't do it."

Daphne was walking figure eights around Stella's legs. Looking around the apartment one last time, she bent to give Daphne a scratch behind the ears, looking not unlike a daughter going off to college.

"Thanks for everything? Is this what you want? You're worth more than this." Mizbie tried to think fast. The two of them moved toward the door. "You hear me, but you're not listening to me, Stella. You're not listening at all." Mizbie saw proof on Stella's shirt, a drop of a tear that had rolled from her cheek. Mizbie was too angry to hear Stella's last words. "Just go then. Just go." Mizbie tried to hug Stella who shrank away, but not before she tucked her email address and phone number into Stella's pocket.

After the door closed behind them, Mizbie imagined what she should have done. She could have pushed Stella's mom away and escaped with Stella to Kalamazoo. Could she become a foster parent? At least she would make sure Stella got her internship. Daphne hopped on the table where the Pablo Naruda poetry book had been. Just last night they had sat on the couch reading "Ode to My Socks" together. "Damn Damn Damn!" she yelled. On second thought, she was glad to think the book was tucked inside Stella's backpack. On her bed, she found a hastily written note:

> *Dear Miz B,*
> *Thanks for letting me stay with you and listening to me when I was hurt, hungry, scared, and mad. I have to believe my mom. She says things will be different this time. So I guess this is it. I'll always remember you and that day you found me in the locker room. I'll come back and see you someday.*
> *Love, Stella*

∽

Jesspin9
toMBax20
8:50 a.m.
June 8

Hey Miz,

My brother, Hank, just sent a high-speed train ticket for me from Milan to Luxembourg. It must've cost him dearly. I'll have to find a way there from where I am now at Lake Como. Elle is due to have her baby on Tuesday, and she wants me there because her family isn't coming over from the states. She's never had a child away from home before and she's pretty homesick. Hank didn't say he wanted me there. Oh well, I can support her, hold her epidural legs, and tell her to push as well as anyone, I guess. I've gotta hand it to her. This will be her third child and she schleps them around Europe, moving every year or less. She's a peach. I've got to say outside of you, Elle's the closest thing I have to a sister. What she sees in my brother, I'll never know.

Jess

At 13:00, Jess was finally on a train that moved. A track problem had caused a half-day delay. Elle called twice, afraid Jess wouldn't make it in time. She felt as if the baby would arrive early, and the doctor said it was a clear possibility. The ride seemed interminable, with each stop seeming to take longer than the last. Jess hadn't slept in 24 hours and was halfway through a second reading of *Angels and Demons* when the train pulled into Luxembourg at 23:00 (or 11:00 at night). Hank picked her up and took her back to the apartment, with barely a word. At the quiet apartment, Elle's warm strong hugs, with her belly that came between them, were followed by stories comparing everyone's level of exhaustion. They had the sofa covered with a down pillow and blanket for Jess.

"You made it. I was really worried I'd have to go to the hospital without you," Elle rubbed her swollen belly. "I'm so relieved you're here." Her tired eyes looked Jess over as if she was a favorite Christmas gift. "Love you. See you in the morning." She gave Jess another hug and disappeared into their bedroom.

Two hours later, Hank opened his bedroom door and told Jess to get up. "What?" Jess tried to prop herself up on the sofa.

"It's time," Elle said, wrapping a sweater around her pajamas. Hank held her bag that had been packed for a week. Their neighbor came to stay with the children whom Jess hadn't even seen yet, and off they went to Ettelbruck Hospital. After seven hours of iPod music, an exercise ball, leg holding, and a birth pool, little Catherine was born.

They had worked together for seven hours, nurses and doctors walking in and out, some who could speak English, some who could not. Between the three of them they pieced together enough French to understand what to do. "Just look at her," Jess was overcome.

"She's finally here," Elle was beaming. "I was afraid it would just be Hank and me when she was born. Everyone is so far away." Catherine lay curled up in the warmth of her mother's arms.

"It's startling when you think about it," Hank said. "Catherine was just waiting for you to get here, Jess."

Jess didn't believe it for a minute. Babies were born in their own time. Still it was a sweet thing for her usually blockheaded brother to say.

"Would you like to hold her?" Elle asked. Hank took a nursery blanket and swaddled Catherine with a practiced hand, holding her out to Jess.

Jess cradled Catherine in her arms. Catherine opened her dark blue eyes for a second, then slept. Playing with a brunette curl over Catherine's ear, Jess looked at Hank. "She's got your hair. Look at this!" She debated whether or not Catherine's hair would be as unruly as Hank's, and her resentment melted away.

"Should we ask her?" Hank looked at his wife and she nodded.

"Elle and I decided it's time to put down roots. Leo would have to switch schools next year and we don't want him shuttled around anymore. I'll still have to travel some, but not so much as I do now. What I'm trying to say is that we're the only family we have outside of Uncle Claud in Chicago. We've found a place in Costa Mesa so I can drive to the bank in Los Angeles. We want you to have a home base with us. It's a big house."

Jess didn't answer.

"Or we'll help you find your own place nearby, if you'd rather. But it's gotta be nearby."

Jess looked at her brother. He couldn't be serious. She waited for a punchline, but there wasn't one. "My kids have to have Aunt Jess in their lives, not just a couple times a year. When the kids get old enough, I'm gonna tell them the crazy stuff we did, and when they don't believe it, you'll be there to back me up."

Jess's mind flashed to a few things her brother didn't know and never would. "I never thought of living in California before."

She looked down at little Catherine and felt the weight of her in her arms as she wiggled and yawned, so content in her swaddling. How could it be possible to feel such love for this little girl the instant she first saw her? Maybe Elle and Hank were ganging up on her. Her defenses were down. She wondered if her brother had ulterior motives, if he was trying to control her, protect her, or keep her from being a professional embarrassment to him.

"A home base. I'll think about it." Thinking or planning beyond her next train trip or cycle path wasn't so bad. "I do want you to know though, when my book becomes a bestseller, I'm buying a summer place in Elk Rapids, right on the lake. You can come and visit."

"Done," he smiled.

"Jess, I can't wait for us to be together. Hank is so miserable when you're at odds with each other, but we can put that behind us." Elle said. Little Catherine began to cry and Jess gave her back. "I can't wait to move somewhere where I actually have family."

"Get ready to attend lots of soccer matches. Leo is quite the midfielder," Hank said.

"And swim meets," Elle added. "Wait until you see Kit dog paddle."

"And maybe a flute recital or two. This one's gonna play the flute." Jess looked down at Catherine. "Look how she holds her mouth!"

Chapter 18

Overheard on the bus –

So when I wear this shirt, I feel like a real guy, ya know? I don't know if it's ironic or not, but this is my real guy shirt.

R enee sat on a student desk in Mizbie's room.

"Have you seen Mark?" Mizbie always organized the students' final exams in her file cabinet on the last day of school. Mizbie talked with Renee about Mark's concern for the future of the science department after more cuts were planned for next year.

"Your work husband! He's gonna miss you this summer!" Renee said.

"He looked terrible. It was his freshmen. His physics and chem averages were well above, but not enough freshmen would do the work. It didn't matter how many sodium and potassium grains they blew up in water or the rocket engines they designed and trajectories they measured in the parking lot. The percentage was so close. He almost made it. And you know what he worried about? How those kids were gonna get jobs with work ethics like that."

"Sounds like Mark," Renee said.

"I tried to think of words to help. I asked him what he was going to do. He hadn't even thought about it. He hadn't planned on retiring for another 10 years. He'll have no pension now, but his wife Margaret still has her job with the power company. He has a wood shop in back of his garage."

Their conversation turned to Stella. "Weren't you always the one who was wary of the responsibility of having someone depend on you?" Renee chided after Mizbie finally told her about hiding Stella. Renee already knew about Stella and wondered when Mizbie would be ready to talk about it. "How do you like it? It hurts, doesn't it? Suck it up, kid. Stella's a survivor. She'll land on her feet, you'll see." She tugged on Mizbie's school lanyard and hugged her shoulder. "She'll be all right."

After Renee left, Heuster stopped by to remind Mizbie he'd be available to knock the block off Bland Man if she needed him, but only after he returned from Extreme Body Camp in two weeks. "Did you hear about Jeff Hines from Brenton? We finally got him. You know he's wanted to come here for a couple years, and he was our first pick after coach's retirement." Heuster looked almost excited at the news.

"Who is Jeff Hines?"

"Only the best football coach in the county. Benton Bulldogs have been state champs the last three years in a row. He teaches phys ed out there. He graduated from Scottsdale and his wife's family is from here too. I guess they've been figuring Coach Maxfield would retire. He needed to cram in some credits so he'd be highly qualified. He's been trying for a few years, took a few classes at Hill College, but couldn't pass. He said he finally found a couple online courses. Some school I've never heard of out in New Mexico? But I guess it's legal."

She thanked Heuster for his offer of brute strength and headed for her appointment with Principal Krahler. "It's Mizbie, the Shakespeare guru," Ryder said walking beside her, running his hand through chronically disheveled hair, its former rich brown color steeled with hints of gray. His mood seemed to match his film-star smile.

Mizbie thanked Ryder for his suggestions and told him her night terrors were fewer than before. "So what's going on this summer?"

"My state of mind is in akrasia, I know it," Ryder shook his head. "But I'm going to New York," he said, strutting his inner peacock. "My last wife is there." Penelope had contacted him for the first time in a year, lamenting the 12-hour days working in the theatre district, watching men in turtlenecks, tweeds, and black T-shirts. She missed her cowboy.

"I'm flying out tomorrow. When the day comes and I find myself standing at God's eternal time clock waiting to punch out, I want to be wherever she is."

Mizbie wished him well when she saw Krahler step out of the wrong office. He had exchanged rooms with the assistant principal again. Krahler liked the natural light better in the assistant's office, but the noise from irritable students who had been sent to the fish bowl awaiting sentencing annoyed him. He decided to change back. Some principals were circus ringmasters, communicators of public relations, promoters of sparkle and dash, others, like Krahler, were country preachers, flip-flopping harbingers of doom and suffering, seekers of sin.

She sat down to wait and saw Singer picking up papers from the office assistant. He looked back. "I guess it's time to say goodbye," he said.

"Not really. You'll be back from college for holidays. I'll see you around town. Play some local shows and I'll see you there too," she smiled.

"I'm going on the road with the band. We've actually got a tour that takes us to Kansas City, Red Rocks Canyon, then Australia and New Zealand. We've got a following in New Zealand. Between tours we'll pick up some local gigs wherever we happen to be."

"Singer, you made your decision." Mizbie was happy for him. "I thought you'd be telling me you'd decided on a college."

"It's partly because of you, Miz B. You always said to explore. You never lectured me about playing it safe or going to college and getting a real job like everybody else. So I'm going for it. If I didn't do this now, if I waited four years, this whole band thing might be over and I'd always wonder what would have been. You know what it's like to write a song and play it for the first time, not knowing how people will react to it, and when they shout and they go crazy –"

"And they chip your tooth."

"Yeah, that too. It's like nothing else."

"That makes me so happy, Singer. Send me a postcard from Australia."

"Miz Baxter, I'll see you now," Krahler said. Mizbie saw a first-year math teacher she'd never gotten to meet, scuttle away from the office with a dour look. Krahler closed the door behind them.

"Desmin didn't pass the state test." Krahler didn't wait for Mizbie to sit down.

"You know he came from Detroit. His reading level jumped three grades this year. He memorized his lines in *Hamlet*! For somebody who spends a third of his time in detention, what did you expect?"

"I'll tell you." He straightened a family picture behind his desk and sat down. "I expect every student to read at grade level and he's still reading at a seventh grade level. Look at your December state test scores." He tossed the form in front of her. "They've plummeted 7 percent since last year, Mizbie, plummeted."

Mizbie recalled the last staff meeting when Krahler announced that those teachers with state exam passing rates averaging below 80 percent would be let go. Grading results would not be shared with the staff. *Why share statistics that would actually help teachers focus on what students needed to learn?* Scores would be published in the local newspaper for parents. Results were kept until year end when termination notices began two days before the end of final exams. She wanted to trust Krahler and didn't think he would really do it. Yet there were the broken promises, the grand plans that hadn't benefited anyone but the superintendent. Was he trying to get his name on the short list for a position with the administrative office?

"Well Mizbie," Krahler adjusted the desk pad in front of him. The plug-in waterfall on a bookcase shelf burbled. "I meant to talk to you about your evaluation before the last day of school, but things came up, you know, with the bomb scare and the protest –"

"I know. It's been a busy spring term. So what do you have to tell me?" She tried to keep her voice calm.

"About your evaluation, I've visited your classroom several times. It's been difficult finding exactly what was needed. I wanted to be helpful to you in any way I could, but I had to find exactly what needed improvement. I think I've found it.

"Yes, you've visited my classroom 17 times this year. Sometimes for 20 minutes or so, sometimes for the entire hour."

"Really? Yes . . . well . . . I see that you've been late for school four times, rushing in just as the bell rings when you're supposed to be in class six minutes early. Preparation is important. Our kids deserve well-prepared teachers, organized and ready to go every day."

"If you'll remember, last Tuesday, when the bell rang, I had picked up muffins for your office assistant's birthday breakfast."

"Yes, well, we have to plan ahead for those contingencies. And in the classroom, I don't see your students responding well to you. We must constantly be aware that our students are paying attention. One time I saw Desmin in the back of the room actually looking out the window before you caught him and redirected him. The results are right here on the evaluation form."

Krahler placed the multipage form in front of Mizbie and pointed to the offending item. There it was. December state test scores. "Test scores. Teachers keeping their jobs for good test scores is like allowing weather forecasters to keep their jobs when they announce sunny days. The neighboring forecaster who has rain, can't control where his weather comes from. He has no power over the low and high pressure systems that feed his rain storm. Do they fire forecasters when there's rain?"

"Well," Krahler cleared his throat. "Mizbie, I could go on, but as you know, this is not the first time we've had disagreements," he said, losing patience and noticeably wanting to get on with it. "You can't slide forever on last year's exemplary evaluation. I've told you I'd help in any way I could. I gave you extra evaluation time in hopes that things would improve, but it just isn't going to happen. You're just not a good fit here at St. Bartholomew's this year. You're highly qualified; that's not a problem. I'll give you a good recommendation. Let me know how I can help you. Good luck."

At that, he abruptly stood up like a wooden soldier and held out his hand for Mizbie to shake. It's a good thing he wasn't a doctor, she thought. His bedside manner stinks.

"Well, Mr. Krahler, I can't say I haven't been expecting this every spring for the past seven years." Some things we would rather not know once we find them out. How could she state her case? "St. Bartholomew's is like family to me. I love this staff and my students still come back to visit me after they graduate –"

"Yes, we know about your annual end-of-the-year student lunches at the Tikki Cove."

"Some of these students have gone on to pursue college majors in English and they say I influenced their lives. I've edited a school news-paper that has won state awards, sells out, and is emulated by other schools. Money from the spring plays supports three after-school clubs. But none of this matters because four students missed one or two questions on a test from last December when I'd only had them four months? These students progressed so much. Doesn't that count for anything?"

Krahler's wooden stare made Mizbie furious. "What about Justin? He can't keep his pants on and he'd never read a whole book before this year. He read *1984*, one of my classroom books, then "lost" it. He couldn't give it back. He discovered books can be a gift, not a punish-ment. That's progress! I can't tell you the number of book thieves I've had. What about Kim from Korea? She could barely write in September, and it took months to get her an English language tutor. She won the Michigan and Me essay contest! That's progress, Krahler, and you won't find it measured on any test, but these kids made giant leaps this year. Maybe Justin and Kim didn't pass with an 80 percent, but I know they'll succeed in English next year and I don't need any damn test results or any administrator out for his own self-interest to tell me."

Mizbie looked at his eyes, riveted pinpoints under wild graying brows. Horseshoe hair a shade too brown curled around a head that grew shinier through the stresses of this afternoon. Krahler controlled his voice with effort. "A good school depends on my continuous effort, evaluation, and finding the sparks before the fire starts so I don't have to put it out after. I never give up or give in. The sparks have to fire in the right direction; I'm tired of cleaning up after the inferno. Mizbie, you are a conflagration. Look at the issue with Stella. Your nurturing is beyond what this fire department can put out." He waited for her reaction. She saw him swallow, the knot in his purple tie inching up.

"You know Stella was living in the girls' locker room. Her foster-home experience was terrifying and she was petrified I would turn her in. She needed me, okay? And maybe I needed her too." Mizbie surprised herself and hadn't expected to say that. A fleeting expression on Krahler's face let her know she slipped. "Besides, she's with her mom now and it's all settled."

"Nonetheless, we cooperate with the DSS. You crossed the line and it reflects poorly on this school and its reputation. We don't invite conflict with parents."

"Conflict! I gave her daughter compassion. That is not conflict, Krahler, that is concern for another human being, something I'm not sure you're capable of now that you're an administrator alone in your office with your statistics and test scores. Just a short time ago you were a teacher in my shoes. Did you forget what it's like? What happened?"

"You mean well. Your motive was what was best for kids. But we got sucked into the Iraq conflict with the idea that it was best for America. We got involved in Afghanistan declaring a war on terror." Krahler's opinions were irrefutable, like quick-drying cement, impossible to move without a jackhammer. "We meant well, but we caused trouble. Our well-meaning actions were a recipe for disaster. You have become St. Bartholomew's recipe for disaster."

"Isn't that quite a leap, comparing me to the war on terror, Krahler?

He turned to the next page of the report. "Look at Isabelle Hollander. She almost didn't get to wrestle because of your grades."

"Izzy needed glasses and no one caught it. I arranged with a local optometrist who was a wrestling fan, and he was happy to fit her with a pair for free. You should see her grades now."

"Regardless, timing is everything. You should have caught it before the December exams. Any girl who can wrestle like that shouldn't be so close to academic ineligibility."

"What about Nick Huntsman? His ineligibility for basketball didn't stop Mrs. Huntsman from getting him off the hook." Mizbie was fighting a losing battle. Her future here couldn't be reversed any more than she could reverse the current of the Grand River. Her offenses flowed and bubbled out of Krahler, as if they had been previously dammed up and waiting for spring.

"I hope Jeff Hines works out for you," she said.

Krahler set his jaw. "What are you talking about?"

"Jeff Hines? The football coach you're bringing in to replace me?" Mizbie hadn't been sure about what Jeff would teach, but Krahler's face said it all. "I hope he can teach the nuances of Shakespeare and the ways that authors craft character and maybe he's read a few hundred books and can match them to his students' individual interests. Maybe students will feel like they can come to him when their fathers abuse them or they're thinking of running away from home, or they're looking for a reason why not to have sex yet. I hope he learned all that in his semester of English correspondence courses. When his kids are sophomores and their teachers come to you saying, 'Why don't his students know how to write? Why can't they support an idea?' You'll know why. This was all about your decision to get a new football coach, and it stinks. Good luck to *you*, Mr. Krahler."

"It's complicated," he said, not admitting or denying anything. "So you're not indomitable. You're still young. Go reinvent yourself. So you got a bad break with the percentages and school politics worked against you." He grimaced. Mizbie pictured Krahler's acid tongue on a platter, suspended in aspic surrounding the new big-fish football coach. "Look around. You'll find a lot of other jobs that involve much less work and much better pay than teaching." He was finished. Krahler stood like a proud athletic supporter, opening the door for Mizbie to leave.

"Have a good summer, Miz." Sonia breezed through the office carrying a box. "I'll probably see you out biking. Mrs. Borrows next door still talks about her son playing in *Hamlet*. Only two more years and my daughter will have you in class. I'll put in a request as soon as she's through eighth grade."

Krahler turned to his office assistant after Mizbie was out of ear-shot. "Call Superintendent Winchell, will you? Tell him Mizbie's out, the new football coach is in, and his favorite Mrs. Huntsman, the basketball player's mom, doesn't have to withhold her athletic complex funding now. I handled it. Don't schedule any more chickenshit meetings for me today. Hold my calls. I'm done." His present mood was a dark energy force splitting further into the school universe. He walked into his office and closed the door. St. Bartholomew's political pendulum had swung firmly to the football side.

Mizbie unclenched her hands that were balled into fists. She had just been tossed out of her niche, skewered and catapulted into an unknown direction, padlocked out as if the last seven years had all been a mistake. How could she tell Renee, Mark, or even Heuster? Their sympathy was the last thing she wanted. How could she force herself to think through this, a punch she didn't believe was coming, a stinging loss? She could feel the worry and anger that was about to cloud around her. But first she needed a place to wallow.

Nick was hanging around outside the office. She detected a smirk when he saw her. "What are you looking at?" She snapped at him. "You say you're obsessed with the certainty that everyone else's life is so much better. You think our lives are fairer than yours?" Mizbie pounded her palm. "There is no fairness, no integrity. Fairness is a breathtaking act of staggering hypocrisy. One moment you feel like you can defy gravity, the next you've got nothing. Nothing! Put that under your hoodie for subtext. Now get out of here," she yelled. Nick was about to say something, but no words came out.

What did she do? He's Nick, but did he deserve that?

∽

The back door slammed. "Good, Nick. You're home." Mrs. Huntsman put her arm around her son and congratulated him for finishing the year. "I have something to show you."

274

"I'm going to Brent's. I'll be home later." Nick dropped his books on the granite-topped kitchen island.

"I've saved this letter for you. I had to take care of some things before I showed it to you. It's very important and I want you to read it before you go." She held it out to him. "Then I'm going to put it in this pot on the cook top and burn it." Mrs. Huntsman walked after him with the letter.

"Later." His voice was loud. He grabbed his backpack from the hallway. Backpacks were forbidden on the last days of school, and his was bulging with shaving cream cans jammed in the night before.

"I mean now." Her tone of voice made Nick drop his bag and take the letter. "No one else will ever see this letter but you and me. Not even your father."

Miller Miller and Smitz
Private Investigation
543 E. Second St.
Astor, Michigan

Mrs. Huntsman:

Although we located your sister, we regret to inform you of her accidental death in West Branch, along with that of her husband. As you can see from the attached reports, their vehicle was demolished by a driver, who was .15 percent over the legal alcohol limit. Trial details for the drunk driver are to be scheduled at a later date. His prison term is expected to be from 15 – 20 years. I will protect your anonymity and confirm the driver's prison sentence after the trial.

On the other matter, the young woman, their daughter, who caused your sister and her husband to flee and break all contact with you, is now an instructor at St. Bartholomew's High School.

She is in the English department, teaching under your sister's married name, Baxter.

Please accept our condolences for your loss. I hope the additional information will be helpful to you in your search for answers to your sister's disappearance.

Sincerely,
J. D. Miller

"So this means Bitch Baxter is related to us?" Nick handed the letter back.

Mrs. Huntsman ripped the letter into strips, struck a match, and held it to one strip. When the fire spread, she dropped the strips in the pot on the stove. "She has never been related to us. Don't you see? She's the reason why I lost my only sister, the aunt you never met." They watched the white strips turn black. "Because of this letter, we know why my sister left, why she wouldn't let us contact her ever again." Because of your Miz Baxter, my sister is dead."

She held her son, her head resting on his shoulder. Nick squirmed.

"But it's okay now." Her voice softened. "Mom fixed everything." She patted his back and looked up. "Miz Baxter won't teach you again. She won't teach anyone at St. Bart's again. I made sure of that." She watched the flames dwindle. Blackened bits clung inside the stainless steel pot on the cook top.

"Nobody liked her. She didn't teach. She didn't care. All she did was give out bad grades." He sniffed the smoky air and tossed the backpack over one shoulder.

"Dinner's at seven. The Orloffs are coming, so no jeans." Mrs. Huntsman opened the window over the sink.

∾

Desmin's aunt waited outside Mizbie's room, still in her prison-guard's uniform.

"Miz B, they found him. They found Desmin. He and his dad got caught in Detroit running from police and they pepper-sprayed him bad. You know how his skin is from the burns. He in the Henry Ford Hospital and I'm on my way to see him, but he asked me to stop by and tell you in person first. I'm glad I caught you. If you'd been any longer, I'd a left. I got to go see him." She wiped her eyes.

"Miz, you just can't stay out of trouble with parents, can you?" Renee interrupted on her way out. "That reminds me," Renee turned, suddenly ignoring Ms Gray. "Remember next week at my house. We'll start around nine, not too early. I'm guessing we'll take about a week to integrate more core standards into the curriculum. Let's put in that interdisciplinary discussion format you made too. Be sure to bring your notes for critical thinking so we can all use them. We'll get it approved by Krahler and be all set for fall. See you."

Mizbie waved goodbye to Renee. "Ms Gray, what happened?" Mizbie imagined the worst.

"He been with his dad for three weeks now, stealin' cars, getting into all kind of trouble. They got caught. I been sleepless with fear. At least now I know where he is." She looked at Mizbie. "There's some peace in that. I talk to him on the phone and he made me promise to come tell you he's sorry. It's not your fault. He say you showed him how to reach deep inside hisself to find his true nature. He said he felt peaceful inside 'cause of you, like he didn't need to be mean no more."

"Poor Desmin. I can't think straight right now." She no sooner had heard Ms Gray and her brain knew Desmin was guilty, but she wished with all her heart he hadn't done it. His aunt probably burst out in a rant, a thunder of rage, a storm of shouting when she found out. Mizbie could relate. His father was another story. Did he know how far Desmin had come this year? "I know you have to go. Wait a minute, please?"

She ran to her bookcase, oblivious to the young man picking through her file cabinet in the back of the room. She found a book she was only halfway through reading. She opened the front page and wrote a note to Desmin. What she had read reminded her of his situation, a hopeful young man who could've lived a hundred years earlier. She gripped it with both hands and offered it to Ms Gray. "Would you give him this for me? For when he feels better," Mizbie said. She wanted to say so much more. She wanted to tell the police that here was a boy who had passion and compassion, a boy who had a loving, *and powerful* aunt, a boy who could have a bright future if he could just have another chance.

"I will make sure he gets it." She looked at Mizbie's red face, then at the title. "*Arc of Justice?* Hunh. We can only hope fo' that. Wait a minute. What's wrong with you Miz B? You got somethin' wrong with you? C'mon, tell me. You don't want to mess with no uppity black woman."

"Me?" Mizbie nearly broke, wanting to spill out the day's U-turn. "I'm okay," she said.

"I don't believe that fo' a minute, baby," she said, wrapping her muscular arms around Mizbie and hugging her. "Not fo' a minute. You take care now."

After the last final exam grade had been bubbled on the grade sheet, she had packed boxes in preparation for summer cleaning. She packed with the idea that if she was let go, she could exit with little fuss, or unpack them easily in the fall. Every June was as unsure as a bird on a wire, until now. She looked at the boxes and thought of her students. She already missed them. Before this she had taken it all for granted, never believing she wouldn't be coming back. She grabbed the masking tape, and heard a voice. "I'm Jeff Hines. I'm the new English teacher here next year. How ya doin'?"

How am I doin'? How does he think I'm doin' losing my job to somebody who had to retake college English online for the purpose of replacing me. "What are you doing back there? What do you want?" Her voice wavered as she came out from behind the desk to face him. She frowned at the stack of papers he had taken from her files, a trove of lessons that worked, depending on the students.

"Well . . ." He looked down, then slowly up from her sandals to her summer dress. Remembering himself, he cleared his throat and kept his eyes on her face. "I got boxes in my Chevy. I'm gonna start movin' 'em in, you know, get a feel for my new room."

Mizbie got the impression this guy never asked permission for anything, just told people what he was going to do. He had the understanding manner of a Mack truck. "I've been here for seven years, and that means I have some packing to do. Why don't you bring your boxes back tomorrow?" She countered.

"Look, they're all in the truck and it isn't covered and it looks like rain tonight, but okay. I'll bring 'em back tomorrow," he said, waiting for her to cave in. She stared at him willing lightning to flash from her eyes.

Mizbie decided to quiz Jeff. "So, who's your favorite poet? William Carlos Collins? Ezra Cummings? E. E. Wordsworth?"

"Yeah . . ." Jeff said. "I've heard of 'em, but I can't say they're my favorites. I transferred mosta my credits from American Studies."

"I see," Mizbie said.

Jeff left and she grabbed a box, slapping on a long strip of masking tape. The way he talked! She felt a pang of guilt turning her kids over to a character like this. But what could she do? She perused the bookshelf. Historical fiction, classics, science fiction – what would she do with all these well-loved classroom books her kids checked in and out? Anything but let Jeff Hines get his hands on them. She packed boxes and forced her mind to think of other things, anything but the afternoon's events. Nothing worked.

"Miz, give me a call next week and we'll go out and do something," Corky called on her way down the hall.

That was it. She had to get out of this place of suffocating salience, find a one-track cycle path, free from damning statistics and football coaches, full of bird song and tire crunch. She dragged herself onto her bike with her full backpack, and escaped from a thicket of tension to the meadow beyond the park.

She cycled the way she used to drive a car. Krahler had used Desmin's test score as an excuse. Desmin was not a political pawn, not a test score. And now his fate lay in the hands of the Detroit Police Department. She had to do something.

Chapter 19

Two caffeinated writers overheard at the Leaf and Bean –
And it needs depth of character, a moral dilemma.
Otherwise it's no better than a Booker Prize winning novel.

Nearly an hour later, her face hot and red, she walked into the Bean and Leaf. She found an empty chair in the corner and collapsed with her legs stretched in front of her. Next year she would incorporate more current events, especially around November before the election. They could stage their own gubernatorial debates around student issues. But there would be no next year. Astoria was a football town. Maybe if more parents had requested her. If she pushed it to the back of her mind before, she felt the brunt of it now.

In seconds she gulped half her iced coffee. Two tables of celebrating high school kids sat nearby. Thankfully she didn't recognize any of them as hers. Sharing goodbyes right now would be too much. She opened the laptop and hit the reply and delete buttons much harder and louder than necessary. A message from Jess popped up.

Jesspin9
toMBax20
11:00 a.m.
June 15

Hi Miz,

You must be just about finished with your school year. I got an extension on my contract, so I'll be here past September. I'm doing a dessert book called Sweet Union (as in European Union). My editor doesn't like the title, but he likes the idea, so I'm funded with another slim advance on a new book. I found a good bike shop here in Pamona, and I'm staying put for 10 days to get my bike checked out. After logging a couple thousand miles on it, it's in need of some TLC. My uncle Claud just got promoted to another level of senior editor. I need the job, but I was so in the mindset to come home. Sure, it's an experience here, but I want to wake up in my own bed and get dressed from a closet, not this backpack. I'm sick of my backpack and the broken zipper held together with safety pins. I know I'm complaining.

My brother and Elle are going to be settled in Costa Mesa soon, and even though I haven't seen the house yet, the idea of having a home base there by Christmas is feeling more appealing. I hate to admit my brother might be right. I need a job where there's something left over at the end of a week, something to show for my work, but mostly I don't want to be the strange relative his kids see on some holidays. I want them to expect me at their soccer games and tap-dancing recitals, some of them anyway. I'm thinking of being a regular part of our family, not a missing part. Not that I'd give up travel writing, but maybe I could be around more to watch Kit and Leo grow up. And now Catherine too.

I think I'll go back to northern Italy – maybe the green belt of Austria in September when the veggies and grapes are harvested. I'm going back to Spain to nose around a few Basque restaurants that have closed. I have to find the chefs and see if they've gone somewhere else, a bit of detective work. Really, they have some of the best food in the world in Spain. I'd like to try Bilbao too. Then there's Portugal and their dessert ice wines.

Too bad you work in September, but you could fly here for the summer. You could research the culinary history of these places, eh? That's what the French say after everything they say in English, eh? Kind of like the Canadians, eh? That research is the last thing I want to do, but the editor loves it, and I know you do, going through archives, reading 100-year-old diaries in town museums. Even if you could come over for a couple months, that would work. I'm sure I could squeeze a few bucks out of Uncle Claud for your research and cowriting.

It's just biking and backpacking and living in hostels, Miz. You can fly to Rome and take a train up to Parma. We can find a bike for you here. I just asked this guy at the bike shop and he said he'd give you a good deal since prices in Italy are always negotiable. It would give you good stories to tell your students. Everybody here has a story, the expats, the locals. You have to hear these people. You have to be here. Can you detect a shard of homesickness in my voice? C'mon over, dear Miz. Just email me back and say you'll come, and you'll never be the same again.

Jess

Mizbie hit the reply button and paused before she typed no. She didn't have to be back in Astor by September anymore. If only Jess was here to talk to right now. Mizbie would tell her that she had imprinted herself into the genetic makeup of St. Bartholomew's like a duck on its mother, and how could she extricate herself? Then she heard Jess's imaginary voice, *It's a job. You have a life. Go live it. Cast off the hamster wheel of school. Grab a bike wheel over here.* This might be the only chance she'd ever have to go to Europe. If she needed to clear her mind, she could clear it in Europe as well as she could wallowing in her apartment, maybe even better. Before she had a chance to obsess about all the reasons why she shouldn't go, she typed a quick, "Yes, I'll come," Before her logic kicked in, she tapped *send*.

She'd pack her backpack, rent a car, and leave it at Detroit Metro. Desmin came to mind, his voice like an earworm she couldn't ignore. She couldn't leave before trying to explain his big heart and potential. Before the flight, she'd stop off at the Detroit Police Department to give them a piece of her mind.

"Ms Baxter?" A familiar voice beside her made her turn. He was a bit older than she was, tall and ruggedly fit, and his jeans were pressed. "May I sit down?" he asked.

Mizbie sat up, the coffee infusing her with enough new energy at least for that. "I know you," she said, focusing on this man with a strong hand nearly strangling his coffee cup.

"I'm Brad Peters, Seth's dad," he said. Brad wasn't the best at reading expressions, but it didn't take much to read hers. The few times he had seen her before with her violet eyes and animation, she was far removed from this woman. Her eyes were now rimmed in red and her arms hung lifeless at her sides. He figured it was a bad time to tell her, and he didn't have a clue how to begin.

Mizbie lowered the laptop lid and reached out to shake his strong hand.

"I just wanted to thank you for teaching my son this year," he said. "He's never talked about school much before, but he sure talks about your class. From what he says, I can tell you care and that means a lot. He said you usually come here after school, so I thought I'd give it a try." He shifted closer, moving over for a woman with four lattes in a holder. "I don't know where to start."

"Sure, sit down, Mr. Peters," Mizbie tried to focus. Not that she wouldn't prefer to stand on the table and throw her shoes if she had the energy, swearing every epithet she ever knew. What could St. Bartholomew's do now? Fire her again?

"He is so thoughtful, Mr. Peters, he really is, organizing that Relay for Life run after his mom died, and running the lightboard for our production of *Hamlet* –"

"Seth has come so far this year. So much has awakened in him and I can see him change, it seems, every day." He took a drink of coffee. "Did Seth tell you about his mother?" he asked.

"A little. He said she was an avid reader and she wanted him to go to college."

"When she found she only had a year left with us, she started teaching him different belief narratives." Brad took Mizbie's ice-cooled hand between his. Karina would take his hand between hers like this and explain how her parents had named her. Her name was Sanskrit for loving compassion, the interdependence of all living things. They'd talk about what it means to have compassion."

He looked at Mizbie's hands, but his eyes were far away. "She told him when he sat down at the kitchen table, she'd be there with him." He returned his hands to the coffee cup. "She said when Seth stood under the mulberry tree at the side of the house, she'd be the breeze in the leaves. He'll stand out there sometimes, and I know he's thinking of Karina."

Mizbie thought about the last time Seth had come to her room after school and pulled up a chair just to talk. That look. There was a give and take of energies in their conversation as there had been with Mara Jade, Desmin, Rashmi, and Singer, a few of her favorite students. She wondered how much Seth resembled his mother. It must have been hard for Brad to see Karina in him every day.

"I can see where Seth's thoughtfulness comes from."

"He has compassion. He can soak it up from other people too. He sure didn't get that from his hardheaded old man," Brad said. "I didn't mean to go into all that. I don't know why I did, but there's another reason I wanted to talk to you. Let me see if I can say this right." He seemed impatient with the direction of their conversation. "It's not just Seth. I think what cinched it was when you showed up at his lacrosse match that night. I was planting and couldn't make it so my neighbors –"

"I remember your neighbors. They seemed to think the world of Seth. Really, I just happened to be in the neighborhood that night. I hadn't planned on seeing the lacrosse –" She didn't finish her thought because she had a sense that she was being watched. Her eyes were drawn to the man in the corner reading the paper. It was the same Bland Man. How long had he been there? *I wish Heuster was here.* Bland Man caught her eye, folded the paper and left. She could use a beer right now.

"Seth talks a lot about you." If Brad noticed she was distracted, he didn't mention it.

"Come to think of it, he's told me about you too," Mizbie said automatically, trying to smile. She just lost her job, for God sakes. *Say something to end this wrenched conversation, go home, and take a cold bath.*

"Well, that night at the lacrosse match my neighbors started talking to Seth and me about how familiar you looked."

"Yes, I have heard that. I don't know what it is, but people tell me that. I really have to go." Mizbie started to gather her things.

"But this was different." He studied her face. "They mentioned your smile and the way your cheek has these lines around it here." He reached out.

Mizbie leaned back in her chair, and she wasn't smiling. She set her feet on the floor and prepared for a quick exit, deciding how she could leave. "This is all very interesting, but I have to leave now," she said.

"No, please wait. I didn't mean to upset you. This all sounds crazy, I'm sure," he said, shifting his chair back in a loud scrape on the floor. "Maybe this will explain what I mean." He reached into his pocket and took out an old picture. "This was taken in 1979. See, these are the people you met, my neighbors."

"Yes, it looks like them," she said, glancing at the picture of a man and woman at a restaurant table, but keeping her eyes on him.

"But look again. Do they look familiar to you at all? She was a little younger than you when this picture was taken. He gripped the picture as if it would make her understand. Seth told us that you said your parents had died in some drunk-driving accident, and when Fran heard that, she couldn't believe it."

Mizbie became self-conscious. She let go of her laptop and finished her coffee. "It's been years since my parents died."

"I'm sorry. But when Fran saw you at the game and brought over this picture for me to show you –" He started again. "What I mean is, she asked if I'd come here and talk you into coming to see them at the farm. She has something she wants to tell you. It's about your family. They asked me to take you to meet them. They can explain better than I can."

"This Fran and Jim are waiting for me? Right now?"

"They are. I have a truck. We can put your bike in the back. I'll have you back in an hour."

She shouldn't have drunk the coffee so fast. Her head swirled with Krahler, Desmin, and now her parents and these farm people. Her face grew hot again and she tried to cool it with her hands.

"Here." Brad gave her a white handkerchief. No one carried handkerchiefs anymore. She was grateful for it, blotting her face and neck, letting her hair fall around her face as a means of some privacy. Brad looked away. The handkerchief was faintly scented with a musky cologne and in her confused state, she felt some comfort from this man and his scented handkerchief.

"I know this must seem kind of sudden to you. Fran and Jim are like family to me. You'll see. They're wonderful people. You won't regret taking the time to meet them."

"I'll be right back. Let me freshen up first," she said. In the bathroom, Mizbie splashed cold water on her face, but it still felt hot. The door was opposite the bathroom. She could easily just walk out and bike home. Maybe these people belonged to some obscure cult. But her laptop and backpack were at the table. What the hell. Whatever happened at Fran and Jim's couldn't be worse than the rest of the day.

"I don't think I'm the person they're looking for, but maybe I can put their curiosity to rest," Mizbie said to Brad as she stepped up into the truck.

"What if I said they knew your parents a long time ago?" Brad secured her bike in the back.

"They knew my parents?"

"That's what Fran says. She knew them when they lived here. I'll let her tell you." He started up the truck, an old Ford that smelled like earth and dog.

"My parents never lived here," Mizbie tried to be patient. They're mistaking me for someone else. I grew up in Alabaster, a little town on Lake Huron. Why would they think that?"

"It was a long time ago before you were born. When Seth told us your parents died, they were really surprised. They were good friends with your parents when they lived here, but Fran and Jim lost track of them when they moved. They wanted to hear about your parents and share what they knew. When I said I was coming to thank you today, they asked if I'd invite you over."

Mizbie searched her memory for any stories about her parents living anywhere else but Alabaster. Then there were the dreams that Ryder had helped with, telling her to get in touch with her past. Since her trip back to Alabaster, the night terrors were fewer. Maybe this visit would help even more. Was there a chance they could've lived here years ago, right where she was working? Why didn't her parents ever mention it? Her curiosity grew. If she didn't meet them, she'd always wonder about Fran and Jim.

"They said your mom was a singer and sang with a band when she was young. They said your mom always sang an old song to you. It was, 'You Are the Sunshine of my Life,' I think."

Mizbie's throat tightened as she looked at this man who breached the chasm between parent and teacher, between present and past. She hadn't thought of the song since she was a child. "I remember," she said, curiosity replacing some of her tension.

They turned onto a gravel road. "You know, I think I saw you last summer on your bike. The trail goes behind my farm. It's not used much, but it's a great path. Just the other side of it is a pond at the back of my acreage. On hot days Seth and I will jump in. It's ice cold and feels pretty good on a hot afternoon in July." His voice seemed to relax now that he'd made his case for Fran and Jim.

Mizbie knew the pond very well. She'd gone skinny dipping there herself on a hot day. It was far enough away from the bike trail that no one could have seen her. The water was surprisingly cold, and she would watch for sunfish nests on the sandy shallows where she stepped in or out. Lying in the meadow grass after a swim, she arranged her hair, fanning it out on her shirt to dry. She looked up at the clouds that spread like a sky of spiked hair, then smoothed into ribbonlike strings. She tried to remember what else Seth had said about his dad. "Seth tells me you sailed to Fiji?" she said, trying to make conversation.

"Yeah, Seth likes to hear about it," he almost smiled. "It was right after MSU. I graduated in agribusiness and my roommate Mike partied hard and played soccer. We were complete opposites, but we figured if we could stand each other in a postage stamp-sized dorm room, we could handle the close quarters in a 24 footer. Mike's stepdad kept his Morgan at Dana Point in California. It had only one mast and a tiny motor. I'd never sailed before, but after a day or two, the lap of the waves and the wind when it hit the sail, the clank of the lines on the halyards, the sea birds – I don't know – I fell in love with the whole thing.

"We'd been out for awhile when we stopped in Tahiti for supplies. The next day we hit a squall with gusty north and west winds that I swear nearly broke the mast in half. Really, it broke the mainsail line. Mike and I spliced it back together, but it was shorter at that point and we couldn't get it trimmed as much as we needed. But by that time, we'd been out a week and we knew how to pull the sail and secure the boat, turning into the wind. When it was over, we were off course and it added some time to the trip."

She watched Brad's faraway look. "So what did you think of the islands? Would you go back?"

"We dove in the Great Sea Reef, that's north of the big island, Vanua Levu. We climbed volcano trails. In the middle of Viti Levu are waterfalls you can swim under. And the people, they talked with us as if they had all the time in the world. I doubt they've eaten anyone in years. Yeah, I'm going back. I'll take Seth with me."

Mizbie told Brad about her trip to Europe in a few days.

"Fran and Jim travel a lot. They have a fifth wheel they take all over in winter. I've never been to Europe either." He adjusted the rearview mirror and his arm brushed hers.

Mizbie got the impression that this farmer was at home on the farm or in a sailboat, but awkward when it came to women. She stretched out in the passenger's seat, looking out the window. Her brain pinballed from Fiji to the Detroit police to Krahler's statistical gibberish. Backpacking with Jess this summer would help clear her mind. It's not that Astor had become so endearing to her, but it had become the closest thing she had to call home. She was freer now than she had been when Stella came to live with her. Stella and their morning diatribe, Stella racing around the apartment playing with Daphne. What would happen to Stella if her mom skipped out again?

Mizbie remembered a couple of no-name papers still in her backpack. It was too late to track down the owners or include them in the last grades. It didn't matter. She had no reason to feel a part of these kids' success anymore –, their fears, their anger, their rushing to tell her about their weekend or cry about it. Would she find a school somewhere that valued her skills over football? She stared out the window at the farmland skimming by, fence posts, occasional dirt crossroads, waving fields of wheat, just getting ready to turn gold.

"This is some good country, good farm land for organic," Brad broke the silence. "I've been certified organic for about 10 years now, mostly tomatoes, blueberries, basil, and strawberries. The orchards on either side of me are organic too, so we don't have to worry about runoff or spray." His gaze stretched far over the fields. "In winter I have a 10 acre greenhouse for hydroponic tomatoes and strawberries. You'd be surprised how many tomatoes you can get from one greenhouse. The taste sure beats those ones with the pasty insides you get from the grocery. And you know those ripe, red strawberries you get at the market at Christmastime? Those are mine."

To Mizbie this farmer was using a foreign language with his talk of runoff and certified organic. Her mind wandered to Jess's fields of sunflowers in Tuscany where she followed a trail to a monastery or some such place. "I have to admit, I'm clueless when it comes to farms," she said.

"Fran and Jim will fill you in," Brad said.

Brad's easy, natural way began to rub off on her. Her wariness of motive and agenda was being won over by his calm assurance. There was no hint of the tension she grew use to with Carl. The window breeze wafted through her hair and down, cooling her neck. She smelled something and sneezed. "You have a dog?

"Just took her home from the vet – had to have surgery. Gabby's only five, a golden lab. Seth loves that dog, so when the vet said there were still lots of good years left in her if we did the surgery, I didn't think twice about it. Doc Walters said the surgery was better than expected and in a month she'll be herding chickens again. She's got stitches from stem to stern, though." He smoothed his hair back and punched a few buttons on the radio until he found a classical public radio station. Violins playing a Vivaldi concerto filled the quiet space between them.

"So Jake's really attached to Gabby?"

Brad lowered the volume a bit. "Oh, she sleeps at the foot of his bed and waits on the porch for him to get home from school. Gabby follows him to the greenhouses when he does his chores. She's his dog. I couldn't see putting Gabby to sleep. That was not an option."

It sounded like Jake wasn't the only one who couldn't put Gabby down. "So you don't get tired of driving so far to get anywhere? I rarely drive anything but my bike. Everything's close to where I live."

Brad wasn't the least offended. "You get use to it, I guess. I wouldn't live in town if you paid me." He took a breath. "Good country air."

He must not smell the wet dog, Mizbie thought.

"I have two porches on the house, one east and one facing west. The east one I have Adirondack chairs for morning coffee. Spring to fall, I'm out there every sunny morning, watching that sun climb over the tomato fields. It casts shadows on the crop and the sky turns all kinds of pink and orange. At sunset I have the west porch, the blueberry field and greenhouse side. Seth joins me sometimes. I have a glass of wine in one hand and check the evening news on the laptop. Seth has a Coke and we have some of our best talks out there. I can't say we're religious people, but it's a spiritual experience, something we couldn't come close to in town." He checked Mizbie's expression to see if she was comfortable with the windows open. "Seth said you have a cat."

"Spoken like a dog person!" Mizbie laughed. "Daphne's very spoiled but agreeable when I'm there, and she takes care of herself when I'm not. She's not mine really; I'm watching her for the friend I'm going to work with in Europe. She's writing a book on backpacking and eating her way through the western EU. So what's your wine, red or white?" She was running out of conversation.

"I've made some dry white table wine from my neighbor's Anjou pears. He likes it pretty well. I like my red rhubarb-plum wine best. It's all organic. I don't sell it, just give it to friends. You like wine? You can try it."

Mizbie was surprised. "Sounds good to me." Her student's father, an organic farmer, dog lover, and winemaker. She pictured Gabby with Seth sitting on the west porch with Dad, talking about her cat.

The road turned to gravel as Brad veered from side to side to avoid ruts. "Normally I'd just drive through 'em. I've got heavy-duty suspension, but you'd probably bounce up and hit the ceiling," he said, swerving a hard right again.

Mizbie planted herself firmly in the seat. Her right arm had already hit the door a few times. At that, they hit a deep rut at highway speed. After driving square into it, he looked over, checking Mizbie's bounce. "Missed one," she said, clearly feeling the seat springs on the way down.

"This is it." They pulled up the long, gravel drive past the centennial farm sign. An older man, probably Jim, was playing catch with a preschool boy in the front yard. The boy hunched forward and caught the ball, holding up a huge catcher's mitt with his thin left arm, throwing it back with his right. Brad parked behind a truck and another car. Jim caught the ball and called out. Two women opened the front screen door, crossed the white wood porch, with its requisite swing, and down the front steps to the driveway, lining up and waiting for Brad's truck door to open.

Looking at the faces, Mizbie saw the older woman, probably Fran, Jim's wife, and a woman close to Mizbie's age. Next to her stood a man with a nondescript face, ivory shirt, and khaki pants. An instant recognition made her stomach churn. It was the voyeur she saw get into the white van at the spring food fest, the stalker at the school parking lot, the damned parasite who seemed to be everywhere she was. At the sight of Bland Man, she forgot everyone else. Before Brad could turn off the truck ignition, Mizbie opened her door and slammed it. She walked up to this man, who had caused her so much irritation, and glared. He was no taller than she was. She was waiting for this moment and here were witnesses. She could yell every foul word she was capable of, or tell him that the school weightlifter was ready to pound the shit out of him. His expression was neutral and unreadable. Everything about this man was infuriatingly benign.

He opened his mouth to speak and Miz released a swarm of curses like hornets in full sting. Her face glowed with heat from her fiery core and her fists circled. With her index finger, she poked a chest button on his no-iron oxford cloth shirt.

"You false, conniving, devious, crooked miscreant . . ."

Glancing at Fran and Jim, she detected amusement at her outburst rather than shock. She continued.

"You foul, contemptuous, underhanded, deceptive, deceitful, reprobate, trying to hoodwink me . . .

I want to know *now*." Her finger continued poking the button, her brows shooting up, then wrinkling together. "Who *are* you, you reprobate . . . nincompoop, and why have you been following me?" She stepped forward as he backed away.

"I was hired by Fran and Jim to find Lauren." He looked to both sides as if he would need a quick exit. "And now that I've found you and identified you, my job is done."

"What do you mean, *find* me?" I'm not lost here. I'm just here to talk to some people who think they knew my parents. What's going on? Brad, who is Lauren?" She turned to look at him. Brad's expression didn't reveal anything. What's this about?" Her voice sharpened.

"I'll be going now. Fran and Jim will tell you." Bland Man backed away.

"You're not leaving. I want an explanation."

"It's not what you think," Brad said, as if she had misread directions and turned the wrong way. "We'll explain –" His anodyne smile added to her irritation.

The two women waited expectantly, everyone wanting to speak, but no one offering up the first words. "Yes . . . well . . ." the agitated Bland Man's eyes darted from Fran and Jim, then back to Mizbie. Without a backward glance, he headed for his car, opening the door.

"Go ahead and sneak off!" Her voice cracked. "Just don't let me ever see you again!" Mizbie's fists clenched, fingers turning from red to white.

"Mizbie, you will not ever see me again," Bland Man stood behind the car door. "Believe me, you're more of a man than I ever hope to be."

They watched him shut the door. He could have asked Brad to move the truck, but he cut a U-turn through the yard and drove away.

"That annoying pipsqueak . . . that pest . . . that sniveling idiot always returning like a bad penny . . ." Mizbie sputtered.

"Well . . ." Fran changed the subject, attempted a hug, tried shaking hands, but ended up clutching Mizbie's arm. It was a gesture Mizbie had used with students, but it had no effect on her. "I believe introductions are in order. I'm Fran Bartner and this is Jim." Everyone said hello breaking the tension. "When we saw you at the lacrosse game and Brad offered to talk to you at the Bean and Leaf, we just thought this would be easier."

"What she's saying is, we wanted to find out what happened to your parents," Jim said. We wanted to find out what you knew about them. And we thought you would want to know what they were like when they lived here."

Mizbie searched his face and detected no artifice or hidden agenda. The fight began to drain out of her.

"C'mon in. I'm sure you have a lot of questions you want to ask us," Jim said.

Fran and Jim led the way, walking shoulder to shoulder with the familiar contentment of an older married couple, ahead of Brad and Mizbie. Brad's giant hand curved around her back, nearly resting on her shoulder in a gesture of comfort. Thinking better of it, his hand returned to his side. Little Wyatt, his adult-sized catcher's mitt nearly dragging on the ground, ran in from the yard followed by his mother. Mizbie thought she heard Fran say, "I know where she gets that temper from."

Mizbie tried to remember which of her parents had the temper. Not remembering annoyed her.

They entered the parlor of the old farmhouse, which smelled of fresh fruit and furniture wax. The wall that led to the dining room was lined with floor-to-ceiling shelves stuffed with books. She browsed the titles and noticed a few from American and European history. "You have the Mark Twain *Autobiography*," she said.

"Yep . . . an affliction. 'Loyalty to petrified opinion never broke a chain –'"

"'Or freed a human soul,'" Mizbie said.

They sat down and attempted polite conversation while Wyatt sat on the floor with a toy kaleidoscope to his eye. He dashed across the room to catch the light.

"I'll get some iced tea," Jim said.

On the opposite wall were pictures of meadows with wildflowers, birches, and ginkgo trees. "I've seen your work in the Astor Art Museum, Fran. The birches –"

Loud, expletives sprung from the kitchen. "Just a little finger slice from cutting the lemon, that's all," Jim called out. "I'm okay."

Everyone was quiet when he brought out the tray of iced tea and a bowl of lemon slices. Mizbie noticed a new bandage wrapping his left index finger.

So many questions she had, but where to start? Mizbie steered the conversation to her life on the lake at Alabaster. They seemed most curious about the jobs she had before teaching. She entertained them with stories about her work at a used bookstore, a go-cart track, and pickle packing with Jess one summer, where they had seen workers drop a pickle, reach down with a rubber glove, and stuff it back in the jar. Finally she exhausted her patience and asked what made them think it was her parents that they knew.

"Remember the lumber company where your father worked? You said he loved wood working. He made this table for us,"

Mizbie walked over to examine the arts-and-crafts style lamp table with a shelf for books or magazines below. She remembered a similar table in her Alabaster home by the living room bay window that overlooked Lake Huron, hand-rubbed cherry, where Mom kept her book next to her chair. Her child self ran her fingers along its smooth top, printing letters in the light dust that invariably settled there. That must've been where Mizbie inherited her housekeeping skills. It looked like something her father could've made, but wasn't unusual in any way. "He even branded his initials inside the drawer here," he said, showing her the initials DB in the drawer's dovetailed corner.

"Dylan made it for us. We admired theirs, so he made this one." Jim was going to sit next to Mizbie but pulled out an ottoman and sat across from her instead.

"He used to be a real-estate appraiser. We were both young married couples and went out on weekends together." Fran talked about how Mizbie's mom, Audra, would go up on stage and sing with bands. Her mom had a good voice, but Mizbie couldn't imagine her mom singing in front of people. Then Jim grew more serious and explained how their friendship changed after Fran had their first child. It was about that time that Dylan had decided to accept a job in northern Michigan somewhere. When Jim and Fran's little girl was nearly two, she disappeared one day. Jim described the devastation they felt and how everyone from police to neighbors searched for weeks. Mizbie's parents had also searched, postponing their move to help. But it was all in vain; they lost touch with their friends when they moved up north. "Then we had Kelly."

Mizbie was beginning to believe that her parents might have been their friends; there was the wooden table, but why wouldn't they have mentioned living in Astor, especially when they knew Mizbie came here to teach? It didn't make sense. "What about that horrible private detective?" She had to know.

"We're so sorry that he upset you," Fran said. "It's just that when we saw you at the lacrosse game, we were so hopeful that you might have a clue, that our daughter might still be alive."

"I'm sorry for your loss, but I can't see how I can help. If my parents had lived here, I'm sure they would've told me." She excused herself to the bathroom.

In the hallway Mizbie passed the wall of family pictures. Glancing at faces in portraits and snapshots of weddings and soccer games, school graduations, new tractors, and anniversaries, her eyes came upon a small picture at the bottom. Three smiling adults stood on a lawn with a toddler. In front was a shadow of the man taking the picture, her father. She focused on the picture, but her mind couldn't accept it. The snapshot was the same size and shape, in the same birch bark frame. Like little Wyatt's kaleidoscope, one look revealed a shift that no amount of turning back would ever replicate. Colors randomly fit together to create a new paradigm. Her eyes focused on the picture and recognized it, but she couldn't see it with all the new patterns crowding their ways through her mind. This shift was one she could not believe, although it was there on the wall in front of her. Here was the evidence but she refused to accept it. Her years growing up in Alabaster were fake, a fabrication, a lie, an incredible secret weight her parents took to their deaths. The same picture, the same frame. She rushed to the bathroom and threw up.

After a time, she heard Brad through the door. "Are you okay . . . Mizbie? You've been in here a long time. Can we get you something?"

"No, I'm not okay. Give me a minute," she said, splashing water on her face and combing her fingers through her hair. She opened the door.

Brad saw the look on her face and instinctively put his arm around her. She was shaking and leaned into him.

They listened to Mizbie talk about her picture in its birch frame. She looked from face to face at the circle of people watching her. Her mom and dad had been her only family and she loved them. They couldn't have been capable of abduction. To even consider the possibility seemed inconceivable. "How can I believe this?" She asked. But there was the picture.

"We tried to think of the best way to tell you. We thought of all sorts of ways, but nothing seemed quite right. Dear, your necklace," Fran said pointing to the silver circle entwined with miniature leaves.

Mizbie reached for the necklace half hidden under a collar. "I've had it since I was sixteen. It was a birthday gift that belonged to my grandmother, but Mom put it on a different chain, she said."

"Do you know what it means?" Fran asked.

"I don't know if it means anything, but it's the only thing I have of grandmother's. We never met."

"It's a framing circle." Fran looked impatient. "It's the idea of a life in time. It did belong to your grandmother, then it belonged to me. I gave it to Audra when they left; that's how much I cared about her," Fran said with great effort. "When my mother gave the necklace to me on my birthday, she said it means you grow up, you find your way, and you come back." She looked at Mizbie. "You've come back now, and the necklace is right where it belongs, on you."

Part of Mizbie wanted to listen to Fran, and part of her wanted to slam the screen door behind her and forget they ever met.

"Mom, remember?" Kelly pointed up to the bookcase.

"Oh, Jim, you were suppose to remind me," Fran said, reaching up to the bookcase and placing in Mizbie's lap a carefully wrapped package tied in a single green satin ribbon. "This is for you, Lauren. Happy birthday. I've dreamed of saying that every year for more than 30 years and now I can say it."

"My birthday's in October," Mizbie said.

Fran was about to say something and changed her mind. "The day you were born was really last Tuesday."

Mizbie opened the wrapping and lifted out a 1934 edition of Robert Frost's *Selected Poems*.

"Seth said you read a few of the Frost poems in class and liked 'em. We thought you'd like this."

Mizbie gently touched the pages and the book fell open to "Mending Wall."

"Look here," Jim said, carefully holding the book and turning it to the inside front cover. There was a name and date on the yellowed page,

Lesley 1965. "Lesley was his daughter, you know. This might be another Lesley, or it might just be her."

Mizbie was touched by their thoughtfulness. "It's a treasure." Her throat caught. "Thank you," she said, holding the book and smelling its old book smell.

One by one, little discoveries began to weigh on Mizbie's balance of understanding. Fran and Jim seemed full of expectation, raw, protective emotion waiting to be let loose on her. Compared to the picture, except for the fine lines around Fran's bright eyes and the dark pools of Jim's eyes, they remained unchanged. How foreign her parents' relationship seemed to this clan. Sonia's horse, Pete, might have felt the way Mizbie did right now before he reared up and dropped Sonia's daughter on the ground.

"You look a bit distraught, dear," Fran said. "Jim, get some crackers and cheese and some grapes. Maybe some of Brad's rhubarb wine."

"How about that goat cheese?" Jim asked.

"Yes, yes. That's fine," Fran answered, not wanting to miss a moment of mothering that could make up for lost years.

Mizbie stood up. Thoughts swam in her head. The parents who raised her, keepers of a secret so dangerous they could have gone to prison. Through kindergarten, braces, driver's training, first dates, and college, they kept the truth from her. She couldn't decide how she felt in the confusion of a life built on fabrication. Was she furious or forgiving? Joyous that her birth family was alive, or full of revenge against people who weren't around to hear it? Here were these loving people, possibly her family, talking about goat cheese and rhubarb wine. "I really need to go."

Fran stood too, trying to get Mizbie to stay longer. "We understand. It's all so overwhelming. Would you like to see your old room before you go?"

Wyatt ran to his mother and held up the kaleidoscope for her to see. "Wyatt stayed in your crib when he came to visit, but now he's graduated to a bigger bed," Kelly picked up her son and held him in her lap.

Mizbie really didn't want to see the room, but she climbed the stairs with Fran behind her. At the top, Fran linked her arm through Mizbie's.

Upstairs were four bedrooms and one small windowless nursery room in the middle, just above the parlor. The nursery was nevertheless cheery with white walls and colorful handmade quilts. It smelled freshly aired. A train decal chugged along the wall opposite the crib, probably added for Wyatt. A shelf of picture books included well-worn copies of *Lengthy* and *Round Robin*. "Those were a couple of your favorites," Fran said.

In the middle of the floor was an iron filigree grate. "Those are common in old houses like these," Fran explained. "It had central heat by the time we inherited it from Jim's parents, but when they owned it, there was a stove in the middle that heated the whole house. This is where the stovepipe came up through the roof. We chose this for a nursery because it was the warmest room in the house. The heat and light came up from the parlor downstairs." Fran reached over to turn on a light, but Mizbie asked her to wait a minute.

As the others waited below, Mizbie stared at the filigree grate, her eyes slowly following the light that came through, creating its filmy lacework on the ceiling. She stood on the grate and watched the spot on the ceiling change its shape as she moved. Could it be? She crouched on her arms and legs looking down through the grate at the others who looked up at her.

"You'd be playing up here and when your dad or I looked up at you from the parlor, you'd call 'ite, ite!' You couldn't say your 'l's' yet. We'd turn the light on and you'd stretch your arms up to make shadows on the ceiling of your room, and you'd laugh. Fran laughed. Everyone below laughed, releasing the tension in the room like a rainstorm on a drought-stressed field. Kelly turned on a table lamp from below and the light shot up intensifying the lacy pattern on the ceiling. Mizbie moved her arms and watched as the ceiling pattern changed.

Downstairs Jim paused before he opened the screen door for Mizbie. "Hot damn, you discovered it yourself. We didn't have to tell you. That's the best. He slapped Brad's back. "Thanks, Brad, for getting

Lauren here so we could –," he looked up at Mizbie and blinked, "– see you again."

Fran reached around and gave Mizbie a hug there was no escape from. Stepping side to side with Mizbie trapped in her arms she said, "I'm sorry about the private detective. So sorry. We just had to know. We've had a few weeks to think about this and imagine what it might be like to meet you, dear. It's all we've thought about. Go ahead. Take some time. Take all the time you need. We'll be here for you."

The little group walked out to Brad's truck where he opened the door for her. "Here's our phone number." Fran held out a piece of notebook paper. "Jim, write the email address on there too. You have a pen?" She gave the paper to him. "You just give us a call whenever you feel like it. Our daughter. Lord, I never thought I'd be talking to you again, and here you are. Do your thinking and give us a call when you're ready. C'mon and see us anytime. How about Sunday dinner?" Fran said.

Fran's intensity made Mizbie feel unraveled. "This is too much. I need some time." Their looks alternating between hope and despair, barely registered with Mizbie. "I have to get out of here, Brad."

"Wait. Please wait a minute," Kelly said, racing to the house, but Mizbie was on her way to the truck. Kelly pushed open the screen door, and it bounced on its springs behind her. In her arm was a brown stuffed rabbit. "Here, Lauren, this is yours. Mom kept it all these years, but you should have it now." She held it out, but the window stayed closed.

"Let's go," Mizbie said, turning away.

She saw him say a few words to Fran and Jim, then uneasily take his place in the seat beside her. She refused to look back at them, but imagined them huddled together, Kelly with the stuffed rabbit cradled in her arm.

They drove in silence. Brad stretched his arm out the window. "You know, the black-capped warbler, this bird in Germany, migrated to southern Europe, but some of the birds go all the way to England in winter, even though they used to go to Spain, where it's warm. Since the 1960s the birds going to England have an evolved wing shape and beak, like Darwin's finches. It seems the Brits have been feeding them from their backyards, and the warbler's wings and beaks adapted to the Brit's bird feeders. They keep coming back."

"You're trying to teach a teacher," Mizbie chided. Her shoulders drooped in tired confusion. "What have I missed these years? I don't even know when their birthdays are."

"I can tell you the last one. Your mom's is July 15th and your dad's is September 27th."

"My mom and my dad."

Brad changed the subject. "A few years back I picked up a '05 Crown Vic from craigslist when Seth and I were in Chicago. It's an old taxi. Those babies never die. It's got 200,000 miles on it. Seth already knew how to fix John Deere tractors, and he couldn't wait to get into this car. We replaced nearly everything but the engine block."

Mizbie wondered why anyone would put so much effort into a decade-old car. "Does it run yet?"

"You could say that. Just about. By the time Seth's a senior, we should have it finished. That's his goal, to take his girlfriend to the senior prom in it. That used to be our Friday night together, ordering pizzas and a couple of two-liter root beers, working on the car. Now Kelsey takes up his Friday nights, but that's okay. She's a good gal, Kelsey. Lost her dad, so they have that in common too." His voice drifted off.

He turned on a classic radio station where Fleetwood Mac sang, "Don't stop thinkin' about tomorrow –" Mizbie thought of Seth and Kelsey, whom Seth didn't recognize with her contact lenses, walking together into her classroom at St. Bartholomew's. Izzy would be going to summer wrestling camp, and Edward's broken hand was probably on the mend. She thought of Brandon and his tectonic plates, hoping he'd be safe in Canada. Rashmi was probably packing to spend the summer in India, and Mara Jade would be working at the comic book shop in New Orleans. Singer would be on-the-road Singer. Would the band get an invitation to their favorite gig, the Gainesville, Florida, music fest?

"Yesterday's gone . . . yesterday's gone . . . ooh . . . don't 'ya look back." A bump in the road jostled her back to their conversation. "I can see the two of them in that old car on the way to the prom. Seth and Kelsey all dressed up."

She told Brad about last summer, when she had turned down Front Street, and found herself in the middle of a procession of classic and muscle cars that Astor residents brought out of barns and from under tarps for the Fourth Annual Astor Cool Cruise. Speakers blared "Just My Imagination" as she cycled behind a black 1930 Ford with a Kermit the Frog character driving, and Winnie the Pooh and Tigger in the rumble seat. Men and women, old and young, made up a collection of ponytails, poodle skirts, leather vests, and muscle shirts. The local hot-dog stand had car hops on roller skates bringing root beer and Coney Island hot dogs to car windows. The next song she recognized was Elvis's "You Ain't Nothin' but a Hound Dog," then three 1958 Corvette convertibles drove by in the other lane, one red, the next white, the last one navy blue with a skull and crossbones hanging from the rearview mirror. Behind them drove a '70s vintage Cadillac hearse, gray with lace curtains. A red '60s Chevy truck with an American flag in the back window honked a horn to the tune of, "My Dog Has Fleas." Hooters, the only chain restaurant Astor would allow in town, had its wait staff in black tank tops and shorts with white knee socks passing out tickets for chicken wings. Mizbie arrived home humming, "Help me Rhonda, Help, help me, Rhonda."

"Seth will be able to have his car in the Astoria Cool Cruise next year," she said.

"His car isn't that old, but he might cruise it anyway," Brad said.

Mizbie's voice was tired. "This morning I had a job, I knew who my parents were, what my name was, what gigs I would play this summer, and where I would live."

"I'm used to hearing Fran and Jim say your name. They've been calling up and saying Lauren this and Lauren that all week." He smiled until his eyes crinkled, a smile Brad didn't trot out too much. "So what are you afraid of?"

"Afraid? Who's afraid, Mr. Psychiatrist? Why should I be afraid of these farm people I've never met before, these intense people who have all these expectations about who I should be, but maybe I'm not? These people who have created a fantasy about who I would be, about the prodigal daughter who returned to her roots. What am I supposed to be afraid of, having a sister? What would we do, bake Christmas cookies together? Does she even like Devo or Sun Ra music or her husband? And a nephew who plays baseball, yuck! I don't give a flying fig about baseball." She strained against the seat belt and tried to order the scattered splinters of ideas. "My life hasn't changed, really. Except everything in my memory is a lie now, and I can't confront the people who created this charade, because all they are now are ashes in my closet. So everything from this point on will finally be real."

She looked over at Brad's shoe on the gas pedal, the olive green shoe that was popular with vegans, no leather or glue holding it together. Was he vegan besides being an organic farmer? She would've asked if she cared.

"How about afraid to admit that the parents you've loved all your life abducted you?"

"Wrong. You are so wrong. That is lame. I don't want to talk about it." Her brain screamed a silent howl, annoyed by his calm. He had known about this for weeks. In his mind, why wouldn't she be happy to discover a whole damn new family? The ride back to the coffee shop seemed interminably long.

"That picture on the wall was taken a couple weeks before the kidnapping. I can't count the times I heard Fran say, "I just stepped up to the house to get her sweater because there was a chill in the air." And when she came back out with it, you were gone, taken from a blanket in your own front yard in the middle of the day. They searched for years. They never gave up. Fran saved all the news clippings. When they saw you at the lacrosse game, they hired the detective who traced you back to Alabaster on Lake Huron. He talked to the people living in your old house and they remembered you coming up and asking questions just last month. Losing you was the biggest regret of their lives."

Mizbie recalled the road in front of Fran and Jim's house, and how it curved around a side yard. The same house that was in the picture, with its wooden screen door. "So their house with the gray and white porch, the house in the picture would've been my home? My parents were never interested in photographs, even when I graduated from college."

What were Fran and Jim like? What was the friendship between the couples like? She thought she knew who her parents were, when in reality they were cons, impostors, charlatans, and fakes. "It's maddening that things fall into place looking back, but you can't live going backwards."

"I think Kierkegaard said something like that. 'Life can only be understood backwards; but it has to be lived forwards.'" He swerved around another bump in the road.

"I know what you did today was done out of caring for Fran and Jim," she said, not feeling a word of it.

Brad searched for words to help Mizbie Baxter/Lauren Bartner retrieve her feisty voice. The violet sparks in her eyes were dulled. She sat next to him looking only vulnerable. "You always told Seth to explore what was possible."

"I tell all my students that."

"You can tell that to yourself now," he said. "You plow the same field, you get the same crops. My acreage had been in soybeans and corn since before I worked the farm. It was time for something different. Maybe it's time for you to plow a new field for yourself."

Mizbie didn't know what he was talking about. If this was a movie, she would have had yet another explosion of conflicting feelings, found her way, and lived happily ever after. Instead she looked at Brad as if he were a spoiled jar of jam, deciding whether to scrape off the bad and keep the sweet part, or just toss the whole jar.

There was the issue of her parents' ashes stored in a wooden box behind towels in her closet. She had kept them, but what should she do with them now? She would go home and scream at them, cry over them. Or she could dump them in the park behind her apartment, working the remnants of ash into the soil until she couldn't even tell they were there. It would be the end of a fake family and the possible beginning of a real one. After Carl, Stella, St. Bartholomew's, and her parents, here was a change with a future.

"I don't cook much, but I grill a good burger," Brad said, thinking he still had so much he wanted to say. "I can take you back to the Bean and

Leaf, or you can join Seth and me for dinner. It's 100 percent organic farm-raised Black Angus beef, grass fed."

There were a hundred good reasons not to have dinner with Brad and Seth. She didn't have a dirt speck of interest in farm conversation, although she realized she would have known everything about it if a certain event years ago had not occurred – all because a mother wanted to protect her toddler from a breeze. Even with the invitation, she felt an easy freedom between the two of them, and it wasn't just about the width of the truck seat. His dinner offer would be better than being alone right now. She would still have time to pack a few T-shirts and shorts in her backpack, negotiate with her landlord, who would probably watch Daphne, and commandeer a bargain fare to Rome, where she would meet Jess in fewer than three days.

"Let's meet Seth for some burgers," she said. "I'll make a seasoning. Do you have some Worcestershire sauce and alderwood smoked salt?"

He laughed. "Just salt and pepper. You answered just in time." He cut the wheel to the right so quickly that Mizbie's shoulder bounced off his arm.

"Take it easy." She rubbed her shoulder.

He heard the strength in her voice. "You bet."

Acknowledgments

T hanks to the many dedicated, creative teachers I've met through the years at National Education Association conventions across the country. Someday their neverending pursuit to strengthen student engagement will overcome short-term political vilification of our profession.

Many thanks to insightful editors Joni and Cynthia and also to my writers group.

Thanks especially to my dear children, Sheila, Sarah, and John, who kept eye rolls to a minimum as I wrote.

Made in the USA
Middletown, DE
13 October 2023

40722282R00187